A Member of the
Local Nine

A Member of the Local Nine

Baseball and Identity in the Fiction of W.P. Kinsella

William Steele

McFarland & Company, Inc., Publishers
Jefferson, North Carolina, and London

Library of Congress Cataloguing-in-Publication Data

Steele, William, 1973–
A member of the local nine : baseball and identity in the fiction of W.P. Kinsella / William Steele.
p. cm.
Includes bibliographical references and index.

ISBN 978-0-7864-6317-6

1. Kinsella, W. P.—Criticism and interpretation. 2. Baseball stories, Canadian—History and criticism. 3. Baseball in literature. I. Title.
PR9199.3.K443Z87 2012
813'.54—dc23 2011037870

British Library cataloguing data are available

Front cover design by David K. Landis (Shake It Loose Graphics)

Manufactured in the United States of America

McFarland & Company, Inc., Publishers
Box 611, Jefferson, North Carolina 28640
www.mcfarlandpub.com

To my wife, **Heather Steele,**
a first ballot Hall of Famer every time,
who gives me her best even at my worst.

To my parents, **John and Linda Steele**,
who give so much and ask for so little.

Table of Contents

Acknowledgments

My father once told me he heard a writer comment, "When people say they wish they could write a book, what they *really* mean is that they had *already* written a book." Looking back on this entire process now, I could not begin to agree more. Former MLB commissioner Bart Giamatti once wrote, "When people win together, the joy is more intense than when any of us wins alone, because part of any true pleasure is sharing that pleasure, just as part of the alleviation of pain is sharing the burden of pain." Any pleasure I have had while working on and completing this manuscript is undoubtedly magnified because of so many friends and family who have had a part in its completion. Sharing this with them makes it all worthwhile, and their help made all of the frustrations and setbacks more manageable than they would otherwise have been. Knowing that I run the risk of overlooking some people, there are many folks to whom countless thanks are due.

My wife, Heather. There are no words and not nearly enough space, so "I love you" and "thank you" will have to suffice on these pages. Your patience and countless hours editing make this finished product as much yours as mine. My two daughters, Molly Reagan and Marianne Elizabeth. You have been incredibly important to balancing my life and I can't imagine it without you. When asked what I should put in this book regarding them, Molly told me "To Molly, who loves milk and cookies and to Marianne who loves cheese." Consider it done.

My parents, John and Linda Steele. All good that is in me is because of you. Your example has touched more people than you can possibly know, and I am blessed to be able to call you my parents. This book started with the love for literature, history and, most importantly, the love of my family identity you instilled in me.

My siblings and their families: my brother J.L. and Lisa, Jessie and Destiny Steele; my brother Eddie, Austin and Morgan Steele and Ryan Baker;

and my sister, Priscilla. There is nothing in this world more important than family and, for all of you, I am thankful. I am indebted to my in-laws, Kelly and Debbie Barker; the Scaramucci family; and the Clark family. The many days of watching the girls so I could have time to work on this book have not gone unnoticed. Perhaps now we can return the favor.

In friendships I have been most fortunate, but never have there been ones whom I would so willingly call my friends: James Carr, Jason Cost, Ryan Lynch, and Chad Wise. Time and distance may separate us more than I would like, but know your ability to remind me of friendship's value has been a blessing throughout this process.

James Carr. I know that you will tell me that lumping you in with Jason, Ryan and Chad doesn't count, so please know that I appreciate your editorial comments and insight on the manuscript.

Scott LaMascus. Your friendship and professional advice has meant a lot to me on many levels. Your edits, insight, and encouragement are all parts of this project coming together, especially in its waning days.

In a broad sense, this book had its origins in research conducted for my master's thesis, which focused on Kinsella's first novel, *Shoeless Joe*. Many thanks to Larry Gentry and Robert Holtzclaw, who served on my committee during that process. More specifically, this manuscript took shape as a dissertation completed at Indiana University of Pennsylvania. I am very much indebted to the dissertation-committee members, whose guidance and encouragement helped me not only get the degree but revise for book publication. Thanks to David Downing, Ronald Emerick and Michael Vella.

The faculty and staff of Cascade College, especially from 2008–2009. It's been said that you don't know what you've got till it's gone. I understand that now and I am blessed to have had some small part to play there. The more I am removed from our work at the college, the more I am certain of one thing: we did good and we did it well. Thank you. Though by no means the only people from there who helped me, special thanks for too many things to mention are due to: Gary Tandy, your personal and professional interest and the advice from your own experience have helped shape much of my work at Cascade and beyond; Ryan Rouse, I can't imagine my time in Oregon as a coach and teacher without your friendship and all you brought to the band; Shawn Jones and Darren Williamson, your friendship and encouragement in things academic, professional, and spiritual mean more than you will ever know and I thank you both for the blessing of your friendship.

I am also grateful in too many ways to mention to my Lipscomb University family, including Denny and Shirley Loyd, Lin Garner, Ed Edgin, Wayne Garrett, Steve Prewitt, Paul and Val Prill, Douglas Morris, Lynn Griffith, Clay Nicks, Kim Chaudoin and the entire cross country program from 1991–1995. My IUP friends, Laurie Cannady, Lauri Chose, Renae Applegate-House, and Lee Hobbs—your friendship and discussion were important aspects of this book being started and made the time in Pennsylvania much more enjoyable. Chris, Mary, Annie, Paul and Molly Masterson and Kathy Reeger—your friendship is among the most treasured parts of us being in Pennsylvania and your encouragement while there was not unnoticed.

Cami Agan, Becky Briley, Merle Gatewood, Bailey McBride, Gail Nash, Frances Sawyer, and Tina Ware. Your encouragement and support during this process have not gone unnoticed. Thank you so very much for the advice, prayers, and kind words in the months leading to the finished product.

Tim Wiles, Claudette Burke, and the rest of the staff at the Giamatti Research Center at the Baseball Hall of Fame and Museum in Cooperstown, New York; thank you for answering every question I had and helping me access the files and archives at the Hall. The librarians at Cascade College—Lindsey Hoffman, Noelle Marler, and Michael Clark—and Oklahoma Christian University—Tamie Willis, Chris Rosser, Lee Anne Paris, and Connie Maple; your help with the seemingly never-ending interlibrary loan requests is greatly appreciated.

Jimmy Young, your technological expertise has saved me and this manuscript more times than I care to count. Jeff Shewmaker, your help in getting my manuscripts sent off so that I could graduate and get to this point is not forgotten. Maggie Reilly, for your proofreading help, I sincerely thank you. Jerica Briggs, your help with my research and copying with so little complaining is greatly appreciated.

Bobby Murcer. A "Yankee for Life" and one of the nicest guys in the game I have ever had the pleasure of meeting. Our conversations about the game were too few, but very much a highlight of this whole process.

Robert Hicks. I am glad to have waited in line to meet you and to have that encounter turn into a friendship. Thanks for your insight, encouragement, and great stories throughout this whole process.

Tom Wolf, Patricia Bryan, Bill Simons, Jim Gates, Bob Cullen, and the rest of the people from the Cooperstown Symposium who have been so encouraging during this project and in other areas of my baseball research. The same may be said of Trey and Geri Strecker, Jean Hastings-Ardell and the folks at the *NINE: A Journal of Baseball History and Culture*'s Spring Training Conference. The opportunities to present and discuss baseball literature at these two very fine forums made my manuscript much richer as so many of you provided helpful suggestions and comments.

In a perfect world there is no artificial turf, no designated hitter, no indoor stadiums, and no errors in published books. I have had no role in the first three imperfections; however, as with any text there are bound to be errors that, as much as I would like to have someone to blame, I must claim as my own and for which I must take full responsibility.

Preface

This book explores W. P. Kinsella's baseball fiction, specifically focusing on three types of identity—community, family and individual identity—found in his five baseball novels and selected short stories and how he uses the game to establish each within the texts. Though I did not realize it at the time, the idea for this book probably began during the summer of 1989 when, while vacationing in Tennessee, I broke from a group of friends and family who went to see *Indiana Jones and the Last Crusade* so I could sit by myself in a theater watching *Field of Dreams*. Later I discovered the novel, *Shoeless Joe*, that inspired the film, and it quickly became one of my favorites even serving as the subject of my master's thesis at Middle Tennessee State University. My focus was the father-son relationships in the novel and film. Over the next several years, I read all the Kinsella works I could find, including his non-baseball collections on Indian tribes from his native Canada. The more I read, the more I became drawn to how deeply ingrained baseball is in each town, family, and person in his novels. After discovering, while at Indiana University of Pennsylvania, that there had been no full-length book on Kinsella since Donald Murray's *The Fiction of W. P. Kinsella: Tall Tales in Various Voices*, a 1987 collection of interviews with Kinsella and reviews of his work, I decided to push ahead with my research. Kinsella had published three more baseball novels since then along with numerous short stories in which baseball plays an important role.

My purpose through this study is to provide a more complete analysis of Kinsella's baseball fiction. The analysis considers four baseball novels set in Iowa—*Shoeless Joe* (1982), *The Iowa Baseball Confederacy* (1986), *If Wishes Were Horses* (1996), and *Magic Time* (published in Canada in 1998 and in the United States three years later)—one novel set in his native Canada, *Box Socials* (1991), as well as a large portion of his short stories as they relate peripherally to the novels and the various types of identity found within both literary genres. Several critical approaches have already been applied to Kinsella's baseball fiction by other scholars; however, one area that has been neglected by these theorists is the manner in which Kinsella uses the game of baseball as a means of establishing for his characters an identity beyond (though connected to) class, race, or gender. Although there are several forms of identity in these texts, my approach focuses on three: national/community identity, family identity, and individual identity.

Kinsella's characters are often based on what they are not rather than what they are. *Shoeless Joe*'s Eddie "Kid" Scissons, for instance, lives a life based on the lie that he played for the Chicago Cubs in the early 20th century. While the Scissons character is the basis of much critical study, there has been no consideration given to how the game plays a role in his developing a false identity or how it helps him deal with the consequences of perpetrating his lie. Other characters in various short stories share similar experiences as they are drawn to the game, not because they have the ability to play it well, but because they are able to find an identity within it. *The Iowa Baseball Confederacy*, *If Wishes Were Horses*, and *Magic Time* are each set in small Iowa towns recognized primarily as the homes of baseball leagues, teams, or individuals somehow involved with the game. Kinsella continually establishes the identities of groups of people or individual characters through the game of baseball and, in doing so, he seems to offer a critique of the sport. The Iowa Baseball Confederacy All-Stars, for example, are identified only by their roles on the team and not by what roles they have within the community of Big Inning, Iowa, in 1908. By using the game as a foundation for his characters' identities, Kinsella is forced to deal with a variety of issues that have blemished the game over the years: its patriarchal structure; the class differences between the owners and the players and the owners and the fans; the reluctant acceptance of minority players; and the lack of accepting openly gay players.

Much of the first chapter is concerned with the scholarship on sports fiction, specifically the sub-genre of baseball fiction and the variety of approaches to reading Kinsella's work. My research of various historical and cultural elements took me to the Giamatti Research Center at the National Baseball Hall of Fame and Museum in Cooperstown, New York, and countless hours obtaining books and articles online and via inter-library loan at Indiana University of Pennsylvania, Cascade College and Oklahoma Christian University.

Chapter Two focuses on the identity of the country/community within the selected texts. While Kinsella primarily focuses on a community (i.e., a small town or rural county), there are also several situations in which he draws upon the American nationalism often associated with baseball. George

B. Kirsch, Albert Spalding, and Charles Springwood have each dealt with various aspects of the game's "American-ness" and serve as the foundation for this chapter. In the four previously mentioned American based novels by Kinsella, small Midwestern towns are identified by outsiders based on the level of community involvement with the game of baseball. The lone exception is *Box Socials*, a novel set in Alberta, British Columbia, and the one novel in which the game is less of a driving force for the overall plot. Since Kinsella often uses his short stories as chapters in his novels, selected shorter works are also examined to trace the development of the communities' identification. Several critics have commented on the fact that the game itself was reluctant to accept non-white players until 1947 and that, to date, no female players have ever played at the major league level. Unlike basketball and football, both of which have professional women's leagues, baseball has had limited success with women's leagues. Kinsella's fiction makes no apologies for these facts, and the communities in his fiction mirror these same characteristics. The towns are often represented as social structures dominated by white, heterosexual male characters who are, at the very least, financially secure. This aspect of his fiction is also developed in this chapter.

The third chapter narrows the focus of identification to specific family units within the community as a whole. Kinsella generally focuses on two relationships within the family: fathers and sons and husbands and wives. Although the families in his short stories have more variety in their backgrounds than do the communities themselves, the families seen in his novels are, with the exception of *Box Socials*, all from Midwestern states, either Illinois or Iowa, and are predominately white, middle-class families with only a father present. The Canadian-based novel, beyond the geographic difference from the other texts, often focuses on families who are impoverished or, at best, lower-middle class. The framework outlined in the previous chapter allows for continuing to discuss identity through the more specific examples of the family units. Kinsella's families often have one of the parents, usually the mother, missing due either to death or abandonment; all of the families, however, become defined in some manner through their relationships with the game of baseball. In some cases, like Ray Kinsella and his father, John, in *Shoeless Joe*, the game ultimately allows them to be reunited years after the father's death. Though their reunion may not specifically be an issue of identity, the manner in which they are reunited, the baseball field on the farm in Iowa, does identify them to other characters in the story. In other cases, such as Matthew Clarke and his wife, Maude, in *The Iowa Base-*

ball Confederacy, the game is one of the things leading to their separation. While the results in these two texts differ, the game lies at the root of what the families become in that, without the game, there would be little common ground for these characters to share and through which to develop. As the game serves as the only means of maintaining the town in *Magic Time*, it inevitably serves as a way to bring potential husbands and wives together, thereby basing the entire family structure on the game. Although Kinsella often identifies the families in his novels through the game, consideration is also given to *If Wishes Were Horses* and *Box Socials,* in which the game plays a significant role, though only in the most remote manner in identifying the families.

The fourth chapter takes the issues of baseball as an identity to an even more personal set of examples: the individual characters in Kinsella's fiction. While the two preceding chapters focus primarily on the novels, this chapter incorporates a variety of Kinsella's short stories as they are used in later novels. The short stories deal primarily with individuals identified by their connection to baseball; in several cases, these short stories are used as chapters within the novels. *Shoeless Joe*, *The Iowa Baseball Confederacy*, and *Magic Time* all have significant portions written originally as short stories. This chapter explores the manner in which individual identities and the role of baseball transform as the short stories are incorporated into the novels and how Kinsella uses the game to clearly establish the characters' identities, including successful players, marginal players, and fans whose lives become dominated by baseball. In all of Kinsella's baseball novels, including those with little connection to his short fiction, the protagonists are often identified by their connection with the game. The traits seen in the larger communities and specific family structures are clarified even more when considering individual characters in each text.

Building on their introduction in the previous chapter, Chapter Five specifically focuses on Kinsella's short fiction beyond those stories that are incorporated into novels. Many of these short stories explore specific issues of community, family, and individual identities; however, unlike the novels, the shorter fiction tends to explore only one of these areas rather than attempting to weave a variety of identities together as in the novels. The brevity of these works allows for a more specific analysis of the game as it is used to identify the specific types of characters Kinsella employs: characters integrated into his novels, notable players from baseball history, and even Kinsella himself.

After examining Kinsella's baseball fiction with regard to identity, it is important to consider how his work fits with the game's modern identity and how the fiction relates to contemporary America. The concluding chapter summarizes the aforementioned areas of critical studies already explored in recent scholarship and demonstrates the need for more definitive, future examinations of Kinsella and his baseball fiction. Finally, this chapter introduces the idea of identity through the game of baseball by examining the United States' identity as a nation through the development of its "National Pastime." Special consideration is given to the ways in which the sport has dealt with labor and class issues, racial conflicts, and gender differences and how these same issues often serve as the framework for Kinsella's fiction.

This book's purpose is to refute a common misconception many scholars have in viewing Kinsella's baseball fiction as a pastoral ideal in which all of the characters are able to find happiness through the game of baseball. While many of the characters do find such happiness, there are no current theorists who consider the fact that minorities, women, and characters from the lower class are often given no opportunity to find such fulfillment. In contributing a dissenting voice to the continuing discussion of Kinsella's writing, I hope to demonstrate the importance of the game of baseball as it is used to develop and establish identities of characters within his texts. Many of the theoretical interpretations of baseball fiction in general and Kinsella's work specifically are used to demonstrate how understanding identity through baseball leads to a greater understanding of his fiction. In attempting to define baseball fiction, David McGimpsey says that "it is not separable from the patterns of fan loyalty and fan identification that keep people tuned in to the real sport" (3). I take this assertion one step further and conclude that baseball fiction, specifically that of W.P. Kinsella, is not separable from the ideas and issues that make us parts of our communities, parts of our families, and who we are as individuals.

Chapter One

The Foundations and Approaches of Baseball Fiction and W.P. Kinsella

Baseball in America

The game of baseball has been a part of American culture since the early 1800s. Although evidence suggests an early version of the sport being played as far back as the American Revolution, baseball's mythical origin is that Abner Doubleday invented the game in Cooperstown, New York, in 1839. Baseball has generally been accepted as America's "National Pastime" since 1911 when Albert G. Spalding published his own biased perspectives in *America's National Game: Historic Facts Concerning the Beginning, Evolution, Development and Popularity of Base Ball.* Some four years prior, The Mills Commission, led by Abraham G. Mills, then president of the National League, declared in its final findings that "'Base Ball' has its origins in the United States" and that "the first scheme for playing it, according to the best evidence obtained to date, was devised by Abner Doubleday at Cooperstown, New York, in 1839" (Kirsch xiii). Although later evidence refutes the Doubleday legend and further suggests that the game developed from the English game of rounders, the notion that baseball is uniquely American remains ingrained in nearly all subsequent studies of baseball in American culture.

Spalding published his book of the game's "historic facts" at a time when the United States was developing into a significantly stronger global power. His text examines the game, not as a version of the British game, rounders, but as a game invented by Doubleday, himself a Civil War hero at the Battle of Gettysburg. Baseball's characteristics described by Spalding reflect those elements he saw in America soon after the turn of the twentieth century:

> I claim that Base Ball owes its prestige as our National Game to the fact that as no other form of sport it is the exponent of American Courage, Confidence, Combativeness; American Dash, Discipline, Determination; American Energy, Eagerness, Enthusiasm; American Pluck, Persistency, Performance; American Spirit, Sagacity, Success; American Vim, Vigor, Virility [4].

As the country expanded westward following the Civil War, the game continued to grow in national popularity as it "[was] the American Game *par excellence*, because its playing demand[ed] Brain and Brawn, and American manhood supplie[d] these ingredients in quantity sufficient to spread over the entire continent" (5). These characteristics linking the game to America often presented to other cultures what it meant to "be American."

Despite the conflicting accounts of its origin, the game continued to thrive in the late nineteenth century. In concluding his study of the game during the Civil War, George B. Kirsch writes, "After 1870 the ties between baseball and American nationalism would grow stronger as the nation flexed its muscles in the international arena. Waves of imperialism and new wars would present renewed opportunities for Americans to use the national pastime to promote American interests abroad — especially in the Caribbean and the Far East" (133–4). Kirsch and other scholars have considered the ways Major League Baseball promoted the game on a global level by taking teams abroad to play exhibition games for countries unfamiliar with the sport. Domestically, the late nineteenth and early twentieth centuries were a time when cities found forms of common identities by aligning themselves with local teams.

In times of war, baseball often plays a significant role, portraying a sense of national pride. Teams frequently held military exercises on the field before games during World War I, and several players either enlisted for or were drafted into military service including Ty Cobb, Christy Mathewson, and Grover Cleveland Alexander, three of the greatest stars of the period who were eventually elected to the Hall of Fame. In 1918, the most difficult year for baseball during the war, General Enoch Crowder, provost marshal of the armed forces, "issued a 'work or fight' order that stipulated that men in nonessential industries either find themselves work related to the war effort or be drafted" (Honing 91). Crowder's order is a striking contrast to the letter President Franklin Delano Roosevelt sent to Commissioner Kenesaw Mountain Landis on January 15, 1942, less than one month after the Japanese attack on Pearl Harbor:

> I honestly feel that it would be best for the country to keep baseball going. There will be fewer people unemployed and everybody will work longer hours and harder than ever before. And that means they ought to have a chance for recreation and for taking their minds off their work even more than before [Honing 245].

Major league baseball did continue, albeit with diluted rosters filled by marginally talented players taking the places of stars who enlisted in the armed forces. Immediately following the United States' declaration of war against Japan, players like Cleveland Indians pitcher Bob Feller enlisted in the military. Others players were drafted into the armed forces, including two of the biggest stars of the day, Boston Red Sox slugger Ted Williams and New York Yankees center fielder Joe DiMaggio. Williams later flew missions in the Korean War, forfeiting some of his potentially most productive athletic years in the process. In many cases, these players became sources of propaganda for the military, often playing exhibition games for the public or the troops stationed overseas. Others, like Feller, requested to serve on the front lines with more soldiers who, unlike him, had no celebrity or name recognition preceding them. In both World War I and World War II, the game and its players were recognizable products promoting the military agenda and nationalistic mindsets of the times as well as helping generate publicity for the game itself.

It was during World War I that two of baseball's most endearing traditions began, traditions that are commonplace in today's game. The 1918 World Series represents the first time that the national anthem was played before a baseball game. This time period also began the pageantry of the President of the United States throwing out the ceremonial first pitch on the season's opening day. These two traditions "intensified the association between the sport and American nationalism" (Kirsch 135). In a similar situation, it was after play resumed following the terrorist attacks of September 11, 2001, that teams added a rendition of "God Bless America" to the seventh-inning stretch. While most teams have since removed the American flags from their uniforms, symbols common on all jerseys in the early days following 9/11, many major league baseball clubs have continued to play the patriotic song as a part of the seventh-inning ceremony.

Although Albert Spalding argues that baseball represents all that is good in America, it has become clear that the game is not without its shortcomings. Many fans questioned the integrity of the game following the 1919 World Series when eight members of the Chicago White Sox were accused of conspiring with gamblers to fix the series against the Cincinnati Reds. While the players were acquitted of any wrongdoing by a jury, newly appointed baseball commissioner Kenesaw Mountain Landis banished all eight of the players for conduct he deemed contrary to the ideals of the game:

> Regardless of the verdict of juries, no player that throws a ballgame; no player that undertakes or promises to throw a ball game; no player that sits in a conference

> with a bunch of crooked players and gamblers where the ways and means of throwing games are planned and discussed and does not promptly tell his club about it, will ever play professional baseball [Honig 116].

Elected by the team owners to help restore the integrity of the game in America, Landis, through his ruling, effectively ended the playing careers of eight members of what was arguably the best team of the period. A similar ruling occurred in 1989 as Pete Rose, Major League Baseball's all-time base hits leader and then the manager of the Cincinnati Reds, was given a lifetime banishment by Commissioner A. Bartlett Giamatti for betting on Major League games, once again demonstrating Major League Baseball's intent to present an ideal game that is incorruptible. The reality, however, is that these two cases demonstrate how the business of baseball is often corrupt to its core.

The game recognized as the "national pastime" was also known, until 1947, for its exclusion of minorities. Within two years of Jackie Robinson breaking the color barrier with the Brooklyn Dodgers in April of 1947, the Negro American League was the only major Negro League still functioning ("Timeline"), and by the early 1960s, the last of the Negro Leagues teams, once the only refuge for players of color, had disbanded ("Negro Leagues History"). In a similar set of circumstances, professional women's leagues began during World War II when a large portion of major league players served in the military. Although a woman has yet to play in the major leagues, it became evident during this time that women also have a place in the game known for excluding them. Today, both minorities and women are recognized in detailed exhibits at the National Baseball Hall of Fame in Cooperstown, New York. Displays include tributes to Latin American baseball pioneers, women's teams throughout the game's history, and tributes to many of the former Negro Leagues players enshrined in the Hall.

Despite the game's acknowledgment of minorities and women in its history, baseball continues to be plagued by controversies of various types. The most recent scandal causing fans to question the national pastime is rooted in the accusations that some of baseball's premier players have tainted the game by using steroids and other banned performance enhancing supplements. Jose Canseco, a former Most Valuable Player, wrote in his 2005 book, *Juiced*, details of his own steroid use during his major league career and accused such marquee players as Mark McGwire and Rafael Palmeiro of doing the same. The fallout from his book led to a Congressional hearing with these three players, in addition to Sammy Sosa, Curt Schilling, and other stars being called to testify in March of 2005.

As with the Chicago White Sox scandal regarding the 1919 World Series and the 1989 decision by Commissioner A. Bartlett Giamatti to impose a lifetime ban on Pete Rose, the revelation that the game's records and its very integrity had been compromised by some of its most successful players threatened the marketability to and acceptance from the very fans who long supported the game. The consequent legal and disciplinary issues were immediate and far-reaching. In March of 2006, following the release of Lance Williams' and Mark Fainaru-Wada's *Game of Shadows*, the book most credited with detailing San Francisco Giants leftfielder Barry Bonds' connection to the Bay Area Laboratory Co-Operative, MLB Commissioner Bud Selig appointed former Senate Majority Leader George Mitchell to investigate the use of performance enhancing drugs (PEDs) in Major League Baseball and to make recommendations to address the problem (Bloom).

In December, 2007, over a year and a half after his appointment, the now infamous Mitchell Report, which named 89 players ranging from potential Hall of Famers to the relatively unknown, was released to the public. Following the release of these names, New York Yankees third baseman Alex Rodriguez admitted before the start of spring training in 2009 that he had used PEDs earlier in his career while playing for the Texas Rangers, and Los Angeles Dodgers left fielder Manny Ramirez was suspended 50 games that same season for testing positive for banned substances. Following his denial under oath during the Congressional hearings of using PEDs, seven-time Cy Young Award winner Roger Clemens was indicted on perjury charges in August of 2010. These ongoing scandals may be years from being resolved, causing fans of the game and cultural scholars alike to question whether or not the game is representative of the American culture or if it has come to represent nothing more than its own self-serving interests and corporate issues.

The myth that baseball was invented by an American without any earlier influence has long been dispelled; however, the idea that the game represents American ideals is still very much alive. The game has transcended the fields on which it is played and is now seen in film, heard in music, and, most important to this study, read in literature. In recent years scholarship regarding baseball in American culture and in literature has become increasingly popular due in large part to the belief that "baseball has in fact gained a highbrow, literary reputation that no other American sport, and very few objects of American popular culture, enjoy" (McGimpsey 2). This reputation emerged because of a belief in the qualities that Spalding presents as inherent to the game and despite evidence — like gambling and drug scandals—contradicting his idyllic description of the same game.

Baseball in the Traditional American Literary Canon

As baseball's popularity and visibility increased following the Civil War, it began to be used in American literature of the period. Writers like Walt Whitman saw value in the game for its physical benefits and its embodiment of nationalistic ideals. Other writers like Mark Twain used the game as a representation of American characteristics portrayed in foreign countries. In the early decades of the twentieth century, writers like Ernest Hemingway and F. Scott Fitzgerald began using the game as a metaphor for larger issues, such as greed or excellence, which lay at the heart of their literature. While these canonical writers did use the game in their fiction, the resulting works are not considered part of the sport's literature or baseball fiction canons. They do, however, indicate the overwhelming wave of popularity the game had over the span of several decades.

Much has been written about Walt Whitman and how man's physical nature is often seen in his poetry. Images and descriptions of men's bodies engaged in various forms of physical activity fill many of his poems. In "The Manly and Healthy Game: Walt Whitman and the Development of American Baseball," Ed Folsom notes that Whitman's writings would "often extol wrestling, track, quoits, sailing, and other sports, but there was only one sport he would return to throughout his life, and that was baseball" (44). Whitman's interest in the game, Folsom concludes, is explained in large part because "his adult life coincides—geographically and temporally—with the development of American baseball from its birth to its maturity" (46). As the country grew and expanded, so did the popularity of baseball as a national game, something Whitman undoubtedly witnessed. His views of baseball's benefits to America are clear: "I see great things in baseball; it's our game—the American game. It will take our people out of doors, fill them with oxygen, give them a larger physical stoicism. Tend to relieve us from being a nervous, dyspeptic set, repair these losses, and be a blessing to us" (qtd. in Leitner 3). The benefits of the game include the sense of community in America as well as the physical exercise itself. John A. Lauricella argues that baseball appeals to Whitman because "[t]he victory of the club is primary, but the efforts of the individual players may, even in a losing cause, be applauded. Congratulation of honest effort is a sign of civility that accords with the spirit of the game" (26). While he dedicates none of his major poems to baseball, Whitman's private correspondence demonstrates that he is one of the early major American writers to be a fan of the game, recognizing the elements that unified a growing national audience.

Though Whitman was an early fan of the game, Mark Twain was "the first major writer to allude to baseball in a significant if ironic manner" (Candelaria, "Literary" 411). Only after the Civil War did American writers begin to use the game within their fiction. Lauricella says, "Baseball was a cipher to virtually all nineteenth-century authors, becoming a national pastime only (and somewhat ironically) during the Civil War and arguably a national preoccupation in 1869" (29) when the Cincinnati Red Stockings became the first professional team in the country. One result of the game's popularity was that writers began using it in their works. Twain's *A Connecticut Yankee in King Arthur's Court* in 1889 used "baseball to mark the American modernness of his hero" (32). In the novel, Hank Morgan replaces the traditional jousting tournament with a baseball game. Twain obviously uses baseball as the game of Morgan's choice in Camelot because, as Whitman previously demonstrated, it represents America's positive and respected national attributes. Instead of playing games that are associated solely with England, Twain comically describes the royalty attempting to play something obviously American and less like its predecessor, rounders. Because the game was still in its relative infancy, Twain had none of its historical significance or tradition which contemporary authors have to use in their fiction. Instead, he uses the game as a way of demonstrating how America began having an identity of its own and was not merely a transplanted version of Great Britain's identity. Lauricella notes that Twain and Whitman both "allude to the game in general terms: A certain amount of history had to happen before the stories that surround baseball became usable material for creative writers" (35). As the game grew and developed its own history, American writers did begin using baseball creatively in their works, though not at the level at which the works would be considered "baseball fiction."

For nineteenth century writers like Whitman and Twain to refer to baseball in their writings and letters comes as no surprise; they were, after all, fans of the game. Twentieth century writer F. Scott Fitzgerald, however, "considered baseball a waste of time" (Lauricella 37). It is interesting to note, then, that baseball plays a rather significant role in his most well-known work, *The Great Gatsby*. While at a lunch with Jay Gatsby, Nick Carraway is introduced to Meyer Wolfsheim. After Wolfshiem leaves, Nick asks who he is:

> "Who is he, anyhow, an actor?"
> "No."
> "A dentist?"

> "Meyer Wolfsheim? No. He's a gambler." Gatsby hesitated, then added coolly: "He's the man who fixed the World's Series back in 1919."
> "Fixed the World's Series?" [Nick] repeated.
> The idea staggered [him]. [He] remembered, of course, that the World's Series had been fixed in 1919, but if [he] had thought of it at all [he] would have thought of it as something that merely *happened*, the end of some inevitable chain. It never occurred to me that one man could start to play with the faith of fifty million people—with the single-mindedness of a burglar blowing a safe [Fitzgerald 74].

While this is one seemingly minor conversation in the novel, it does demonstrate how Nick's optimism and faith in America are shaken because his faith in its pastime is similarly disrupted. Most Americans considered baseball to be beyond reproach until the 1919 White Sox scandal showed how corrupt the game could become. Fitzgerald could have used another sport, like horse racing or boxing, to convey the country's corruption, but he chose baseball since "Nick regards baseball as something more than an inconsequential diversion and the World Series as more than a string of boys' games" (Lauricella 44). The very ideals that drew Whitman to the game are now questioned by Fitzgerald as Nick Carraway's very faith in the national pastime is in doubt. The game that represented the ideals of America to Whitman and Twain now becomes corrupted by gamblers and con men in Fitzgerald's fiction.

Unlike Fitzgerald, who rarely uses athletic references in his fiction, Ernest Hemingway often refers to various sports in his work. Bullfighting, hunting, fishing, and boxing are all employed in various Hemingway texts, but perhaps his greatest use of sport takes place with his use of baseball references in *The Old Man and the Sea* (1952). Lauricella maintains that theorists have divided "the baseball content of this novel into two unequal parts: Santiago's invocations of 'the great DiMaggio' while at sea, and the more specific baseball talk between the old man and the boy" (99). While several critics have already dealt with the baseball references in the novel, it is important to notice that Santiago's benchmark of excellence is always Joe DiMaggio. He refers to DiMaggio playing through the pain of bone spurs in his heel, and he compares himself to the Yankee great: "But I think the great DiMaggio would be proud of me today. I had no bone spurs. But the hands and back hurt truly" (97). For Santiago, fishing while in great pain compares to DiMaggio playing through his ailment. Baseball's importance in the novel becomes further clarified as Santiago sails on after killing the great fish and tells himself not to think: "But I must think, he thought. Because it is all I have left. That and baseball" (103). The other people in the village have given up hope that Santiago will ever be able to be a great fisherman again; only the boy believes in Santiago, so the bond between them is strengthened by the one thing they have in common: baseball.

The Emergence of a Baseball Fiction Canon

Bernard Malamud's *The Natural*, published in 1952, the same year in which *The Old Man and the Sea* was released, marks the beginning of what many consider to be the start of serious baseball fiction. Since *The Natural* (1952) and Mark Harris's *The Southpaw* (1953), the genre has evolved into an area of literature complete with its own canon of "classic" texts. This is not meant to imply that no legitimate baseball fiction written prior to the 1950s exists; rather, the earlier fiction is primarily intended for a juvenile audience. From the late nineteenth century until *The Natural* and *The Southpaw* were released, baseball fiction was rarely considered to be "serious" literature. With the exception of sportswriter Ring Lardner, whose *You Know Me Al* in 1914 is considered by the majority of scholars to be the first adult work in baseball fiction, most writers within the genre based their stories on the model of the "boy-heroes" found in Thomas Hughes's British work, *Tom Brown's School Days* (1857), a text "[b]ased on the author's experiences as a boy at Rugby" and which "is structured around the protagonist's gradual introduction and integration into school life" (Evans 105). Several subsequent British texts follow the general format of the Hughes text in that the protagonists are young boys who overcome adversity throughout a variety of areas in their lives, with athletics always playing a role. By the late 1890s this genre had gained immense popularity in the United States. Perhaps the most popular American stories of this kind were those based on the Frank Merriwell character, by Gilbert Patten; Baseball Joe books, by Lester Chadwick; and Matthew M. Colton's Frank Armstrong stories (Evans 106). While there are countless examples of juvenile sport fiction and those texts dealing specifically with baseball, there are few legitimate examples of adult baseball fiction until after World War II.

The Malamud and Harris novels of the early 1950s are widely regarded as the beginning of adult baseball fiction because they "were recognized as literary novels despite their baseball content" (McCue 9). Though postmodern literary scholars contest the designations themselves—canon and literary being highly suspect—the use of baseball in fiction was thus viewed by critics of the day as a detriment to the texts rather than something worthy of consideration itself. Andy McCue argues, however, that Malamud and

Harris "opened the baseball novel to serious literatures. Novelists began to use baseball to explore established themes and questions in a new way" (9). The resulting canon of literature is examined in such studies as *Diamond Classics: Essays on 100 of the Best Baseball Books Ever Published*. While this collection does not include the aforementioned juvenile fiction, it is no coincidence that all but two of the one hundred books mentioned were published after 1950 (xiv). Although the sub-genre of juvenile baseball fiction is worthy of serious academic consideration, my own specific approach focuses on an area within the narrower sub-genre of adult baseball fiction. Soon after the publication of *The Natural*, Norman Podhoretz referred to it as the first "serious" novel about a baseball player since Ring Lardner's *You Know Me Al* in that "'serious' means simply that the book appeals to a wider range of emotions and ideas than those which hang on winning or losing a game" (321–2). Building on this definition of "serious" baseball fiction, a wide range of texts was included in the genre in the post–Malamud era.

Perhaps the most problematic issue when studying this sub-genre is determining what exactly is meant by the term "baseball fiction." Simply mentioning the game of baseball or one of its players does not constitute a work of baseball fiction. In *Seeking the Perfect Game: Baseball in American Literature*, Cordelia Candelaria defines baseball fiction "as poetry and prose literature that derives its primary subject and controlling metaphors from the sport of baseball, its history, or its particular ambience, [it] occupies a valuable place in our literary and cultural history" (146). As the adult baseball fiction sub-genre has continued to develop since the 1950s, other writers have contributed to the canon of baseball fiction. Timothy Morris, in *Making the Team: The Cultural Work of Baseball Fiction*, defines the commonly accepted canon as "six or seven texts whose literary status is well respected" (1). This canon coincides with Candelaria's text as well as Deeanne Westbrook's *Ground Rules* and is comprised of Malamud's and Harris's novels; *The Great American Novel*, by Philip Roth; Robert Coover's *The Universal Baseball Association*; *Shoeless Joe* and *The Iowa Baseball Confederacy*, by W. P. Kinsella; and Eric Rolfe Greenberg's *The Celebrant*.

Critical Approaches to Baseball Fiction

In the past 50 years, baseball fiction has emerged as a sub-genre through which its writers have used the sport to deal with such issues as race, gender, socio-economic conflicts, class struggles, and religion. As a result, contemporary scholars study baseball and its subsequent literature through a variety of critical approaches. Christopher Evans and William Herzog, Allen Hye, Brian Aitken, and Linda Joffe all examine some aspect of baseball and/or its fiction as it portrays religious characteristics of America. Michael Oriad, Deeanne Westbrook, and Bryan Garman consider baseball fiction to be a modern creation of epic myths and the heroes found therein. Kathleen Sullivan Porter and David McGimpsey examine baseball fiction and the ways in which it portrays the gender differences in the game. Bobby Fong and Neil Randall view various works in the canon of baseball fiction as extensions of fantasy literature. Critics such as Timothy Lord apply Marxist theory to the genre, while others such as Jules Tygiel, Christian Messenger, and John Lauricella view the fiction as a representation of American values and social structure.

Criticism of baseball literature has grown considerably since 1952, when Bernard Malamud published *The Natural.* In his essay, "Horatio at the Bat; or, Why Such a Lengthy Embryonic Period for the Serious Baseball Novel," Mark Harris echoes McCue's aforementioned assertion, claiming that Malamud's novel is the first serious work of fiction about baseball, breaking free from the earlier writings that are more juvenile in nature. Richard Peterson expands on Harris's ideas, going so far as to call 1952 the "annus mirabilis" of serious baseball writing (89). In *Diamond Classics: Essays on 100 of the Best Baseball Books*, only two books of baseball fiction published prior to 1950 are included for consideration. Since Malamud is one of the earliest writers of adult baseball fiction, *The Natural* paved the way for Mark Harris, David Carkeet, William Brashler, Philip Roth, and other contemporary writers within the genre, including W.P. Kinsella, whose baseball fiction—both novels and short stories—has dominated the genre for the majority of years following the 1982 release of *Shoeless Joe.*

The earliest theoretical approaches to baseball fiction are a minute portion of broader studies of sport in American society or general sport literature. Although they do not focus solely on baseball, in his overview of early critical studies within the genre, John A. Lauricella says, "These books have helped to legitimize sport literature criticism and deserve notice" (221). While Lauricella considers a wide range of texts dealing with sport literature, my own study only refers to these as they relate to the more specific study of baseball fiction, even more specifically that of Kinsella's fiction. It is worth noting, however, that theoretical approaches to both the broad area of sport literature and the narrow area of baseball fiction have come in two seperate waves. The early approaches began in 1975 with Leverett T. Smith's *The Amer-*

ican Dream and the National Game and Wiley Lee Umphlett's *The Sporting Myth and the American Experience*. In 1981, one year prior to *Shoeless Joe*'s publication, there were three significant books published which narrowed the focus from the general area of sport in America as a nation to the specific area of sport in American fiction. Neil Berman's *Playful Fiction and Fictional Players*, Robert J. Higgs's *Laurel and Thorn*, and Christian K. Messenger's *Sport and the Spirit of Play in American Fiction: Hawthorne to Faulkner* all contributed to the growing trend of examining sport in specific works of American literature. These approaches deal with the early texts from serious baseball novels—post–Malamud—while also considering more traditional texts that have elements of sport in them such as stories by Washington Irving, James Fenimore Cooper, Ring Lardner, F. Scott Fitzgerald, and Ernest Hemingway (Lauricella 226).

While these critics began to apply various literary theories to sport literature and, specifically, baseball fiction in journal articles dating back to the 1950s, it was not until the 1990s that book-length studies of the genre, the second wave of critical approaches, began being published. Bridging the gap between the earlier studies and those dealing only with baseball fiction are Christian K. Messenger's *Sport and the Spirit of Play in Contemporary Fiction* (1990) and Michael Oriard's *Sporting with the Gods: The Rhetoric of Play and Game in American Culture* (1991). With the earlier works, as Lauricella notes, "each of the foregoing studies takes as its subject sport literature and/or sport in literature" (231). While such texts do provide an important critique of the broad genre of sport literature or sport as it appears in literature, none provides significant analysis of the narrower area of baseball fiction.

Since the 1980s, scholars have published an overwhelming number of critical studies dealing solely with baseball fiction. The release of several baseball films during the eight-year period between 1984 and 1992 led to an increase in closer interpretation of baseball literature, specifically fictional works. *The Natural* (1984), *Bull Durham* (1988), *Eight Men Out* (1988), *Field of Dreams* (1989), *Major League* (1989), and *A League of Their Own* (1992) all contributed to baseball literature's resurging popularity. Of these six films, half are based on works now in the canon of baseball literature: *The Natural* from Malamud's novel, *Eight Men Out* from Eliot Asinof's book on the 1919 Chicago White Sox World Series scandal, and *Field of Dreams* based on Kinsella's novel, *Shoeless Joe*. It is, therefore, no coincidence that the late 1980s gave birth to a new wave of criticism of baseball film and literature, scholarship that reflects the types of films and the books from which they were taken.

One of the first critical texts dealing with baseball fiction as its own genre is Cordelia Candelaria's *Seeking the Perfect Game: Baseball in American Literature* (1989). Candelaria explains one of the most problematic obstacles for critics when she says, "the multifarious nature of baseball fiction makes it elusive of neat conceptual categories and, in fact, its multilayered literary texture makes it richly amenable to multiple interpretations" (2). Realizing the difficulty of dealing with the variety of issues and layers found within the genre, Candelaria chooses to explore "the baseball imagery and metaphor found in U.S. American literature" and "to explain how this figurative treatment of the sport creates its own framework of the imagination, its own fictive universe" (2). Her study, pioneering such a clearly directed approach towards baseball fiction, opens with the early development of the game itself as well as the resultant folklore and literature. She continues her study, not allowing the genre to be categorized as "the romantic escapism of juvenilia" (3), by exploring Ring Lardner's fiction and his role as the savior of baseball fiction. Candelaria then traces the use of metaphor in baseball fiction through minor and major writers, beginning with Mark Twain and continuing through the late 1980s. Her study delves into the game's mythic qualities and how they are portrayed by the authors from within the genre, beginning with Bernard Malamud. This text also explores the game's metonymic properties, specifically through the Henry Wiggen novels by Mark Harris, before concluding with how Candelaria herself personally views the development of the genre through Robert Coover's *The Universal Baseball Association, Inc., J. Henry Waugh, Prop.* (1968) and *The Great American Novel* (1973), by Philip Roth. Although her text does serve as a solid foundation for the criticism of baseball fiction in American literature, Candelaria neglects to examine any recent baseball novels from the 1980s, including Kinsella's first two baseball books—*Shoeless Joe* (1982) and *The Iowa Baseball Confederacy* (1986)—which had been published prior to her study.

Candelaria's text opened the door for critics to approach baseball fiction as an area worthy of traditional scholarly research, but it was not until the mid–1990s that others began to follow her lead, dealing with the baseball fiction canon in great detail. While Candelaria deals with a variety of issues and approaches in her study, Deeanne Westbrook chooses to deal specifically with the mythic aspects of baseball in her 1996 book, *Ground Rules: Baseball & Myth*. Perhaps the greatest difference between Westbrook's text and Candelaria's chapter on myth is that Westbrook goes into much greater detail concerning the theoretical foundation for the study of the modern myth. Westbrook applies traditional literary theorists including Claude Levi-Strauss, Sigmund Freud, Eric Gould, Northrop Frye, Friedrich Nietzsche, and Roland Barthes to the novels in the baseball fiction canon. She broadens her study, however, to include contemporary fiction often associated with other genres, specifically August Wilson's play *Fences* and William Kennedy's novel *Ironweed*. This study also considers such areas as the monomyth, the metaphysics of baseball, and the "relationships among myth, religion, and art ... as these converge in the literature of baseball" (Westbrook 13). While the scope of this approach is obviously limited to myth and its role in baseball fiction, the depth of research and theoretical applications provide a clearer understanding of baseball fiction as a vehicle for conveying modern myths. More narrowly focused approaches like those by Candelaria and Westbrook demonstrate that rigorous critical analysis, traditionally reserved for the accepted mainstream canonical texts, may be applied by other critics across a wide range of theories and academic disciplines.

One of the leading scholars in the field of baseball fiction, Timothy Morris, contributed to the expansion of baseball fiction criticism with his study, *Making the Team: The Cultural Work of Baseball Fiction* (1997). Unlike many of the critics within this emerging genre who view juvenile baseball fiction as "far less respectable" (1) than adult baseball fiction, Morris sees an important relationship between the two areas. His text, therefore, argues "that despite this well-policed boundary, the cultural work and ideological constructions of adult baseball fiction are continuous with those of juvenile baseball fiction" (3). The four themes Morris considers as he examines the various novels are assimilation, heterosexuality, language, and meritocracy. While these four themes are imperative in gaining a greater understanding of baseball fiction as a serious genre, Morris clarifies that these four areas "do not exhaust the things that baseball fiction means or does" (3). Unlike the previous critical approaches, Morris chooses to focus on "what [baseball fiction] texts do" and not on specific authors themselves (9). He bases his entire study on the thought that "[a]cademic criticism routinely proposes that adult texts do unintentional cultural work; most readers and authors of scholarly books agree that it is all right to see multiple meanings in the serious text" (9). Morris thus approaches his four chosen thematic areas well aware that his methodology and interpretation are only one of several possible ways by which readers may consider the texts from this genre.

While Morris focuses on the broad area of culture in baseball fiction, David McGimpsey takes a narrower approach in his study, *Imagining Baseball: America's Pastime and Popular Culture* (2000), choosing to discuss "the tropes in baseball's cultural products" and "how certain expressions signal conflict and how this conflict informs any understanding of the acculturation of baseball" (2). While his examination of baseball and popular culture centers on this key issue, McGimpsey challenges one of the great barriers keeping baseball fiction from entering the traditional literary canon: the implied differences and values implicit in designations such as "high" and "low" culture. The effectiveness in the approach lies in the balancing of issues in baseball fiction (a term that McGimpsey himself finds difficult to define) and those found in American culture, both high and low. In an attempt to present baseball as being something worthy of academic consideration, many writers and critics tend to focus on the elements of the game that make it appealing to the masses while ignoring the problems that are inherent in the game and its history. McGimspey's entire study deals with these often overlooked areas: scandals in the game's history; the pastoral conventions and how they play a role in framing the issues in baseball fiction; the fact that the game has often been defined by gender and racial differences; and the issue of the generational gap that is found in several forms of American popular culture. While focusing on these issues as they relate to baseball fiction, this study also connects with several film versions of the various texts and how the visual medium differs in dealing with said issues as plots are condensed and characters are altered to tell the cinematic version of the story.

In light of the growing amount of criticism regarding baseball fiction, Richard Peterson's *Extra Innings: Writing on Baseball* (2001) attempts to "provide a commentary, in form and content, on the way baseball writing—from personal and historical essays to realistic and fantastic stories—has shaped our understanding and misunderstanding of the game" (xiv). Although he has written various critical essays in *Aethlon: The Journal of Sport Literature* and *Elysian Fields Quarterly* and has spoken at the annual *Cooperstown Symposium on Baseball and American Culture*, Peterson uses *Extra Innings* to separate his position from traditional critical approaches by writing "[his] essays on baseball writing with a minimum of critical apparatus" (xiv). The result is a collection of essays dealing with the first standard baseball histories, the combining of fantasy and reality, baseball short stories, baseball novels, postmodern baseball writers, and a defense of the legitimacy of the literature. Peterson examines the role baseball fiction plays in the generally accepted traditional literary canon and how it has emerged as a sub-genre in its own right, worthy of significant literary scholarship.

The various approaches used in all of the previously mentioned texts deal with specific issues or texts as they are read and interpreted by the critics who are writing them. In 2002, Mike Shannon compiled the second edition of *Baseball: The Writer's Game*, the first edition of which was published ten years earlier. As the canon of baseball literature, consisting of fiction and non-fiction alike, has grown, Shannon includes "specifically the authors of at least two great baseball books" (ix). Knowing that his criteria were subjective, Shannon writes, "I have never stated or meant to imply that the 15 subjects in the original book were the only authors of great baseball books on the face of the earth" (x). His second edition expanded to include 17 writers, including W. P. Kinsella. In his introduction Shannon presents his biased view of the game: "Baseball is the greatest game, and it is a fitting honor that it was invented and nurtured into perfection in the greatest country in the world" (xi). His comments fail to mention, however, the fact that the game most likely evolved from the English game of rounders, that its "perfection" for many years denied minorities the opportunity to participate, and that it has been riddled with corruption, gambling, and, most recently, evidence of players using performance enhancing drugs. Despite the shortcomings of his own definition, Shannon's text does provide to several significant writers in the broad genre of baseball literature the opportunity to explain their places within the canon. In fact, Kinsella uses this venue to reveal that after the publication of *Shoeless Joe*, "[he] discovered that there was a market for baseball fiction, that there were lots of people out there willing to read it, and that it was an area of fiction that hadn't been well explored" (156). Subsequently, following *Shoeless Joe* and prior to the end of his writing career, Kinsella published four more novels and dozens of short stories in which baseball plays a significant role in the plots. Shannon's collection provides a more thorough examination into the area to which Kinsella has been the major contributor for nearly three decades.

One of the more recent critical approaches to baseball fiction reverts to dealing with a single issue used within baseball fiction's contemporary texts. Allen E. Hye explores the area of religion as it relates to baseball and the fiction based on the sport. While his book may be read as an extension of some themes found in Robert Higgs's *God in the Stadium*, a text dealing with sport as a religion in America, Hye's *The Great God Baseball: Religion in Modern Baseball Fiction* (2004), deals only with religion as used in a specific selection of novels. This study emerged as a result of an attempt to show that "contrary to popular notions, baseball and fiction about baseball can be the object of serious academic inquiry" (Hye 165). Hye delves into baseball, religion, and serious adult fiction, three areas he sees as overlapping to form "a solid body of literature that greatly informs our understanding of modern American culture" (165). Taking issue with the notion that baseball, until the 1950s, "was not considered a fit topic for works of literary rank," Hye deals specifically with several texts now considered to be a part of the baseball fiction canon, including Kinsella's *Shoeless Joe* and *The Iowa Baseball Confederacy*. The examples on which he focuses demonstrate that

> The cultural interaction of baseball and religion, and the game's dual role as national pastime and civic religion, eventually captured the imagination of America's literati. This produced a distinctive subgenre within the excellent, if underrated, body of adult baseball fiction that emerged in the latter half of the twentieth century [166].

The Great God Baseball is an extension of the blossoming criticism dealing with this unique collection of novels.

As the baseball literature canon, specifically baseball fiction, has grown during the past 50 years, critics have obviously begun considering these texts as they deal with themes usually associated with more traditional genres of literature. Although these texts all prove useful in examining the breadth of baseball fiction available today, a relatively small portion of these texts focus on specific authors; instead, critics focus on specific themes or other commonalities within their selected texts. While there have been several journal articles and presentations at sport literature conferences dealing with specific writers and their texts during the past two decades especially, the formats in which these are presented limit the depth of criticism towards the subject matter and rarely focus solely on W.P. Kinsella and his contributions to baseball fiction.

W.P. Kinsella's Place in the Baseball Canon

As the sub-genre of adult baseball fiction has grown since 1952, a wide range of writers have contributed to its canon. The popularity of the literature has been aided by the film adaptations of several of these texts. Bernard Malamud's *The Natural* was made into the 1984 film of the same name starring Robert Redford as Roy Hobbs; William Brashler's *The Bingo Long Traveling All-Stars and Motor Kings* was a 1975 feature film starring Billy Dee Williams as Bingo; and Robert DeNiro played Bruce Pearson as the dying catcher in *Bang the Drum Slowly*, based on Mark Harris's novel of the same title. While the films provided a greater audience for the novels, none of these writers have eclipsed the popularity of William Patrick "W.P." Kinsella, whose first baseball novel, *Shoeless Joe* (1982), served as the basis for the 1989 film *Field of Dreams*.

Long before his success as a baseball fiction writer, Kinsella established himself as a Canadian short story writer who published three collections of stories primarily dealing with contemporary North American Indians. Going against his success in this specific area, Kinsella wrote a short story, "Shoeless Joe Jackson Comes to Iowa," intending to have it published in the *New Yorker* until they called the story "too sentimental" (Dahlin 6). Subsequently, the story appeared in "Aurora: New Canadian Writers 1979" and caught the attention of an editor at Houghton Mifflin, who suggested that Kinsella expand the short story into a full novel. Although several critics and scholars have already addressed Kinsella's process of writing the novel, it is worth noting that he had no intention of becoming so productive within the genre: "if *Shoeless Joe* hadn't been successful, I probably wouldn't have written any more baseball fiction" (Shannon, *Baseball* 156). Kinsella's comments about the lack of quality in baseball fiction are neither surprising nor new to criticism of the genre. One of the early reviews of the emerging canon, written only six years after Malamud's novel was published, mentions, "The list of good writing about baseball is short.... Writers must view the game afresh as a complex as well as colorful human situation" (Farrell 5). Since 1982, Kinsella has proven to be the leading contemporary writer of baseball fiction, helping to give the genre a widely accepted place in the study of literature.

With the exception of Mark Harris, who wrote four novels of baseball fiction, Kinsella is the only author in the baseball fiction canon to contribute more than one work. Timothy Morris has considered the variety of writers, both well-known and obscure, who are contributors to the genre, and he concludes that Harris and Kinsella are the most productive members of the group and "the bulk of each author's work is decidedly outside the genre" (152). Following *Shoeless Joe*'s publication, Kinsella wrote four more novels with baseball as a foundation—*The Iowa Baseball Confederacy*; *Box Socials*; *If Wishes Were Horses;* and *Magic Time*— and dozens of short stories involving the game.

Though now most often considered a "baseball writer," Kinsella argues that his fiction, while using the game, is not about the game: "I am someone who writes peripherally about baseball. I agree that the best sports literature isn't really about sports. I, for instance, write love stories that have baseball as a background" (Horvath and Palmer 186). With this in mind, one must consider the fact that Kinsella's baseball fiction is also often categorized in the fantasy genre, demonstrating that the material appeals to an audience larger than readers of only sport literature. All of his novels include some aspects of mythology and fantasy, resulting in several scholarly approaches to his texts as examples of this literary genre. This mixture of fantasy and reality, "magic realism," is the subject of other critical readings of Kinsella's fiction.

More often than not, Kinsella's baseball stories do not deal with players of great significance. Two major exceptions are *Shoeless Joe* and "Searching for January," both of which deal with former major league players whose careers were cut short: Joe Jackson's due to his permanent banishment by Commissioner Kenesaw Mountain Landis, and Roberto Clemente, who died on New Year's Eve in 1972 en route to aiding the victims of a Nicaragua earthquake. In these two cases, players are literally brought back to life by Kinsella with the hopes that they will one day play the game again. In fact, Kinsella realizes that the idea of hope often fuels his fiction: "There are so few novels with happy endings and baseball is a happy-ending kind of game" (Dahlin 7). The hope of which Kinsella speaks is not reserved for those players who have achieved athletic greatness; to the contrary, his protagonists are often athletically inept or simply fans of the game with little playing ability at all; such is the case with Ray Kinsella in *Shoeless Joe* and Gideon Clarke in *The Iowa Baseball Confederacy*. Characters such as "Truckbox" Al McClintock in *Box Socials* have only limited success on the field as they play only for the joy of the game and not for professional teams. Those characters who do play the game, however, such as Shoeless Joe Jackson and Stan Rogalski, Gideon's best friend and fellow time traveler, have significant character flaws (taking money from known gamblers) or athletic shortcomings (a perennial minor league player). A connective link for each of these types of characters in Kinsella's fiction, however, is Joe McCoy, the protagonist in *If Wishes Were* Horses, a pitcher who initially had great success at the major league level and then, due to a series of misfortunes and personal issues, finds himself outside the game as an investigative reporter for a Los Angeles newspaper. The commonality with all of Kinsella's characters, though, is the love for the game itself and a belief in the hope associated with it. Regardless of the level of success his characters have found in the game, if they even play the game at all, Kinsella's characters share a deep love and respect for the sport and what it represents to them.

Kinsella speaks of hope in the game and the reasons he sees for the success of its use in fiction:

> I think baseball is conducive to fiction writing because of its openendedness. The other sports, football, basketball, hockey, are twice-enclosed: first by time limits and then by rigid playing boundaries. In contrast, there's no time limit on a baseball game, and the true baseball field has foul lines which diverge forever, eventually taking in a good part of the universe; and that's what a fiction writer is looking for [Shannon, *Baseball* 160].

His admitted "canned answer" is telling in that the qualities that set baseball apart from other sports for writers are also those qualities which marginalize people often neglected by the game. The timelessness of the game, for instance, is also indicative of the problems within the game. That the game encompasses, by Kinsella's definition, a large portion of the universe, means it would therefore include the negative issues such as racial divisions and gender inequities. For far too long, minorities were banned from Major League Baseball and were forced to play in leagues by themselves for far less than what their white contemporaries were being paid. Similarly, a female player has yet to break the gender barrier at the major league level. The universe that Kinsella's diverging foul lines encompass is not immune to problems of racism, gender discrimination, or class struggles; while Kinsella's fiction often glosses over these issues, many critics of the genre, including myself, choose to explore these marginalized characters as they relate to the white, male protagonists in his works.

Due to an accident in 1997 when a car backed into him, causing him to hit his head on a sidewalk, Kinsella has impaired senses of smell and taste and, most unfortunately, had lost his impulse to write creatively until the highly anticipated 2011 release of his first baseball novel in well over a decade, *Butterfly Winter*. While this unfortunate turn of events has left readers with a gap in the baseball fiction Kinsella will contribute to the genre, it also gives scholars the ability to analyze his texts to date as a collective group, in their entirety; therefore, the time has come for a more complete consideration of Kinsella's baseball fiction and the issues and themes found therein.

Recent Critical Approaches to Kinsella's Fiction

As a result of the popularity following the publication of *Shoeless Joe* and the 1980s release of several baseball films based on various novels, the past several years have produced a resurgence in baseball fiction criticism, specifically concerning Kinsella's works. A large portion of these approaches is found in the broad collection of sport literature criticism discussed earlier in this chapter, but a significant number of critical approaches dealing specifically with W. P. Kinsella are found in a variety of literary journals and other publications. In spite of his contributions to the genre of baseball fiction and the fact that he has been the most productive contributor within the genre over the past three decades, there has been only one in-depth examination of Kinsella and his writing, Don Murray's *The Fiction of W. P. Kinsella: Tall Tales in Various Voices*, published in 1987. The main objective of my research, therefore, is to more fully consider Kinsella's contributions to the area of baseball fiction regarding his use of the game as a means of establishing various forms of identity.

A former professor at the University of Calgary and a graduate of the University of Iowa Writer's Workshop, Kinsella is familiar with the world of literary criticism in academics. Much has been made of his apparent disdain for theorists and how they often interpret, or misinterpret, his texts. In an interview with Don Murray, Kinsella comments, "I actually enjoy reading good critical work, especially academic criticism. I am often extremely critical of academics" (Murray 51). His frustration with critical approaches to his texts stems from reading critics who "probe for hidden meanings which you had no intention to hide" or a "critic [who] devises an interpretation based on writers that you've never read or even heard of" (51). Since 1982, Kinsella has been afforded the opportunity to read a broad range of critics who have explored his fiction from a postmodern viewpoint, through a feminist lens, as a commentary about religion, or as it relates to gender. While none of these approaches clearly define the fiction, they all contribute to the ongoing narrative which considers Kinsella's writing, providing readers of baseball literature greater depth in understanding his fiction.

Brian Aitken argues that one unique aspect of Kinsella's fiction is "the mythical element in [his] baseball stories that conveys his religious vision and offers some insight into how sport can be a doorway to the sacred" (64). He then compares the baseball fiction to Joseph Campbell's *monomyth*, "a paradigm of myth that is repeated over and over again in a thousand faces and a thousand contexts" (64). This comparison is applied primarily to the two earliest Kinsella novels, *Shoeless Joe* and *The Iowa Baseball Confederacy*. Aitken's conclusion that these stories "indict organized religion" (73) is an idea already approached by other critics and by Kinsella himself. Timothy C. Lord extends Aitken's idea even farther by examining *Shoeless Joe* as a fantasy story in which "baseball becomes both a metaphor and a replacement for religion and the religious life" (43). Lord's study transcends fiction and delves into the ideas of Hegel and Marx as they each relate to the religious ideology as presented by Kinsella in his fantasy. Instead of religion being "the opium of the people," Lord claims that *Shoeless Joe* uses baseball in this role; the game "dulls Ray's responses to fundamental injustices and oppressions within society, making it seem as if practical action to bring about social change is futile and the only refuge must be found in a higher realm isolated from the social realm where material problems are rooted" (48). The most glaring deficiency of this study, however, is that Lord examines only one Kinsella novel, *Shoeless Joe*, without considering the two subsequent novels, *The Iowa Baseball Confederacy* and *Box Socials*, both of which had been published before the essay's publication.

Perhaps the most notable element of Kinsella's fiction contributing to his popularity and the uniqueness of his writing is his use of "magic realism" where elements of fact and fiction blend together so closely that the reader is often unable to tell where one ends and the other begins. As a writer, he views his job as being to "liven up the dull, tone down the bizarre until it is believable" (*Thrill of the Grass* x). For Kinsella, this usually involves connecting actual people and events to fictitious characters and places. Ray Kinsella sees Joe Jackson play baseball over a quarter of a century after Jackson's death; Gideon Clarke and Stan Rogalski become transplanted back in time 70 years to participate in a game against the 1908 Chicago Cubs; and a fictional version of Kinsella himself signs a contract to play with the New York Giants and witness the 1951 "Shot Heard Around the World." Robert Hamblin considers all of these examples and others from the stories of magic realism as what "places [Kinsella] squarely within the mainstream of the literary movement that is commonly identified by the term *metafiction*" (9). As Hamblin's title implies, Kinsella's use of magic realism is a "split fingered fastball," an overpowering pitch in his literary arsenal making his works unique to the literary world.

Kinsella's works are included in nearly all of the contemporary critical approaches to the canon of baseball fiction. David McGimpsey, Timothy Morris, Richard Peterson, and Deeanne Westbrook have all written detailed studies on baseball fiction and how the literature fits into a variety of areas including myth, popular culture, and the study of literature. None of these texts, however, dedicates more than a chapter or two to Kinsella, and those chapters predominately focus on his first two novels and their comparison to other works within the genre. The eclectic range of approaches, though, reinforces Kinsella's own thoughts on the genre: "There are no limitations, at least to baseball fiction" (Horvath and Palmer 188). The limitless nature of the texts gives way to an equally limitless number of approaches to the canon of baseball fiction. Though not yet canonical to baseball literature, Marilyn Robinson's *Gilead* and *Home* are more recent examples of novels which use baseball extensively and, like most of Kinsella's baseball fiction, are set in Iowa. The variety of critical approaches specific to Kinsella's work continued to blossom following the release of *Field of Dreams* in 1989. Since then, scholars have considered Kinsella's texts and how the film deals with the variety of issues already mentioned. My approach is written in an attempt to fill some glaring gaps in the study of Kinsella's baseball fiction and to continue the discussion pertaining to his body of work within the genre.

Chapter Two

"Is This Heaven?": Kinsella's Idyllic Community

Phil Alden Robinson transformed W. P. Kinsella's fantasy baseball novel *Shoeless Joe* into the film *Field of Dreams* (1989) in which the protagonist, Ray Kinsella, builds a baseball field on his Iowa farm, enabling his dead father and his father's hero, "Shoeless" Joe Jackson of 1919 Chicago "Black Sox" infamy, to reemerge from the rows of corn in the outfield and finally fulfill their dreams of once again playing the game of baseball. Although there was a large amount of baseball fiction before Kinsella's novel, including Ring Lardner's stories from the early twentieth century, Zane Grey's formulaic baseball novels, Mark Harris's series, and Bernard Malamud's *The Natural*, Robinson's film caused a renewed interest in the literary sub-genre of baseball fiction. Following the film's release, literary and film critics alike explored the connections between baseball and American ideologies more deeply. While some studies focus solely on the film versions of various baseball novels, others compare representations of the game and nation in the texts with the film versions of the same subjects. One area that has, until now, gone largely unexplored is the way in which Kinsella's use of baseball, as portrayed in four of his novels set in the United States, serves as a representation of the collective nation and many of its ideologies; the fifth novel, *Box Socials*, set in Canada, uses the game in a different manner and may be read as a contrast to the American imperialism often associated with the game. While the broad field of cultural studies is applied in this chapter, it is important to trace the issues of race, gender, and class which combine to define who America and its communities are as a culture as well as how this culture is identified, in Kinsella's fiction, by the game of baseball.

In *Shoeless Joe*, Ray Kinsella, an Iowa farmer who has plowed under his only crop in order to build a baseball field, kidnaps reclusive writer J. D. Salinger and brings him to the farm so that Salinger may reconnect with the game he loved in his youth. During the climactic scene in which Salinger tells his version of the field's purpose, he explains the role of baseball throughout American history, emphasizing how the game has been "the one constant through all the years," marking time's passing "while America has rolled by like an army of steamrollers" and reminding "us of what once was" in the nation's past (252–3). Though America has moved forward, Salinger argues that the game is a cultural phenomenon anchoring it to the past and to the ideals on which the national identity was founded. Salinger's description, however, implies that the game is the one great unifier in the nation's history, ignoring the divisiveness it has created through corruption, gambling, drug use, racism, and gender imbalances, issues that continue to resonate in the twenty-first century. Building on the pastoral landscape that serves as the setting for Salinger's soliloquy, his narrative focuses on the game's unifying aspects, completely ignoring the issues contrasting his view.

More than any other sport played in the United States, baseball has taken on both mythic and religious characteristics, traits that many scholars have considered in their works on the game and its impact on the nation's cultural dynamic. In *The National Game: Baseball and American Culture,* John P. Rossi says that the game "has formed an intimated link with American history and culture for more than a century and a half. No other sport has embedded itself so deeply in the national psyche or has generated such a large body of serious literature" (3). The game has, therefore, evolved far beyond a form of simple entertainment; it has become a way for the people of this country to identify with each other as a nation and to relate with other cultures in the world that have since been exposed to and have also adopted the game. Perhaps no better example of this global identity can be found than by watching the World Baseball Classic, played for the first time in 2006 between teams of major league talent representing individual countries from around the world. The team representing the United States was comprised of players who were both American by birth and those who immigrated to the country and later became citizens.

Although certainly influenced by the English game of rounders and varieties such as "town ball" and "old cat," the game's prevailing mythical beginning is that Abner Doubleday, a Civil War hero at the Battle of Gettysburg, invented it in Cooperstown, New York, in the summer of 1839 (Rossi 3–4). It seems then that this myth, which credits the game to an American's own ideas with no European influence, is used to break from the association with the English games. In light of the fact that America was its own country at this time, the Doubleday story enables the United States to have a game that is its own with no connection to the colonizing British. In fact, Mark Twain referred to various teams from America who toured the world, using the sport as a way of bridging the cultural gaps between other nations with a uniquely American game. At a dinner in New York honoring Albert G. Spalding's team that played in, among other countries, Australia, Italy, England, Scotland, and Ireland, Twain praised Spalding for taking the game to other parts of the world, referring to the sport as "the very symbol, the outward and visible expression of the drive and push and rush and struggle of the raging, tearing, booming nineteenth century" (qtd. in Zoss and Bowman 395–96). As the game was used to cross cultural barriers, however, it also began to embody specific traits through which America defines itself—traits which writers and scholars have dealt with in various manners for over a century.

An overwhelming number of contemporary studies focusing on baseball and American culture refer to Jacques Barzun's line from *God's Country and Mine* in which he offers his explanation of the importance of the game in this country: "Whoever wants to know the heart and mind of America had better learn baseball" (159). While most critics cite only this portion of the quote, it is important to note that Barzun's line continues, "land do it by watching first some high school or small town teams" (159). This oft overlooked part of the quote is perhaps the most telling when discussing America and its connection to and obsession with baseball; the basic understanding of the nation comes not from watching a game of multi-millionaire players on television or being one of tens of thousands of fans in Yankee Stadium on an October evening. Instead, to "know the heart and mind of America" is to know the game as played on any one of the countless fields spread across the country's landscape. The baseball of small town America is precisely what W.P. Kinsella deals with in his fiction. Rarely in his short stories and never in his novels do the protagonists play at the major league level; rather, they are either mediocre minor league, semi-professional, collegiate or high school players, or obsessive fans of the game who are drawn to baseball for its simple pleasures and not for the amount of wealth or fame it may bring them.

Although Kinsella is Canadian "by accident of birth" (Murray 32), he considers "[himself] a North American writer" (32), and while the majority of his Indian stories are based in Canada, nearly all of his baseball fictions are based in the United States: "Baseball is an American game.... It would be fatal if I set the baseball stories in Canada" (33). In fact, of his five novels in which baseball plays a significant role in the plot, four of them are set in the United States, specifically in Iowa. The lone exception is *Box Socials*, a novel in which the game plays an important role in only one of the characters' lives, making it the book that relies least on the sport. In Kinsella's short fiction, there are rare instances in which his baseball stories are set in Canada; however, the players in these stories are American players who happen to play or live north of the border separating the United States and Canada. Of his five novels in which baseball plays a role, only *Box Socials* casts the game in a significantly less important role in the storyline than in his other four novels in that it is neither the catalyst for conflict nor the motivating element for the protagonist. Kinsella, therefore, recognizes and emphasizes the definite connection between the traditionally American game and its fans, a connection he displays through the small town settings in which the game, its players, and the fans play mutually important roles, further establishing the identities of the communities in his fiction.

The role of sport in a community can be traced back at least as early as the ancient Greeks, when wars were put on hold so that the athletic abilities of the armies could be showcased at the original Olympic Games. Throughout history, people have identified themselves by their allegiances to specific athletes or athletic teams. In *Take Time for Paradise: Americans and Their Games*, A. Bartlett Giamatti, a former President of Yale University as well as the Commissioner of Major League Baseball in 1989, considers the relationships between American sports fans and their teams:

> Very soon the crowd is no crowd at all but a community, a small town of people sharing neither work nor pain nor deprivation nor anger but the common experience of being released to enjoy the moment, even those moments of intense disappointment or defeat, moments made better, after all, precisely because our fan is a part of a large family of those similarly affected, part of a city of grievers. When people win together, the joy is more intense than when any of us wins alone, because part of any true pleasure is sharing that pleasure, just as part of the alleviation of pain is sharing the burden of pain [32].

The concept of sports fans being a part of a community was stronger in the days before the combination of cable television and internet broadcasts made every major league team's games available to fans around the world, but there are still clear markers indicating community loyalty to specific teams. Red Sox fans, the "Red Sox Nation," felt a connection to each other in 2004 after breaking 86 years of frustration at the hands of the "Evil Empire," the New York Yankees. Fans of the former Brooklyn Dodgers still agonize over the heartbreak of having "their" team moved to California to become the Los Angeles Dodgers. Pittsburgh Pirates fans who remember sharing in the joy of Willie Stargell and the "We Are Family" team of 1979 winning the

World Series also share the bond of disappointment in remembering the team's demise in the playoffs of 1990–92 and more recently suffering through watching the franchise set the record for the most consecutive losing seasons of any major professional sports team.

In 1911, Albert G. Spalding published his *America's National Game: Historic Facts Concerning the Beginning, Evolution, and Development and Popularity of Base Ball,* in which he propagated several myths about the game, including the Doubleday legend that has long since been debunked by historians of both the nation and the game. Spalding, however, does outline his justification for baseball being America's pastime: "Base Ball is the American Game *par excellence*, because its playing demands Brain and Brawn, and American manhood supplies these ingredients in quantity sufficient to spread over the entire continent" (5). His consideration of the game's characteristics extends beyond the lines on the field; Spalding asserts that "Base Ball is American as to another peculiar feature. It is the only form of sport known where spectators have an important part and actually participate in the game" (10), including actively participating in keeping scorecards, something rarely if ever seen at other sporting venues. The connection between the game and its fans was obvious even at the developmental stages of professional baseball in the early years of the twentieth century, a period from which Kinsella frequently draws in *Shoeless Joe* and *The Iowa Baseball Confederacy*. This connection continues today with neighborhoods and entire cities being defined by the teams playing within their geographical boundaries.

Baseball and Community in Kinsella's Fiction

Attempting to address the relationship between baseball and community identity in Kinsella's novels becomes problematic because the definition of community is constantly changing and evolving. The United States often defines community by generic geographical boundaries. If one happens to reside within the boundaries of New York City, then he or she may be considered as a part of the community for that reason alone. Within larger communities like New York, however, there are more specific geographically based communities such as The Bronx, Queens, and Harlem, each of which has its own unique features separating it from the larger general community of New York City.

A community may also be defined by more specific elements although, in many cases, these elements form any number of combinations. Community may be defined by racial or ethnic characteristics (African-American community, Hispanic community, and Asian community), religion (Jewish community, Muslim community, and Christian community), sexual orientation (homosexual community, bi-sexual community), and economic status (wealthy, middle, and lower classes). In any case, defining community by one standard definition is an impossible task. Each geographical location may have dozens of combinations of other smaller communities within it. For instance, someone may be a part of the Muslim community and the African-American community simultaneously. Being a part of one community, perhaps geographically, does not necessitate being part of another community within those boundaries.

The most obvious community structure in Kinsella's baseball novels is based on geographic location. The four American-based novels, *Shoeless Joe* (1982), *The Iowa Baseball Confederacy* (1986), *If Wishes Were Horses* (1996), and *Magic Time* (1998 [Canada]; 2001 [U.S.]), are all set in rural Iowa farming areas generally located in or near a small town. While *Shoeless Joe* focuses more on the familial relations that are discussed in the following chapter, the three later novels demonstrate his use of baseball as a means of establishing or enhancing the communities in these stories. Even in *Box Socials* (1991), the novel set in Canada in which the game is used the least, baseball serves as a way for an ethnically and economically diverse community to share in the communal experience of watching one of its own citizens play in an all-star game against major league talent. The game and the towns in each novel often reflect both the positive and negative characteristics found in baseball and in the various communities. Much has already been written on the American-ness of baseball and its attributes; some of these characteristics are more closely examined in the following pages. Albert G. Spalding and Charles Frueling Springwood both explore the ways in which the game mirrors the positive elements often associated with the United States. Both writers, and many like them, agree that baseball, unlike other sports, has a history deeply rooted in the country's landscape and structure. Richard Alan Schwartz considers the characters in *Shoeless Joe* and how fact and fiction are intertwined before concluding, "[b]aseball, because it is something that they all share, dream about, and love, synthesizes these levels of reality and serves as the medium through which they exist harmoniously and coherently. In this respect, it functions very much like a myth" (144). Kinsella's myths, like those of the ancient Greeks, provide stories that represent many generally accepted standards and beliefs of a society and often rely on the game to create a bond between individuals and groups of people. Sharing the game of baseball is tantamount to sharing in the myth and, as Schwartz suggests, "[s]hared myths establish human bonds" (138). If no other element provides a sense of community to those reading Kinsella's fiction, the game of baseball serves as a unifying link for everyone.

A. Bartlett Giamatti asserts that "sports flourish in, and are in every sense most deeply allied with, the City" (48), but he clarifies that "[a] city is not an extended family. That is a tribe or clan. A city is a collection of disparate families who agree to a fiction: They agree to live *as if* they were as close in blood or ties of kinship as in fact they are in physical proximity" (50). The differences between the towns and the families in Kinsella's novels are more clearly seen in the next chapter where the concept of baseball and family identity is discussed in greater detail; however, like Giamatti, Kinsella often describes his towns as a tribe sharing common interests, the most important of which is baseball. In recent years, with the expansion of mass media markets from cable television and the internet, the notion of a baseball team being an identity for a city is not as strong as it once was; however, it is still a significant part of the game today and one that figures into Kinsella's fiction on a regular basis.

Kinsella's baseball novels are prime examples of how America's national pastime is instrumental in establishing the identities of the nation and the communities found therein. Over the past three decades baseball has shifted from a game controlled by the wealthy proletariat owners who, for all intents and purposes, owned the players to a game where players now command multi-million dollar contracts from these same owners. During this same period, the game has gained greater popularity around the world and teams from other countries have quickly equaled and, in venues such as the Olympic Games and the World Baseball Classic, surpassed the American teams on the field of competition. Despite these changes, however, the game is still identified with the United States and represents the country as a large, all-encompassing community. By using rural Iowa locations as the backdrop for the four novels set in America, Kinsella presents the reader with a microcosm of his American community and how the game aids in establishing the identity commonly perceived by the rest of the world. The communities of Onamata, Big Inning, Grand Mound, and Lone Tree, Iowa, are conveniently and generically structured by geographic boundaries and then by the racial, gender, and class guidelines already represented by the game of baseball in America, boundaries that have in some manner marginalized various groups of people for decades. Through the small Iowa towns in his fiction, Kinsella emphasizes the game's traditionally positive traits of inclusiveness while ignoring the exclusive elements read in the game's history that have not afforded certain peoples within the culture equal opportunity.

Though set in Canada, *Box Socials* is narrated by Jamie O'Day, whose parents are both transplanted to Alberta from the United States. Though Mr. and Mrs. O'Day are originally from South Carolina, the family now considers Alberta, Canada, home. The novel serves as a counter narrative to the four imperialistic novels set in Iowa. While the communities in these four novels are largely identified by their connection to and involvement in the game, only one character in *Box Socials*, Truckbox Al McClintock, has any strong connection to the game, though many in the area surrounding the small village of Fark travel to Edmonton to watch him play in an all-star game against major league players. Lacking the passionate connection to the game, *Box Socials* and its lack of emphasis on baseball reiterates the significance of its role in the American identity. Despite being set across the Canadian border, *Box Socials* does participate in the view that baseball is not purely or exclusively American, even though it may be the most distinct representation of the United States to other countries; furthermore, by setting the game against the backdrop of the Canadian landscape, in a community dominated by Eastern European immigrants, Kinsella implies that the game does have *export* value, taking Spalding's version of the American ideal to the Northern neighbors.

Race and Baseball in Kinsella's Communities

The myth that baseball originated in 1839 in Cooperstown, New York, is telling in that it suggests the game comes from a rural, predominately white setting. Joel Zoss and John Bowman suggest that "Americans want to believe in a simpler rural society that produced baseball, but Americans also want to believe that they have always been receptive to different types" (116). While this idealistic belief may be the goal of many Americans who buy into the notion that baseball is a true representation of equality, the reality is that for many years, non-white players were marginalized or, in most cases, banned from competing by the various leagues owned by white businessmen. Albert G. Spalding boldly proclaimed in 1911 that "all America has come to regard Base Ball as its very own, to be known throughout the civilized world as the great American National Game" (13). What Spalding fails to mention is that, during the time period in which he was writing, there were few if any players from Italian heritage on major league teams, and the year his version of baseball's history was published was the same year that the first two Hispanic players, Cubans Rafael Almeida and Armando Marsans, appeared on a major league roster (Zoss and Bowman 131). Coming "to regard Base Ball as [the country's] very own," therefore, was limited primarily to white players. It was not until 1947, when Jackie Robinson first played a game with the Brooklyn Dodgers, that African-American players were permitted in the major leagues, and not until 12 years later, during the 1959 season when the Boston Red Sox added Pumpsie Green to its roster, that every roster had at least one black player. Spalding, therefore, would have been more accurate in saying that the baseball of his time was the great *white* American game.

The lack of minority players in the game's early history is mirrored in *Shoeless Joe* as the players who are afforded an opportunity to play on Ray's field are those from the pre-integration days. Shoeless Joe Jackson and the rest of the banned White Sox players, former New York Giants outfielder Moonlight Graham, and the Chicago Cubs, for whom Eddie Scissons imagined pitching, each represent the game as it was before African-American, Latin, Hispanic, and Asian players were afforded an opportunity to play in the major leagues. It is not until Kinsella's 1996 novel *If Wishes Were Horses* that teams from the post-integration era are brought back to life on Ray's mystical baseball diamond. In this case, Joe McCoy is given the chance to see himself pitch for Lone Tree High School against Sioux City, a way for him to rewrite his personal history by playing in a game in which he had originally refused to pitch, thereby changing the course of his life. Interestingly, however, the novel's plot allows a specific play to right a wrong from his own past, yet Ray's field never allows minority players the chance to correct the racism in the game's past. Ray Kinsella's field, though, is not the only case of W.P. Kinsella's fiction exploring baseball's history when juxtaposed with the modern game.

Gideon Clarke, the protagonist and narrator of *The Iowa Baseball Confederacy*, is transported with his best friend, Stan Rogalski, from Onamata, Iowa, in 1978 to seven decades earlier when the town was known as Big Inning, Iowa, and where he is given the opportunity to prove the existence of a league, the Iowa Baseball Confederacy, and an all-star game that was played against the Chicago Cubs on July 4, 1908. With the exception of the inquiries made to the Cubs' front office from Gideon and his father, Matthew, and the Milwaukee Braves game at which Matthew is killed by a foul ball, there is little mention of players from the game during Gideon's lifetime.

Instead, the accounts of the game as it relates to the town of Onamata/Big Inning, Iowa, are primarily based in 1908, before non-whites were seen on major league rosters. In fact, with the exception of Drifting Away, a Native American whose battle of wills with the tribal Grandfathers results in the epic 40-day game between the Cubs and the all-stars and who ultimately wins the game for the all-stars with a pinch-hit home run, all of the players on both teams are white and no mention of non-white citizens of the town is ever given.

Onamata, Iowa, as described in Gideon's narration, is "two miles south and west of Iowa City, a hundred miles east of Des Moines" (Kinsella, *Iowa* 22) and, according to his copy of *Place Names of Iowa*, "Origin unknown. Possibly a corruption of the Black Hawk Indian word for magic. Town established in 1909" (22). Perhaps not surprisingly, the town's name comes from a Native American word, yet the town is identified by Matthew and Gideon Clarke through its connection to a game that, as emphasized by the warrior Drifting Away in the novel, was invented and developed by the white man. It is only after the flood during the game in the summer of 1908 that washes away the town of Big Inning, literally and figuratively, that Onamata magically appears. An understanding of how baseball serves as a means of identifying racial roles in the community is problematic in that the two versions of the town, Big Inning and Onamata, are represented differently based on the town's relationship with and identification of the game of baseball. While Onamata has only the Baseball Spur as a reminder of the railroad line that used to run to the baseball field, Big Inning and its league are identified by people from outside the community only through the game of baseball. Onamata, then, is no different from the other small farming communities in Iowa while Big Inning is known for the epic game between its all-star team and the Cubs. That the focal point of the novel is a game played between two completely white teams in an era before minorities had the opportunities to play at the major league level is key in understanding the racial dynamic of the area in which the story is set. Although the game represents an epic struggle between Drifting Away and the Native American grandfathers, minorities were not afforded opportunities to play in this specific game because they had generally limited opportunities in America during the early twentieth century. It is only when Drifting Away literally takes matters into his own hands, grasping a bat to stand in against the Chicago Cubs, that a non-white takes the field in the game. Despite the shortcomings in the game's past regarding its acceptance of ethnic minorities, Drifting Away still acknowledges that baseball is the one thing that the white culture has "done right" (166). Tellingly, it is this one non-white player whose hit wins the game for the Confederacy.

With the majority of the novel set in 1908, the emphasis rests on the community of Big Inning rather than Onamata, the name of the town in 1978 where Gideon Clarke lives. During the course of his narrative Gideon often quotes from his father's master's thesis, which was unanimously rejected by the history department at the University of Iowa. Proving the facts in this thesis is what Matthew and Gideon Clarke have spent their entire adult lives attempting to do. It is within this thesis that Drifting Away, the warrior who is locked in a test of strength with his tribe's grandfathers, is given a voice. As he surveys the impact of the whites on his land, Drifting Away understands the differences between the Native Americans who find power in the circle and the white settlers who base their structure on the rigid squares: "Squares have no power ... Power lies in the circle. Everything in nature tries to be round" including the world itself, all celestial bodies, birds' nests and eggs (44). Drifting Away then sees the power of the circle in nature being broken by the whites: "But the whites carved the land into squares" in order to claim it as their own, "though everyone knows you cannot sell the land upon which the people walk" as none of creation is a commodity to be bought or sold (44). Though he sees the land as a resource for all people who inhabit it, Drifting Away is soon told by the colonizing whites, who view the land as a commodity to be owned rather than shared, to leave his own land under penalty of death. By the time Gideon and Stan travel 70 years back through history, Big Inning is clearly a white community; however, it is only such due to the displacing of the Native Americans from their homes to reservations set aside by the colonizers.

After the native tribes are removed from the land, the white settlers establish their own communities and institutions, specifically the institution of baseball. Matthew Clarke's thesis recounts a large Indian figure seen by the men who were constructing the baseball diamond on the outskirts of Big Inning. Though they never saw a clear image of Drifting Away, the workers often hear the coyote or bird sounds he makes or feel his presence as he passes by their construction of the baseball diamond. It is at these moments that the racial divide in Big Inning is most clearly seen as the men refer to the native warrior as a "damn Indian" and being able to "smell his ornery hide" (59). For Drifting Away, the game represents the culture that has displaced him and his people, yet this same game is what he sees as being the closest to perfection that the colonizing culture will ever attain: "Baseball is the one single thing the white man has done right" (166). When Gideon reminds Drifting Away that the game is based on the squares and lines that represent the rigid structure of white society, the warrior encourages him to consider the game's circular elements such as the ball itself, the bat's circumference, the outfield extending to the circular horizon, and the very act of running the bases. Because so much of the game incorporates circular shapes and activity, it "is as close to the circle of perfection as white men are allowed to approach" (167). The game that Drifting Away uses as a contest with the tribal Grandfathers, baseball, is a paradox of the only good thing whites have done and the dominant culture that led to his wife's death and his own quest to be reunited with her.

That Kinsella chooses to focus on the racial relationship between American Indians and the white settlers is unique because the majority of baseball fiction in which racial conflict plays a role focuses on the struggle of African-Americans or Hispanics within the game. While recent years have seen protests against mascots such as these of the Cleveland Indians and Atlanta Braves, "American Indians occupy a special niche in the history of baseball," specifically that Native Americans "were accepted in professional baseball early on — accepted, in fact, at the very time that the last Indian wars were being fought (Wounded Knee was in 1890) and that blacks were being pushed out of organized baseball" (Zoss and Bowman 125). The elements of perfection Drifting Away sees in baseball, a game that was more accepting of his people than people of other races, are tainted by the fact that the game in Big Inning, Iowa, in which he plays a principal part is the national pastime of the very people who marginalized and displaced his tribe as the settlers moved westward. For Drifting Away to get the game-winning hit that reunites him with his wife, Onamata, while depriving Gideon of his relationship with Sarah Swan, is a small way for Kinsella to allow the Native Americans to reclaim that which was rightfully theirs before the white community established its dominance of the land.

Following the success of his first two baseball novels, both of which employ the use of magic realism to present an idyllic version of the game, Kinsella's third novel in the genre, *Box Socials*, is removed from both the elements of fantasy and the use of the game and its history; moreover, Kinsella sets this novel in one set time period, 1945–46, and in Alberta, Canada, making this the only one of his five baseball novels not utilizing Iowa as its setting. In a 1987 interview with Don Murray, Kinsella explains that baseball "is an American game; consequently, all but one of my baseball stories have been set in the U.S." (Murray 33). Though the entire novel is set in Canada and the town rallies around Truckbox Al McClintock, the one player in the town to have any success in the local baseball leagues, his own inadequacies as a hitter are revealed when he strikes out looking, taking three pitches from Cleveland Indians pitcher Bob Feller. The United States' superiority in the game is reinforced in this novel as a team of all-stars comes to Canada and reveals their dominance north of the border. The Canadian community in *Box Socials* sees baseball as little more than a form of entertainment available for the community, while for the Iowa towns in Kinsella's other four novels, it serves as the dominant trait by which each community is identified.

Unlike the novels set in Iowa, *Box Socials* has a community dealing less with racial conflict than with national and class conflict. Primarily comprised of immigrants from Scandinavian countries who came to Alberta in the late nineteenth and early twentieth centuries, there is no mention of anyone from the area known by its inhabitants as the Six Towns—New Oslo, Sagnundo, Fark, Venusberg, Magnolia, Doreen Beach, and Bjornsen's Corner*—who is non-white. The narrator, Jamie O'Day, is the only son of two South Carolinians who, through a variety of events in their lives, settled down to live in Canada. Although baseball is used less in this novel than in any of the five Kinsella has written, the dominant narrative voice is still that of someone whose family comes from the United States. Although the O'Days' roots are in the South before World War II, none of them mentions any type of racial division or even of the existence of a racial minority in the area. Instead, Jamie quotes his mother who says, "We're hillbillies [...] only difference is we know we're hillbillies, and we won't always be that way, unlike some we know" (4). Calling her family "hillbillies," Jamie's mother reinforces the notion that class identity is the key conflict in the novel. The reference to the "some we know" alludes to three of the families in the area, all of whom come from Scandinavia and are, in Mrs. O'Day's mind, beneath her family on the social scale. Noel Schraufnagel maintains that in this novel, "[i]n contrast to *Shoeless Joe* and *The Iowa Baseball Confederacy*, the game is de-emphasized" (120). By diminishing the importance of baseball in the plot, Kinsella also removes the types of racial divisions seen in the majority of his other novels. Following this novel, however, Kinsella returns not only to the Iowa setting of his first two novels but to the racial tensions within the small Midwestern setting.

The 1996 novel *If Wishes Were Horses* not only returns to Iowa, but

*Jamie O'Day explains the seventh name in the area known as Six Towns: "Ejornsen's Corner was just a place, not a town, or even a post office, so didn't officially count ... (18)."

incorporates the landscape of both *Shoeless Joe* and *The Iowa Baseball Confederacy*, the same location that is used again in Kinsella's most recent novel, *Magic Time.* In fact, both Ray Kinsella and Gideon Clarke reappear as narrators, reinforcing, along with *If Wishes Were Horses*' primary narrator, Joe McCoy, the dominant white voice in the story. McCoy finds himself on a quest to meet both Ray and Gideon as he searches for a way to reclaim the life he lost when he chose not to pitch in the Iowa state baseball championship game during his senior year because he did not have his preferred four days' rest in between games. Knowing the reputations of the two other men, McCoy seeks their assistance in replaying the game, this time with him pitching.

Playing on Ray's field once again supports the overwhelmingly white history of the game. Searching for Ray out of "frustration at not being able to repeat [his] journey to the past," McCoy admits that he has "heard [Ray's] baseball field has healing properties" (15). Intentional or not, however, the only players who have been afforded an opportunity to participate on the field are white. Though his high school team competed in a time that was decades after the game was integrated, McCoy makes no mention of minority players on the team, implying that, much like the communities already described in the earlier novels, the players were all white.

The two teams playing in the 1908 exhibition in *The Iowa Baseball Confederacy* are understandably all white and represent the culture of the game 39 years before its highest level was integrated. The Grand Mound Greenshirts from *Magic Time*, however, are integrated and have players of Hispanic and Asian heritage. This racially diverse team does not mean that the Grand Mound community is without prejudice. Though the team itself is more accepting of racial minorities, it is clear that some of the townspeople are uncomfortable with having non-whites in their community.

On his first day in Grand Mound, Mike Houle reads an article in the local newspaper, the *Grand Mound Leader*, announcing the arrival of new players in the town. Houle is one of three new team members, the others being Daniel Morgenstern, a New Jersey native with dark hair, and Stanley Wood from San Francisco, of whom there is no picture available. The initial newspaper article and accompanying pictures reflect no racial tensions by themselves, but evidence of the limited racial tolerance is quickly made known as Mike meets his two fellow arrivals to the team. Wanting to share their initial reactions to the town and its citizens, Houle seeks out Wood, who immediately shares some of the racial comments that were directed at him by his teammates during the inter-squad game. Wood explains that he is Taiwanese and his family name, Woo, was changed by his father to Wood so "business associates wouldn't find out [they] were Asian until they had to look [them] in the eye" (106). The racial tension noticed by Wood's father on the west coast is also apparent in Grand Mound as Stanley's host family is "horrified" to discover he is Asian and that it "apparently never occurred to anyone in Grand Mound that Stanley Wood of San Francisco, California, would not be white" (105). The implication, then, is that the town is accustomed to having a predominately white team and that what minorities there are on the roster were known as such before they arrived. The town's racial bias is reinforced when Stanley reveals to Mike that his ethnicity was unknown to everyone in town before his arrival, including the baseball team's management. Based on the reception from his host family and the players already on the roster, there is no indication that had the community been aware of Stanley's ethnicity, he would have been offered a place on the team; in fact, based on their behavior once Wood arrives in Grand Mound, all evidence suggests the contrary. The town, therefore, clearly demonstrates an intention to remain predominantly white while ensuring that any minorities who are welcomed into the community are carefully screened and selected by members of the Booster Club and its host families.

Despite the obvious examples of racial tension and struggle in both baseball and communities like Grand Mound, where baseball serves a central role, the game and such communities are often presented as idyllic representations of a world without racial divides. Justin Birdsong, the agent for Mike Houle, Dan Morgenstern, and Stanley Wood, directs his clients towards the town, but being African-American alienates him from the team and town. Telling Mike of the conversation he had with a member of the Grand Mound Booster Club, Birdsong is drawn to those things he sees as advantages to living in a small town until he remembers various aspects of segregation from his own childhood, including his sitting in the balcony of a movie theatre as a boy, living in a town where he recalls separate washrooms and water fountains to accommodate both the black and the white populations in the "separate but equal" South. Able to offer Grand Mound players to fill its team roster, Birdsong is aware that this is the only connection he has with the town, a connection through the game of baseball. Ironically, the African-American agent who never physically appears in the novel is responsible for at least one minority player being invited by the Grand Mound Boosters to join the predominantly white team.

When studying baseball's development in America and the ways in which it came to include peoples of various races, it becomes clear that the early years of the sport, even as late as the early 1900s, were dominated by whites. Although a variety of leagues were started in the early twentieth century to provide playing opportunities for minorities, the major leagues were filled with players of predominately white ancestry with a few notable exceptions of Native American players. It has been estimated "that over 90 percent of the professional baseball players into the early 1900s were from only three groups—old-stock Americans, Irish-Americans, and German-Americans" (Zoss and Bowman 122). While it may be argued that many of the minority groups that are a part of baseball in America today had not yet come to the United States in the nineteenth century, it is clear that "[t]here has been more than enough prejudice and discrimination to go around in America, and baseball has been very much a part of that scene" (125). The whiteness of the game represented through the 1919 Chicago White Sox in *Shoeless Joe* and in the 1908 Chicago Cubs in *The Iowa Baseball Confederacy* may be attributed to the lack of diversity in the game during those times; the marginalized treatment of the minority players in *Magic Time*, however, reminds the reader that baseball, even in Kinsella's utopian Iowa communities, has a history that is marked with racial imbalance and injustice.

Gender and Baseball in Kinsella's Communities

While players from all ethnicities and races now compete in major league baseball, there is still one group of Americans who are left, literally, on the sidelines watching the game rather than being afforded the opportunity to compete in it: women. Albert Spalding, having neglected to mention any specific racial constructs in his early history of the sport in the United States, left no question as to how he saw women fitting into the game of baseball:

> Neither our wives, our sisters, our daughters, nor our sweethearts, may play Base Ball on the field. They may play Cricket, but seldom do; they may play Lawn Tennis, and win championships; they may play Basket Ball, and achieve laurels; they may play Golf, and receive trophies; but Base Ball is too strenuous for womankind except that she may take part in grandstand, with applause for the brilliant play, with waving kerchief to the hero of the three-bagger, and, since she is ever a loyal partisan of the home team, with smiles of derision for the Umpire when he gives us the worst of it, and, for the same reason, with occasional perfectly decorous demonstrations when it becomes necessary to rattle the opposing pitcher [11].

Continuing to marginalize the role women may have in the sport, Spalding further asserts that "spectators of the sterner sex may play the game on field, in grandstand or on bleachers" (11). While non-white players finally claimed their rightful places on the rosters of major league teams beginning in 1947, women still are noticeably absent on all rosters at the sport's highest level and in the overwhelming majority of front office positions in the game. With the exception of the All-American Girls Professional Baseball League (AAGPBL) established during World War II in 1943, when many teams' rosters were depleted with players serving in the military, and continuing through 1954, few outlets have been offered to women to play baseball professionally. The most recent women's baseball team to achieve any degree of success and notoriety was the Colorado Silver Bullets who, from 1994–97, competed against "men's teams within the ranks of minor league, semi-pro, college, and amateur baseball," compiling its only winning season in 1997 with a record of 23–22 (*Colorado Silver Bullets*).

In an examination of the role that baseball or any sport has in a culture, the roles of the people within the culture must be defined through the sport itself; therefore, in the case of baseball as a national identity, it is important to consider the role that women have in the culture. As sport is often associated with the masculine members of society, evidenced by Spalding's comments about the "sterner sex," it is imperative that this examination include the role that women have in the game of baseball and in the fiction that is based on the sport. Kinsella's writing often deals with the subject of fathers and sons, an area that is more completely discussed in the following chapter, and how baseball connects these two representations of the male character together. Consequently, the female voice appears, at first, to be lacking.

David McGimpsey, in *Imagining Baseball: America's Pastime and Popular Culture*, writes that "[b]aseball's cultural products, like baseball itself, are predominantly male. Similarly, there is no resolute correlation of, or alibi for, the gender imbalance in baseball's fiction reality. The women are, with some notable exceptions, in the background of the texts that form the body of baseball fiction" (13). Cordelia Candelaria echoes this idea while including other assertions about the game and its fiction: "Mirroring the pervasive ethnocentrism and male chauvinism of American society, baseball fiction is, with few notable exceptions, largely about white men participating in a closed activity of the dominant—that is, white, male Christian, and capitalist—culture" (*Seeking* 3). Even today, with a broad spectrum of nationalities and cultures represented in the major leagues, women are noticeably absent. With the exception of select instances, there have been few female owners. No woman has played in a Major League Baseball game, although there have been those leagues throughout the game's history which have afforded women's teams opportunities to compete against one another. In fact, it was not until late in the twentieth century that pitcher "Ila Borders became the first woman to pitch and win [in] a men's professional baseball league, debuting in 1997 and earning her first win in 1998" (Mandel 131). Mike Veeck, the team owner who signed Borders to play for the St. Paul Saints of the Northern League, an independent baseball league unaffiliated with any major league teams, also made headlines in 2009 when he hired Justine Siegal, believed to be "the first female coach in men's professional baseball," for the Brockton (MA) Rox. Recognizing the rarity of a female coach at any level, specifically a professional team, Rox bench coach Ed Nottle says, "people have to be given opportunities. No matter how this turns out, I think it's going to mean a lot to all the young girls out there. For that reason alone, I'm behind her" (Buckley B16). While a female presence may be emerging in more levels of the sport, the game's literature is only now starting to reflect this shift. The lack of female voice in what Kathleen Sullivan calls "the 'boys only' club that seems to be baseball literature" (4), specifically Kinsella's, is representative of the gendered culture of the sport which, in turn, mirrors the culture of many Western societies, including the United States.

Poet Donald Hall has examined the game of baseball and what it means to Americans, and he concludes that the sport is unable to be separated from the country's history, a history told from the colonizer's point of view, a view that is predominantly male: "like nothing else among American things, an endless game of repeated summers, joining the long generations of all the fathers and all the sons" (46). The game, often compared to religion by authors and critics alike, has become a series of traditions that are continued not out of belief, but simply to serve as a link to the past. The aspects of the game that represent the white culture to Drifting Away as his tribe is overtaken by white colonizers in *The Iowa Baseball Confederacy* have now become ways in which the prevailing society connects with its roots. Beyond society, though, Hall goes on to write that the connections are predominately, if not exclusively, male: "Baseball connects American males with each other, not only through bleacher friendships and neighbor loyalties, not only through barroom fights, but most importantly, through generations" (49). While the game is again seen as a connective thread linking America's present to its past, that connection seems limited only to the male members of the dominant society.

In explaining why baseball makes such a useful tool in his writing, W.P. Kinsella says that the game is important to his fictional stories because of "its open-endedness. The other sports ... are twice enclosed: first by time limits and then by rigid playing boundaries" (Shannon, *Baseball* 7). Though every other major sport in the United States is confined by spatial limitations—out of bounds, lines of scrimmage, foul lines, half-court—baseball remains the only game that is spatially open: "Baseball ... knows no time limits, and on the true baseball field, the foul lines diverge forever, eventually, because of their sheer numbers, taking in most, or all of the universe" (7). Following Kinsella's assertion, it is clear that baseball is the most colonizing of all American sports, resulting in the patriarchal structure that mirrors many national ideological institutions. As the foul lines, in theory, diverge forever, crisscrossing one another in space, the game has already conquered the entire planet. The fact that the game is not controlled by a clock, but by the players as long as the game remains tied, the domination can hypothetically continue forever. Kinsella himself gives readers a taste of limitlessness in *The Iowa Baseball Confederacy* when two teams play for over one month as an act of ultimate male supremacy in the midst of a flood of Biblical proportions. It is important to note, however, that the game of baseball in this and other examples is not dominated by "Father Time" and is generally associated with "Mother Nature" as a pastoral game. George Bowering argues that baseball "is just about signifier, [and] very little signified" (119), while Nicholas Mount counters that the game "signifies a host of referents ... [it] symbolizes youth, nostalgia, springtime, harmony, simplicity. In a word, baseball signifies pastoralism" (62). The game, as a pastoral signifier, is associated with the rebirth of a new season, spring, paralleling the renewal of "Mother Nature" herself. While the game, in everyday life as well as in baseball fiction, may be male dominated, it is shown to have very feminine traits and associations.

Kinsella's fiction, dominated by male characters playing the game or attempting to connect with those who play the game, is saturated with imagery that is expressly feminine in nature. Even while sitting with his daughter, Karin, watching Joe Jackson play on his field early in the novel *Shoeless Joe*, Ray Kinsella uses feminine language and references to the two females in his life in responding to Jackson's assertion that the field and farm must be Heaven: "No. It's Iowa," Ray tells Jackson, feeling "the night rubbing softly against [his] face," watching his daughter sleep in his arms, thinking of his wife, Annie, and her love that awaits his return to the house, and smelling the fresh-cut grass hanging in the air, all the while watching the left fielder position himself for the next pitch. While watching the very much male dominated game, Ray is drawn to the feminine representations that surround him: his wife, his daughter, and Mother Nature. The balance found in the text provides an extremely important role for the feminine in a world that is largely masculine. In Ray's personally constructed world built on the family farm, neither masculine nor feminine elements are able to be complete without the other. The masculine game, for instance, is only complete when united on the field with Mother Nature.

Despite Kinsella's heavy reliance on pastoral descriptions and feminine references, many critics of his novels take him "to task for the inadequacies of his female characters" (Cameron 46). Annie, Ray's wife in both *Shoeless Joe* and *If Wishes Were Horses*, is steadfast in her love towards her husband, never questioning his hearing voices or his plowing under the cash crop on their farm to build a baseball field. It is Ray who takes the initiative to build the field, and it is he who does all of the physical labor on the field, referring only to his wife as a support structure who tells him, "Oh love, if it makes you happy you should do it" (4). In her study *Women Characters in Baseball Literature*, Kathleen Sullivan writes that Annie "defends her home for her husband ... allowing Ray Kinsella a safe place to return after his cross country journey" (137) and "possesses the qualities of Hestia because she maintains their home, making it a place of refuge for her family during their tremendous financial struggles" (143). Intentionally or not, Annie enables Ray to assert his patriarchal dominance, putting his family and its financial future in jeopardy by plowing under his crop in order to build the baseball field, the sole motivation for which is to bring back to life Joe Jackson and his own father, John Kinsella. However, as Sullivan concludes, eventually Ray is only able to save the family farm because Annie "unconditionally supports her husband's plans, which often conflict with logic and appear to place her home and family in danger" (144).

Perhaps the passage most telling of Annie's role in the novel is when Ray describes when they first met; he was a student in college and she was the young daughter of his landlady. When Ray overheard a conversation between Annie and her girlfriends in which they were talking about their future plans, Annie proclaimed that she would, once she grew up, marry Ray. Although her friends all mentioned very specific occupations for their adult vocations, Annie named being with Ray as her life's goal. Through Annie's support of her husband's quests to build the field, kidnap J.D. Salinger, and travel to Minnesota in search of a player who has been dead for several years, her identity expresses itself only through her relationship with Ray. She is identified as Ray's wife and Karin's mother, nothing else; in fact, nothing more is known of her beyond her unfailing love and support for Ray, their daughter, and his project. Annie Kinsella is only one of several marginalized females in Kinsella's novels, each of which is told from the viewpoint of a masculine narrator.

The uniqueness of *Shoeless Joe* in Kinsella's canon of baseball literature exists because there is a female character from whom, however marginalized she may be, the protagonist draws motivation and support. In *The Iowa Baseball Confederacy* this supportive female character is noticeably absent from the narrator's life, and in *Box Socials, If Wishes Were Horses* and *Magic Time*, the females fill the traditional roles assigned by the dominant males: mothers, wives, and girlfriends. Gideon Clarke, a man who, like his father before him, is on a quest to prove the existence of the Iowa Baseball Confederacy and to find evidence of a game played against the 1908 Chicago Cubs, is the sole remaining member of his family in Onamata, Iowa. His mother has long since abandoned the family, and his sister, an urban guerrilla named Enola Gay, is on the run from the FBI and contacts her brother only when she threatens him for not providing her with financial support. Gideon, however, describes the influence of his deceased father as "a giant smothering me with his shadow" (*Iowa* 45). His own wife, Sunny, provides no background information on her life before they are married and refuses to offer any more insight after they are married. Just as his obsession with proving the Confederacy's existence to the people who have laughed at his family name for years mirrors his father's obsession, Gideon finds himself being drawn towards the same types of women as his father; the smothering shadow of his father, therefore, is inescapable in both the good — the obsession with the league — and the bad — the women whom they love and who ultimately leave them. In each instance of these relationships, Gideon is alienated from the females in his life and is motivated, not by a female character as was Ray Kinsella, but by the need to validate his father's story of the Confederacy.

Even with Gideon's separation from his family in Onamata, he is able to find a female character with whom he connects on a physical and emotional level when he and his friend, Stan, are transported 70 years back in time to July of 1908, the summer in which the Confederacy All-Stars played the Chicago Cubs. Sarah Swan, the sister of an All-Star playing in the game, is courted by Gideon as he lives in this parallel time period. Physically, she reminds Gideon of his transient wife, Sunny, who constantly drifts in and out of his life at her own discretion. Sarah, however, becomes so closely connected to Gideon that she is willing to leave her life in Big Inning, Iowa, and take the train from the Baseball Spur to start a new life anywhere outside of the only place she has ever lived. Kinsella's recurring motif in the story of Gideon losing all of the women in his life is continued as the Indian spirits, who are using the game in the flood as a test of wills, root Sarah to the ground in the midst of the rising waters. Ultimately, the day after the game ends, Gideon witnesses the first automobile fatality in Big Inning, Iowa, with Sarah as the victim. In each case — as mother, sister, wife, or lover — Gideon's ideal female remains, for him, unattainable. Only in the other novel in which his character appears, *If Wishes Were Horses*, does he finally find his ideal woman, Francie Bly, who is literally and figuratively delivered to him by former pitcher Joe McCoy.

While first reading *The Iowa Baseball Confederacy*, it appears that Kinsella purpose shows his female characters alienating themselves, leaving the story to be driven by the masculine members of the culture in which the story is set. A closer reading, however, clearly demonstrates that the entire novel centers on the male-female relationships. The epic game that Gideon witnesses to prove the league's existence is actually a battle of wills between Drifting Away, a Black Hawk warrior, and the tribal grandfathers against whom he finds himself pitted. When Drifting Away stopped to sleep only a half a day's ride away from his wife, Onamata, for whom the town was renamed in 1909, white men came and killed her; in return, the grandfathers had her remains scattered to the four corners of the Earth. If Drifting Away is able to aid the Confederacy in winning the game against the Cubs, the grandfathers will allow him to be reunited with his wife, as they have declared the time has come for the warrior and Onamata to be together. The game, based on his unique vision, is what will lead to that reunion: "Because my power vision was of baseball, the game is the thing" (208). The underlying story, then, is not the game itself, but the potential reunion between the two separated lovers. Were it not for the opportunity to gain redemption for his physical weakness that led to his wife's death, there would be no significance to the game other than as a form of entertainment during the Fourth of July festivities in Big Inning. Instead, the game takes on Albert Spalding's definition of the game: "Base Ball is War!" (7). With echoes of the game's imperialistic traits, seen as the two teams are locked in an epic on-field struggle, Drifting Away conveys the significance of the game as a war to Gideon, saying the game will last "[u]ntil one of us wins," emphasizing that, because of the patience both he and the grandfathers have demonstrated thus far, the contest could continue for years to come (210). Drifting Away's long-awaited reunion is a battle between two groups of men, "the greatest baseball team in the world" and "a group of farm boys" that compares to "the cavalry fighting the Indians" (208), in a game most often described in feminine terms and language. The key character, therefore, is not one of the male players, Gideon, or Drifting Away, but Onamata and her representation, the Black Angel. Without her separation from Drifting Away, no contest between the grandfathers and her husband, exemplified in the game, would exist.

For Gideon Clarke, his life lacks a continually stable female character. His mother abandoned him and his father; his sister has no relationship with him as she, too, left the male members of the family and became a fugitive of justice; the girl with whom he falls in love in 1908, Sarah, is killed by a car as she tries to walk across the street towards him; and his wife, Sunny, repeatedly tells him that she will not remain captive to him or the life in Onamata, eventually leaving him for good upon his return from the journey 70 years back in time. As she leaves Gideon for the last time, and as he tries one last time to keep her in Onamata, Sunny, like Sarah years before, is presumably struck and killed by a passing vehicle. The only female in the novel on whom Gideon can rely is Missy Baron, the mentally handicapped daughter of John and Marylyle Baron and the only female in the novel who remains with Gideon. Like the game of baseball itself, in which women lack a place equal to that of men, Kinsella's town of Big Inning/Onamata marginalizes women by limiting the roles they may take. Though the game centers on the resurrection of Onamata, the contest between the All-Stars and the Cubs is carried on by the male players, leaving her fate in their hands. The patriarchal structures of the Native Americans and the white settlers' societies combine to control the destiny of Onamata and her reunion with Drifting Away.

Contrasting Gideon's inability to find a stable relationship with a female character in the novel is his best friend, Stan Rogalski. At age 33, a time at which a minor league player is no longer considered a legitimate prospect for the major leagues, Stan continues to play minor league baseball in the hopes that he will soon be called up to the game's highest level to fill in a utility role. While Sunny comes and goes from Gideon's life, Stan's wife, Gloria, not only remains with her husband, but encourages him in his increasingly unrealistic pursuit of his baseball dreams. Much like Annie Kinsella does with Ray, Gloria tells Stan that she will remain with him after he informs her during his brief retirement two years earlier that he wants one more opportunity to join a minor league team. Gideon and Stan both share a passion for baseball and each of them individually is identified by his relationship with the game; however, Gideon must fight, not only the stigma within the academic community of his researching a supposedly nonexistent league, but he must do so without the support of his wife while Stan is able to continue only because of the strength and support drawn from Gloria.

Continuing its role as the antithesis of Kinsella's baseball novels, *Box Socials*, though not presenting universal equality between men and women, does reflect a structure in which women characters fill a more assertive, even preferred role. Feminine assertion beyond the home and hearth exists, in Kinsella's novels, only in Canada. Though his father traveled throughout the United States playing baseball and working following World War One, Jamie O'Day is never able to "establish who he played for, or who with, or for how long" (38). Unlike Ray Kinsella and Gideon Clarke, both of whom have specific details regarding their fathers and the role each had in the game of baseball, Jamie has no such information. Now living in Canada, where the game plays a far less prominent role in the Six Towns culture, dominated by families of Scandinavian descent, Jamie lacks the strong relationship with his father, based on the game, that the narrators of the two previous novels had. When various families from the community meet in the O'Day home to discuss the possibility of having a box social event for the area children, Jamie confesses that he "was more interested in the women than the men; the men tended to discuss matters that didn't interest me a lot, or that I didn't entirely understand," matters like farming, vehicles, and stories of sexual prowess (77). By rejecting an opportunity to sit with the men, deciding instead to sit in the kitchen corner listening to the women gossip, Jamie is the only one of Kinsella's narrators to prefer the company of women who were "much more interesting than the men" (78). This apparent emasculation is further supported when the reader recognizes that, unlike the rest of Kinsella's male narrators—Ray, Gideon, Joe, and Mike—Jamie is the only one who has no strong connection to the game, attending only the game in which Truckbox Al bats against Bob Feller.

Despite the diminished presence of baseball and the increased voice provided to women in the novel, *Box Socials* also demonstrates once again the sexist and arguably misogynistic tradition of the game. Feminist theorists Sandra Gilbert and Susan Gubar argue, "[i]t is debilitating to be *any* woman in a society where women are warned that if they do not behave like angels they must be monsters" (2029). While Jamie describes his mother in a manner more likely to place her in the angelic role, Louisa May Sigurdson may be read in the more monster-like role as the reason for Truckbox Al McClintock's failure in the all-star game against major league pitcher Bob Feller. Upon meeting McClintock for the first time and asking him if he is "the guy's going to Edmonton to play baseball," Louisa May offers, in return for

Al taking her with him, away from the Six Towns area and into the larger city, sexual favors that will "both curl his toes and rot his socks" (74).

Fulfilling her promise to Truckbox Al on their first night in Edmonton, Louisa May rejects his offer for another sexual encounter, deferring until after the game is over and she can witness for herself his athletic ability. After striking out against Feller, Al returns to the dugout in time to see her leave the ballpark "with at least one, and maybe two or three, American soldiers" (221), never to return to the Six Towns area. With the baseball game serving as a field for sexual competition, a competition Truckbox Al also loses when Louisa May leaves with the soldiers, the female character is finally given a position of power within Kinsella's work. As an observer of a game that has for years limited the role of females in its construct, Louisa May Sigurdson sees Al McClintock as nothing more than a resource to be used as a means of escaping the rural confining community to a much larger city, affording her the opportunity to escape with the American soldiers, once more reinforcing the dominance of not only the male voice, but the American male voice. Whereas the female characters in Kinsella's other novels are absent from the male narrative, Louisa May Sigurdson represents a shift to a female character who is present until her goal of exploiting Truckbox Al's success for her own advancement is achieved. Rather than, as in many of the other novels, a woman being used as, at best, a peripheral character who fills the needs of the husband, Louisa May fulfills Al's sexual needs only as a means to escaping from the Six Towns area.

Though it differs from his other novels in a variety of ways, *Box Socials* provides Kinsella several key opportunities to show alternate patterns at work in his body of fiction. Shifting the setting from Iowa to Canada and incorporating a stronger, more autonomous female character into the plot necessitates that baseball be more peripheral than in the other novels. Continuing to rely on baseball's existing constructs for women would have further marginalized the women within the Six Towns community; however, by changing the setting to a place where baseball is not seen as a method of identifying the community as a whole, the female characters are not oppressed by any such existing roles and expectations found in the game.

Following his only novel involving some element of baseball to be set solely in Canada, Kinsella's fourth novel, *If Wishes Were Horses*, returns to the Iowa landscape that serves as the backdrop for many of his short stories and nearly all of his novels in which the game is used. Beyond simply returning to Iowa, however, Kinsella incorporates the narrators from his first two novels, Ray Kinsella and Gideon Clarke, and sets the story in the town of Lone Tree, presumably a place within a reasonable distance from the settings of the earlier books. While a casual reader unfamiliar with the first two books may not grasp the significance of this novel's setting, the return to the rural, predominantly white communities already used in his earlier fiction, Kinsella reinforces those societal paradigms already discussed. Similarly, the gender issues from within the communities of *Shoeless Joe* and *The Iowa Baseball Confederacy* reemerge and are often strengthened in *If Wishes Were Horses.*

Although three characters—Ray Kinsella, Gideon Clarke, and Joe McCoy—share the role of narrator in the novel, the plot centers on McCoy's lives in parallel dimensions of time and how he tries to amend for his mistake in high school of refusing to pitch in the state championship game on less than four days' rest, a decision that costs his team a title, but provides him an opportunity to continue playing in college and, eventually, in the major leagues. In his post-baseball life as an investigative reporter in California, McCoy encounters an extraterrestrial form that causes him to suspect that he has been living simultaneously in two dimensions of time and place—one based on his refusal to pitch in the game and the other as though he had pitched the game and never left Iowa.

Most of the novel is spent with Joe McCoy and Francie Bly, a woman with whom he falls in love, on the run with a baby mysteriously left in their care in the Los Angeles airport. As a result, the plot lacks the strong connection to the Iowa community that is found in the first two novels; however, weaving the narrations of the three men together, Kinsella is able to introduce a new community to the reader, a community of three men, all of whom share a love for the game and what it brings to their own lives. That the entire novel is told from three males voices once again removes any significant female voice, thus marginalizing their roles in the novel.

Of the female characters who are mentioned in the book, only two are developed with any great detail and both of them are described in Joe McCoy's narrative. Maureen Renn, McCoy's high school girlfriend, is a casualty of his decision to put his own baseball career ahead of the high school championship. Once he decides to save his arm to continue pitching at the college and professional levels, McCoy leaves Lone Tree, never to return for more than the briefest and most infrequent of visits, the last being when his mother dies and he returns for the funeral, yet another case of an absent mother in Kinsella's texts, though not one of significance to the plot of this novel. When first meeting Gideon and Ray, McCoy says that he would prefer to live his life over so that, among other things, he could "marry [his] high-school sweetheart ... and live happily ever after" (28). Despite the dominant presence of the male voice, the novel's protagonist recognizes that his life is not as fulfilled as it could have been had he placed Maureen and their relationship above his own interest in the game and his career. At the end of the novel, as Maureen lies in the hospital dying from cancer, Joe McCoy is able to change his life's trajectory by reliving the high school championship on Ray's baseball field, thereby saving Maureen and giving him the life he feels has always eluded him.

The second female character in the novel, Francie Bly, leaves her fiancé, who is also the brother of McCoy's love interest in Los Angeles, and runs off with McCoy as he travels to Iowa in the search for the life he left behind in high school. Though he initially feels as though he is falling in love with Bly, often dreaming of her, McCoy's dreams and thoughts soon begin to turn more towards Maureen; thus, Bly's role is more of an aid in assisting McCoy to reach the life to which he is trying to return. Although both women are often described as hypersexual instigators in the relationships with McCoy, they are described as such by McCoy himself, who can shape the narrative to fit his own male dominated agenda. Further reinforcing this concept, when McCoy arrives at Ray's farm to begin reversing his life by replaying the championship game, Francie Bly falls in love with Gideon Clarke. After losing both his wife, Sunny, and Sarah Swan, with whom he falls in love in 1908 Big Inning, Gideon has been left with no female presence other than his guardianship over Missy Baron, the mentally handicapped woman with whom he is entrusted at the end of *The Iowa Baseball Confederacy*. He has his own desire for a woman to love fulfilled once McCoy brings Bly to him in Iowa. In both cases, Bly and Renn are described as commodities through which Gideon and McCoy find personal and sexual fulfillment. Despite the lack of a central community as in earlier novels—much of his story, in fact, takes place while McCoy and Bly are traveling across the country attempting to avoid capture—the ideas of the patriarchal dominance and privileging of the male voice once again solidifies these same structures found in the Iowa communities previously used by Kinsella.

Unlike the females in Big Inning/Onamata, Iowa, where the game is driven by the relationship between a husband and a wife, the women in Grand Mound, Iowa, the setting of Kinsella's most recent novel, *Magic Time*, are used as little more than commodities whose purpose is to help draw unsuspecting baseball players to the town. The Grand Mound Booster Club that lures players of marginal ability to town to play on the Greenshirts is comprised only of men; there are no women who offer input into the decision-making of the group inviting players into the community. After only a few weeks in Grand Mound, Mike comes to view Marge Powell as "the mother [he's] never known" and Tracy Ellen as a girl with whom he envisions a romantic relationship (83). His father, after visiting the town only a few times, is "seduced by [the town] and by Peggy McNee" (183), a widow in the community. Similarly, when the groundskeeper Roger Cash originally comes into town to hustle a game against the Greenshirts, he is injured and becomes "seriously involved with Janet," another local widow (209). Several times during his initial stay in Grand Mound, Mike is told that a large majority of the players are drawn to the town for baseball before eventually settling down to marry local girls and start new lives of domesticity. The females in the town, therefore, are presented as commodities offered to the players in an effort to sustain the town's existence. Women are offered both sexually and socially to the players, pandering to the male needs within Grand Mound. Women are given no positions of power, nor are they included in the business of the Booster Club that decides on the players to be scouted and invited to join their team. Though scholars of the game assert that "women are much more a part of the organized sports world than ever before in history" (Zoss and Bowman 196), Kinsella limits the role of women within the game's structure to that of spectators while they serve outside of the game as the excuse for the players choosing to settle in the town. Females, therefore, are unequal with males in their level of importance as the team's decisions and structure are dominated by the Grand Mound patriarchs.

Social Class and Baseball in Kinsella's Communities

Throughout baseball's rich and often tumultuous history, the game has both unified and divided the country that claims it as the National Pastime. In his essay "The Nationalist Pastime: The Use of Baseball to Promote Nationalism Globally," Russ Crawford argues that baseball was unable to hold the country together before the Civil War, but the war "was instrumental in spreading the popularity of the sport to men from all sections of the nation" (126). While most studies of nineteenth century America may focus, rightfully so, on the strained relationships of the Northern and Southern states and their clashing ideologies, Crawford further asserts that in the antebellum years, "before the war spread the popularity of the sport, the celebrated match between the old-stock Protestant middle class Excelsiors and the Irish Catholic working-class Atlantics demonstrated the tensions that could arise when class, ethnicity, and nationalism formed the milieu in which the game was played" (128).

The class divisions in contemporary baseball continue to take on new dimensions as fans of small- and mid-market teams like the Pittsburgh Pirates with low payrolls and limited on-field success bemoan the fact that larger-market teams like the New York Yankees, who have virtually unlimited financial resources, enjoy unparalleled success in the postseason. Cutting across these obvious class differences, however, the game's historical narrative has emphasized the traditional Puritan work ethic of the colonial times. While the disproportionate payrolls between such teams does not necessarily indicate that only wealthy fans will identify with the Yankees or that only lower income fans will identify with the Pirates, it does show the ways in which the perceptions of the "haves" versus the "have nots" seen on an individual level also manifest themselves at the major league level.

When asked why baseball has "generated such a large body of quality fiction" as opposed to other sports, Mark Harris, author of multiple novels within the genre, responded that "baseball was always available to poorer people, whereas football for many years was just for college people. And certainly tennis and golf were not the common man's games. Golf clubs and tennis clubs by their own rules excluded anybody but white males, etc." (Horvath and Palmer 187). It has also been argued that "[o]rganized baseball may be the most perfectly meritocratic social organization in modern America. Better players rise higher in the organization, become more famous, and make more money" (Morris 116). This idealistic view of the game, however, ignores the fact that for many years the game was limited to white males. Admittedly, baseball also has a past of excluding non-whites and still marginalizes the roles of women in the establishment; however, the game is perhaps the first sport available for participation to people of all classes in America. This ostensible classlessness is structural, in part. According to George B. Kirsch, who has detailed the history of baseball during the Civil War, the democratic aspect of the evolving game in the mid–nineteenth century is rooted in the fact that "[b]aseball had no clear fixed or privileged positions," including the pitcher, "who was supposed to throw 'good balls' that players could strike" (24). Unlike individual sports where the emphasis is on one-on-one competition, baseball was the first sport in the country to distribute the responsibility of offense and defense evenly to each member of the team. Every position player in the field on defense has the opportunity to score runs while taking a turn at the plate. The expectation to contribute to the good of the team, therefore, rests not on just one player but on each player as an individual.

Beyond structural classlessness, baseball's relationship with its audiences and communities has also included significant elements of more romantic notions. As the game developed through the nineteenth century and spread during the Civil War and into the Reconstruction Era to parts of the nation that had been unfamiliar with the game before the war, it was viewed "as an urban phenomenon, better suited to the values and needs of merchants, clerks, journalists, skilled workers, and other townspeople than to those of slave masters or rural folk" (Kirsch 25). By the early twentieth century the game was seen developing a "brilliant array of ... men of eminence in all the professions and in every avenue of commercial and industrial activity" (Spalding 5). Following the acceptance of players from all social classes, it is clear that the game came to be viewed by many as an urban sport to be played by workers from within the labor community. Contrary to this view, the game has often been perceived by critics and scholars as a pastoral symbol found within the urban setting. Bryan K. Garman argues that, even in contemporary society, "the most aesthetically pleasing of the major league ball parks, particularly those that have maintained natural grass playing fields, serve as respites from the homogeneous urban concrete and the city's morally complex and hectic pace" (47). The game, therefore, is a melding of the pastoral characteristics that are largely romanticized by fans and writers of the game and the urban framework in which the game is so often set.

While baseball in Kinsella's novels often marginalizes or even disregards minorities and women, the novels participate in a romanticized, classless view of the game, allowing everyone within the communities to participate on some level, either as members of the team or part of the community of spectators in the stands who are represented by the players in the game. Though the first collegiate game was played between Amherst and Williams in 1859 (Kirsch 73), the game's popularity quickly grew to the point where Americans from all walks of life, not just those in college, became connected with the game. In the crucial developmental years during and immediately following the Civil War, "Native and foreigner, young and old, white and black, male and female, craftsman and clerk, merchant and manager, affluent and humble, all took part in the action [of baseball]" (70). This acceptance of all classes of people in the game is in stark contrast to Albert Spalding's reminder "that the men who first gave impetus to our national sport ... were gentlemen 'to the manor born,' men of fine tastes, of high ability, of upright character" (51). While baseball's history demonstrates that professional teams in the major leagues were not inclusive towards minorities, even after Jackie Robinson broke the color barrier in 1947, the game, unlike football, golf, and tennis, did start to blend players from all social classes once team owners realized that many of the blue collar or factory workers might have the physical abilities needed to win games for them. Though Kinsella's communities are predominately white and patriarchal in structure, the towns show little if any evidence of social class division and, in the case of Grand Mound, Iowa, appear utopian in their organization.

Within the two communities of Big Inning and Grand Mound, baseball is an integral part of the identity of the towns as a whole. Without the game, neither of these towns has anything to separate it from the rest of the farming towns dotting the Iowa landscape. Kinsella uses the game to eliminate the class distinctions that have defined so much of America's development and expansion, echoing the sentimental and idealized descriptions of America and the myths of the game voiced at least a century earlier by Walt Whitman and Albert Spalding. In Big Inning/Onamata, Iowa, of *The Iowa Baseball Confederacy,* the game validates the existence of the town and the league itself, something that Gideon Clarke and his father have spent their entire lives attempting to prove. In Grand Mound, Iowa, the game is the only element keeping the town from fading away. In both novels baseball reflects characteristics that define the society — without social classes in an idealistic utopian community.

Gideon Clarke's description of Onamata, Iowa, is vague in its consideration of the townspeople. The 1978 version of the town "consists of thirty houses, a general store, a café, a Conoco service station, a John Deere subagent, and the Clarke & Son Insurance Agency" (22). There is no mention of the people who inhabit the town, but the description clearly indicates that the town's economy is based on the agriculture of the area. The only business that Matthew Clarke's insurance agency generates is through walk-ins or by his casual encounters with his existing customers when he reminds them of their various policies coming up for renewal; Clarke's business is not motivated by financial gain, yet he is able to exist by attending to the basic insurance needs of the farming community.

The only details given regarding Onamata's inhabitants are in Gideon's story of when his mother, Maudie, moved into the family home formerly owned by Matthew's parents, who had moved to Florida. Gideon says his mother had no friendships in town because the younger people all lived on farms outside of town and those people who did live in close proximity to the Clarkes were retirees who had no children living at home. As the only businesses in town mentioned by Gideon provide for the fundamental needs of the farming community, it is obvious that the entire town revolves around various aspects of the agricultural industry. The town's rural setting bears a striking resemblance to the setting Kinsella describes in *Shoeless Joe*, *The Iowa Baseball Confederacy*, *If Wishes Were Horses*, and *Magic Time*. The reliance on the pastoral setting is clarified by David McGimpsey as he compares Major League Baseball's attempt to recreate a rural, pastoral setting in a contemporary urban environment to "the pastoral response in English literature" which is "often less a celebration of rural life than a creation of an imagined, nostalgic place where the unpleasant demands of society can be avoided" (62). Kinsella's use of the rural locale in his baseball novels, clearly evidenced in Onamata/Big Inning of *The Iowa Baseball Confederacy*, enables him to create imagined communities where issues of class can be ignored if not altogether eliminated. Baseball is then presented as an economic development tool, a form of community "boosterism" on which these communities rely on for vitality, growth, and, ultimately, embodies the ideals of class-free capitalism.

Placed in the same geographical location in 1908 as he left in 1978, Gideon is able to experience a completely different community in Big Inning when he is transported through time at the abandoned railroad line, the Baseball Spur. Big Inning is the original version of Onamata before the flood of 1908 literally wiped the town off of the map and out of the minds of nearly everyone who had lived there. In 1909, the town reemerged as Onamata, Iowa, in which Gideon currently lives. Gideon Clarke himself realizes that the two towns share little else other than the plot of land on which they sit as he tells his time-traveling companion, Stan, that the towns are the same only in the sense that they share the same physical location. The houses he sees in Big Inning obviously differ from those in 1978 Onamata because, as Gideon reminds the reader, "There *was* a flood" (128). Unlike the generic description of the townspeople of Onamata, however, Gideon quickly discovers some unique characteristics of the people from the Big Inning area.

As he is introduced to the Twelve-Hour Church of Time Immemorial, a denomination that worships and lives 12 hours ahead of the rest of the community, Gideon is told the congregation will be playing the hymn "I Shall Not Be Moved." The song has "become the theme song for Big Inning," reflecting the town's stubborn nature as it continues to exist even after the railroad's main line bypassed the community, leaving it only with one spur line (144–5). The characteristic resiliency of the town and its inhabitants is represented most clearly in the steadfastness of the unique religion of the church and in the baseball team, both of which are representations of the town as a whole. The Iowa Baseball Confederacy All-Star team plays an exhibition game against the Chicago Cubs that lasts 40 days and 2,614 innings in the catastrophic flood, further demonstrating the firm resolve for which the town is known. Unlike the church, however, the town gains recognition from the newspapers and word of mouth to the point that President Theodore Roosevelt and Leonardo DaVinci appear to watch part of the contest. The town's identity, therefore, is apparent more in the game's characteristics than in the farming industry or religion of the same area. Seventy years later, once all evidence of the team and its legendary contest with the Cubs has literally been washed away by a flood, farming has supplanted the game as the trait for which the town is most known by people both in and out of the community. The "boosterism" that the all-star game brought into Big Inning is also washed away in the flood, eliminating the town's identity in the game as it transforms into Onamata, a town with no baseball history left on its landscape other than the vague evidence of which the Clarkes alone have been made aware.

Although the town is represented through its unwavering citizenry, there is no indication that there is any form of class distinction within the group itself. Gideon's perspective, while somewhat limited, does provide a glimpse into what the town's social structure is like as he and Stan live in the area for over a month as the game is played. At the end of the first day of the exhibition game, the town gathers together at the Big Inning Community Hall where there is a dance and celebration for Independence Day. During the celebration, and in subsequent dinners hosted by the townspeople in the evenings during which the game is played, members of the community rally around the team with no mention of political or social turmoil. The social and economic utopia engendered by baseball is enduring, but Kinsella's characters allow a few glimmers of insight in the cracking facades of the classless society of baseball's America. In a later discussion with Joe Tinker of the Cubs, Gideon is told that the connection between citizens and baseball players is obvious even at the major league level. While recognizing the ideals often associated with professional baseball players, Tinker keenly understands the reality that mere athletic talent is not enough to transcend the barriers dividing the lower class players from the higher class fans and owners between whom baseball is the only common denominator.

Like the All-Stars, the Chicago Cubs are treated with high regard by the area they represent; unlike the All-Stars, however, the Cubs are also viewed under a watchful eye by members of the same city that basks in the team's glory. Unlike the major leagues, Kinsella's rural teams face little evidence that the citizens of Big Inning, Iowa, view the players as anything other than heroes. There is no obvious upper class to treat the All-Stars as suspect, as the Cubs are treated in their hometown. In fact, Big Inning is an anomaly in that the people of the area rally around the team, farming, and religion, with no apparent division within their ranks. Conversely, the Cubs are rallied around only when they win; otherwise, there is a clear distinction between upstanding citizens, the "muck-amucks" and the players, who are "suspect" (215). Interestingly, the city of Chicago would, less than ten years later, be identified by its other baseball team, the White Sox, for eight of its players being accused, acquitted, and later banished for their role in conspiring with gamblers to fix the 1919 World Series against the Cincinnati Reds, the event that inspired Kinsella to write "Shoeless Joe Jackson Comes to Iowa," the foundation for the later novel, *Shoeless Joe*. Tinker's comments seem to foreshadow these events in which baseball players present themselves as being even more "suspect" to those from outside the game.

Kinsella's use of the rural settings in his novels lends itself to a nostalgic, idealistic representation of American communities without class divisions or hierarchal structures that echoes the early days of the game in the United States. In analyzing the history of the game in the mid–nineteenth century, George B. Kirsch details the fact that "[a]ll of the baseball cities had their predominant white-collar clubs of merchants, managers, lawyers, doctors, clerks, actors, and petty professionals" (86), and that "large numbers of middle- and upper middle-class men joined these white-collar clubs" while "an equal or greater number of blue-collar players formed working class clubs" (87). The game in Big Inning is contested between two teams, one amateur and one professional. The Iowa Baseball Confederacy all-stars have no apparent class divisions that separate them from the community they represent, while the Cubs clearly understand that their equality with the upper classes of Chicago extends only as far as the team wins. For Kinsella's communities, no such class division exists as his towns use the game of baseball to demonstrate unity rather than division.

The fact that *Box Socials* is similarly set in a rural community, though in Canada, illuminates even more the one area in which the Six Towns area differs from the other settings—the absence of an overwhelming presence of baseball. The class divisions here, while present, have nothing to do with the game and, therefore, lack the parallels shared by the other novels. Despite the differences between the Canadians, the transplanted Americans, and the European immigrants, the Six Towns area does present itself as a unified community, although only for a brief period, when the citizens take up a collection to send Truckbox Al McClintock to play in the all-star game with many of the citizens following him to Edmonton to watch the game. The differences are noted even by someone as young as Jamie O'Day, who comments on the "English-speaking people" in the area who are "a minority in the Six Towns area," yet who "considered [their] rites, and rituals, and ceremonies, more sensible" than those of the European immigrants (127). The social divisions within the community, then, are predominantly based on language, between the English-speaking citizens and the Norwegian-speaking people.

Despite the language differences that led to this noticeable division, Jamie's mother notes that most of the people living in that area "were hardworking farmers who made a marginal living in good times, but were presently mired in poverty because of the Depression" (139); however, she is careful to note that three specific families, including the Sigurdsons, whose daughter, Louisa May, trades sexual favors to Truckbox Al in exchange for his assistance in getting her to Edmonton, are "all lazy, shiftless, sorry, and ungrateful" and would stay in poverty where they had always been (139). Baseball in general, but specifically in much of the fiction within its genre, often reinforces the disparity between social classes, i.e. the haves vs. the have nots; however, because this specific novel is set in Canada where there is no strong connection to the game, the sport actually reverses this dynamic and, instead, is used to unify a community of diverse nationalities and, at least marginally, financial means.

During the wedding celebration at which Louisa May makes her proposition to Truckbox Al, the community in attendance donated money "from many and various pockets" (204) to pay for his bus fare and hotel accommodations during the weekend for the all-star game. Additionally, an oldtimers' game had been played, the proceeds from which are given to Truckbox Al's father, Curly, who spends the money to buy his son a new uniform for the game. Despite a strong connection to the game and no real sense of community identity rooted in baseball, the people of the Six Towns area realize the significance of the event and rally to support their lone representative in the game, many of them going so far as to spend even more money to travel to Edmonton to watch the game themselves. With an ongoing depression and all of the people lacking sufficient financial resources to justify giving to Al's fund and attending the game, the citizens rally to support the cause, thereby attaching their entire community's identity to Trucknox Al's growing fame. Unlike the other novels in which there is a specific team around which to rally — the White Sox on Ray's field, the Confederacy All-Stars against the Cubs, the Grand Mound Greenshirts, and the Lone Tree high school team — the Six Towns area has no signifying team of their own; therefore, they are only able to identify with one player instead of an entire team. Unfortunately for both Al and the members of the community, his ability to succeed is shown to depend on facing teams from Indian reservations, none of whom know enough about his inadequacies as a player to throw anything other than fastballs. Once his weaknesses are exposed against Bob Feller, there is no indication that the citizens continue to support his athletic endeavors, thereby severing their connection to his identity. Significantly, then, Kinsella's use of the game in this manner demonstrates a unifying and highly nationalistic aspect of the sport not often seen in his fiction.

The town of Grand Mound, Iowa in *Magic Time* is similar to Big Inning from *The Iowa Baseball Confederacy* in that neither place has an apparent division between social classes; however, Grand Mound's identity through the game of baseball is so strong that the game turns the town into an idealized community in which there is no class conflict and everyone works together for the good of the citizenry as a whole. Kinsella utilizes the same type of setting by placing Grand Mound in a rural farming town in Iowa, but Mike Houle, *Magic Time*'s narrator, unlike Gideon Clarke, becomes a citizen of the town rather than being a passer-by in the community. This role allows Mike to present a more intimate view of the town and its relationship with the game of baseball and the league of which it is a part, the Cornbelt League.

In the opening pages of *Magic Time*, Houle recounts the first time that he heard of the community of Grand Mound, Iowa, from his agent, Justin Birdsong, who describes the town as "the perfect place to play baseball" (7). The town's team is part of the Cornbelt League, a semi-professional league unaffiliated with any larger, more established organizations and one in which each team supports its own players, making the individual clubs within the described league their own unique communities. Mike identifies other locations in which he has dreamt of playing as a means of making it to the major league level — Des Moines, Vancouver, and Japan — through their connection to baseball; having never heard of Grand Mound, Houle has no preconceived notions of what the town has to offer other than the chance to play the game. Its only identity, therefore, is that of a location where he can play the game until a major league scout comes to see him play and signs him to a professional contract with more promise than playing exhibition games against members of his own team. The only verification of the town is in an old copy of a road atlas Mike consults before making the trip to Grand Mound; the league itself is unknown in any of the sources he locates or to a sportswriter from the *Chicago Tribune* who says that various amateur and semiprofessional leagues not attached to specific major league organizations largely exist in rural American locations, "especially in the Midwest and South" (61). Grand Mound's identity is similar to that of many Midwestern American towns in the early twentieth century where companies hired players to work during the day and play on the company team in the evenings and on the weekends. These teams, however, combined the financial prowess of the bourgeois employers with the physical abilities of the proletariat players, whereas Grand Mound's team is, in the truest sense, "a loose cooperative, jointly looking after their best interests" (74), where the emphasis is not on wealth or prestige, but on a united community founded on baseball.

A clear connection between the community in *The Iowa Baseball Confederacy* and the community in *Magic Time* is presented as Emmett Powell, the father of Mike's host family with whom he will stay during his time in Grand Mound, tells him that the town name has no intentional connection to a pitching mound. Powell, whose description of the town's name echoes a similar analysis from Gideon Clarke, does tell Mike that another Iowa town was named Big Inning because it *was* connected to the game. Presumably, this Big Inning to which Powell refers is the same Big Inning that was washed away by the flood Gideon details in *The Iowa Baseball Confederacy*. Kinsella's reference back to his earlier novel presents the importance of the names of the towns and how each is connected with the game. Big Inning was named because of baseball, yet it is washed away by a flood and renamed Onamata. Grand Mound, however, is identified solely by its connection to baseball, yet its name has no connection at all to the game. Also serving as a connective thread linking Kinsella's novels is that Ray Kinsella and Gideon Clarke are both narrators in *If Wishes Were Horses*, helping former high school baseball start Joe McCoy return home to the same general vicinity. Knowing that Ray and Gideon are both from the same general area in which he was raised links the novels, not just through the game but through locale as well. The fact that several geographic locations—Johnson County, Lone Tree, Onamata, Big Inning, and Grand Mound—are mentioned in various combinations of all four of Kinsella's Iowa based novels simply reinforces the idea that the identity of the communities, then, is not in the name but in the role baseball plays within the framework of the community as a whole and as an active ingredient in an ostensibly classless society.

The relationship between baseball and Grand Mound is outlined by Emmett Powell who, like Matthew and Gideon Clarke, is an insurance agent. Evidenced in both cases, playing on their professions, the game "insures" both Powell and the Clarkes have an identity within the game, outside of their roles as insurance agents. In the most revealing passage of the town's relationship with the game, Powell explains to Mike the Grand Mound Booster Club's intention of reversing the trend in Iowa where small farming towns disappear as larger corporate farms take over. Expressing no concern about Grand Mound's demise, Powell claims that the town is one of only a few in the state to have shown a population growth "every year for the past five years" (74). This success, minor as it may be with the population being "about the same as it was fifteen or twenty years ago," is attributed to "having a team in the Cornbelt League" (74). The economic revitalization in the community has nothing to do with the agricultural industry and everything to do with presenting the fictional league to the arriving players in Grand Mound. The uniqueness of the Grand Mound Greenshirts is that they only play intra-squad games and are not at all affiliated with an actual league. This information, however, is only revealed to the players as they become woven into the fabric of everyday life in the town and decide to settle down to a permanent residency there. The formula for maintaining the population of the town is implemented by Powell and the rest of the Boosters as they form the co-operative structure for the team and the town in which both institutions work together for their mutual benefit. The game, therefore, is used as bait to lure the players to the town with the hopes that an idyllic Midwestern American lifestyle will be appealing enough for the players to permanently settle into the community. A truly utopian community in which social perfection is achieved in nearly every possible manner, Grand Mound draws on the talents of all who are imperfect, most notably the baseball players notorious for choking in the "real world," combining their talents to form a highly efficient, nearly perfect, harmonious community for all of its citizens.

After his discovery of the town's actual relationships with the game, Mike confronts one of the members of the Boosters, Roger Cash, who reiterates the reasoning behind using the game to lure the players in, saying small towns around the country, even those outside of Iowa, were running the very real risk of dying off as younger people grew up and moved away. The solution, then, was to recruit young baseball players to Grand Mound "who, if we made life attractive for them, would stay with us, marry into the community, keep the faith, so to speak" (203). The community then worked together in a utopian manner in which all of the citizenry labored for the good of the entire town and not just for themselves or their families and presented to the young players the ideal place in which they could exist — a world centered on baseball. The communal elements of the game are such that, even during the daily practices and intra-squad exhibitions, the entire town shows up to demonstrate its support, not for individual players, but for the team as a whole. In Kinsella's setting, supporting the team is intertwined with supporting the town; neither one would be able to exist without the other, making the identity of the town and the identity of the team one in the same.

Though the intentions of the people in Grand Mound may be admirable, Mike Houle comes to the realization that the entire Greenshirts baseball team is comprised of players who are unable to achieve success in a traditional league because they have a common tendency to fail in clutch situations. The Boosters intentionally invite these players into the fictional league where they are told there is no danger in their being cut from the roster. With no pressure to perform, the majority of the players rise to exceed even their own expectations. By foiling the baseball's economic basis and corporate baseball, Grand Mound emphasizes the game's most fundamental trait: its enjoyment. After discovering the reality of Grand Mound and the Cornbelt League, however, Houle attempts to mask the type of player he was in college by offering statistical evidence showing his success. The response to these facts clarifies that there are multiple versions of reality: "Statistics lie, Mike ... Your stats may have looked okay on paper, but what did you do when the pressure was on?" (201). Houle then understands that the identities of the town and its players are not quantifiable by statistical evidence; rather, their identities are based on each person's connection to the fictional league. The townspeople all have roles in presenting the town and its team to new members like Mike Houle, Dan Morgenstern, and Stanley Wood and then doing what they can to ensure that the players become connected to the town enough to make it their home. Unlike Big Inning, Iowa, where the team represents the best players from several communities in a league that already exists, Grand Mound's team plays only intra-squad games and represents only the people within that community.

The most striking difference between the two Iowa towns in *The Iowa Baseball Confederacy* (Onamata/Big Inning) and *Magic Time* (Grand Mound) is the manner by which each chooses to accept and identify with people from outside the town structure. The exhibition game in Big Inning is obviously the main social event of the year as trainloads of people flock to the field to watch the contest against the Cubs. Gideon and Stan are immediately welcomed into the town and, not long after, onto the team. The Baron family offers them a place to stay, and members of the Twelve-Hour Church of Time Immemorial treat them as members of their denomination and not as outsiders. The lack of clear social class divisions in the town is reflected in the way the town equally treats both its own citizenry and outsiders who come into the community. There is no mention of socioeconomic divides that alienate some people while welcoming others.

Grand Mound's community initially appears to have the same modus operandi as Big Inning, welcoming and including outsiders into its fold; however, the townspeople take significant measures to ensure that the players who are invited to play in the league fit the mold of what the town wants in its additions. When Mike Houle discovers that the town does not actually play in the Cornbelt League and his chances of being scouted by a major league team are non-existent, he is reminded of what a magical place Grand Mound is and exactly how baseball determines the town's identity: "look at what's been accomplished in Grand Mound. The people who came up with the idea were years ahead of their time" (203). Realizing that small towns and the ways of life found therein were in danger of being lost as people moved away to larger cities, the citizens of Grand Mound, rediscovering utopia within their town, decided to use baseball to lure the types of people they wished to have in their midst, hoping those players would permanently move to the town, marry into the community, and actively participate in the Boosters' plan of continuing the town's existence through baseball. As the early players left town once they realized it was not a part of a competitive league, the town cultivated the concept of pursuing baseball players who had statistics comparable to other professional prospects but who, like all of the current Greenshirts players, failed to perform in high-pressure game situations. Taking these types of players who would have otherwise been, at best, marginal in a more mainstream league, Grand Mound began to be identified by an unlikely type of player: players who have trouble performing under pressure, but who fit the mold of small-town America set forth by the townspeople.

Because Stanley Wood is a late replacement for the player who was originally supposed to be on the roster, the townspeople do not have ample opportunity to scout him and discover that he is Asian. Generally, however, the various families take every precaution to guarantee the players in the league will be viable additions to their idealized community. Although Mike

Houle senses that the Powell family has somehow discovered personal information about him, it is not until Roger Cash, the groundskeeper whom Mike met as a young man, tells him that the family actually traveled to Louisiana to scout Mike in college that he begins to understand the complexity of the town's exclusiveness. Roger tells Mike the town's secret to finding people who will blend into the community is that everyone from Grand Mound does their research on the players, scouting those prospects who best fit the mold of the idyllic setting for which the citizens strive, so that the team and, therefore, the town will continue to exist in coming years. Cash's comments explain the reasoning behind Jewish players being housed by Jewish families, gay players being housed with families who have eligible gay sons, and single players, like Mike Houle, being housed by families like the Powells who have daughters who will soon be eligible to marry. With every person and family doing their own research with the town's common goal in mind, the players find their religious, familial, and social needs addressed even before arriving in town. It is the ideology of sport which drives these plots and characters in Kinsella's novels, particularly regarding social and economic class.

In his foundational work "Ideology and Ideological State Apparatuses," Marxist critic Louis Althusser outlines the basic difference between an Ideological State Apparatus (ISA) and a Repressive State Apparatus: "Repressive State apparatus functions 'by violence,' whereas the Ideological State Apparatuses *function 'by ideology'*" (1490). Among those institutions labeled by Althusser as ISAs, "a certain number of realities which present themselves to the immediate observer in the form of distinct and specialized institutions," are the family ISA, the communications ISA, and the cultural ISA which includes "Literature, the Arts, [and] sports" (1489). It is by employing these specific ideological structures available to it through baseball myths that Grand Mound is able to thrive in a time when other towns its size are dying off. Unlike some places where ISAs promote more class-stratified agendas, Grand Mound's family, communications, and cultural ideologies are all based on the game of baseball. These ISAs are only able to succeed in the novel because of the history of the game as such an important aspect of American culture.

Baseball's ideological roles in American culture continue to be toward democratizing and, although other sports in the United States have risen in popularity during recent years, baseball is still the sport through which America is most often identified. That baseball is considered America's National Pastime dates back to the years following the Civil War when Walt Whitman called it "our game — the American game" (qtd. Folsom 50) and

Albert Spalding determined that "Base Ball is the American Game *par excellence*" (5). The characteristics seen by Whitman and Spalding in the game as being representative of those positive attributes of the American way of life are the very foundation of this nationalistic mindset. The people of Grand Mound, Iowa, see these same characteristics enabling the community to maintain its existence, yet the nationalistic and democratizing framework is often lost in the isolationist means of producing the utopian community which they so desperately seek. Baseball is the sport that most often identifies America as a country, but Kinsella's community in *Magic Time* intentionally shuts itself off from the outside baseball world. When asked where he can obtain a copy of *USA Today*, a national newspaper, Emmett Powell says, "we don't have much call for outside newspapers like that," but that Mike may purchase local papers, the *Des Moines Register*, from the town's drugstore and that a regional newspaper like the *Chicago Tribune* may also be available on occasion (102). The most telling comment from Powell demonstrating the solitary nature of the community is when he continues to reinforce the town's isolationist perspective: "we have the *Grand Mound Leader* every day, and ... we're more interested in what's happening in Grand Mound than anywhere else" (102). By regulating what news from outside the town is made available, Grand Mound's leaders control the flow of information the new players may receive, demonstrating the success of the communications apparatus the townspeople have set in place. This enables the town to establish the utopian perfection they seek to have in the community, one rooted in baseball. The newspaper itself may therefore be read as an example of utopian fiction as the truth regarding the town and its role the Cornbelt League is hidden behind the agenda-laden prose of sportswriter Dilly Eastwick. In fact, the *Grand Mound Leader*, as a way of continually promoting the game's role in the community, recycles descriptions and nicknames of the players as some players retire to live in town as private citizens and others are added to the roster to take their places. The information in the paper, then, is nothing more than propaganda used to promote the game to the new players and to reinforce the continued indoctrination of the townspeople as a whole. As such, Kinsella's novel demonstrates the limitations of baseball as an American ideology as the facts and descriptions of each team offer nothing unique and are simply regurgitations of what Eastwick has already written.

In their efforts to control the outside influences coming into the town, Grand Mound regulates not only the media available to the citizens but the flow of visitors into the community as well. When Mike's father announces his intention to visit his son and watch him play baseball, it becomes evident that the town has taken precautions to control the people allowed into the town as there is no lodging available for non-residents in the town except for those homes opened to outsiders. As Marge Powell tells Mike, the town has no hotel of its own and the nearest motel is outside of the city limits by the highway. This option, she feels, is not helpful as she is sure the motel "isn't the kind of place [Mike's] father would want to stay" (131). Though she has never met Gil Houle, she is adamant that the only place he will be welcome is in the home of a widow neighbor. Mike's father, like Mike himself, comes to the town for reasons directly connected with the local baseball team, and like his son, he will eventually choose to make a life in the town for reasons other than the game. By not having a hotel, the people of Grand Mound have effectively closed themselves off from random passersby; instead, they have again found a way to control who stays in the town by limiting the places available to stay and regulating them by setting the standards by which the visitors will be allowed to stay. This subtle method of controlling outside influences through the family ISA keeps the utopian structure by which the town exists in place.

Grand Mound's attempt at creating the perfect society founded on baseball limits any influence from the outside world. Those who are admitted into the community, however, find themselves in a place of utopian purpose and structure, eliminating any type of social class division amongst the masses. The Grand Mound Boosters, made up of prominent businessmen and selected officials, control every aspect of the league, including how it presents itself to the world beyond the borders of the insular community. The town's survival is based on the existence of a baseball team that presents itself to potential players as a part of the Cornbelt League although it has actually never been a part of any league. As the players grow accustomed to living in the idyllic town of Grand Mound, they learn that the common bond between the townspeople extends beyond baseball and is evident in other areas of people's lives with no regard for a hierarchal framework within the community. During his first afternoon practice with the team, Mike has a conversation with Emmett Powell and Roger Cash in which Mike is shown some pebbles hidden in the dugout that he may scatter in the infield as he leaves at the end of an inning to increase the chances of the opposing second baseman making an error in the game. This advantage, he is told, will only be used once the actual season starts and that no such manipulation is used during these intra-squad games between the Greenshirts players. Not yet knowing that all he will play in Grand Mound are intra-squad games, Mike is unaware that none of the ballplayers will have an advantage over the others;

there is no hierarchal structure in the league as all of the players were scouted by the town to ensure they would be comparable with one another, and each of the intra-squad teams is purposely divided to offer an equal chance to both sides.

Away from the baseball field the town is similarly structured, with each person in the community contributing for the benefit of the entire society. When it is discovered that left fielder Felix Rincon has a wife and family in Vera Cruz, the Grand Mound Booster Club — the "state" in control of the citizenry — suggests that he move the family into the community. Various members of the community then find a home to be restored, and Dilly Eastwick, the newspaper editor, enlists the help of Senator Tom Harkin, who helps get visas for Rincon's family. As citizens of the town and the members of the team repair the house, Emmett Powell explains to Mike that the Boosters are generally "a pretty prosperous lot" who are "able to trade things in a little earlier than some folks" (170). Though it appears that this example of the distribution of wealth is evidence of class division, Powell explains that the club members are able to distribute items to families like the Rincons, benefitting everyone involved. Despite Powell's attempt to claim otherwise, this does in fact signify class division as the Booster Club controls the housing, wealth, media, and representation to the world outside of Grand Mound. Though families like the Rincons and individual players like Mike Houle do benefit from the town's structure and organization, it is only through the manipulation by the ISAs— media, family, and even baseball — that the Boosters are able to convince players to consider even visiting the town.

Mike is told that "[i]f Grand Mound were a country, the Booster Club would be the cabinet" (179), yet the members of the club are intentional in not using their positions within the community to gain some advantage over other townspeople. Instead, their positions of power are used only to aid in maintaining the class-free structure within the masses and the communal atmosphere of the town. While Timothy Morris argues that baseball "may be the most perfectly meritocratic social organization in modern America," in which "[b]etter players rise higher in the organization, become famous, and make more money" (116), Kinsella's community of Grand Mound, Iowa, illustrates opposing forces within American culture. As all of the players invited into the team are known for failing in intense game situations, there is no danger of anyone gaining a place of prominence over other players on the team. Since the Greenshirts are not a part of a league, the players never have to concern themselves with succumbing to the pressures of game situations. The players, like the members of the community itself, are equally balanced with the other members of the society. The game of baseball used by the Booster Club to maintain the community is not one of meritocracy but one of equality; the emphasis is not on fielding the most competitive team but on offering marginally successful players the opportunity to become a part of an idyllic, imagined community grounded in baseball.

Kinsella's Community as Representative of America

In his close examination of *Shoeless Joe* following the success of the film *Field of Dreams*, Bryan K. Garman argues "that Kinsella engenders a culturally conservative world, which reflects the historical circumstances of the 1980s and reproduces the ideology of Ronald Reagan's presidency" (41). Garman's essay focuses on Kinsella's use of baseball to reflect back on a simpler, more idealistic time whether such a time actually existed or not. This motif is not unique to *Shoeless Joe* and is repeated in *The Iowa Baseball Confederacy* when Gideon Clarke's travel through time back to Big Inning, Iowa, in 1908, Joe McCoy's journey back to his hometown in the area in which Ray and Gideon both live, and Mike Houle's idealistic utopian community in Grand Mound, Iowa. Of Kinsella's five baseball novels, only *Box Socials* breaks from this trend. Set in Canada in an area inhabited mostly of immigrants from European countries, this novel further demonstrates that baseball's impact is more significant to those from the United States than it is to its northern neighbors. The game in the four remaining novels is presented not as a fallible representation of America, but as a symbol of all that is right in the nation. Kinsella's fiction confirms that baseball and the functions of ideological class are only active within American culture, something demonstrated in all five novels. Garman writes, "[in] the same way that Reagan's masculinity and appeal to nostalgia absolved the sins of America's recent past, Ray's field wipes away the transgressions of baseball's history and returns the game to its fabled innocence" (45). Baseball's innocence in each of Kinsella's novels set in the United States binds the communities together and defines who they are as a collective group. Kinsella's emphasis is not on the shortcomings of the game — though they often reveal racism, sexism, homophobia, greed, and a rampant drug culture — but on the qualities of a meritocracy and a democracy that appear to provide opportunities to everyone within the community, regardless of what other issues or characteristics may divide them.

Robert F. Burk argues that "professional baseball provides to spectators and players alike sport's nonthreatening outlets for emotional exuberance, individual expression, competitive fervor, and communal dedication to team and city" (xi). In his baseball novels, W.P. Kinsella often uses the game to unify the inhabitants of his rural Iowa towns. The game, however, extends beyond a simple means of unification; the identity of Kinsella's towns is usually contingent on the game of baseball, the basis for each town. The patriarchal, racially biased, seemingly misogynistic, homophobic societies of the towns are often masked by an attempt to portray a community without class division, a community whose divisions and inequalities are hidden by the lack of class conflict. While he does not go to the extreme of Albert Spalding's "Base Ball is War!" quote, Kinsella does use the game's shortcomings to reflect the inadequacies and conflicts within the communities while conversely using the game's timeless pastoral qualities to reflect an idyllic representation of America's positive attributes. These binary oppositions within baseball are both positive and negative characteristics of how identity functions in Kinsella's communities and lay the foundations for those families living within the towns. The negative traits so often associated with the sport — sexism, misogyny, racism, drug scandals, and gambling — actually solidify the more positive traits from the game, traits towards which Kinsella's communities are drawn and on which they often thrive — rebirth, forgiveness, and meritocracy. Only by recognizing the possibilities within baseball can Americans truly understand identity in the communities within Kinsella's baseball fiction.

CHAPTER THREE

"We Are Family!": The Familial Paradigm

Dating back to Walt Whitman, who saw baseball as a national game, an idea Albert Spalding propagated in his biased history of the game, *America's National Game*, the sport has for years been used to describe and reinforce the positive elements of American society. Using small Midwestern towns as a microcosm of the nation, Kinsella's novels often continue to convey this message to readers. In an even more specific method of reinforcing the American ideal, Kinsella often identifies many of the families within the communities by their connection to the game. The relationship between family and baseball is not unique to fiction, however. In fact, writers like Roger Kahn, Roger Angell, and Donald Hall have explored the role that the game has had in connecting and reinforcing relationships within each of their own families.

My earliest baseball memories are of my brothers and me taking turns having Dad pitch to us in our backyard, each one of us assuming the role of one of the 1979 Pittsburgh Pirates, the team that had adopted Sister Sledge's song, "We Are Family," as its unofficial theme song. My older brother, J. L., was long-legged and fairly quick at the time, so he usually acted the part of base-stealing outfielder Omar Moreno; my younger brother, Eddie, already showing the physique that would help him years later to become a solid offensive lineman, chose to be Ed Ott, the reliable catcher; and I, naturally, chose to pattern myself after another player named Willie, first baseman and future Hall of Famer Willie Stargell. This game that we shared between us was the same game that our great-grandfather, John Lewis Steele, told us about watching while he was a young man following the careers of Ty Cobb and Honus Wagner, and the same game that my nieces and nephews all enjoy playing and watching themselves. More than any other sport in America, baseball lends itself to connections with familial relationships. As Stephen Jay Gould writes, "I can make no meaningful contact with football and basketball players of my grandfather's generation, for I do not grasp their different games, while the numbers attached to their performances permit no comparison with modern assessments" (303). Baseball, however, because it is essentially the same game as it has been since the late nineteenth century, allows for more accurate comparisons and assessments with today's game. Baseball's literature, memoirs and fiction alike, is largely based on a connection to the past and a link to the future within the family structure not unlike that in my own experiences.

A close examination of baseball literature's canon clearly shows that many authors have the same connection with baseball as I do when considering the game and how it connects on some level with family. An overwhelming number of the family stories written using baseball as a vehicle emphasize the relationship between fathers and sons. Before being named the United States' poet laureate in 2006, Donald Hall contributed to the growing amount of baseball literature beginning in the 1970s when he wrote an essay, "Fathers Playing Catch with Sons," describing his George Plimpton-esque participation in spring training with the 1973 Pittsburgh Pirates following the untimely death of their team leader, Roberto Clemente, whose airplane taking relief supplies to victims of a Nicaraguan earthquake had crashed into the ocean just weeks earlier. Hall explains that his "friendship with Dock Ellis, a product of that week, led [him] to spend parts of two seasons with the Pirates" and resulted in a book about Ellis (5). Subsequently, Hall began writing reviews of baseball books and other sport assignments for various publications. He argues that "[b]aseball connects American males with each other, not only through bleacher friendships and neighbor loyalties, not only through barroom fights but, most importantly, through generations" (49). The timelessness of the game coincides with the lack of boundaries of time linking generations of families. In contrast with sports such as football, basketball, and hockey, Kinsella often comments "there's no time limit on a baseball game" (Shannon, *Baseball* 160). This open-endedness sets the foundation for what Hall sees as an important part of the genre: "In baseball history writers find connection with the past that most Americans, most of the time, ignore or deny" (129). Gender critic Michael S. Kimmel recognizes the role baseball played in reconstructing masculinity in America during the late nineteenth and early twentieth centuries, arguing "that baseball — as participatory and spectator sport — was one of the chief institutional vehicles by which masculinity was reconstituted and by which Americans accommodated themselves to shifting structural relations" (56).

Despite the perceived shifts in these structural relations, Kinsella's use of baseball in his novels defines the family as being ruled by a patriarchal figure with a marginalized or an entirely absent female presence, much like the game itself is structured.

This motif is utilized in four of five Kinsella novels. In *Shoeless Joe*, Ray's mother is mentioned as still living, but she is never brought to the field and she never appears in the storyline other than when her son remembers events or conversations from his past in which she played a part. *The Iowa Baseball Confederacy* has a noticeably absent mother who has chosen to abandon her husband, Matthew, and their son, Gideon. Following in his father's footsteps, Gideon falls in love with a woman, Sunny, who much like his mother, also chooses to leave him, reinforcing the reliance on the male figures in the novel. *Magic Time* shows Kinsella once more removing the matriarchal character from the novel in the opening chapters when Mike Houle recalls the events of his mother's death as she was hit by a car and the subsequent impact on the remaining family members, all of whom are male. In *If Wishes Were Horses*, Joe McCoy remembers his mother when she was alive, but so sick that she is never able to attend his baseball games, including the state championship game that played such a role in changing the course of his life. He later recalls returning home for her funeral. His wife, Marueen, who exists in the parallel life he tries to reclaim on Ray Kinsella's field of fantasy, is dying of cancer, and it is only through his reclamation of this parallel existence that he is able to save her, once more illustrating the preferential treatment given to Kinsella's male characters. In a common refrain, *Box Socials* is the exception to this trend. The narrator, Jamie O'Day, not only has a family with both parents, but he often describes spending more time in the kitchen with his mother and women who visit their home than he spends with his father and the other men who spend their evenings drinking and telling off-color stories. Jamie mentions this preference, saying, "To be honest, I was more interested in the women than the men; the men tended to discuss matters that didn't interest me a lot, or that I didn't entirely understand" (77). In addition to this shift in emphasis from the male to the female, unlike the other novels, the narrator in *Box Socials* has no real interest in the game beyond that of the most casual fan, and his family's identity is not contingent on baseball.

While serving a prison sentence in Nebraska, former state senator and Little League coach Kurt Hohenstein wrote a book focusing on the lessons learned from baseball, specifically at the Little League level, and how they apply to life outside of the game. Although he has both a son and a daughter, Hohenstein dedicates a chapter to the father-son relationship, qualifying his decision to do so: "By illuminating the father-son relationship, I do not suggest any others are less significant or less important. Mothers and daughters, fathers and daughters, mothers and sons—it is not the genealogy that charts the course, as all of these relationships are in their own way vital and valuable" (94). Like Hohenstein, I have chosen to explore the family relationships in baseball in their broad sense while focusing more specifically on the relationships between fathers and sons for two reasons: first, my own experience as a baseball fan began with family trips to Three Rivers Stadium as a child and continued, as with many boys and their fathers, when my father coached my Little League team; and second, Kinsella's novels focus primarily on the male relationships, though there are peripheral females in the families who must also be considered.

All four of Kinsella's Iowa-based baseball novels share several common themes and motifs, the most obvious of which is their reliance on the male relationships grounded in the game of baseball. Again, *Box Socials,* has multiple father figures in the story, but none of them have an identity that is as clearly based on the game as in the other texts. In these four novels, however, he establishes the importance of the father-son relationships over any other in the family structure early on in the narratives. The use of baseball to establish the male relationships has been explained by the game being, as Elspeth Cameron observes, "a striking metaphor for male bonding" (46). In considering Kinsella's fiction, Cameron notes that "[s]ome reviewers have taken Kinsella to task for the inadequacies of his female characters" (46). While this chapter further examines the marginalized roles of females in Kinsella's novels, it will do so in consideration of the assertion that "such quibbling may be irrelevant," while answering the question, "If women writers such as Alice Munro and Sylvia Plath can deliberately define the sensibility of women, why can't male writers [like Kinsella] explore the lives of boys and men?" (46). This chapter, then, is not intended to trivialize the female members of the families in Kinsella's fiction; rather, it considers the family dynamic as a whole through the various specific relationships within each novel. The overall emphasis in Kinsella's novels, however, is on the patriarchal figures and the relationships between the fathers and sons in each text.

Defining Family

In "The Death of the Hired Man," Robert Frost writes, "Home is the place where, when you have to go there,/ They have to take you in" (38).

Home and family are often used interchangeably to describe the specific construct from which one emerges. Frost's version of home demonstrates the notion that family, out of a sense of obligation more than nearly anything else, serves as a support structure for members of the unit who choose to separate from the unit as a whole. His description is supported by several sociologists who argue that "[t]he family is a place where one is unconditionally accepted, something almost unknown in the worlds of business and politics" (Bellah et al 87). That the family construct is described as a place and not as a group of people reinforces the assertion that family and home are inseparable; the two terms are signifiers for the same concept. Kinsella weaves the members of the physical family into descriptions of home so often that there is little if any separation between the two in his fiction as well. As with establishing a definition for community, defining family becomes problematic because of the variety of definitions employed by different cultures: "In more complex societies that remain traditional, kinship may provide a rich vocabulary of relationship that can be extended fictively to people who are not related" (114). While it is certainly acceptable to consider parts of a community or society with no biological connection as family, my approach separates the community identity dealt with in the previous chapter from the biological family units whose stories often serve as the framework in Kinsella's fiction.

To establish what constitutes a family in Kinsella's novels it is necessary to first analyze the basic foundations of the unit: the mother and the father. The relationship between these two parties stands "[a]t the crux of family life" (Bellah et al 88), and "love that unites the marriage partners grows into the love between parents and children" (88). The love demonstrated by various members of the families in each of Kinsella's baseball novels is represented by the love each has for the game of baseball. The love for the family and the love for the game enhance each other and strengthen the ties between the fathers and sons, fathers and daughters, and husbands and wives. A 1994 study concerning sport in America resulted in the conclusion that "a majority of respondents ... felt that sport competition is good for children because it teaches them to strive to do their best, it reduces delinquency, and it is likely to bring the family together" (Miracle and Rees 14). There is a clear reliance on sport to aid in the development of children in ways that have traditionally been controlled by the parents. Furthermore, "if delinquency is viewed as a result of weak social controls exerted on youth by the family or other institutions, then it may be assumed that the strict regimen of athletics and the discipline of the coach may provide the necessary antidote" (105). For Kinsella, only baseball serves as the sport used to fill this role in the family, and it oftentimes works in place of absent family members to maintain the family structure. Though Kinsella's families often have absent patriarchal figures, the game fills these voids so that the family structure may be maintained or to allow family members to be reunited.

Characteristics of Kinsella's Family

The use of baseball when dealing with family issues in literature is not unique to Kinsella's fiction. In fact, several of the canonical texts from baseball literature deal with some element of family. Bernard Malamud's *The Natural*, Mark Harris's Henry Wiggen series, William Brashler's *Bingo Long and the Traveling All-Stars and Motor Kings*, August Wilson's *Fences*, and David James Duncan's *The Brothers K* all deal with various elements of familial relationships while using baseball as a means of either unifying or dividing people within the family units. Much of the criticism dealing with baseball literature echoes Bryan Garman's exploration of *Shoeless Joe*, which shows a "nostalgic world ... characterized by a mythic history of consensus, a fraternal and patriarchal order, and discrimination based on race and gender" (41). The perceived discrimination, however, is little more than a reflection of the game's shortcomings and is not intended as a commentary on the abilities or supposed foibles of female members of the family; rather, baseball literature, written predominately by men, is based on the world with which they are most familiar, a world of fathers and sons and brothers connected by the game of baseball.

Baseball is the most obvious choice of American sports through which to deal with issues of the family because the game is as constant and timeless as the linking of families through generations. While the rules of basketball and football have changed significantly since those sports originated — it was several decades before the NBA adopted the slam dunk and the three-point line and an equally long time before the NFL saw the forward pass— baseball has remained true to its roots with only minor changes. Instituting the designated hitter in 1973 and adopting inter-league play in 1997 have been the most noticeable changes, yet neither one of these has tampered with the basic rules set forth in the early to middle part of the nineteenth century. It is no coincidence that baseball is also the American sport with the longest season, making it as much of a routine as traditional family life. While the National Football League has a 16-game regular season and the National Basketball League and the National Hockey League both play 82-game seasons, Major League Baseball plays 162 regular season games, nearly twice that of the next closest major sports.

Former Cleveland Indians pitcher and 1962 Hall of Fame inductee Bob Feller has said, "Every day is a new opportunity. You can build on yesterday's success or put its failures behind and start over again. That's the way life is, with a new game every day, and that's the way baseball is" (qtd. in Plaut 47). With a season lasting from March until October and games played nearly every day during that time, it is by far the most routine of the major sports, mirroring the everyday routine of family life. The lack of emphasis on time in the game and throughout the season is frequently used by Kinsella to show the timelessness of the familial issues found at the heart of his novels. One of the more frustrating elements for many non-fans and for television audiences is the leisurely pace at which the games are conducted; that this game is not controlled by a clock as in other sports, however, simply reinforces the manner in which it replicates the timeless aspects of paradigms outside the game, specifically that of family.

Much like the history of the game itself, Kinsella's baseball novels are always narrated from a male perspective. Each of the five novels, including *Box Socials*, is told from the viewpoint of a son within a family. Ray Kinsella, Gideon Clarke, Jamie O'Day, Joe McCoy, and Mike Houle all tell stories relating to their specific families, yet the versions of the stories are incomplete because the only female representation comes from stories told from this masculine viewpoint, thus the first-person voice and viewpoint are lacking in the narratives. The reader's only glimpses into the matriarchal elements of the families are what fundamental information is provided by the sons from the families. The game's history is told, like Kinsella's novels, from a male perspective. Despite female leagues that existed in the country during and immediately after World War II and the growing numbers of females who are playing the game at its grassroots levels, the game is still overwhelmingly presented in the male voice.

In contrast to the strong male presence in each of the novels are the shared elements of an absent matriarchal figure and a marginalized wife in the stories. Ray Kinsella's mother is alive and incorporated multiple times into his narrative, yet she appears only as Ray recollects events from his youth and from one telephone conversation he has with her, inviting her to come to the field. The driving force behind his building the field is the hope that he will provide his deceased father the opportunity to once again play baseball. In *The Iowa Baseball Confederacy*, Gideon Clarke, abandoned by both his mother and wife, attempts to prove the existence of the Iowa Baseball Confederacy to justify all that he and his father worked for, to "show everyone who ever laughed behind his hands at" either Matthew or Gideon (130). Joe McCoy, the protagonist and predominant narrator of *If Wishes Were Horses*, refers to his sick mother who is too ill to attend his high school baseball games and whose only advice to her son comes to him in the form of a dream vision he has years later, after her death. Mike Houle in *Magic Time* tells of his experience growing up with a father who raised two sons after his wife died, a childhood filled with only success on the baseball field. In each case, though the families differ in various ways, Kinsella emphasizes the male voice and male relationships by eliminating or marginalizing the characters of wives and mothers. Once again, *Box Socials* serves as the antithesis to the others novels as the narrator Jamie O'Day's mother is the only consistent female presence appearing in Kinsella's fiction, going against the commonality of an absent or marginalized wife/mother usually read in his novels.

Though there are female characters in the roles of wives or girlfriends, Kinsella provides them with virtually no voice in the novels and usually shows them as being little more than supporting figures for the male narrators in the stories. This combination of absent mothers and marginalized wives may first appear to be yet another representation of the misogynistic aspects of the game itself; however, a closer examination of the families within Kinsella's novels shows that this lack of voice from the female characters provides more of a voice to the game's feminine qualities. In an ethnographic study exploring the relationships between fans and workers at the closing of two major league ballparks, scholars have concluded "that some of the qualities associated with this seemingly male-dominated ballpark are stereotypically *feminine* in nature" (Trujillo and Krizek 323, n.), and "some of the 'male bonding' that occurs at the ballpark does so through a structure that is identified with feminine labels and through processes that are guided by traditionally feminine values such as warmth, openness, supportiveness, and sentimentality" (323, n.). As detailed in the previous chapter, Kinsella relies on the feminine references to nature and the pastoral elements of the game in his novels, due in large part to the absent female characters. The female voice, therefore, is projected by baseball itself and not from traditional female characters—wives, mothers, and sisters—from within the family structure.

In the majority of his novels, each of Kinsella's families shares a strong connection with baseball in some form or another. Though each family is identified differently through the game, all four of the novels set in Iowa emphasize the importance of the relationship between fathers and sons more than any other set of dynamics within the family. Nick Trujillo and Bob Krizek's study on baseball stadiums and personal identity determines "that males generally attributed more personal significance to baseball and to the ballpark than did females" (323, n). With this in mind, the five novels examined here, including the anomaly *Box Socials*, have five separate and unique representations of the family structure: *Shoeless Joe* shows the Kinsella family as a "blessed nucleus ... where domestic life is presented with Norman Rockwellian cuteness" (Murray 60); the Clarke family in *The Iowa Baseball Confederacy* is dysfunctional in that Gideon's mother, sister, and wife all abandon the male members of the family; Joe McCoy's mother's illness makes her noticeably absent from his high school experience, and the females in his parallel lives, wife Maureen and love interest Francie Bly, both have issues that risk their place in the family; and the Houles in *Magic Time* combine the elements of the absent mother figure with the wholesome idyllic characteristics of Kinsella's first novel. Continuing the pattern already seen in reading Kinsella's novels together, *Box Socials* demonstrates an example which breaks the mold established in the other novels. The O'Day family has both parents in an apparently strong relationship, sharing the responsibility of raising their only son, Jamie; however, as this family has little more relationship with the game other than as casual fans of one player from their hometown, their identity has nothing to do with the game and is not considered in any detail here. Though John O'Day, Jamie's father, played semiprofessional baseball as a young man, the game's relative absence within the family during the novel allows Kinsella to develop the family identity with baseball as a peripheral element rather than as the dominant means of identification. This absence, then, demonstrates the maturation of the baseball novel in which Kinsella uses the game as *a* component rather than *the* component by which a family is known. Despite the different variations of the familial structure in his novels, however, Kinsella always shows a strong bond between the father and at least one of the sons. This is the strongest of the family characteristics seen in each of the texts.

Each of the families in the novels examined in this chapter shares the timelessness of the game, a strong male voice and an absent or marginalized female one, and a strong emphasis on the father-son relationship, but the family dynamics present obvious differences that Kinsella employs as a means of arriving at a common result—a sense of belonging in a home or home-like setting. While *Shoeless Joe*, *The Iowa Baseball Confederacy*, and *If*

Wishes Were Horses all rely on the fantastic element of time travel and resurrecting of the dead, *Magic Time* emphasizes more the idealized characteristics of life in small town America. Once again proving to be the exception in Kinsella's five baseball novels, *Box Socials* has no families in the story whose primary identity is based on the game, though this absence itself allows the O'Day family to gain its own unique identity. In the remaining four novels, however, baseball is the common ground on which each of the family units is built and through which each is identified.

Baseball and Family Identity in Kinsella's Fiction

Although the families would continue to exist without the game's presence, it is clear that Kinsella uses baseball to shape the identities of these families as they are viewed by the characters outside of the families and by the readers. While each of the families in the novels is unique in its own way, there are multiple elements that each shares: Kinsella's families are patriarchal in structure, they often have noticeably absent matriarchal figures, and those female characters who are included in the family unit, at best, play peripheral roles. In each case, however, baseball is the one constant that defines and unifies the family while mirroring the game itself in both positive and negative aspects.

Perhaps the most noticeable commonality in Kinsella's introductions to the families in his novels is that each family is introduced to the reader by referencing some element of the father's presence. In introducing the title character of *Shoeless Joe*, Ray Kinsella says, "My father said he saw him years later playing in a tenth-rate commercial league in a textile town in Carolina, wearing shoes and an assumed name" (3); Kinsella's second baseball novel opens with the narrator introducing himself and his father simultaneously: "My name is Gideon Clarke, and, like my father before me, I have on more than one occasion been physically ejected from the corporate offices of the Chicago Cubs Baseball Club" (*Iowa* 3); and in the most recent novel, *Magic Time*, the narrator opens with a prologue in which he and his father are playing Scrabble, setting up the first chapter which begins, "My father is a remarkable guy" (11). In the opening pages of these novels, Kinsella reveals the importance of the father figure and of the father-son relationship. As each novel continues, Kinsella uses this common trait as the foundation for the various familial identities that take shape in the stories. A close examination of these three novels and the families therein shows the game as it becomes the most important identifying trait of each specific family; furthermore, Kinsella uses the concept of home plate in baseball to reinforce a variety of familial issues and concerns regarding home as a characteristic of the family unit, specifically in *Shoeless Joe* in which Ray's father, who was once a minor league catcher, is brought back to life on the field.

That each of the three novels begins with references to the fathers in the families from the narrators, males themselves, lays the foundation of dominant patriarchal power in the familial structures of each story, an aspect that also appears in *If Wishes Were Horses*, although this specific novel lacks the opening reference to the father found in the other texts. Though the issue of gender has already been considered in the broad sense of the game and community identity, Kinsella's novels narrow the focus to specific families within those communities whose identities are established by their connections to the sport; and while a family structure dominated by male characters is not unique, Kinsella's use of the game to demonstrate this dominance is an element that is specific to his fiction. As a result of the male dominance seen in the novels, there is an obvious lack of female presence in both the symbolic and the physical sense. Each of these aspects of the family is contingent upon the other, and both are deeply connected to the game of baseball upon which the identity of the family units rests.

In the opening pages of the aforementioned novels, Kinsella establishes the dominant presence of the father and, conversely, the absence or marginalization of the mother. Ray Kinsella's father, John, is dead, yet his unfulfilled dream of playing professional baseball is one of the driving reasons for Ray being led by the Voice to build the field. Though Joe Jackson, a player whose story was passed from John to Ray during Ray's youth, is the first of the players to appear on the field, Ray's thoughts are immediately drawn, not to his baseball hero, but to his deceased father, expressing his wish that his father could be with him at that very moment so that they could share in the experience together. Jackson informs Ray that the other players who were banned by Commissioner Landis from ever again playing professional baseball are available to play on the field once each of the areas of the field is completed, and Ray again thinks of his father. Since the catcher from the 1919 White Sox, Ray Schalk, was never connected with the conspiracy to fix the World Series, he was never suspended and, therefore, is not a part of the group Jackson proposed reuniting on the field. Ray, however, offers a solution to the missing catcher: his father. "I know a catcher. He never made the majors, but in his prime he was good. Really good. Played Class B ball in

Florida and California" (19). Ray is motivated on his quest to build the field, not by the possibility of having the banned players being brought back to life to play, but by Joe Jackson's promise that Ray's father will be given a fair opportunity to play with them. While Ray mentions bringing his mother, who is still very much alive and with whom he maintains contact, to the field, the primary ambition is to assist in resurrecting his dead father to afford the family patriarch the chance to play again.

The driving presence of Ray's father is made even clearer by the absence of Ray's mother, whose name is never mentioned throughout the novel. The references to the father in the family, who has been dead for several years, clearly overshadow the few instances in which Ray mentions his mother, who is still living and with whom he remains in contact. Expressing his frustration at not having his field built and all of the players playing on it, Ray remembers his mother quoting the axiom, "Rome wasn't built in a day" (27). This initial description of his mother as a widow, who will, from time to time, watch a World Series game, is based on a connection to his father. Despite the fact that John Kinsella has been dead for over 20 years, Mrs. Kinsella — identified only by her married name — recalls how he loathed the New York Yankees, wishing aloud during one broadcast that they will "break a leg," looking to Ray for his approval of his hope (28). Ray offers no connection with his mother other than what they share through the game of baseball, a game that links them both to the husband/father, John Kinsella.

Much has already been written — academically, culturally, sociologically, and creatively — about the timelessness of the game and how it mirrors the seasons of nature, yet Kinsella uses these same characteristics in what is the most important instance of the patriarchal dominance over the matriarchal characters in the novel. Before leaving on his trip to kidnap J. D. Salinger, Ray purchases a gun and remembers his childhood when he once killed a bird and proudly took it to show his mother. Rather than praising Ray, his mother told him to "bring the creature back to life" and that, unless necessary for obtaining food, he should never again shoot another creature (36). Ray remembers this advice as he builds the field that ultimately brings his father and many other former players back to life, where they are afforded the chance to fulfill their greatest dreams. When Ray calls his mother to reminisce about her advice to him, she is certain that the advice was directed towards Ray's twin brother, Richard, and that Ray had never killed the bird. Lacking this connection to his mother, Ray's only justification for the field is not to give life as his mother told Richard, but to offer new life to his father, John, by providing him the opportunity to play as a member of his favorite team.

Following the success of *Shoeless Joe*, W.P. Kinsella once more explored the connection between baseball and family in his 1986 novel, *The Iowa Baseball Confederacy.* Similar to his prior baseball novel, Kinsella's narrator begins the story with a reference to his father and how the game links them together. Their confrontations with the Cubs, which Gideon details in the novel, occur after Matthew Clarke, Gideon's father, and Gideon himself repeatedly attempt to prove the existence of a game between the Iowa Baseball Confederacy All-Stars and the Chicago Cubs in July of 1908, a game of which no one else, including the Cubs organization itself, has any record. As with Ray Kinsella and his father, Gideon Clarke and his father share the common bond of baseball, the bond that makes them unique to those from outside the family structure. Gideon realizes the stigma that is attached to his family by members of the community because of the interest in the game and, specifically, a league of which there is no evidence: " 'Like father, like son,' the people of Onamata say about me," continuing on to call both Matthew and Gideon "right odd" (14). His eccentric nature is passed to him like an heirloom and is rooted in the knowledge he shares with his father about the Confederacy and the game against the Cubs. Unlike Ray Kinsella, who has a daughter with whom he shares his passion for and love of the game, Gideon has no children, meaning that his obsession with the Confederacy and its game against the Cubs rests on him as the sole "heir" to the family legacy.

For Ray Kinsella, the presence of the father is an element of his field that he intentionally seeks on the farm, asking Joe Jackson to give a younger version of his father a try-out; Gideon Clarke, however, feels the presence of his father in a way that is far more oppressive, despite his admiration and love for him. Referring to his father as both "a giant smothering me with his shadow," and a "Cyclops, a colossus," (45) Gideon's description presents a darker, more oppressive version of the father figure than shown in *Shoeless Joe.* Like his father, who suddenly possessed enough knowledge of the Iowa Baseball Confederacy to write a thesis on the subject after being struck by lightning, Gideon's mind is filled with the knowledge of the league at the exact moment his father is killed by a line drive foul ball from Bill Bruton off of a Harvey Haddix pitch at a Milwaukee Braves game. Gideon confesses that he is the only person who knows that his father's death by leaning into the errant ball, a death that appears to everyone else to have been an accident, was in fact a suicide. Gideon immediately inherits the task of proving the existence of the league and the game against the Cubs to others, much the way Ray attempts to prove the magical qualities of his field to those, like his brother, Richard, and his brother-in-law, Mark, who cannot initially see the players emerging from the outfield. In both novels, the game serves as both a blessing and a curse to the protagonists; it blesses Ray and Gideon as both men are able to fulfill their family dreams and destinies, yet the curse is that not all with whom they attempt to share their connections with the game — on Ray's diamond and in Gideon's trip back in time — are able to see it as they do, if at all.

Once Gideon's mind has been filled with the historical and statistical information heretofore known only to his father, he realizes that "[w]hatever had been visited upon [his] father was now visited upon [him]" (46). Baseball is what links the sons/narrators to the fathers in both novels, but Gideon lacks the freedom afforded Ray as his farm is transformed into a baseball stadium. When the Voice offers instructions and Joe Jackson asks for various parts of the field to be built, Ray has the freedom to decline and continue farming. He pursues the opportunities so that he may see Shoeless Joe play ball and so that he may be able to provide his father with the chance to play with the White Sox. Gideon, however, is filled with his father's knowledge of the league, with no chance to decline fulfilling his father's pursuit. In both families, the presence of the patriarchal characters dominates the family structure, leaving little room for a female presence, a void that is filled by the game.

For Ray Kinsella, the family matriarch is still alive, yet he only connects with her or mentions her if she is able in some way to magnify the bond between the male members of the family. There is no evidence that Ray has a strained relationship with his mother; in fact, he invites her to the farm so that she, too, may see what her son has "brought to life" (*Shoeless* 203), though this is secondary to his securing a tryout for his father amongst the ghost players on his field and, no mention of her visiting ever appears in the story. In the only example in which Ray's mother is described as having any interest in baseball, she watches the occasional World Series game on television, only choosing a specific team for which to cheer if the New York Yankees are playing, at which point she hopes they "break a leg" (28). Despite her husband being gone for more than two decades, she roots against the Yankees because he did, giving them a shared bond in the game even after his death. This seemingly insignificant comment also allows Ray to connect with his mother through a shared dislike for the New York Yankees, a trait passed on to both of them by John Kinsella. In contrast to this relationship, Gideon Clarke has limited contact with his mother, Maude, about whom little is known and who left her husband and son and moved with her daughter, Enola Gay, to Chicago where she remarried. Gideon knows little about his mother beyond what his father has been able to tell him, and his father, Matthew, only knows what she told him about herself before they were married: "My name is Maude Huggins Clarke. I'm nineteen, and I used to travel with a carnival" (28). These sparse details are all Matthew knew of Maude before their marriage; they are the only information about her personal life that she ever shares with her husband. The implied reason for her abandonment is that Matthew became obsessed with verifying the existence of the league; the game that connects Matthew and Gideon ultimately leads to the separation of the male and female members of the family.

Philip G. White and Anne B. Vagi have explored Dorothy Dinnerstein's assertion "that resolution of the competing desires for female emotional sustenance and identification with men comes through gaining control over women and therefore one's own sense of vulnerability" and offer that "[t]his sense of control may be achieved by rejecting women, by denying them equal status in relationships, or by otherwise downplaying the role women take in meeting men's emotional needs" (74). Kinsella uses the baseball league and the quest Matthew and Gideon share to overshadow the role that Maude plays in the family, leading to her abandonment of the traditional motherly role. White and Vagi argue that throughout history "the mothering role has been performed by females" (73), yet Maude Clarke, the character on whom this role would traditionally be placed, leaves her husband and son alone with little more than memories of her, Enola Gay, and the shared obsession Matthew and Gideon have in the league. The game once again assumes the role of mother as it is the one area in which the male Clarkes may seek refuge in their lives from the abandonment of the female family members.

Continuing the trend of serving as a novel which subverts the roles baseball plays in establishing the various forms of identity, none of the families in *Box Socials* have any strong connection to the game other than as casual fans. The only example of a family member, other than Truckbox Al McClintock, who has any deep interest in baseball is Jamie O'Day's father, John Martin Duffy O'Day, who played years earlier, before becoming a husband and a father, on semi-professional teams in Florida and California. Once more, Kinsella's Canadian baseball novel demonstrates a shift away from his use of the game as a means of identifying specific characters or groups, in this instance choosing not to base an entire family identity on baseball, either as players or as fans.

All of Kinsella's Iowa-based baseball novels have an overwhelming emphasis placed on the male characters which results in a marginalized or an absent female presence. His most recent and presumably last novel, *Magic Time*, continues this trend, albeit through a slightly different approach in which the father lives and the mother dies. Described by his son, Mike, as "a remarkable guy" (*Magic* 11), Gil Houle keeps the memory of his deceased wife alive for himself and his two sons as they grow older. Fulfilling the role of both mother and father in the family, Gil explains the manner through which he courted his wife to his son: "In baseball, you make the same play thousands, even hundreds of thousands of times, [though] each one is unique. But it's patience and persistence that carry you through. The same patience and persistence that won over your mom" (11). Though his mother has no direct connection to the game, the relationship between Mike's parents is described by his father in terms that Mike can understand, terms related to the game of baseball and a language that father and son share with one another. Baseball vernacular, in this case, becomes the interpretive key for males seeking to understand familial life. Consequently, Gil conveys his marital relationship in language that his son will understand: baseball. As with the first two novels, Kinsella establishes the foundation of the family through the game. The novel continues with Mike's narrating how he and his father are changed by the game as they both move into the town of Grand Mound, Iowa, demonstrating once more a family whose identity is established by and reflects the characteristics of the game of baseball. The family identity in the game is further reinforced when Gil eventually marries the widow in whose home he stays during his first visit to town. Although there is no indication that she is more than a fan of the game, baseball is what brought them together and, as Gil is offered a coaching position for the Greenshirts, it becomes one of the factors in his decision to stay in town, being able to work with his son on the baseball diamond.

Unlike *Shoeless Joe*, where the mother is alive but rarely mentioned, and *The Iowa Baseball Confederacy*, where the mother and daughter leave the family, *Magic Time* revolves around a family in which the mother, though dead, is still loved and admired by the husband and sons. The emphasis on masculine dominance in *Magic Time* is one that lends itself less to a misogynistic interpretation than the two earlier novels. While baseball assumes the nurturing role of a feminine character for Ray Kinsella and Gideon Clarke, Gil Houle assumes both masculine and feminine roles for his family. Refusing offers from various female relatives to help raise his sons, Gil decides to be both mother and father to his boys. It is in this dual role that Gil, who played in a commercial baseball league as a young man, signed

Mike up for Little League, where his son immediately proved his talent on the field as being far superior to all other players his age. The same feminine qualities of baseball used in the earlier novels to replace an absent matriarch emerge in this novel as Kinsella once more employs the game as a means of filling the void left by Gracie Houle.

Of the four novels set in Iowa, three of them —*Shoeless Joe, The Iowa Baseball Confederacy,* and *Magic Time*— deal with family identity as a major part of the storyline. Ray Kinsella's quest to build the field begins as a way of allowing his dead father an opportunity to once again play the game he loved during his life. Gideon Clarke's proving the existence of the Iowa Baseball Confederacy legitimizes the decades of work both he and his father put into researching the league, despite negative reactions from friends, family, and everyone to whom they presented their work. Mike Houle is able to find a perfect place in Grand Mound, not just for playing baseball, but more importantly, for settling down and raising a family. *If Wishes Were Horses*, however, primarily focuses on the individual, Mike McCoy, though references to his families in his parallel lives are mentioned. Woven into McCoy's own narrative are the chapters narrated by Ray Kinsella and Gideon Clarke, both of whom McCoy seeks out upon deciding to return to his hometown of Lone Tree, Iowa.

During their initial meeting, Joe McCoy asks Ray if he is familiar with the phrase "Things are out of kilter in Johnson County" to which Ray responds that his own wife often uses the phrase, explaining that "her family have been here for generations" (4). Though the reader familiar with *Shoeless Joe* will remember that Ray's immediate family is from Montana, his identifying with his wife's family in this example shows the deep roots he has with the area. Whereas Ray's family connection to Iowa is through his wife's family, Gideon Clarke's entire life has been spent in Iowa. In his first narration in *If Wishes Were Horses*, he explains that his validation of his father's work has made Matthew Clarke's work "one of the finest pieces of baseball research ever documented" (10). Though his father is dead and his wife has left him, Gideon still identifies himself through the work on which he and his father collaborated. Despite his early concern that his journey to 1908 and back again causes him to lose any ability to love someone again, he ultimately becomes enamored with Francie Bly, who accompanies McCoy back to Iowa. Gideon's dreams and fantasies soon become dominated by images of Francie moving in with him, thoughts that, upon McCoy's replaying of his high school championship on Ray's field and the reunion with Maureen, allow Gideon to find love once again. Francie's role is twofold: first, she and the kidnapped baby provide a reason for McCoy's fleeing to Iowa; and second, she provides Gideon a relationship that allows him to make amends for his failed marriage to Sunny and for losing Sarah Swan in 1908. Arguably, then, the replaying of the baseball game that brings McCoy to find Ray and Gideon also allows Gideon to find the one thing which he most desperately seeks in his life: love.

In a unique use of the family paradigm, Kinsella utilizes the game in *If Wishes Were Horses* to demonstrate the family dynamic between people who share only the love of the game and no blood relation. Because of their own unique quests that were doubted by friends and family alike, both Ray and Gideon relate to Joe McCoy's wish to replay a game from his senior year in high school, and they both agree to assist him in whatever ways possible. As they grow closer together while discussing his parallel lives and the problems with which he's confronted, McCoy alludes to the three men as becoming something beyond the traditional male friendship: "We three baseball outcasts have developed a rapport, like brothers, I suppose, fictional brothers ... here we are, sharing camaraderie of soldiers? Convicts? Teammates?" (101). This unique family is based solely on the game as Ray and Gideon's reputations for the supernatural events involving baseball in their own lives are what lead Joe to find them. In Kinsella's other novels, the biological family structure is already in place and baseball simply solidifies that system; however, in this case, the game is what draws these three strangers together into a system that becomes, to McCoy at least, very much like a family.

In developing the family structures within his novels, Kinsella most often emphasizes the patriarchal influence, always described by a male narrator. Focusing on the masculine relationships through baseball's lens is not unique to Kinsella, as other writers, of fiction and non-fiction alike, also explore this element. David James Duncan's novel *The Brothers K*, Roger Kahn's memoir *The Boys of Summer*, and Donald Hall's collection of essays *Fathers Playing Catch with Sons* all incorporate the father-son relationships within the narratives. In the novels studied here, however, the father-son construct dominates each plot so much that a more rigorous examination of this specific dynamic is needed to better understand the ways in which fathers and sons participate in a reciprocal relationship with baseball as its unifying element.

Fathers and Sons in Kinsella's Families

Kinsella's emphasis on the male family members in his novels naturally leads to a specific focus on the close relationships that are formed between fathers and sons in his fiction. While most of these novels do have families with daughters, with *Box Socials* once again being the exception, the focus on interfamilial relationships is overwhelmingly on those of the fathers and sons. The novels examined in this study further support Donald Hall's observation that "baseball is continuous ... an endless game of repeated summers, joining the long generations of all the fathers and all the sons" (46). Though many writers and critics within the genre focus on the male relationships that are established and strengthened by the game of baseball, it is imperative that the game "is a sport that women can identify with" (Zoss and Bowman 226). The game, then, is a means through which Kinsella is able to relate the intricacies of the father-son relationships to female readers. Like Hohenstein, Kinsella does not consider the father-daughter relationships or mother-son relationships to be unimportant; in fact, Kinsella's fiction often includes relationships of these types as well. The most emphasized relationship in the family dynamic in each of his novels, however, is that of the father and son.

In his consideration of sport in the United States, *Power Plays, Power Works*, John Fiske says:

> The intense significance of sport serves local rather than national relations and identities, and works to form felt relationships either with the locality of city or region, or within the more immediate locale of family. Family relationships can often be enhanced by sharing an experience that matters so intensely. Sport commonly provides fathers and sons with an intimacy that their masculinity often prevents them expressing directly. But sport's relational terrain extends to include all members of the family, all relationships [90].

As the previous chapter demonstrates, Kinsella uses the sport of baseball to define the communities in his novels; however, it is also clear that he, like Fiske and Donald Hall, recognizes the significance of sport in the family structure, specifically in the relationships between fathers and sons. Kinsella's novels are prime examples of Charles Springwood's observation that "[b]aseball has frequently been viewed as offering space for a gentler, more flexible range of masculinity" (164). Springwood argues that, following the release of *Field of Dreams* in 1989, "this father-son paradigm was applied to baseball with yet greater enthusiasm" (165). The focus on this specific family dynamic extended beyond films like *Field of Dreams* and *The Natural*, and it reached into the genre of baseball literature to explore similar relationships in the novels on which those films are based and in other texts from its literary canon.

Following the success of *Field of Dreams*, critics began giving serious consideration to the relationship between Ray and his father, John, in the film before applying their approaches to *Shoeless Joe*, the source of Phil Alden Robinson's screenplay. In a classic example of life imitating art, fans of the film began flocking to the town in which the movie was shot simply to walk on the field or to have a game of catch with family members. Charles Springwood has examined the ways Dyersville, Iowa, the filming site, and Cooperstown, New York, the site of the National Baseball Hall of Fame and Museum, each approach the game and its fans. Both sites are "where baseball is seen as the substrate for the emotional bond between males—father and sons" (Springwood 165). Similarly, the relationship between Ray Kinsella and his father in the novel is based on and defined by their mutual love for the game of baseball. The game, after all, is what sends Ray on his mythic quest to build the field, kidnap J. D. Salinger, find Moonlight Graham, and bring Kid Scissons back to the farm before finally reuniting with his brother and a younger version of his father.

There have already been a considerable number of critical approaches to *Shoeless Joe*, *Field of Dreams*, and how Kinsella and Robinson each represent the family structure against the backdrop of the 1980s. These approaches, however, focus on how baseball defines the biological families in Kinsella's fiction, while understanding that there are certainly important and substantive relationships between Ray and men who fill the void left by his father—J. D. Salinger, Eddie "Kid" Scissons, and Archibald "Moonlight" Graham. The parameters for this examination, therefore, are limited to the biological fathers of each narrator in each novel.

Ray Kinsella hears the voice of an announcer at a ballpark give him three directions throughout the novel: "If you build it, he will come" (4), "Ease his pain" (31), and "Go the distance" (93). In each instance, Ray is directed to perform tasks involving baseball which, though they provide opportunities for other characters, ultimately serve to reunite Ray with his father. The specific element of the game that binds Ray and John Kinsella together is their shared interest in Shoeless Joe Jackson and the Chicago White Sox. The novel opens with Ray remembering his father telling stories of the great player: "'No one has ever been able to hit like Shoeless Joe'" (3). A prime example of a "die hard" fan, Ray's father "quickly learned to live and die with the White Sox" (6), dying a little when the club lost the 1919 World Series against the Cincinnati Reds and dying even more when the following year saw eight members of the White Sox accused of purposely fixing the Series. John's love for the team, and even more specifically, his love for Joe Jackson, is passed along to his son, who unquestioningly follows the Voice telling him to build the field so Jackson can return.

John Kinsella is the only character in the story whose passion for the game is equal to Ray's. Shortly before John's death, he and Ray share the story of the 1919 Black Sox Scandal one last time before John, who had visited all of the major league ballparks in existence during his lifetime, passes a unique inheritance to his son: "I've been in all sixteen major-league parks. I want you to do it too. The summers belong to somebody else now, have for a long time" (15). Rather than leaving Ray with property or a monetary bequest, John leaves his son the thing most important to both of them — the game of baseball. The field that Ray builds then becomes a tribute to his father, who instilled in his son the love for Shoeless Joe Jackson, the Chicago White Sox and, most generally, the game of baseball. Like a birthright passed through generations in a family, Ray's love for the game is returned to his father in a very tangible way as John is literally brought back to life through the game on the magical field.

Kinsella's emphasis on the importance of the father-son relationship in *Shoeless Joe* is further magnified when considering the relationship between Eddie Scissons, the man from whom Ray leases the farm, and his daughters, who are not fans of the game. Though he claims to be the oldest living member of the Chicago Cubs, a story Ray knows to have been fabricated by the elderly man, Scissons's description of his life and love affair with the game further enhances the shared bond between John and Ray Kinsella. Telling Ray that the Cubs "have been [his] whole life," he claims to have worked in Chicago so that he could live in close proximity to his beloved team (171–2). Later, working as a school principal in Iowa, Scissons remembers that he "still had the summers" for going to watch games at Wrigley Field, with his only regret being that he never had a son with whom he could share his love of the game (172). Rather than expressing his pleasure at having three daughters, Scissons laments that he never had a son who could inherit his own passion for the game. It is after he remembers hearing this story for the first time that Ray returns home from his quest with Salinger and Graham to discover that his estranged brother has come to the farm and his long-deceased father has finally been afforded the opportunity to play on the field with the White Sox. The lack of a father-son relationship in Scissons's family, serving as a thematic parallel, further emphasizes the strong relationship between Ray and his own father. It is only on Ray's field that these incomplete relationships are made complete; Ray and his biological father are brought together on the field in the same way in which Scissons (as a surrogate father) and Ray (as the son Scissons never had) are united.

These two conversations retold by Ray are revealing in another important way—both of the older men, John Kinsella and Eddie Scissons, speak of summertime as though it is a commodity to be used or to be passed along for someone else's consumption. Ray's father tells him that "[t]he summers belong to somebody else now" (15), implying that the baseball season is now something which Ray must consume (it, like summer, "belong[s] to somebody else") and experience by visiting all of the same stadiums his dad visited. Scissons, however, still claims the season as his own—"But I still had the summers"—because he has no son with whom he can share and to whom he can pass on his love of the game. For both men, summertime is represented by baseball and is something to be experienced and shared, something they both convey to Ray, whose field forever captures the pastoral qualities of this season and shared experience.

Unlike Ray and John Kinsella's relationship, in which both men share a fan's love for the White Sox and for baseball in general, Matthew and Gideon Clarke in *The Iowa Baseball Confederacy* have a relationship based on the need to prove the existence of a league for which there are no surviving records. While both novels begin with the sons as narrators telling a story about their fathers and baseball, the Clarke family and its father-son relationship differs from what Donald Murray calls "the blessed nucleus" (60) of the family in *Shoeless Joe*. Because Matthew's wife and Gideon's mother, Maude, and the daughter/sister, Enola Gay, have left the family for vague reasons which become exacerbated by Matthew's obsession with researching and proving the existence of the Iowa Baseball Confederacy, the close connection between Matthew and Gideon is obviously moved to the forefront of the novel. Gideon recalls his father's commentary on family after visiting his own parents who left Iowa, never to return: "We are haunted by our past ... [o]f the past, the mystery of family is the most beautiful, the saddest, and the most inescapable of all" (24). As Matthew and Gideon are the only two members of the family left in Iowa, their relationship, based on a baseball league mysterious in its own right, becomes the focal point of the story; yet, despite this being the only familial relationship left for either of them, the reader knows little if anything about their relationship that is *not* rooted in the game.

Similar to the inheritance passed from John Kinsella to Ray, a passion for the game of baseball, Matthew Clarke's obsession is transferred to Gideon. Though W.P. Kinsella includes this commonality in both relationships, he shows a clear difference between the two families regarding the manner in which the inheritance is passed from father to son. For Ray, the recollection of having his father pass the summers and the love of baseball to him is a pleasant memory that solidifies the already strong bond between father and son. For Gideon, however, his role of carrying on his father's interest in the game, specifically in proving the league, is more immediate and less pleasurable than Ray's experience. While attending a Milwaukee Braves game with his father, Gideon sees Matthew lean into a foul ball and die. Gideon immediately knows his father has died because at that very moment, his own mind is filled with the information about the Iowa Baseball Confederacy and the one game against the Cubs. This information was known for years only by Matthew and, upon his death, it is transferred to his only son, who then assumes the burden of proving the league's existence and validating all his father has spent years trying to do. Unlike Ray, who is there to talk with his father during the passing of the inheritance, Gideon's father dies suddenly, immediately filling his son with the knowledge of the league that plagued him throughout his own life and led to both his dismissal from his academic career and the dissolution of his marriage. Gideon now assumes the role his father had of being the only person to publicly acknowledge the existence of the mysterious baseball league. After traveling back in time and seeing the game his father spent a lifetime trying to prove took place, involving an all-star team from a league in which only Matthew and Gideon believed, Gideon reflects, as does Ray upon first seeing Joe Jackson on his field, on how he misses his father and how he wishes his father could be with him to share in the experience. Despite the fact that Kinsella himself sees this novel as being "a much darker book than *Shoeless Joe*" (Shannon, *Baseball* 160), and the ways in which possessing the knowledge of the league and the game cursed both Matthew and Gideon, Gideon understands that their relationship was unique because it was based on the game and that, like the game itself, their relationship transcends both time and death.

While Ray and Gideon are both clearly motivated in their individual quests by their fathers' legacies, only Ray has a choice available to him. When Ray's father passes on his love of baseball to his son—"The summers belong to somebody else now, have for a long time"—it is a hope that his son will share the passion for baseball which he had. Gideon, however, is filled with the knowledge of the Iowa Baseball Confederacy at the same moment his father is killed by an errant foul ball in Milwaukee. John Kinsella's blessing to Ray offers two choices—to visit or not visit the ballparks. Matthew Clarke bestows no such blessing; instead, his knowledge of the Confederacy and the exhibition game is passed on to Gideon more as a curse. Gideon has no say in whether or not he wants the information and, once he has it in his mind, he becomes the same type of fanatic, driven by a desire to prove the information as factual, as his father had been for so many years.

In *Shoeless Joe* and *The Iowa Baseball Confederacy*, both narrators are sons who use some aspect of baseball to connect with their dead fathers; however, Kinsella's fourth American-based baseball novel and his fifth overall, *Magic Time*, focuses on the relationship between Mike Houle, a player for the Grand Mound (Iowa) Greenshirts, and his father, Gil, who eventually moves to the town as well. Although the novel opens with this father and son playing a board game — not baseball, but a game nonetheless— when Mike receives a call from his agent letting him know about the interest from the Cornbelt League, their relationship is not so rigidly defined by baseball as are the relationships in the two earlier novels. Unlike the narrators' descriptions of their fathers in the first two stories, Mike Houle initially describes his father by relating the story of his parents' courtship. It was, however, Mike's father who signed his son up in Little League, where Mike first gains notoriety as a player, proving himself better than everyone else in the league, thus introducing his son to the game that would eventually lead to both of them settling down in Grand Mound, Iowa.

Having raised two sons on his own following his wife's death, Gil Houle has an obviously strong bond with his boys. Mike's absence at home motivates Gil to call his son to announce a trip to Grand Mound, taking his first sick days in seven years. Kinsella offers the reader a brief glimpse at what is the shared bond between them when Gil tells Mike that he is coming to visit, not just because he misses his son but also because he misses seeing a "well-played baseball game" (129). Once more Kinsella uses the game as a means of reuniting father and son, providing them both "space for a gentler, more flexible range of masculinity" (Springwood 164) that allows them to express their love for each other in terms of the game. The pastoral game leads them both to the idyllic setting where they are presented with opportunities to become parts of families that have a female presence, something often lacking in Kinsella's novels. Though Gil has a second son, Byron, who lives in their family home, he decides to move to Grand Mound where he will be a first base coach for the team, allowing him to share in the game with Mike.

Though the families in Kinsella's novels vary in structure and in the ways that the game is used to establish their identities, nearly all of the families in the five novels emphasize the father-son relationship. The game allows each narrator/son an opportunity to right past wrongs or to offer a chance at making amends with the father figures. Ray Kinsella provides his father with an opportunity to play the game with his hero, Shoeless Joe Jackson; Gideon Clarke is given the chance to travel 70 years back in time to prove the existence of the Iowa Baseball Confederacy, thus legitimizing the years of frustration suffered by him and his father; and Mike Houle is offered a contract to play for a team that is unaffiliated with any league, but which gives him and his father a complete family structure for the first time since his mother's death. For each of these families, the chances to atone for imperfections and shortcomings are found between the baselines of the game and lead each of the narrators to a greater realization of the importance of home.

Home Is More Than Where the Heart Is

Kinsella's fictional families, though varied in their relationships and in the ways by which they are defined through specific elements of baseball, share one vital aspect of the game: for each narrator representing the families in the novels, home is the end goal of his quest. Despite risking his livelihood and the existence of the field he was called to build, Ray Kinsella sets out on a quest that takes him to New England and Minnesota with the ultimate end being a return to the field. Gideon Clarke is able to slip through a crack in time to be transported back to 1908, only to return after the all-star game has concluded to the very spot he left. Jamie O'Day, while narrating the story that least relies on baseball within the plot, spends an overwhelming amount of the novel describing his home community and his own family's house in Alberta, Canada. Mike Houle moves to Grand Mound believing that it will be one of several stops through the minor league circuit on his journey to reach the major league level. In the end, he decides that making a home in the small town and having a family of his own is more important than pursuing his elusive goal. In nearly every case, baseball guides the men on their quests, eventually bringing them home; in *Box Socials*, the fact that Jamie and his family only leave their town once, to watch Truckbox Al McClintock play in the exhibition game with the all-stars, reinforces the concept of a physical home and its importance in the stability of the family structure as seen in the other four novels.

The concept of using the game as a guide for the protagonist is not unique to Kinsella's novels, but its applications may be used in a close examination of many baseball texts. Charles Springwood says that the idea of home is only natural when dealing with the sport of baseball:

> The assemblages of baseball action are suggestive of a narrative of travel, since the progression of play is marked by a batter facing a pitcher at *home* plate, whose ultimate goal is to safely negotiate a circular journey, base by base, in order to return finally to the starting point—home plate [177].

Using Springwood's observation as a lens through which to read Kinsella's novels demonstrates the importance of both the quest and the subsequent return home for each of the narrators in the novels.

In examining four novels from the baseball fiction canon, John A. Lauricella observes one specific commonality: "the quest for home" (10). Though none of Kinsella's novels are included in this particular list, four of the five novels examined in my study—*Box Socials* using the game in a different way to reinforce the importance of home—certainly continue that theme. Since baseball's emphasis is on "going home," it comes as no surprise that home plate is the only one of the four bases on the field that has a unique shape; "regarded from its front end—from fair territory—home plate resembles a child's drawing of a house" (Lauricella 13). The symbolism of home in Kinsella's novels is accentuated by his use of the imagery of the game as it relates to the various families in his fiction. In the novels studied here, home is an essential element of the plot and the end goal for most of the characters within the families. Even *Box Socials* focuses on Jamie's connection to and emphasis on home, though the game as used in the novel does not reinforce this idea as in the remaining four texts.

The field Ray Kinsella builds on his farm is originally constructed with the purpose of providing Shoeless Joe Jackson a place where he can once again play baseball; however, the more important reason in Ray's mind is for his father to get an invitation from Jackson to try out for the team. Of the eight players suspended by Commissioner Landis, none of them played catcher. Ray's father, however, is described as "a better-than-average catcher" (8) who is ultimately given the tryout promised to Ray. The role of the catcher is literally to protect home; he serves as the last line of defense for preventing an opposing runner to score. John Kinsella, serving in the traditional fatherly role of protector, fills this same role on the field Ray built. His performance is "more than adequate behind the plate" (219), and Jackson compliments John to Ray, saying, "You have good judgment when it comes to catchers" (219). For a player of Jackson's caliber to make such a comment validates John's roles as a catcher and, more importantly, as a father. Ironically, accepting John as catcher means not affording the catcher on the 1919 White Sox team, Ray Schalk, the chance to play. Schalk, who was known for his defensive prowess in the dead ball era in which he played, was one of the honest players on that year's team, with no evidence linking him to any of the gamblers' payoffs in the attempt to fix the outcome of the World Series. Choosing John Kinsella over a Hall of Fame member in Schalk suggests that John was better than "more than adequate" both as a baseball player and as a father.

Although Ray is never given permission to join the players as his father is, he does fill a separate role of protector on the field. When his brother-in-law, Mark, arrives on the farm to present Ray with a court order giving them control of the farm, he and his business partner threaten to "knock down that eyesore of a fence and that pile of rubble you call a bleacher" (241), thus threatening the field into which Ray has invested so much of himself. Ray's only option is to get the gun he purchased on the way to kidnap Salinger and fire off a warning shot. In the ensuing chaos, Ray's daughter, Karin, slips from the bleacher and falls to the ground unconscious. It is at this moment that all thoughts of the field become inconsequential to Ray, Annie, and nearly everyone else on the field. When Moonlight Graham steps from the field and into the stands to help Karin, he is transformed into the older version of himself, a doctor, and saves Karin's life. This self-sacrifice presents another example of someone on the field fulfilling an obligation as a father, giving up his life as a young ballplayer on the field for the good of the child. This example, however, occurs only because Ray stands up to the partners who are trying to take his home. Ray's defense of his home and his farm is a reflection of his own father's role as protector of home within the confines of the baselines. It is within this role of protector that he defends his home as property, his home as family, and perhaps most important to him, his home as tradition.

Due in large part to the amount of criticism applied to *Field of Dreams*, much of the scholarship written after 1989 pertaining to the novel focuses on the areas common to both forms of the story. Subsequently, one of the most overlooked characters in recent criticism is Richard Kinsella, Ray's twin brother, who does not appear at all in the film. While Ray and his father have a strong relationship, Richard runs away on his 16th birthday after fighting with his father, never returning to reconcile with the patriarch. Like Ray, Richard claims to have heard a voice guiding him on a quest that ultimately leads him to the farm and the field his twin built. Though not yet able to see the players on the field, Richard pleads with his brother to "teach [him] how to see" (239). Once again assuming the role of a father-figure, Ray gently guides his brother to a reunion with the younger version of their father on the field.

Initially, Richard's inability to see any of the players makes him completely unaware that his father is the catcher on the field. When Ray asks his brother what he would do if presented with the opportunity to meet their father, years of anger and alienation are put aside and Richard says, "I'd go to him ... [and] become his friend" (250). While the film version of Ray

Kinsella is a son who uses the field to repair a broken relationship with his father, the novel presents two sons, each of whom has a different relationship with the father, but both use the field and the game to reunite with him. Like the Biblical story of the prodigal son, Richard is a son whose pride causes him to leave home and sever ties with his family. The game, however, calls him to Ray's farm where Richard is able, through the help of his twin brother once again playing the protector role, to reconcile with his father.

For Gideon Clarke, the issue of home is problematic in that he travels back in time to Big Inning, Iowa, while the physical location remains the same as his modern day home of Onamata, Iowa. Slipping through the crack in time near the Baseball Spur, Gideon and Stan are magically transported to 1908, the night before the exhibition game between the Confederacy All-Stars and the Chicago Cubs, the very game whose existence the Clarke men spent their lives attempting to prove to the rest of the world. Although his father is not there in physical form, his presence is nonetheless felt by Gideon as he remembers the amount of research he has done to arrive in this place: "I followed in my father's footsteps ... feeling close to him" (129). The sole purpose of his mystical journey initially is to clarify and explain the rumors and mystery surrounding the Iowa Baseball Confederacy, thus validating all his father and he had worked for. Once the game ends, Stan and Gideon have no reason to stay in the past, so they retrace their steps along the Baseball Spur to leap forward in time to their natural period of existence. No longer driven to research the league he has been witness to for the past 40 days, Gideon is no longer motivated by the desire to continue in his father's footsteps; yet as the novel closes and Gideon meets a contemporary version of Drifting Away, he recalls his father telling him about "there being a moment when each of us wants to be forever frozen in time" (291). With the quest to prove the league's existence behind him, Gideon has found the moment of perfection of which his father spoke: the moment when he finally returns home, where he assumes the roles of protector and caregiver for Missy Baron, John and Marylyle's mentally handicapped daughter.

Kinsella continues his emphasis on the importance of home to the families in his fiction with the Houles in *Magic Time*. Though the novel begins shortly after the annual major league draft, held in the early part of June each year, and ends before the Fourth of July celebration in Grand Mound, Mike and his father both become connected to the town quickly enough to leave their home in a Chicago suburb and become permanent citizens of the baseball community. That baseball brings them to the town is common to Kinsella's fiction; *Magic Time*, however, is unique in that Mike regularly participates in the game, an active part of the game's goal of returning to home plate, while Ray and Gideon, with the exception of Gideon's one pinch-hit appearance, are removed from the actual field of competition. Mike, then, has a dual interest in home—first as a player on the field and second as a part of a family construct in Grand Mound. That reaching home is the baserunner's goal is obvious, yet Mike's interest in Grand Mound as home is not nearly as well-defined as are the rules of the game.

When first presented with the option of becoming a member of the Grand Mound team and community, Mike tells his agent, Justin Birdsong, that with no other options for continuing to play available to him, he will move to the town sight unseen and play for the team. Before he moves to the town, Mike relates the stories of his parents' courtship and marriage, of a con man who comes to town to hustle the locals in a baseball game, and of tales of growing up without a mother in the Chicago suburbs before going to play college baseball in Baton Rouge, Louisiana. From the first moment Mike arrives in town, he is constantly bombarded by the patriarch of the family, Emmett Powell, with whose family he is boarding, with the merits of living in a small town, summarized by a comment reminiscent of Shoeless Joe Jackson's observation about Iowa from Kinsella's first novel: "Small-town living is heaven on earth, Mike" (62). For the Powells and the rest of the families in Grand Mound, the idea of home takes such a priority that they have established a team unaffiliated with any league, all with the intent of luring players who fit their mold of ideal members of the community into moving there with the hope that those players will eventually settle in the area, helping them to perpetuate their representation of the ideal home.

After discovering that he has been misled into thinking that Grand Mound offers the possibility of being scouted by a major league team, Mike makes the decision to leave the town to join another minor league team in Knoxville, Tennessee, that is affiliated with a major league club — not because he knows he will succeed, but because he feels betrayed by the townspeople. Before leaving Grand Mound, Mike tells the groundskeeper, Roger Cash, that the town is "too pat, too perfect" (205). While Ray Kinsella and Gideon Clarke embrace idyllic places and moments as they occur, Mike attempts to break free from this embrace so that he can find another form of happiness outside of the town, happiness he envisions in a baseball life in which the major leagues are a more realistic possibility for him.

After only three weeks in Knoxville, Mike realizes that the game, despite his having the potential to progress to the highest professional level, is not as enjoyable for him as it was in Grand Mound, and his father suggests that he return to Iowa where everybody misses him and hopes for his return. After another game in Knoxville, Mike decides to return to Grand Mound, where he is welcomed "home" by his father. Though his father has only lived in the town for a few weeks after a lifetime of living near Chicago, he clearly establishes that Grand Mound is his home and Mike is a part of the family residing there. When asked when he knew he was going to return, Mike says, "I think, deep down, I've known all along" (223). As with Ray and Gideon in Kinsella's earlier novels, Mike feels an inherent need to return home. Returning to Grand Mound, like Ray's field and Gideon's Onamata, is the fulfillment of Mike's quest and, like home plate in baseball, the objective of his entire journey.

Within each of the geographical communities in Kinsella's fiction are families whose identities are defined as much by baseball as anything in their genealogies. Like the communities, Kinsella's families often reflect the same white, patriarchal dominance that the game has shown throughout history. Each of Kinsella's novels examined here deals with the concepts of family and home in its own unique way, yet the majority of them share the common bond of the game establishing the identities of the families found therein. Lauricella argues that:

> In itself, baseball means nothing. It is beautiful to watch, exciting to play, but its meaning comes from without, from the imaginative responses of its players and fans. A novel can never be about baseball in the sense that it can be about love, greed, the soul's own pain. Baseball is not a theme, it is not a character, it is neither an ideological position nor a system of ethics. Baseball is a game. It is a game played by men who contest its outcomes with competitive passion and physical pride, and the conflicts inscribed in its play are momentarily resolved, pitch by pitch. For these conflicts to be meaningful, they must refer to a concern beyond strikes and outs, hits, runs, and errors. The revolution, which the reader prospectively contemplates as he reads, must convey the sense of something greater at stake than the final score [219].

Kinsella's novels use baseball not as a character or theme, but as a means of conveying the "something greater at stake"—family. Baseball is the vehicle by which Kinsella identifies his family and deals with the more important underlying issues within the familial structure. When asked about the role of baseball in his writing, Kinsella says, "I am someone who writes peripherally about baseball. I agree that the best sports literature isn't really about sports. I, for instance, write love stories that have baseball as a background" (Horvath and Palmer 186). The love stories Kinsella writes all center on the family; the game serves as a way to establish throughout the text the family and its common goal.

Charles Springwood says, "'family,' as a category of anthropological and sociological analysis, has a long history and should not be accepted as given or unproblematic," and he recognizes that a variety of anthropologists "have struggled to test the universality of the family across cultures" (154). As is the case in defining community, familial terms may be applied to those outside of the biologically related structure. Kinsella often includes characters from outside of this structure to emphasize the importance of family roles in a general sense, reiterating the concept that "family is a complex and loaded term, used conceptually at different times for different purposes" (154). In any case, most of the biological families in the novels studied here, like the communities examined in the previous chapter, rely on baseball for their definition and mirror the game in their structure. At the foundation of both of these units—community and family—is the most fundamental and clearly defined of all the elements defined by baseball in Kinsella's fiction: the individual.

The identity of an individual is most often determined by the circumstances from which the individual emerges: "Like other core elements of our culture, the ideal of a self-reliant individual leaving home is nurtured within our families, passed from parent to child through ties that bind us together in solitude as well as love" (Bellah et al. 62). Understanding the ways in which Kinsella incorporates baseball into the families in each novel leads to an exploration of the more specific ways in which the game is used to establish the identities of the self-reliant individuals within the family structure and those who are not bound in a parent-child relationship.

Chapter Four

Putting the *I* in Team: Individualism in the Group Construct

At the border of Royston, Georgia, stands a large sign reading, "Welcome to Royston — Home of Baseball's Immortal Ty Cobb." The accompanying picture — an image of Cobb in full stride, rounding third base and heading towards home plate — towers over the two-lane road at its base. For all that Cobb did for his hometown, including building a hospital and establishing a scholarship fund for disadvantaged students, the sign at the city limits recognizes only his accomplishments as a baseball player and none of his philanthropic endeavors which benefited the community. Cobb's most identifiable characteristic, that of being a baseball player, is not unique to Royston; towns across the United States recognize in some fashion their native sons who have played at the major league level. My own high school in Washington Court House, Ohio, has space in its trophy case honoring Jeff Shaw, who broke into the major leagues with the Cleveland Indians, but gained his fame as a relief pitcher for the Montreal Expos, Los Angeles Dodgers, and Cincinnati Reds, being named to the All-Star team in 1998 and again in 2001. Though now retired from the game and still living in that small town, Shaw is arguably known more for his former career rather than for any of his current activities within the community.

Similarly, in W. P. Kinsella's baseball novels the communities and families have their identities established in some way by baseball, but the root of each community and family are the individuals around whom he builds his fiction. It has been said that "[i]ndividualism lies at the very core of American culture" (Bellah et al 142), and that American society is one "in which the language of individualism allows people to develop loyalties to others in the context of families, small communities, religious congregations, and what [has been] termed lifestyle enclaves" (250). In *Shoeless Joe, The Iowa Baseball Confederacy, If Wishes Were Horses, Box Socials,* and *Magic Time,* several characters clearly have deep loyalties to various towns and specific families, but Kinsella uses the game of baseball to establish the identities of these characters as individuals, laying the groundwork for each of the identities of the communities and families.

For one to be individually identified through the game is not to say that one must have played the game professionally. Ring Lardner, one of the earliest writers in the baseball literature canon, was first known for his columns in the *Chicago Tribune* and the *Chicago Examiner* dealing primarily with the White Sox. Red Barber became known, not for any on-field accomplishment, but for his longevity as the radio announcer for the Cincinnati Reds, Brooklyn Dodgers, and New York Yankees from 1934 through 1966. Mel Allen, the radio voice for the New York Yankees from 1939 until 1964, also became known for his weekly highlights show, *This Week in Baseball.* Bill Klem, a major league umpire from 1905 to 1941, known for his fairness and honesty and one of the many characters from baseball's history used by Kinsella in his fiction, appears as an unbiased umpire in *The Iowa Baseball Confederacy.*

For a growing number of former players, there are multiple ways by which the game allows them to remain in the public spotlight. Steve Blass first gained fame as a pitcher on the 1971 World Series Champion Pittsburgh Pirates and is now known as the color commentator for the team's local television affiliate. Former players like Dusty Baker and Lou Piniella are now known for their roles as major league managers. Others, like Bill "Spaceman" Lee and Jim Bouton, pitchers for the Boston Red Sox and New York Yankees respectively, are now widely read authors within the genre of baseball literature, specifically memoir, with Bouton gaining fame for *Ball Four,* his 1970 groundbreaking account of pitching for the Seattle Pilots and the Houston Astros during the previous season. These few examples illustrate a minute number of the thousands of players, umpires, writers, and broadcasters whose individual identities are grounded in some aspect of the game.

More than any of these people who are identified by their lives in baseball is a group that chooses to be associated with and identified by the game: baseball fans. Though the majority of fans have never played the game beyond their youth, all of them connect with a specific team or an individual player, making that connection to the game a part of their own identity. Frank McCourt, the owner of the Los Angeles Dodgers, has observed this connection between individuals and the game and understands why there is a strong kinship with baseball and its fans:

> It is everyman's sport still. It really does have an aspect to it, a quality to it, because many people have played it. When they were little, they picked up that ball, hit it, threw it, and ran the bases, played the games and had the experiences. The game is not something that is foreign to almost anyone. It is something that is very familiar to them and brings back a lot of great memories. Therefore, they're knowledgeable about the game, and so there is that notion that people like a player because "he plays the game the way I would play the game if I could be out there." There is that kind of identity, and they can live vicariously through their favorite teams' and players' experiences [qtd. in S. Sullivan 117–18].

Kinsella's characters are primarily fans of the game, but even the players he does incorporate into his novels are, more often than not, marginally successful at best, with the exceptions being the real-life players like Joe Jackson and Roberto Clemente whom he folds into his stories. Regardless of their level of playing experience, all of Kinsella's main characters are on some level identified by their relationship with the game. By choosing fans as the protagonists within his novels and most of his short stories, Kinsella presents an "everyman" narrator with whom his audience is more likely to relate.

Wilfrid Sheed suggests that "[t]he experience of sports can be blindingly intense such that at its peak even a grown-up can't always be sure what's important and what isn't.... Strength of response, as one learns eventually, has only a hit-or-miss connection with what really matters to you" (25). Nearly all of Kinsella's individual characters are adults who have the ability to reflect on the game as it deeply shapes their intellectual and moral character in their childhoods and how it continues to play a significant role in their adult lives. Players like Joe Jackson, Stan Rogalski, Joe McCoy, Al McClintock, and Mike Houle, and fans like Ray Kinsella and Gideon Clarke each experience baseball intensely in their own unique ways, with their responses to the game differing greatly as Kinsella uses his characters to approach a variety of "what really matters," including family, friendship, and love. W.P. Kinsella says that he writes "love stories that have baseball as a background" (Horvath and Palmer 186); in his stories, the importance of the game, to players and fans alike, is merely a means through which they address the larger issues of love, forgiveness, redemption, and hope so often connected to the game's idyllic pastoral history.

Types of Players in Kinsella's Fiction

This chapter explores a small sampling of Kinsella's short stories as well as the five novels already considered in previous chapters. The short stories are essential to analysis of identity because chapters from each of Kinsella's novels, more so with *Shoeless Joe*, *The Iowa Baseball Confederacy* and *Magic Time*, were conceptualized or originally published as short stories focusing on individual characters instead of their roles in the lengthier novels. A more detailed consideration of Kinsella's short stories appears in the following chapter in which selected stories which have not been used in his novels are examined.

Each of the novels has a central figure who is first and foremost a fan of the game. Beyond the identities of these characters, however, are three types of players used by Kinsella: marginally talented players who are easily forgotten because of their inability to consistently perform well at the major league level; talented players who have some tragic flaw preventing them from realizing their full potential; and retired or banned major league players who are for whatever reason afforded the opportunity to once again return to the game after time away from it.

John Fiske argues that "[p]layers are known statistically by the age, height and weight of their bodies" and that "performance is known by the statistics" (83). Similarly, team uniforms with individual names and numbers "serve first to individuate this body from others and then to insert it into the bank of statistical knowledge" (84). The identity of a player, however, is based on more substantial characteristics than a uniform or statistical entry on the sports page. Baseball literature, both fiction and non-fiction, often presents a more accurate representation of individual identity than that found through statistics. A large portion of the canonical literature deals with a season or a career of a player who has achieved a considerable level of success at the major league level. Roy Hobbs in Bernard Malamud's *The Natural*, Bingo Long in William Brashler's *The Bingo Long Traveling All-Stars & Motor Kings*, and Joe Hardy of *The Year the Yankees Lost the Pennant*, by Douglass Wallop are just three popular examples of fictional players who gain notoriety because of their playing abilities.

While Kinsella occasionally writes about players of considerable talent, the majority of the players, both real and fictional, in his novels are marginally talented at best. Oftentimes, his players are talented enough to perform in the minor leagues, but not quite gifted enough for the major leagues. These specific characters emphasize early America's role as, and contemporary America's empathy for those who are considered, underdogs. Among the most notable examples is Archibald "Moonlight" Graham, a player whose name was taken by Kinsella from *The Baseball Encyclopedia* and who played two innings of a game for the New York Giants in 1905 without ever having an official at-bat. Despite a successful minor league career, including his hitting .335 for the 1906 champions from Scranton of the New York League, Graham's only major league appearance was in the single game against the Dodgers one year earlier. Similarly, many of Kinsella's fictional players also display marginal talent at the professional level. Stan Rogalski in *The Iowa Baseball Confederacy* and Mike Houle in *Magic Time* are both talented enough to earn roster spots on minor league teams, but they do not perform at a level where they will ever reach the major leagues. *If Wishes Were Horses* has a more complex plot in which Joe McCoy has parallel lives—one in which he has a mediocre pitching career in the major leagues and the other in which he pitches in the state high school championship game, thereby effectively ruining his opportunity for a college scholarship and a professional baseball career—and his ultimate decision to choose the less glamorous of these lives reinforces Kinsella's use of mediocre or failed players in this fiction. By focusing on players not caught in the trappings of major league fame and fortune, Kinsella's novels clearly focus on the baseball's attributes that endear the characters and the readers alike to the game.

In addition to the marginal players in his fiction, Kinsella also utilizes players who demonstrate immense talent, yet who have a perceived flaw in their characters, leading to a separation from their teams or from the game itself. Many of the characters in this category are found in the short fiction, several examples of which are discussed in greater detail in this and the following chapter; however, a large portion of these short stories are later incorporated into the novels examined here. "Shoeless Joe Jackson Comes to Iowa," the inspiration for the novel *Shoeless Joe*, obviously focuses on the most famous of the eight banished members of the 1919 Chicago White Sox. Despite the facts that Jackson was one of the leading hitters of his era and his performance in the 1919 World Series offers no support to the claim that he did anything other than play to the best of his ability against the Reds in that year's Fall Classic, Jackson's legacy has been forever tarnished by the scandal that marked the end of his career. His infamous decision to accept $5,000 following the series completely overshadows his on-field performances.

As with the marginal players like Rogalski, McCoy, and Houle, Kinsella's players often demonstrate some attribute viewed as a flaw by either the player himself or by his teammates, something which separates them from the game in some aspect. In both "The Darkness Deep Inside" and "Lumpy Drobot, Designated Hitter," a player's conversion to Christianity alienates him from other members of the team. Though not traditionally considered a fault, the Christian lifestyle clearly divides the players from their teammates, disrupting the familial-type camaraderie often associated with the clubhouse life of a baseball team. In *Magic Time*, Kinsella once again uses a characteristic that, while not necessarily considered a flaw, leads to a player's isolation from his team. Barry McMartin, perhaps the most talented player on the Greenshirts, has a career tainted by volatile behavior and physical confrontations. His behavior, however, serves as an attempt to mask the fact that he is the only known homosexual on the team. The result of McMartin's attempts to conceal this part of his identity through fighting and overly aggressive behavior on the field prevents him from being added to a major league roster.

Kinsella's last category of players is that of former players from major league history who are brought back into the game in some manner. With the exception of Moonlight Graham, the players Kinsella chooses to incorporate into his short fiction and into his novels are high-profile individuals, most of whom are members of the Hall of Fame or who, like Joe Jackson, have Hall of Fame credentials. In "The Fadeaway," Christy Mathewson, one of the original five members of the Hall of Fame elected in 1936, appears as a voice on the dugout telephone to teach manager Tag Murtagh how to coach his legendary "fadeaway pitch." Roberto Clemente, the Pittsburgh Pirates' right fielder who died in 1972 while on a relief mission to Nicaragua, reappears in "Searching for January" on a beach in 1987, thinking only a few days have passed since his plane crashed. In two novels, Kinsella blends actual teams from the early 20th century with his fictional characters as the 1919 Chicago White Sox and the 1908 Chicago Cubs play primary roles in *Shoeless Joe* and *The Iowa Baseball Confederacy* respectively. Incorporating players like Mathewson, Clemente, and Jackson allows players whose own playing careers or lives were cut tragically short an opportunity to reclaim the years denied them by fate. Using entire teams in his novels demonstrates the timelessness of the game and how it inextricably links generations of fans, thereby allowing them to compare contemporary teams with those legendary dynasties from the game's past. Regardless of what type of player or team Kinsella uses in his novels, each category presents a unique perspective on how the game plays an undeniable role in establishing and forming a player's identity.

Individual Identity and Baseball in Shoeless Joe

As the first of Kinsella's baseball novels and the only one to date to have been made into a feature film, an overwhelming amount of critical approaches focus on *Shoeless Joe*; the majority of recent scholarship, however, focuses on the film version of the text, *Field of Dreams*, or on comparisons between the two versions of the story. What many of these critics fail to consider are the characters who were not included in the film adaptation. Brett Mandel does recognize the differences in the two versions of the story, describing the novel as one which "weaves a tale of baseball and fantasy and suggests that people can make their dreams come true, have second chances, and use the universality of baseball to form bonds they don't have the words to produce" (44). Kinsella's structure of the novel guides the reader to a consideration of specific individuals in the text; various characters use baseball's universality as a way of forming bonds with other characters and as the primary way through which they establish their own identities within the plot. The five divisions in the novel consider four characters and how each is defined by the game: "Shoeless Joe Jackson Comes to Iowa" is the short story that inspired the novel and serves as the novel's introductory chapter; "They Tore Down the Polo Grounds in 1964" and "The Rapture of J. D. Salinger," the second and fifth chapters of the text, focus on the reclusive Salinger; "The Life and Times of Moonlight Graham" is a chapter in which Kinsella takes an obscure player from baseball's long history and weaves him into a fictional story; and "The Oldest Living Chicago Cub" dedicates itself to a lifelong fan of the game who convinces the people with whom he comes in contact that he once played for the Cubs and was a marginally successful pitcher. The one character connecting this wide variety of people is the novel's protagonist, Ray Kinsella. These players' personal identities in the novel are based on their relationships with baseball, each in a unique way, and all of which are tied together on Ray's baseball diamond.

In *Collision at Home Plate: The Lives of Pete Rose and Bart Giamatti*, James Reston, Jr. recounts an episode from former Major League Baseball Commisioner Bart Giamatti's boyhood in which the fathers of Giamatti and his friends, fathers who were both Italian immigrants, were bound by their paths to the United States as well as by their love of the game: "Baseball brought them together. It gave them a sense of belonging, of participation in the American experience" (19). Similarly, in his analysis of sport in American society, John Fiske writes that "social identities and social relationships are lived in places" and "[s]port identifies place, gives it a significance that works only for those who live in it" (91). More than any of Kinsella's novels, *Shoeless Joe* strongly relies on a sense of place. Narrowly focusing on Ray's field on the farm, Kinsella presents a microcosm of society and various relationships found therein through the players who are brought to play on the field. Fiske also writes that the "experiential knowledge of sport is known in and through the body. Its affective intensity provides vital experience around which fans can organize their sense of the personal histories and relationships, and in which it becomes possible to experience identities that are their own" (91). Players and non-players alike in *Shoeless Joe* experience the game in ways that allow each individual identity to develop uniquely on its own and together with others' identities on the field. The sport is not an abstract concept debated amongst the characters; rather, the sport specifically presents itself on the field Ray builds, the field on which players and fans, living and dead, share in the knowledge of and appreciation for baseball.

"Shoeless" Joe Jackson

In examining Shoeless Joe as he appears in the novel and in the subsequent film, C. Kenneth Pellow argues that an important element of the novel lacking in the film "is that Ray Kinsella feels that Shoeless Joe needs to be exonerated, just as he feels that he still owes something to his father, the proto-typical advocate of Jackson. Therefore, [Ray] is psychologically and politically pre-disposed to desire a miraculous resurrection" (19–20). Ray hears The Voice tell him to build the field, and he immediately interprets its purpose to be providing Jackson an opportunity to return and play the game from which he was banished by Judge Kenesaw Mountain Landis in 1921; Ray never sees Jackson as anyone other than the former ball player who was forced to play under assumed names following his exile from the game. If the 1919 Black Sox Scandal, as George Grella says, "may have been more important than World War I in educating the nation in the dubious lessons of disenchantment" (560), then Jackson and the other seven banned players were the nation's most important teachers of the decade. Unfortunately for Jackson and his implicated teammates, they are remembered not only as baseball players, but as the players who conspired to fix that year's World Series. Due in large part to Jackson's illiteracy and rural background, he has long been portrayed as someone who accepted money for the fix but never agreed to fix the games. Though he did accept $5,000 from teammate Lefty Williams after the Series had concluded (Evans & Herzog 121), there is no evidence that Jackson conspired to fix the outcome of any of the games against Cincinnati; in fact, his .375 batting average during the Series was the highest among players from both clubs. The end result for Jackson, however, is one that continues to be debated today. "Jackson, along with the other principals of the so-called Black Sox scandal, was acquitted of criminal charges; yet in the end, he was penalized by the baseball patriarchy for his unethical practices, and despite his resplendent playing career, he was never elected to the Hall of Fame" (Springwood 121). In the novel, Kinsella uses Jackson's life as a baseball player and the role he may have played in the scandal as a catalyst for inspiring Ray to build the diamond on his farm, leading to the emergence of the other players, most notably Jackson's banished teammates, and various fans in the story.

Ray's introduction to Joe Jackson was through his father, John Kinsella, who told him stories of seeing Jackson some years after being banned from the game by Commissioner Landis, "playing in a tenth-rate commercial league in a textile town in Carolina" under "an assumed name" (*Shoeless* 3). Despite Jackson's name change, being overweight and running slower than he did while in the major leagues, Ray's father was obviously still able to identify the former White Sox star: "he could still hit. Oh, how that man could hit. No one has ever been able to hit like Shoeless Joe" (3). Kinsella's trademark magic realism is a mixture of fact and fiction; however, Jackson's reputation as a hitter is one of the clearest markers of his true identity as evidenced by statistical support from the game's history. Ty Cobb, an inaugural member of the National Baseball Hall of Fame and a contemporary of Jackson's, was known to have "paused to admire the poetic purity of Joe's lash at the plate" (Honig 106). While Kinsella does note that Jackson changed his name in order to continue playing baseball, he also indicates that the name itself is not what identifies the player. His identity lies in his ability to swing a bat, something that remains in spite of a name change or an altered physical appearance. As a result, John Kinsella was able to identify Jackson as a player despite the assumed name under which the exiled legend was then playing.

Any study of Joe Jackson, including one like this which explores his role in a fictional context, is incomplete without examining his perceived role in the Black Sox Scandal of 1919, "a centerpiece for discussion about baseball's place in America" (McGimpsey 51) and "a stain on sportsmanship [which] exists in baseball mythology as a fall from grace" (Candelaria, *Seeking* 12) because "[t]he story of Joe Jackson and [the scandal] are intricately woven, and it is difficult, if not impossible, to discuss Shoeless Joe without engaging the larger issue of the fix" (Herzog 97). This element of baseball history has been analyzed at great length because of its uniqueness in the world of sports: "Professional basketball and professional football do not have (meta)fictional narratives about corruption as embracing as the Black Sox Scandal" (59). Writers such as Eliot Asinof and William Herzog each deal with the scandal, its major players, and the subsequent punishments in great detail, but for W.P. Kinsella, it serves merely as a justification for Ray building the field on his farm. In Ray's mind, the field provides his father's hero a location to once again play the game in which he was long denied the opportunity to openly participate. Ray's only mention of the event is when he remembers the stories his father told him; rather than being raised on children's stories, Ray is raised listening to stories about each of the eight players from that White Sox team who were later banned. With Ray's father specifically focusing on Jackson's alleged involvement, the leftfielder became symbolic "of the tyranny of the powerful over the powerless" (7), a description that is loaded with John Kinsella's obvious Marxist telling of the story with White Sox owner Charles Comiskey as the evil bourgeois and Jackson the most visible of the oppressed proletariat. Ray's connection with Jackson is rooted in their shared love of the game and not the scandal that has forever tarnished Jackson's reputation and the reputations of the other players connected to the fix. The ringleader of the group, first baseman Arnold "Chick" Gandil, spoke years later about how the scandal forever served as an identifying trait for those players: "people didn't remember us afterward for our playing. They remembered us only as the 'Black Sox'" (62). Unfortunately for Jackson, "the scapegoat for the entire affair" (Herzog 99), and third baseman Buck Weaver, who also proclaimed his innocence until his death, their identities remain based on their alleged dealings with players like Gandil who openly admitted his personal guilt in the conspiracy.

Throughout the course of the novel Ray watches Jackson play multiple times, yet he never asks the left fielder about his role in the fix or about his relationships with the other players. Ray briefly considers approaching Jackson about the subject only once — on the first night Jackson appears on the field. Knowing a movement to have Jackson's record cleared was taking place shortly before the player's death in December, 1951, Ray muses that, had Jackson lived, perhaps he would have been reinstated in the game: "I wanted to ask, but my instinct told me not to. There are things it is better not to know" (17). For Ray to discover that Jackson may have had a role in the conspiracy would have altered his perception of Jackson from a player with Hall of Fame credentials wrongly accused to a player who tarnished the game by fixing the World Series. Identifying him only as an exceptional player, Ray chooses to allow Jackson's playing credentials to stand as the only trait by which he is identified. By never asking about Jackson's role in the scandal, Ray is able to connect more deeply through the game with his hero with whom he already shares one important trait: both men are victims of a wealthy ruling class—Jackson as the subservient player on Charles Comiskey's team and Ray as the serf working the land threatened by takeover from the corporate farms owned by his brother-in-law. The game brings them together in a more positive manner, and in doing so, illuminates the game's redemptive powers in each man's life.

As Ray never approaches Jackson about the scandal, neither does Jackson offer any information about the conspiracy to Ray. What is understood, however, is that Jackson's role in the scandal serves as the reason for him being given the opportunity on Ray's farm. At the conclusion of his first game on the field, Jackson approaches Ray about the possibility of returning. When Ray assures him that he is always welcome, Jackson tells his host, "There are others," continuing by naming seven of his teammates from the 1919 White Sox roster—first baseman Arnold "Chick" Gandil; shortstop Charles "Swede" Risberg; third baseman Buck Weaver; utility infielder Fred McMullin; starting pitchers Eddie Cicotte and Lefty Williams; and outfielder Oscar "Happy" Felsch (18). The seven players were teammates implicated in the scandal and banned by Commissioner Kenesaw Mountain Landis from ever again participating in the game; as a result of Ray building the field, all eight find redemption through the game. While history may remember these names for their connection to the scandal, Jackson sees them as he sees himself—as ballplayers. For Joe Jackson, his identity is not based on the punishment handed to him by Judge Landis; rather, he is a player who "loved the game" (15). For W. P. Kinsella, the only relevant aspect of Jackson's identity is as a player who embraces the game and wishes to play again on Ray's mystical field.

J. D. Salinger

After being approached by Larry Kessenich, an editor at Houghton Mifflin who had read "Shoeless Joe Jackson Comes to Iowa," about turning the story into a novel, Kinsella says he began thinking about "how to combine an expanded story with [his] interest in J. D. Salinger" (Murray 48). Kinsella was interested in the writer because

> [Salinger ...] makes himself conspicuous by hiding. If he didn't want to be in the limelight he could give one interview a year to some second-rate magazine, and he would have been forgotten about years ago. Instead he gives no interviews, and everytime someone mentions his name he threatens a law suit, which has kept him in the public eye. I mean, how many living writers who haven't published since 1962 manage to keep their names in front of the public for almost 30 years

and continue to do it? So I knew that was an interesting phenomenon I wanted to investigate [Shannon *Baseball* 158].

Though Kinsella chose to incorporate Salinger into the plot because of characteristics related to his lifestyle and his decision not to publish, in the novel Salinger's character is identified by Ray through their shared love of baseball. When searching for something that would connect his eclectic group of characters together in the novel, Kinsella "found the key to the problem when [he] went back and reread all of Salinger's collected and uncollected work and discovered that he had used two characters named Kinsella in his work" (158). With the Kinsella name used as a way to send Ray on a quest to find Salinger, Salinger's character is then described only by terms of his relationship in some fashion with the game.

Known as much for his reclusive lifestyle as his fiction, Salinger, "[d]espite all his efforts ... cannot avoid being talked about, even preached about" (French 34). Salinger continues to be one of the most analyzed writers of twentieth century American literature in large part because "[his] life (or what we know of it) and his work cast such intriguing shadows upon each other" (Grunwald 3). It is this intrigue that led Kinsella to include Salinger as such a significant character in the novel. For all of his interest in Salinger's writing and private lifestyle, however, Kinsella does not base the author's identity in the novel on what is known about him; instead, the Salinger of *Shoeless Joe* is identified more through his connection with baseball than through his writing career or reclusive nature.

After Ray builds the field, allowing Joe Jackson and the rest of the banished Chicago White Sox to return to the sport, he hears The Voice telling him to "Ease his pain," instinctively knowing that the pronoun refers to Salinger, someone with whom Ray has no apparent connection (31). When Ray has a dream of himself and Salinger at Fenway Park watching a game, he feels called to research all he can on Salinger, something W. P. Kinsella himself did while working the author into his novel. Though Kinsella incorporates a variety of known facts about Salinger into his novel—his chosen lifestyle of seclusion in New Hampshire, his lack of publishing anything new after "Hapworth 16, 1924" in 1965, his initial reluctance and later refusal to give interviews, and his hesitation to allow his fiction to be anthologized (32–33)—he diverts Salinger's identity from being solely a writer to being a baseball fan who happens to write. This transformation from writer to fan happens when Kinsella concocts a fictional interview from an unknown magazine in which Salinger is portrayed as a devoted and knowledgeable fan of the game who has a copy of the *Baseball Encyclopedia* readily available and who, though partial to the Boston Red Sox, watches any game that happens to be televised (33–34). By connecting this fictional article with the fact that "there's a Richard Kinsella that Holden talks about in [*The*] *Catcher* [*in the Rye*]" and "the boy telling that story ["A Young Girl in 1941 with No Waist at All"] is named Ray Kinsella" (Shannon, *Spitball* 58), W.P. Kinsella is able to begin shifting Salinger's identity from the real-life representation to the fictional one he creates of the writer as a baseball fan. Naming the novel's protagonist Ray Kinsella and his twin brother Richard, W.P. Kinsella provides a link between his characters and the very real J. D. Salinger, a link strengthened by the mutual interest in baseball.

After reading the interview, Ray comments that the reclusive writer was at least familiar with the game of baseball and that the interview itself "established a vague kinship between [them] ... for [Ray has] always been a little eccentric where baseball is concerned" (34). The most poignant passage of the interview for Ray is when Salinger comments that his greatest wish as a boy, more than anything else he could think of, was "to play at the Polo Grounds," but that he has grown too old to realize that wish being fulfilled, because the Giants had moved to San Francisco and the Polo Grounds were demolished in 1964 (35). For Ray, Salinger's sentiment deepens the connection he feels with the writer and moves him emotionally. Ray no longer identifies Salinger through *The Catcher in the Rye* or through the rumors surrounding his reclusive lifestyle; instead, Ray identifies Salinger through their shared love of and sentiment for the game of baseball.

Once Ray journeys to New Hampshire, kidnapping Salinger to attend a Red Sox game, both men share a moment when The Voice speaks to them, telling them to "Go the distance" (93), and the statistical entry from the *Baseball Encyclopedia* for Archibald "Moonlight" Graham is flashed on the scoreboard, an experience that Salinger keeps to himself until Ray prepares to leave him. When Ray confronts Salinger about the interview that led him to kidnap the writer, Salinger emphatically tells his kidnapper that he has never given an interview about the game, nor is baseball "a passion in [his] life" (97). He claims to have attended only a few games in recent years and only sporadically follows the game on television or in the newspapers. Although Salinger denies giving the interview, something which he later admits at the novel's end, the shared experience of attending the game at Fenway Park and being given the vision of Graham's statistics further solidifies their relationship in baseball. Salinger goes so far as to express envy at Ray's identity in the game and the quest on which the Voice has called him: "I wish I had your passion for baseball.... If I had my life to live over again, I'd take more chances.... You keep on listening to your voices, even if they're wrong. Keep on doing what it is you do.... Keep on taking risks" (98). Just as Ray identifies Salinger by the writer's love of the game and the experience they have at the ballgame, Salinger identifies Ray not as a farmer or family man, but as a fan who has unparalleled passion for the sport. This relationship is what ultimately leads them together to find Moonlight Graham and return to Ray's field in Iowa.

While beginning their pilgrimage to Chisholm, Minnesota, in search of Graham, Ray questions why Salinger never wants to discuss his writing, to which Salinger replies that, despite farming being his only occupation, Ray never discusses the day-to-day routines and challenges of agriculture. Both men have occupations *outside* of baseball, but they identify with each other and come to be identified by others *because* of baseball. Ray realizes that he lacks sufficient knowledge about farming to carry on anything more than a casual conversation about it, despite the fact that it is his primary occupation back home in Iowa, but that he can and does spend the majority of his time discussing baseball and the field he built on the farm, further demonstrating that who he is as a person remains grounded more on baseball than anything else, including farming, a realization that Salinger also experiences by joining Ray on the quest to find a minor footnote from baseball history, Archibald Graham, witnessing Ray's passion for the game.

Archibald "Moonlight" Graham

The player of greatest notoriety in the novel is Shoeless Joe Jackson, who had a successful major league career (.356 avg., 1,772 hits, 785 RBI) over 13 seasons ("Joe Jackson Stats"); however, Kinsella, as he often does in his fiction, incorporates another player into this novel though, unlike Jackson, he is one who has only become known to the general public because of his role in the novel and film — Archibald "Moonlight" Graham. Graham's statistical information, revealed to Ray and Salinger on the Fenway Park scoreboard, one career game played for the 1905 New York Giants with no at-bats, is taken directly from Major League Baseball's official records. That W. P. Kinsella chooses to incorporate two polar opposites of the major league experience, one player who had legendary success and another who played in only two innings of one game, solidifies the assertion that the game may be used as a means of identifying and connecting people regardless of their level of success in the game. Despite playing in just one major league game as an outfielder for the New York Giants, Graham held a special interest for Kinsella, who intentionally researched the former player with the purpose of including him in the novel: "I knew that I had to write something about 'Doc' Graham, whose wonderful nickname, 'Moonlight,' I'd once found in a baseball encyclopedia. I even did research on Graham in the small town in northern Minnesota where he spent his last years" (Murray 48). Through his research of a typically overlooked former major league player, Kinsella presents the reader with a character who is as much identified by the game as is a higher caliber player like Jackson.

Kinsella's including Salinger in the novel entails various contrived aspects of Salinger's character that are then blended with what is factual about his life. The result is a writer whose identity in the story relies primarily on baseball. When incorporating Graham in the novel, however, Kinsella adheres to factual information about his life and career, inventing only "how he got his nickname" (Shannon, *Spitball* 59), and the obviously fictional conversations that take place with Graham and the various characters in the novel. While considering who was then perhaps the most obscure player in baseball history, Kinsella "knew [he] wanted to write something about Moonlight Graham because of his one line in *The Baseball Encyclopedia*. [He] wanted to know how playing one instant of major league baseball and never coming to bat had affected his life" (Shannon, *Baseball* 158). In the most insignificant of entries, Graham is shown to have played in one game for the New York Giants, though never getting an official at-bat. Graham's player file at the National Baseball Hall of Fame and Museum in Cooperstown, New York provides more detailed information, including a clipping from the *Evening Telegram* from June 29, 1905 that states, "The game gave the champions a chance to try out some of their bench warming talent ... and Archie Graham had two joyous innings [in] the right garden" (Graham). This account of Graham's lone appearance in the major leagues differs slightly from Kinsella's version, in which Graham played only one inning of a game, told by Graham's character in the novel. Also included in the player file is an interview with Graham by Ernie Accorsi in which Graham recollects that he drew a base on balls in his only plate appearance before breaking his leg and leaving the sport. This account, however, is not found in any official record of the game, nor is it supported by any statistical information found in the Hall of Fame archives. Regardless of the validity of Graham's account, a base on balls is not statistically recognized as an official at-bat in a game, only as a plate appearance; therefore, Kinsella's reason for researching and including Graham in the novel—that he never had an official major league at-bat — is still legitimate and allows for Graham's identity to be shifted from his role as a medical doctor, a role that lasted nearly all of his adult life, to his role as a neglected major league baseball player, a role that lasted for only a small portion of one relatively insignificant game.

Connected by the bond of baseball, Ray Kinsella and J. D. Salinger continue their pilgrimage to Chisholm, Minnesota, where Graham lived the majority of his life after leaving the game. With no guidance other than the minimal information provided in their shared vision on the scoreboard, the pair begins their research in the town at the office of Veda Ponikvar, the publisher of the *Chisholm Free Press*, where they read an editorial Ponikvar had written, "His Was a Life of Greatness," an editorial that actually appeared in the local paper following Graham's death in 1965. Though drawn to Graham's hometown because of the baseball connection, Ray and Salinger find that Graham's identity within the town is that of a doctor who provided, in many ways, necessities for the citizenry. In the novel, Kinsella quotes directly from Ponikvar's prose:

> As the community grew, Doc became an integral part of the population. There were good years and lean ones. There were times when children could not afford eye glasses or milk, or clothing because of the economic upheavals, strikes and depressions. Yet no child was ever denied these essentials, because in the background, there was a benevolent, understanding Doctor Graham. Without a word, without any fanfare or publicity, the glasses of milk, or the ticket to the ballgame, found their way into the child's pocket [qtd. in Friedlander and Reising 172].

Unlike Jackson, defined only by his role in baseball and the scandal of 1919, Graham compares to Salinger in that he, like the writer, is identified by the majority of people by an occupation other than something associated with baseball. Salinger is known to most as a writer and Graham is known as a doctor. By blending reality and fantasy into his trademark magic realism, W. P. Kinsella once again reveals the identity of a character as it relates to the sport.

Though Kinsella uses the one game in which Graham played for the Giants as the catalyst for including him in the novel, he recognizes that Graham's life as a baseball player is relatively unknown to the people within the small mining town: "No one had ever heard him called Moonlight. And he didn't talk about his baseball career.... A few people knew ... and all of them thought he played much longer than he had" (Shannon, *Spitball* 59). Rather than embellishing Graham's life as a ballplayer, Kinsella shows the doctor as a man who, though happy with his life in the community, still identifies a part of himself as a baseball player, demonstrating the game's enduring role as an identity marker. Joe Jackson's identity as a baseball player is clouded by the regret of becoming involved with the scandal, and J. D. Salinger expresses regret at never being able to play baseball at the Polo Grounds;

Graham, however, expresses no apparent regret at only playing in one game with no official at-bat, nor does he inflate his role in the major leagues into something which it was not. Instead, Graham becomes a leader in the community and lives a happy and productive life as a husband and doctor. It is obvious by the ways the citizens of Chisholm remember Graham that he is one of the "people [who] not only helped one another and enjoyed one another's company but also participated mutually in enterprises that furthered the common good" (Bellah, et al. 116). One such enterprise is the blood pressure study on school children started in 1926, leading to a 1945 publication in *American Journal of Diseases of Children*, and continuing for the rest of his professional medical career, studies that benefitted "[c]hildren on every continent and in every nation" which continued to be referred to by medical professionals as recently as a 1990 article in *Clinical Pediatrics* (Friedlander and Reising 143). Jackson, guilty of throwing the World Series or not, is forever blemished by the allegations of selfishness in accepting money to betray the team and its fans; Graham, however, though also a member of the baseball fraternity, is known for his selfless identity in which he abandoned his baseball pursuits so that he could benefit the people of Chisholm and children around the world.

The concept of one's identity is twofold: how a person identifies him/herself and how other people identify the person. Salinger, for example, expresses frustration at the variety of rumors from the outside world surrounding his reclusive lifestyle and his decision to no longer publish any of his works while viewing himself as a person content to live alone in New England. That the town collectively identifies Doc Graham in a positive manner reflects his contributions as a doctor and civic leader. This identification, however, does nothing to distinguish him from any other person in a similar role. After spending time researching Graham's life in the community, Salinger tells Ray that a large number of communities across the country have citizens similar to Doc Graham. After all their time in Chisholm visiting with the people who knew the obscure player they knew only as Doc, Ray and Salinger have only discovered positive memories from the citizens, memories that would be indistinguishable from similar people in other small towns. The aspect of his identity that sets him apart from other characters of such backgrounds is the fact that he realized the dream of playing in a major league game, if only for the briefest time possible.

Unable to sleep one night, Ray walks the streets of Chisholm, feeling as though he may have "crossed some magical line between fantasy and reality" (139) as he meets Doc Graham, who has been dead for over a decade.

Referring to the doctor by his baseball nickname, "Moonlight," Ray is told that "[he] must be a fan of the game to know about that" (138), further establishing Ray's own identity in the game as he begins conversing with the former player. Though clearly established as a doctor, Graham relates to Ray the story behind his baseball nickname and declares that he has been a lucky person to have spent his life doing the two things he most enjoys—being a doctor and playing baseball. Unlike Jackson, whose entire identity is established through the game, Graham has two equally important identities, one as a doctor and a lesser-known role as a ballplayer. Though Shoeless Joe earned a reputation as one of the game's greatest hitters, Graham, as Ray says, "brush[ed] against fame like a stranger hurrying past in a crowd" (146) during the appearance in the 1905 game. Rather than being consumed by what might have been, Graham explains that he gave it little if any thought that day because, like most people, he failed to recognize the most important moment of his life while that moment was taking place: "I figured there'd be plenty more days.... But looking back, I can see that I knew ... I was a minor leaguer in a major-league park.... But you don't admit something like that to yourself when you're young and full of hope" (146). This realization led Graham to shift who he was as a marginally talented professional baseball player to being a significantly more talented medical doctor. Fifty years later, though, as Ray questions him about his playing career, Doc confesses that his days as a ballplayer have had more of an impact on him that he likes to admit. Despite his success as a doctor and the fact the he never achieved the level of success for which a player like Jackson is known, Graham realizes that the game did significantly impact his life.

Had Graham been more successful in his lone major league appearance, there is a possibility that he may have prolonged his playing career, an issue explored more in *Field of Dreams* than in *Shoeless Joe*; however, Graham's realization that he was never going to be a successful member of the Giants led him to pursue his far more successful medical career. Ray Kinsella can only see the apparent tragedy of coming so close to realizing the dream of playing professional baseball, but the Doc Graham of 1955 is able to put into perspective the identity of Moonlight Graham of 1905, saying that the true tragedy would have been if he had only been a doctor for such a short period of time: "I love the game, but it's only that, a game" (149). Graham's identity, therefore, is a combination of the two professions—baseball and medicine—although the townspeople only see him as a doctor and Ray can only see him as a player. The baseball aspect of his identity, though, resurfaces after 50 years as Ray questions Graham about the doctor's unfulfilled dream on the baseball diamond, to which Doc Graham replies, "to hold a bat in a major-league game" (151), something that becomes a possibility as Salinger and Ray offer a ride back to Iowa to a young hitchhiker, a young man named Archie Graham. Perhaps more than any of Kinsella's characters, Graham demythologizes baseball and its universalizing influence on male identity, showing that Graham's achievements as a doctor far surpass anything he is able to achieve on his Homeric baseball quest, even on Ray's field.

Graham's dual identity as a player-doctor is reduced to that of only a player once he arrives, resurrected in the form of a young man, on Ray's farm. Shoeless Joe tells Graham that he has been expected and that he should come to the field and start warming up immediately for that night's game. As the younger version of himself, Graham has no idea that he will be a doctor, only that he has been added to the roster of Jackson's team in Iowa. Ray observes that when Graham crosses the fence to enter the outfield, shaking hands with Joe Jackson, "he ceased to be one of us ... and became one of them" (203). The transformation on the field alters Graham's identity from "Doc" to "Moonlight," from elderly doctor to youthful ballplayer. A similar transformation takes place when Graham leaves the field to help resuscitate Ray's daughter, Karin, who is choking in the stands on a hot dog. Without looking back at the field, Moonlight Graham returns to the side of the fence from which he originally came—a place, Ray observes, where none of the other players ever walk—transforming into the Doc Graham whom Ray had met during the night in Chisholm, Minnesota. Once this final transformation has taken place, however, Ray senses that it is irreversible and that Graham will never again appear on the field as "Moonlight," having "violated some cosmic rule that [Ray] know[s] vaguely exists" (249), though he cannot even begin to comprehend. While Graham could have continued his life on the field as a successful ballplayer, he sacrifices this dream so that he can fulfill the role in which he saw his greatest abilities being used: as a doctor. Graham's transformation leads Ray to the understanding that one's identity is never necessarily fixed in one place; Graham is both player and doctor, though he chooses the latter as his primary role when presented with the decision of selecting the one for which he will be most widely identified forever after.

Eddie "Kid" Scissons

Of all of Kinsella's baseball novels, *Shoeless Joe* uses the broadest range of players employed as characters. Jackson represents a successful major league player, Graham a marginally successful major league player, and John Kinsella, a solid minor league player. Perhaps the most intriguing character of the novel, however, is Eddie Scissons, who leads people to believe that he is a former major league pitcher and the oldest living member of the Chicago Cubs. Scissons's reality is that he was only a mediocre minor league player, and he creates the story of his days with the Cubs to portray the career he wishes he had rather than the one that actually occurred. His identity in the novel, therefore, is a false identity which he assumes by his own volition. Although the identity he projects to those around him is based on deception, Scissons's lies are explained by Richard C. Crepeau and Rob Shienkopf in their study based on what they refer to as "the Eddie Scissions [sic] Syndrome": "We remember events in which we were involved and our role in them. Over time our role becomes enhanced. The events take on a more favorable cast than they originally had. Time clouds and distorts. Our desires cloud and distort" (181). The lies comprising Scissons's character have become so deeply ingrained in his identity that he no longer separates truth from fiction. Both are blended together so closely that his identity is based on these very lies, making him the representation of Kinsella's own use of magic realism in so much of his baseball fiction.

The most obvious omission from *Shoeless Joe* in *Field of Dreams* is the Scissons character. Richard Crepeau argues that this fate is a result of Scissons "turn[ing] out to be a fraud" (Crepeau and Sheinkopf 176). Despite the fact that his character is the only one in the novel who lies about his role in the game, Scissons is also shown to be the game's most passionate and emphatic fan. Kinsella uses the game as a means for Scissons to present a false identity to the world around him; as a result, Scissons has two identities which rely on the game — the false identity as a player and the real identity as a zealous fan of the game. Patricia Hampl argues that "[w]e only store in memory images of value" (63) and that "[i]nvention is inevitable" (65) in memory. For Scissons, a man whose daughters are unable to share his love for the game, he values a false image of being someone who was able to realize his life's dream of playing for the Cubs. As Scissons lives his lie for four decades, his false identity becomes an invention which he presents to those around him as being truth. Eventually, even he himself seems to believe the lie, thus transforming, in his mind, fiction into truth.

Defining the role baseball plays in Scissons's identity within the novel becomes problematic when it is revealed that his true identity as a fan of the game is overshadowed by the façade his lie of being a former player for the Cubs creates. Though mentioned only peripherally by Ray in the early stages of the novel, Eddie Scissions emerges as a primary character on the field when Ray returns with Salinger and Graham from their journey, stopping to pick up the elderly man from Iowa City, where he resides, spending most of his days in the Bishop Cridge Friendship Center. Though Scissons no longer lives on the farm and despite Ray not revealing that he already knows of the old man's deception, the two men are kindred spirits in the game. In her critical essay, "*Shoeless Joe* as an Allegory: A Framework for the Writing of Fiction," Rebecca Easton says that Eddie "had sensed the magic of baseball and the farm while still a young man, but he never acted. He could talk the lingo, but he never built the diamond" (123). Scissons, then, is also an expression of deep longing for baseball as a mythos powerful enough to organize lifelong identity, even if it is an identity rooted in untruth. For Ray, bringing Scissons back to the farm serves as yet another way in which he shares his love for the game with someone like-minded in his identity. Ray's having both Scissons and Graham — in addition to J. D. Salinger — in the same vehicle arriving at the farm is telling in that Doc Graham's "restrained behavior contrasts with Eddie's lifetime of stories and Ray's endless retelling of his experiences" (Beach 91). Though all share the common bond of baseball that defines who they are, bringing Scissons to the farm demonstrates the ways in which the game is a part of each one of their lives.

That Eddie Scissons presents himself as a former Chicago Cub is a way through which he can set himself apart from the people with whom he comes in contact. It is his fictional identity that initially draws Ray Kinsella to him on the streets of Iowa City. Scissons, however, intends to play the role beyond his time on Earth, telling Ray that his wish is to be buried wearing a Cubs uniform. His false identity, however, is publicly exposed by Ray's brother-in-law, Mark, who promised Scissons he would not tell the truth of the old man's identity if he and his partner were allowed to purchase the overdue mortgage on the farm, and labels Kid as "a fraud" (216). Mark further explains that Scissons's lie, which Ray has already discovered but kept to himself, is that for which the old man is actually known rather than his being a Cub: "[Scissons is] a joke ... [people] humor [him] because it would be too embarrassing to call [him] a liar to [his] face" (217). Ray, however, assures the old man that he was already aware of this information and that none of it matters to his friends, motioning to all of those in the ballpark on the farm. It is at this moment that Scissons's identity is no longer connected to his lie; instead, he is now identified by his passionate love for the game, a love that connects him to everyone else who has been drawn to the field.

Although his façade as a former major leaguer is no longer being presented, Scissons's real identity includes playing in the minor leagues on a part-time basis for one year on a low-level team in Montana. Like Ray's father, John, the highest level of Scissons's career in the game was in the minor leagues. Since he has no legitimate credentials in professional baseball as do Jackson and Graham, Scissons is relegated to telling stories of his days playing in the West. While Ray has no playing experience at even the minor league level, he and Scissons share an identity that Ray himself sees as being the bond that secures their relationship:

> I understand Eddie Scissons ... I imagine [he] has decided, "If I can't have what I want most in life, then I'll pretend I had it in the past, and talk about it and live it and relive it until it is real and solid.... Once I've experienced it so completely, no one can ever take it away from me [218].

Nearly all of the characters who are drawn to the field attain some form of redemption through the game. Ray is afforded the opportunity to build the field and reconnect with his father; Shoeless Joe is given redemption by the game from which he was banished in 1921; J. D. Salinger is allowed to become a spectator of and a participant in the game he loved as a young man; and Doc Graham is given the unique chance to become Moonlight Graham once more and bat in the major leagues. Scissons, however, is allowed only to see his false identity as a major league pitcher deconstructed and forever destroyed, leaving him with only his role as a fan in the game. This falsehood is a burden that must be shed for Scissons to have the sense of redemption afforded the other players on the field. This seemingly negative experience does not diminish his love for the game; instead, the love is reinforced by what he experiences on the field at Ray's farm.

Before the revelation that his stories of playing for the Cubs have been known by everyone in the community to be fraudulent, Scissons shares with Ray the origin of his love affair with the team, saying that he has been a fan for eight decades, since he was seven years old. Like Ray, who was introduced to the game by his father, Scissons's early involvement in the game is due to a family member. Unlike Ray, however, the retired farmer has no family with whom to share his passion for baseball. While Ray shares his field with his wife and daughter, and eventually his estranged brother and dead father, Scissons laments that his greatest regret is not having a son to teach his love of baseball and to share his joy in watching the sport. Instead, he is the father of three daughters, all of whom are deeply religious and none of whom share his passion for the game. Much has already been written concerning the religious comparisons to baseball in the novel and Scissons's evangelical fervor with which he expresses his love for the game, yet virtually ignored by critics has been his transformation from a fan to one who is given the opportunity to have his life's greatest wish fulfilled on the field, thus gaining him acceptance from those whom he has long admired — established professional baseball players.

During all of the games on Ray's field, the White Sox have played a nameless and faceless team differing from those of the previous games only in that they have different uniforms and batting stances; however, following the exposure of Scissons's lies, the opposing team emerges as the very Chicago Cubs team of which Scissons for years claimed to be a part. Watching the game between the two legendary Chicago teams, Eddie Scissons relates stories of his own brief, unimpressive minor league career until a younger version of himself, Kid Scissons, is announced as the relief pitcher for the Cubs. Like Jackson, Graham, and Ray's own father, Scissons is able to experience the realization of his dream in the game; however, unlike the other players, Scissons's dream soon turns into an embarrassing nightmare in which he surrenders the lead and fails to retire a single batter. Once again, Kinsella allows two versions of a character to emerge — Kid Scissons, the pitcher who fails in his dream to throw in a major league game, and Eddie Scissons, the elderly fan of the game who has witnessed his lifelong dream unravel in front of him. Similar to Doc Graham who gives up his identity as a player to save Karin, Scissons is stripped of his assumed identity as a player, leaving him only with his identity as a passionate fan of the game, an identity not unlike Ray's own. Left only with his true identity, one of which he has no reason to be ashamed, Scissons prepares to die, leaving Ray's farm in neither body nor spirit as both will continue to hold a place with those who are drawn to the field.

On the day before his death, Eddie Scissons appears alone on the bleachers, dressed in the Chicago Cubs uniform in which he wishes to be buried. No longer able to live through his false identity, Scissons calls together all of the ghost players and fans for his proselytizing on "the word of baseball" (227). Unlike Graham, who was able to put his baseball career behind him and establish an identity through medicine, Scissons is haunted by his failed career and the burden of living for 40 years with his lies about being a Cub. Despite the performance his younger self gives on the field, Scissons is able to find fulfillment in the game: "I got what I wanted, but it still wasn't what I needed to make me happy.... It takes more than an infinite ERA to shake my faith" (230). His failure on the field, while fulfilling his life's dream of playing for the Cubs, is not what offers him happiness; however, he understands that baseball represents those qualities that offer him the possibility of the happiness for which he has desperately been searching. Only in baseball is one able to realize new opportunities on a daily basis.

Hall of Fame pitcher Bob Feller also understands this concept: "Every day is a new opportunity. You can build on yesterday's success or put its failures behind and start over again. That's the way life is, with a new game every day, and that's the way baseball is" (qtd. in Plaut 47). The chance for redemption so inherent to the game is an ideal quality for Scissons, who has lived his life with a false identity, only to see that façade fall short of his expectations on the field. Shortly before his death, he realizes that the magic on Ray's field has existed for years, probably acting as the motivation for his own move to the farm so many years before. Sharing with those assembled on the field the faith and optimism he sees in the game, Scissons encourages them with a fervent sermon in which he praises baseball's ability to "set captives free," "open the eyes of the blind," and "raise the dead" (229). Speaking as a prophet proclaiming the healing and restorative powers of the game, Scissons is not discouraged by his own failures in the game; instead, he encourages the congregation of players and fans at the field to embrace the game even more than they already do, imploring them to embrace the "word of baseball," making it a part of their lives, having it live inside each of them, and using it to reach out to those in the world who do not yet have a similar passion (229). Though his dream to play for the Cubs is fulfilled on the field, Eddie Scissons understands that the realization fell far short of his expectations; however, the redeeming characteristics of the game endure and sustain him throughout his life. Echoing the New Testament language in the Gospel of John describing redemption through Jesus Christ, baseball serves as "the Word" for Eddie Scissons, the one thing bringing, despite his performance on the field, peace before he dies.

Before burying Scissons in left field, Joe Jackson summarizes his identity as it relates to the game: "[Scissons] loved the game as much as anyone can..." (235). Though Jackson and the rest of the players far exceed Scissons in playing ability, the old man was every part their equal if not their superior in his love for the game, a trait that is not lost on those who share his love and passion for the sport. Eddie Scissons's identity as a fan, therefore, supersedes his identity as a failed pitcher. While Ray feels as though Scissons's name and record would now appear in *The Baseball Encyclopedia* if he were to search for it, the old man's identity is no longer based on a real or an imagined career with the Cubs; instead, he will be forever remembered as one who is unsurpassed in his love of and devotion to baseball.

Ray Kinsella

Besides baseball, the one common thread linking together Jackson, Salinger, Graham, and Scissons is an unassuming farmer with no playing background in the game — Ray Kinsella. Ray's love for the game and belief in its restorative qualities has led him to plow under a large part of his cash crop so that he can build a baseball field on his farm for Jackson and the rest of the players. His faith in the game's ability to restore the lives and baseball careers of Jackson and his father, among others, transcends his faith in the land's ability to make him money as a farm. Though he is not known for his playing abilities, Ray is known as a fan of the game by those with whom he comes in contact and brings back to his field. His primary identity in the novel is not as a father, husband, or farmer, but as the man who built the field. When Ray's brother-in-law, Mark, and his partner, Bluestein, arrive with a court order giving them temporary control of the farm, Ray still refuses to deviate from his role as a fan; he defends the field, but not the crops. He is no longer a farmer; he is the baseball fan responsible for resurrecting the baseball careers of, among others, the other three players studied in this chapter.

In the short story, "Shoeless Joe Jackson Comes to Iowa," the narrator is never named. In fact, more personal information is given about his father, a former minor league catcher, than about the narrator himself. It has been argued that "[s]pecific places and dates are assigned to the dead in the story, most notably to Shoeless Joe, in order to underscore their magical rebirth in the Iowa cornfield" (Murray 38); however, as Kinsella expands the story into the novel, he provides the narrator a name, Ray Kinsella, and offers more details about his family and background. The lack of any more than basic information about Ray further emphasizes the fact that baseball is his primary identifying trait. In the novel, when he returns to the farm after his trip to New England and Minnesota, Ray's own daughter, Karin, questions his identity, thinking that Ray may actually be his identical twin, Richard, who has, without his brother's knowledge, recently arrived on the farm: "It is really you, isn't it?" (151). Though the physical characteristics make it difficult for Ray's own family, including his wife and daughter, to distinguish him from his brother, Ray's love for the game and for his field from which he has been apart clearly identifies him from his sibling, who has no such passion and only a passing interest in the game.

Several scholars have explored the way in which Ray Kinsella acts as a Homeric hero on a quest throughout the novel; however, Ray is more than a means through whom the dreams of others—Jackson, Salinger, Graham, and Scissons—are fulfilled. By building his field, Ray achieves a level of personal success that directly impacts those able to share in its magical qualities: "The self-interest demanded by the individualistic pursuit of success needs to be balanced by voluntary concern for others" (Bellah et al. 199). By following The Voice's commands to build the field and search for both Salinger and Graham, Ray is clearly able to find the balance between his own goal of reuniting with his father and helping Salinger, Graham, and Scissons each achieve his own dreams on his field. While he certainly remains concerned with the individual characters already examined in this chapter and their identities in the game, Ray's own character is defined by his connection with baseball and its role in his quest. Providing a venue where the 1919 White Sox can play, offering an opportunity to have an at-bat for Moonlight Graham, giving Salinger a chance to reconnect with the game he once loved, and sharing a kinship in the game of baseball with Eddie Scissons, Ray certainly understands the value of the game and its timeless qualities; however, he has no dreams himself of playing the game like Jackson or Graham or assuming a false persona as does Eddie Scissons. Ray is interested in the game in large part because its open-endedness and elements of anticipation provide for needs of the people drawn towards his farm.

W. P. Kinsella says that it is "the open-endedness of the game that makes it so conducive to fiction writing," and that "[t]here are no baseball fans without imaginations" (Shannon *Baseball* 160). With Ray Kinsella's character, W. P. Kinsella is able to utilize these two characteristics of the sport and show how they form the identity of an otherwise unassuming protagonist. Though he fills the roles of husband, father, son, brother, friend, and farmer at various points in the novel, Ray's established identity in the story is that of a fan and, because of this, as the provider of others' dreams in the game. Ray's happiness lies not in the fulfillment of his own dreams, though he certainly wants to be reunited with his father on the field, but in the fulfillment of others' dreams on the field. While some scholars have explored the relationship between Ray and his identical twin brother, Richard, little has been explored regarding the one element that sets them apart: Ray's passion for baseball. When Ray finally approaches their father at the end of the novel, Richard is only able to see thin shadows of the players on the field. Realizing that everyone's dreams have been fulfilled and that the people who are arriving to visit the field will help him financially to save his farm, Ray walks on the field with his father and brother, thinking of the conversations he will have with his father in which they will talk about "love, and family, and life, and beauty, and friendship, and sharing" (255). All of the characteristics he lists have been defined through baseball during his quest and return home. Every aspect of his life has been enriched and defined to the outside world because of the game. Ray is not seen as a family man or as a father, but as a fan so devoted to the game that he jeopardizes his home and farm to build a field so that those who love the game may have a place where, as Salinger muses, they can "watch the game, and it will be as if they have knelt in front of a faith healer" (252). Ray's identity, then, emerges as a fan who wants only for those who share his love for the game to have a pastoral place of refuge from the oppressiveness of the outside world. If, as Nick Trujillo and Bob Krizek claim, "[t]he ballpark is the place where ... fans locate many of their childhood, adolescent, and adult memories" (306), then Ray's identity is based on his being the one person through whom the other characters' wishes and dreams are fulfilled; and in doing so, he is able to reconnect with his estranged brother and dead father, identifying him with his family.

Ray Kinsella's field provides a place for baseball, "a male-dominated social space" (Springwood 167), to serve as a means of establishing clear individuality for the variety of men who are brought to the farm. The identities formed on his field foreshadow those formed by the visitors to the film set of the field in Dyersville, Iowa: "visitors are constructing identities that seem to contest grand nationalisms, displacing them with more inward-looking formations around family, gender, and cultural values" (Springwood 112). The identities of Jackson, Salinger, Graham, Scissions, and Ray Kinsella himself are clearly introspective as each man uses the game to define his individuality with no consideration for his role in a larger society or community. In his tell-all book exposing many of the realities inside the major league clubhouse, former pitcher Jim Bouton writes, "you spend a good piece of your life gripping a baseball and in the end it turns out that it was the other way around all the time" (406). Each one of the characters in *Shoeless Joe* has his identity shaped by the game because of the grip it has on him; how their identities are interpreted by others is contingent on their individual grips on the game. Regardless of the relationship with the game, each character remains in the game's clutches, a game that Viveca Gretton says "signifies as the major symbolic referent for the privileging of white masculine subjectivity" (73). As mentioned in previous chapters, however, Kinsella's characters are not inherently racist, or misogynistic for that matter; they simply reflect the identity of the game that was reluctant to accept minorities and still lacks significant representation of women. These qualities seen in the identities of the characters in *Shoeless Joe* are important points of reference in examining the issues found in Kinsella's subsequent baseball novels.

Individual Identity and Baseball in The Iowa Baseball Confederacy

When Kinsella published his second baseball novel in 1986, Jeffrey Wallach observed that it "employ[ed] baseball as a magical vehicle for self-discovery across the realistic limits of time" (8). Perhaps even more than with *Shoeless Joe*, baseball is used to establish the identities of specific individuals in this second novel. Whereas Kinsella's first novel shows baseball as a blessing that enables Ray to reunite with his father and to provide several other characters the opportunities to live or re-live their dreams of playing the game, baseball in *The Iowa Baseball Confederacy* is a darker representation that arguably curses the Clarke family. *Shoeless Joe* also has characters like Joe Jackson and the rest of his White Sox teammates whose identities are based on their success at the major league level; conversely, Kinsella uses the game in *The Iowa Baseball Confederacy* to construct the identity of a journeyman, mediocre minor league player, Stan Rogalski. Despite the different ways in which Kinsella uses the game in this novel, however, the identities of Matthew Clarke, Gideon Clarke, and Rogalski are directly determined by each man's relationship with the sport.

Matthew Clarke

In *Power Plays, Power Works*, John Fiske says that

> [M]ale fans will often use their expertise to "argue" with the official experts—the commentators. For male fans sport is a field of knowledge which they can know as master, rather than one by which they are known and mastered. But it is an unofficial knowledge: it has no links with institutionally validated knowledge such as that produced by the educational system [87].

What Fiske fails to recognize is that the study of sport is in fact as much a part of academia as any of the more traditional subject matters. Projects like my current study, while a part of the larger, more academically accepted areas of literature and anthropology, are links between the two areas Fiske mentions. The implied divide, however, is at the root of Matthew Clarke's identity within Kinsella's second novel. Until his death by an errant foul ball, only Matthew possesses complete knowledge of the Iowa Baseball Confederacy and its 1908 exhibition game with the Chicago Cubs. His master's thesis is unanimously rejected by his committee in the University of Iowa history department because it lacks any verifiable historical evidence, echoing Fiske's definition of "unofficial knowledge." Only after his death does the knowledge become verified by Gideon and Stan, thus posthumously validating his identity.

Like Ray Kinsella, who is given a vision of a baseball field on his farm and is guided by a mysterious voice to accomplish various tasks on his quest, Matthew Clarke is chosen by a supernatural power to become the recipient of all information relating to the Iowa Baseball Confederacy and the game its All-Stars played against the Chicago Cubs on July 4, 1908, facts that have been mysteriously erased from history and from the minds of the people involved. But while Ray is given the freedom to pursue his quest, Matthew has the task of proving the existence of the league thrust upon him with a bolt of lightning, filling his mind with all of the knowledge and statistics regarding the various teams and people involved from 70 years earlier.

During the summer of 1943, Matthew has just graduated from the University of Iowa with his degree in history and has to choose between the military or enrolling in graduate school. Searching for the woman who would become his wife, Matthew is struck by lightning, the result of which is every detail concerning the Iowa Baseball Confederacy's history, teams, and players being burned into his mind. Before he is filled with this knowledge, there is nothing to indicate that Matthew Clarke is any different from any of the other young men of his age during that time. Following this traumatic event, however, Matthew begins what his son, Gideon, later calls a "quest" that turns him into a "troubled man" (4) who is "plagued" (13) by the truth of the Confederacy. Even after assuming the family insurance business from his own father, Matthew's neighbors identify him by his relentless, obsessive pursuit of the baseball league's existence, despite all evidence pointing to the contrary.

As the local insurance agent in Onamata, Iowa, Matthew never makes an effort to fit into the identity left to him by his father, who founded the business. Unlike his father, whose only role in the community was that of the sole insurance salesman, Matthew's only effort in the company is not actively pursuing new business but only reminding his current clients that their various policies are up for renewal. Seen as an honest man, Matthew

Clarke is, nonetheless, viewed by the townspeople as an eccentric who has wasted his life chasing his dream of proving the existence of the league of which he possesses knowledge. This obsession drives away his wife and daughter, leaving him with nothing more than his knowledge of the league and his son, with whom Matthew, upon his own death, leaves this knowledge.

Reflecting back on his father's life years later, Gideon explains that Matthew had become somewhat reclusive, having few friends, and living his life in relative solitude except for the three things that filled his life: his insurance business, his graduate work, and his overwhelming obsession with the Iowa Baseball Confederacy. The result of his Spartan existence was that he came to be identified solely through his search for evidence of the league. Family friend, Marylyle Baron, tells Gideon that his father "was a fine man, a bright young man too" until he became consumed by his quest to validate the existence of the Confederacy and its history (36). Unable to escape this identity, Matthew commits suicide by leaning into a foul ball at a Milwaukee Brewers game, "thus ending his long and unsuccessful struggle against his tormentors" who never accepted the league's existence, despite the information Matthew continually offered to them (46). This struggle is not unlike Ray Kinsella's fight against the corporate-controlled farming system championed by his brother-in-law and the bank that forecloses on his farm; however, unlike Ray, who is able to use his identity as a fan to provide a place of community on his field, Matthew Clarke's identity as a fan ultimately isolates him from most people and leads to his death, leaving his son, Gideon, with the family curse: the knowledge of the Confederacy.

Gideon Clarke

In "Myth Building and Cultural Politics in W. P. Kinsella's *Shoeless Joe*," Bryan Garman writes that "[m]ost young baseball fans share their earliest experience of the sport with their fathers, and attendance at any game during adulthood invariably summons associations which cause the fan to remember the simplicity and dependence of his or her childhood" (48). Gideon Clarke, the protagonist in *The Iowa Baseball Confederacy* who reappears in *If Wishes Were Horses*, and Ray Kinsella share the fact that their fathers each introduce them to the game. Although they share similar memories as adults of attending games in their youths, Gideon's identity is far less idyllic than Ray's. For Ray Kinsella and his father, John, baseball serves as the common bond which ultimately leads to their reunion on the field; Matthew and Gideon Clarke are also joined by the bond of baseball, but theirs is akin to a family curse passed on from one generation to another. As his father lies dying, Gideon is immediately "overflowing with knowledge, and boiling with righteous indignation because not a soul in the world cared about what [he] knew" (46). Until he slips through time back to 1908, the quest becomes for Gideon what it was for his father, "just out of his reach, the uncatchable mechanical rabbit of his dreams" (47). While the knowledge of the league is a legacy passed to him from his father, his immersion into proving the league's existence becomes as much a part of his identity as his family name.

As is the case with his father before him, Gideon Clarke assumes the role of the local insurance agent for the town of Onamata, Iowa; however, he more fully devotes himself to discovering evidence of the Confederacy by giving his father's business manager, Mrs. Lever, the business itself, with the only stipulation being that she leaves the Clarke family name on the business. With the exception of his efforts to pursue the league, keeping the Clarke family name on the business is the only reputable form of identity Gideon has in the community. Forfeiting the family insurance business allows Gideon to assume the legacy left by his father, the only identity he has left and one not respected by most of the townspeople. Although Gideon's mother and sister are still alive, they have severed nearly all ties with him, leaving him alone in his seemingly hopeless pursuits. Like his mother, Gideon's wife, Sunny, is restless and often leaves him for weeks on end. The end result is that, like Matthew, Gideon becomes wholly consumed by the Iowa Baseball Confederacy to the point that he has no other identity than that of a fanatic for a seemingly fictional league.

For Ray Kinsella, his baseball obsession is a blessing that connects him with not only the variety of players and J. D. Salinger, but with his deceased father. Gideon Clarke's obsession with the game, though it serves as a connection to his father, is a curse through which he sees his identity being negatively changed. The opening lines of the novel focus on the similarities between father and son and how they have both "on more than one occasion been physically ejected from the corporate offices of the Chicago Cubs Baseball Club" (3). Gideon describes his father's quest to prove the league's existence as a "problem" with which he himself sympathized (4). While Ray Kinsella inherits his father's love for the game and, specifically, the Chicago White Sox, Gideon inherits from his father the league's historical and statistical information, known before only to his father, as well as the deeply rooted obsession to prove to everyone else the Confederacy's existence. As Gideon has eliminated all other distractions from his life, including his role as an insurance agent, his entire existence is consumed with two things: his wife, Sunny, and the Iowa Baseball Confederacy.

In addition to the knowledge of the Confederacy, Gideon and Matthew Clarke shared "something [Matthew] must have passed to [Gideon] through his genes: a fatal fascination for transient women" (76–77). Like his mother, Maudie, Gideon's wife is prone to prolonged absences from the family in Onamata. Sunny's decision to leave Gideon for what will ultimately be the last time provides the window of opportunity through which he is able to travel back in time to Big Inning, Iowa, of 1908. Her absence, however, also strips Gideon of his identity as a husband, further emphasizing his identity as a baseball fanatic obsessed with proving the mystery of the league. Realizing the obvious comparison between himself and his father, Gideon understands that his father's personality and obsession with the league made him difficult to live with and that his mother "had some justification for her extended absences" (76). The compulsion that Matthew and Gideon share drives away their spouses, demonstrating yet another way that the game serves as a curse on their identities, rather than the blessing seen in *Shoeless Joe*. It is also another way for the game to continue to assert the dominant male role while marginalizing the women in the novel. In continuing his father's legacy, Gideon clearly recognizes that his eccentric lifestyle, caused solely by his obsession with the game, becomes the foundation for the identity through which he is known. People in academia as well as those who work in the game all consider Gideon "crazy [for] pursuing the Confederacy," saying that he has "spent most of his life on some crazy research project. Something to do with baseball," an obsession that has led to his living alone after Sunny leaves him (79). At the root of his individual identity is the fact that he, like his father before him, has allowed his obsession with the league's history to consume him, to the point where that maniacal consumption is the only thing by which he can be identified.

At various moments in time throughout the novel, people recognize Gideon Clarke by his unique physical characteristics: lengthy white hair, skin made pale by its lack of pigmentation, and pale blue eyes. Mistaken for an albino many times, Gideon is often initially identified by his physical attributes. Upon arriving at the field in 1908 for the game against the Cubs, he is forced into the role of mascot for the Confederacy. Players, superstitious by nature, rub Gideon's hair before each at-bat, giving the historian a unique, but seemingly significant role on the team: a good luck charm. Once he is transported 70 years into the past—where he witnesses the league and the event that have taken him a lifetime to prove happened—Gideon's identity as an eccentric loner who is a baseball fanatic becomes replaced by his role as a symbol for the team. While his identity in 1978 Onamata, Iowa, is as a misguided fanatic, in 1908, players and spectators alike identify him as the team's mascot. In both instances, however, his identity specifically relates to the game and overshadows any of the other aforementioned traits.

As with his father before him, nearly all of Gideon Clarke's life has been defined by his relationship with baseball and proving the existence of the Confederacy. Unlike Matthew, however, Gideon is able to realize his life's dream, much like Eddie Scissons in *Shoeless Joe* witnessing the younger version of himself pitch against the White Sox. After Drifting Away wins the game for the Confederacy, Gideon realizes that he himself will soon drift away to 1978 and promises himself that, having realized his dream of validating the research he and his father did, "[He] can move. [He] can change. [He] *will* change [... He'll] destroy all [his] material on the Confederacy. [He'll] burn it all while Sunny watches [him]. [They'll] get on with [their] lives" (281). Upon his return, though, Sunny leaves Gideon for the last time, his mother and sister have been killed by the FBI, and John Baron, the remaining player in Onamata who played in the epic game, has killed himself. Gideon recognizes, "[His] life is being stripped clean" (284), making him, for the first time since he was filled with his father's knowledge of the league, able to forge a new identity unrelated to baseball. Since Gideon has no reason to continue searching for evidence of the league and the game with the Cubs, his identity, like the town of Big Inning in the flood, has been washed away. Left only with the Baron's mentally handicapped daughter, Missy, Gideon is left at the novel's end with the freedom of establishing a new identity less entrenched in the game. In the closing lines, however, he encounters a contemporary Drifting Away who indicates that Gideon may be given an opportunity to return to Big Inning after Missy is gone. Gideon's response is that he will take along with him a copy of *The Baseball Encyclopedia* to serve as "[a] passport" (292). Even with the obsession of the league behind him, Gideon realizes that his new identity will continue to be based on some element of the game. The game serves as the only consistent element between Big Inning of 1908 and Onamata of 1978; his choice of items indicates that this consistency is the foundation of who he is in both time periods, the same consistency that links Matthew, Gideon, and Stan with the game from the early twentieth century.

Stan Rogalski

Kinsella's fiction is often filled with players who made significant contributions to the game—the 1919 Chicago White Sox, the 1908 Chicago Cubs, Christy Mathewson, Roberto Clemente, Leo Durocher—but he also creates fictional players like Stan Rogalski, who travels back in time with Gideon and participates with the All-Stars in the exhibition game against the Cubs, performing well enough that he is offered a contract by Hall of Fame first baseman/manager Frank Chance to play for the Cubs after the game ends. In both worlds in the novel, Onamata of 1978 and Big Inning of 1908, baseball remains the most significant aspect of Stan's identity, though it is not until the travel back in time that he has the opportunity to play at the major league level. Stan, "a friend whose quest for a baseball career is as tenacious as Gid's is to authenticate the Confederacy" (Kellman 410), has his identity within the past, present, and future grounded in different roles within the game, first as a marginal player, then as a player who finds success on an All-Star team, and, finally, as a former player who dreams of coaching. In each case, Stan's identity relies on the game.

With the exception of John and Marylyle Baron and their mentally handicapped daughter, Missy, with whom Gideon lives following his father's death, Stan is the only person Gideon mentions as a friend. Like his father, Gideon has alienated the majority of the people around him, including his own mother, sister, and wife, in order to pursue evidence supporting his father's claims about the league; Stan Rogalski, however, is the sole supporter of Gideon's quest, sharing a love for the game that equals his friend's. Stan, an adequate minor league player, dreams, at 33 years old, of one day making the roster of a major league team. Though his best friend, Gideon, is captivated by a baseball league from 70 years earlier, Stan equally obsesses with his own dream of being a major league player. Each man approaches the game with a different dream, yet both are identified and validated by one another through the other's relationship with the game.

Gideon's first mention of Stan, and the only time both men appear with their wives, occurs as he hears Stan lamenting seeing Walt "No Neck" Williams, a former major league star for the White Sox, who, though only two years Stan's senior, is retired, while Stan is "still strugglin' to make the Bigs" (60). Gideon's supportive reaction—"You'll make it, Stan"—is one that has been well rehearsed as he has made the same affirmation to Stan "every year for over half [Gideon's] life" (60–61). The only bond establishing their friendship is the game; Gideon pursues his lost league and Stan continues working to make "the Bigs." Without the game, Gideon and Stan are polar opposites. Gideon's wife constantly leaves him, but Stan's wife, Gloria, is supportive of his baseball goals. Stan realizes that he has to work a steady job in order to provide for his family, while Gideon is able to live off of his family wealth. Stan, however, like his best friend, is identified completely by his connection to the game.

Two years earlier, Gloria was able to talk her husband into retiring from the game he had spent the majority of his life playing. Settling into a warehouse job, Stan began playing in a local softball league. Gloria quickly realized how much a part of Stan's life baseball was: "It was sad to watch him. I mean, he was the star of the team ... [b]ut it wasn't baseball. It didn't mean anything to him" (77). Soon after discovering Stan's unhappiness with his new lifestyle, Gloria supported him taking a spot on yet another minor league roster. Though he finds success on the local team with his co-workers, Stan Rogalski is unhappy because his identity as a professional baseball player, albeit a mediocre one at best, has been stripped from him. Being defined by even limited success in the game is what draws Stan and Gloria back to another attempt in the minor leagues at making a major league roster.

While Stan is able to continue playing for two more years, his identity as a player is once again taken from him when he receives his release from the team for which he has been playing. In an effort to convince himself that he still has an identity in the game, Stan looks to Gideon for reassurance: "I've still got a few years left in me, haven't I? Thirty-three ain't too old, is it? (81). Joe Jackson is an established major league star who has an opportunity to play again on Ray Kinsella's field, and Moonlight Graham and Kid Scissons are each able to see their dreams of playing in the major leagues fulfilled; however, Stan Rogalski's identity as a player is quickly disappearing, leaving him nothing else through which he may be known. Moonlight Graham became Doctor Graham and Eddie Scissons became known by his false baseball identity, but Stan has no identity other than as a baseball player. It is only through his trip with Gideon back to 1908 that he is able to have his identity in the game transformed.

When Gideon is approached by John Baron about going back in time to Big Inning, Iowa, in 1908, he tells the elderly ballplayer that he is going to bring someone with him for the journey: Stan (113). Baron accepts this proposal by recognizing Stan: "He's a baseball player, all right" (113). Recognizing Stan as only a player is key to understanding how others in the novel see him. Even as Gideon approaches Stan and Gloria about the journey, he tells Gloria that only her husband is invited because, like Gideon himself, "this guy's a dreamer" (117). Though their dreams differ greatly, both men's aspirations are deeply rooted in baseball. Even after their trip 70 years into the past, when they have the option of assuming the identities of their choosing, Gideon introduces Stan to a much younger Johnny Baron, saying that his friend plays baseball and came to see the Cubs play, "hoping to catch on" (133). Even in a setting where they are unknown except to each other, Stan is viewed only for his ability to play the game.

Approached by the Iowa Baseball Confederacy All-Stars about being the team's mascot, Gideon agrees with the stipulation that they allow Stan a place on the roster for the game against the Cubs that day. Although neither Stan nor Gideon is in danger of being recognized by people living nearly three decades before they will even be born, Gideon provides his friend with an alias when asked what his name is. Rather than providing Stan's real name, Gideon recalls that whole teams and even individual players, Shoeless Joe Jackson among them, played the game for various reasons "under a variety of aliases and assumed names" (141). Claiming that Stan has been banned for playing baseball in the South and in an attempt to mask his mysterious true identity, Gideon introduces him by the name by which he is known for his entire stay in 1908: the Left-handed Farmhand. Similar to Joe Jackson changing his name to play in semi-professional leagues following his exile from the major leagues, changing the name by which Stan is known in no way changes his identity as a man or as a player. Known for his ability to hit, he quickly shows his prowess to the team during batting practice, after which they offer him a position on the team. Even playing under an alias, Stan is recognized by those around him and the other members of the team as someone gifted in the game.

Only in 1908 is Stan Rogalski given an opportunity to play against major league competition. Locked in an epic contest which lasts for 2,000 innings played over more than a month, Stan recognizes that the talent being demonstrated in this game is equal to that found at the highest levels of professional baseball, evidenced by his success at the plate against Mordecai "Three Finger" Brown, a future Hall of Famer. Stan's play has been of such high quality that Frank Chance, the player/manager of the Cubs, offers him a position on the Chicago roster following the completion of the exhibition game. This opportunity supports Stan's personal assessment of his identity as someone who has been talented enough to play in the major leagues for years, but as one who gets his chance only by going back in time. To Stan, the quality of baseball in 1908 is at least equal to that in the major leagues 70 years later, and the relatively unchanged game lends itself to a realistic measuring of his abilities in 1978 to those he has in 1908:

> Think about the game you've been watching, Gideon.... They're playing the same game I was playing last month in Salt Lake, or that all the big-league teams were playing. That's what makes baseball the most wonderful game in the world. Move the Confederacy or the Cubs back to 1978, or bring one of those teams here, and they'd basically be equal ... in baseball I'm a marginally good player here, just like I've always been a marginally good player [237–38].

In the same way that the trip through time has given legitimacy to Matthew and Gideon Clarke's lifetimes of proclaiming the existence of the league, it also legitimizes Stan's identity as a player. He has been given the opportunity to realize that his talents are comparable to those playing at the major league level. Though he could choose a new identity in Big Inning, he finds happiness continuing with the only identity he has ever known—as a baseball player. Rogalski fits seamlessly with the All-Stars because he does not have to change his identity. Unlike Gideon, who assumes a false identity as a newspaper reporter and gains an identity as the team mascot, Stan remains a baseball player despite the changes in both time and place. His experience with the Confederacy justifies the lifetime of work and sacrifice it took for him to play at that level; however, it also helps slightly transform his identity upon his return to his natural period of existence in 1978, where he returns, still cut from the minor league roster. No longer afforded an opportunity to compete at the level from which he just returned, Stan tells Gideon of his new desire to coach young talent at a small town high school, similar to Onamata, hoping to send some of his players to the major leagues, allowing them to achieve the identity so long denied him in the game. Stan realizes that he will have to assume a different role in life now that his playing career is over, yet he also understands that his identity as a hitter will now be used to teach younger players the tools of the game. Despite this transformation of his identity, from player to coach, who Stan Rogalski is continues to be solidly grounded in the game on which his entire life has been based.

In contrast to the eclectic blend of characters on Ray Kinsella's baseball field, the three characters in *The Iowa Baseball Confederacy*, whose identities are formed through their relationships with the game, lack any major league experience. Joe Jackson, Moonlight Graham, and even Kid Scissons are afforded the opportunities to play the game at the major league level against the highest quality competition. Matthew and Gideon Clarke and Stan Rogalski, however, have no such opportunity, though by going back in time Stan *is* able to play on an amateur team, testing his mettle against a major league lineup. Kinsella's emphasis in his second novel is on the game at the minor league level. Although the Confederacy All-Stars play an epic game against the Chicago Cubs, they are still a collection of sub-par talent who would have lost the game to the Cubs much sooner had it not been for the magical influence Drifting Away had on the contest. The identities of these three characters, like the identities of the characters in *Shoeless Joe*, are defined by the game; however, their identities emphasize more of the fan's appreciation for the game rather than some success at the major league level.

Individual Identity and Baseball in Box Socials

A complete reading of those Kinsella novels in which baseball plays at least a peripheral role clearly shows that *Box Socials* has a unique place among these books for a variety of reasons. As previously noted, the third of Kinsella's baseball novels is the only story set outside Iowa, entirely located in Alberta, British Columbia, Canada. Additionally, female characters have a much stronger place in the story line and are, in fact, among the strongest voices in all of his fiction, baseball or non-baseball. While the other four novels rely quite heavily on magic realism as a stylistic device—including using time travel, bringing dead players back to life, and allowing for parallel universes to exist simultaneously—*Box Socials* asks for no such suspension of disbelief from the reader. However, as Noel Schraufnagel posits in *The Baseball Novel: A History and Annotated Bibliography of Adult Fiction*, the majority of this novel "consists of whimsical anecdotes of Canadian folk life" (119); the most significant difference between this text and Kinsella's first two novels (and, arguably, his two subsequent novels). is that "the game is de-emphasized" (120). In all of his novels, Kinsella bases multiple characters' identities on the game; however, only one character in this particular novel is identified by the game. As baseball is does not have popularity in Canada as in the United States, this lack of reliance on the game simply reflects the culture in which the story is set.

"Truckbox" Al McClintock

Unlike Kinsella's four other novels, in which baseball plays a significant role in establishing various community, family, and individual identities,

Box Socials has only one character whose identity within the story is contingent on the game: "Truckbox" Al McClintock. In Kinsella's first two novels and in his final novel, *Magic Time*, the narrator begins with some reference to the patriarchal figure; however, *Box Socials*' narrator, Jamie O'Day, opens with a line that is repeated multiple times throughout the book: "This is the story of how Truckbox Al McClintock almost got a tryout with the genuine St. Louis Cardinals of the National Baseball League, but instead ended up batting against Bob Feller of Cleveland Indian fame" (3). While all of Kinsella's other novels focus solely on story lines which are centered on baseball, Jamie opens chapter five by introducing a separate story that has virtually nothing to do with any aspect of baseball other than Truckbox Al appearing from time to time, though not as a baseball player but as one of the town's younger citizens, like Jamie himself. Jamie's narration in this chapter once again demonstrates the lack of reliance this novel has on the game and how the community, families, and, with the exception of McClintock himself, the individuals have little more than a passing interest in the sport. "Besides being the story of how Truckbox Al McClintock almost got a tryout with the genuine St. Louis Cardinals of the National Baseball League, this is also the story of a couple or ten things that happened to be before, and at about the same time" (75). The fact that O'Day's narrative tells the entire story, unlike the other novels in which narrators who are immersed in the game dominate the plot, further reinforces the limited role baseball plays in the novel, but the fact that he immediately identifies Truckbox Al by his role in the All-Star game demonstrates the way in which even Kinsella's Canadian characters can be identified through the United States' national pastime.

The opening reference to McClintock being provided an opportunity for an at-bat against Bob Feller is the result of McClintock gaining notoriety for his ability to hit five home runs in five plate appearances during a game between his New Oslo Blue Devils and "an all–Indian team from the reserve at Lac Ste. Anne" (5). This is a marker of how pervasive baseball is and of its cultural resilience as the major league players identified in the opening line are known only for their roles in the game. Based solely on this one game, Truckbox Al is "seduced into playing the remainder of the summer for the Sagundo Mustangs" (5), with a veiled promise for a tryout with the St. Louis Cardinals. Unlike individual characters like Ray Kinsella, Gideon Clarke, Joe McCoy, and Mike Houle — each of whom has an identity rooted in baseball from early on in their lives— Al McClintock's identification through baseball comes not until he is a teenager and is, compared with these other characters, somewhat fleeting.

Before the aforementioned game against the Indian team on the reservation, Al McClintock was known by those within the Six Towns area as the oldest son of Curly McClintock and Gunhilda Gordonjensen McClintock, "a classic mixture of Norwegian and Irish stock that made [him] the baseball player he was" (8). Described as both "slow-moving and slow-thinking" (9), Alvin Olaf McClintock was bestowed his unique nickname while still a toddler because his uncle and father concluded that the "boy is built like the box on Daddy's dump truck" (15). Though he is known by everyone within the community as "Truckbox," none of the townspeople refer to him by the moniker while he is in their presence until *after* it is announced that he will play on the All-Star team against Bob Feller. Rather than being offended, he takes "readily to the name" as he feels it gives "him a certain quality of bigness," something that girls were interested in boys having (69).

Only after demonstrating his prodigious ability to hit home runs do the people who have known him since birth—friends and family alike—identify him as someone other than the "slow-moving and slow-thinking" McClintock son. In fact, after people begin to identify him as a baseball player, albeit one who has only shown success against teams of limited ability, Truckbox Al is able to parlay his on-field success in to a sexual relationship with one of the young women in town, something he had never before been able to achieve. The entire novel focuses on a Canadian community of six smaller communities filled primarily with immigrants from various European countries. The community's most celebrated events are the box socials, at which the men bid on box dinners made and decorated by the local women, and weddings. Until his success as a baseball player becomes that for which he is most known in the community, Truckbox Al is unable to have any romantic/sexual success with local girls.

Throughout the entire novel, the only time he is able to attract any attention from women in the town is at the wedding of an American soldier whose incapacitated truck had left him in town for several weeks, and Lavonia Lakusta, one of the daughters of a local Ukrainian family. Truckbox Al's growing fame makes him, according to Jamie O'Day, "the most important person at the wedding and the following reception" other than the bride and groom (68). In fact, it is because the game is that very weekend that Al, despite his unsuccessful advances towards girls at the earlier box socials, is approached by Louisa May Sigurdson, who initiates the conversation by asking him, "You the guy's going to Edmonton to play baseball?" (71). Even beyond the world of American men in which Kinsella's other novels are set, baseball continues to act as a socially organizing force within the community, allowing Truckbox Al to forge an individual identity within the game.

Although both Al and Louisa May spent their entire lives in the Six Towns area, she identifies him based solely on his fairly recent fame as a baseball player, the only one from the community who has the opportunity to take his fame to a much larger venue at the game in Edmonton. Other than a comment about the size of his muscles, the only specific quotation from the conversation the reader is made aware of come when she asks, "How you gettin' to Edmonton?" and once that question is answered, "If you was to get me to Edmonton, too, I might do something for you?" (73). When he expresses interest in her proposition, Louisa May informs Al that "what she was going to do for [him] would both curl his toes and rot his socks" (74), before gripping him tightly as she initiates a long kiss.

The identities of other characters in Kinsella's fiction are often based on a deep appreciation for the game and its history (Ray Kinsella and Gideon Clarke), an ability to play to game at its highest level (Shoeless Joe Jackson and Moonlight Graham), or a desire to continue playing with, at best, marginal playing abilities (Stan Rogalski, Eddie Scissons, and Mike Houle). As the antithesis of these characters, however, Truckbox Al McClintock seems more concerned with using the trip to Edmonton for the game to score sexual favors from Lousia May than he is in performing well on the field. As there is no competition from the Six Towns area able to play on his level, he feels no such pressure to meet the standards of the townspeople in the sense that Mike Houle feels in *Magic Time*.

Once his bus leaves town, the first stop it makes is one mile down the road when Louisa May flags down the driver, climbs aboard, and Al immediately pays her fare. During the entire ride, she continually comments on his physique and "how far he must be able to hit a baseball" (211). Again, the emphasis is on nothing more than his ability to play the game, something that presumably reflects his sexual prowess that she also hopes to see on display in Edmonton. Once she achieves her goal of leaving her hometown for a bigger city, she does "[fulfill] her obligation to [him]" (212), something before which he had no idea as to its meaning. Although the sexual favors were provided only in exchange for the bus ride to Edmonton, she does elect to attend the game to watch the local hero play against the best pitcher in the major leagues during the 1940s, Bob Feller. When McClintock awakens on the morning of the game and attempts to seduce Louisa May one more time before leaving for the stadium, she promises him that she will "show him a couple of other tricks that would curl his hair, as well as curling his toes, and rotting his socks" (213) provided he is able to hit one of the home runs on which his local celebrity it based.

Unfortunately for him, Truckbox Al McClintock's fame in baseball and the sexual relationship promised by Louisa May were both short-lived once the game was played. Coming off the bench as a pinch-hitter in the bottom of the sixth inning, and despite the fans from the Six Towns area who had made the trip cheering for him, Truckbox strikes out on three fastballs from the future Hall of Famer. No sooner does he get back to the bench and sit down does he see his sexual partner of only hours before "leaving the ballpark, with at least one, and maybe two or three, American soldiers" (221). In another representation of a dominant male identity within the game, it takes as many as three American soldiers to replace the one (albeit an unsuccessful one) baseball player. His identity as a home run hitter in the Six Towns community brings him some degree of notoriety and, for one night at least, sexual favors based solely on his ability to play the game. Like Moonlight Graham, Truckbox Al gets only one at-bat against a major league pitcher; unlike Graham, however, Al does not leave the game on his own terms.

The novel's closing paragraph describes McClintock's tryout the following spring with the New Edmonton Hotel Eskimos where, after quickly discovering his inability to hit a curveball, he is one of the first cuts made from the roster. The remainder of his baseball career, then, is when he plays only a few times each summer at community sports days and picnics. While there is no indication of what takes place in his life after he is cut from the roster, other than the few games he plays each year at the local level, it is quite evident that, once the true level of his ability is exposed, he never again has the fame and respect his hitting abilities once provided for him. Baseball, therefore, exposes his parochial identity for what it is, relegating him back to the local ball fields and away from the spotlight of a stage like that of the all-star game.

The individual characters in Kinsella's novels often have connections to the game—fan, highly successful, marginally adequate, or woefully inept player—that develop into an identity for which they are most known in the immediate community or, in some cases, to fans of the sport. In *Box Socials*, however, only one character, Truckbox Al McClintock, has any significant connection to the game and an identity based on that relationship. As Canada is, by Kinsella's own admission, not a place where baseball is as popular as in the United States, McClintock's brush with fame, much like that of Moonlight Graham's, would not hold the same mystical fascination for those who know him. Instead, Al's identity as a player lasts barely longer than the time it took for Bob Feller to strike him out. Once his true identity, that of a physically strong though not very intelligent or talented person, is exposed, he is left with nothing more than the role he had before hitting five home runs against the all–Indian team, an identity that the game cannot change.

Individual Identity and Baseball in If Wishes Were Horses

After turning from the Midwestern landscape and the magic realism of his first two novels to explore a storyline in Canada relying less on baseball, Kinsella's fourth novel not only returns to Iowa. But for the only time in his novels, he weaves primary characters from earlier books into secondary characters in *If Wishes Were Horses* in a fantasy tale of a former major league pitcher who finds that he has a parallel life, ultimately having to decide between them; this "existence in parallel worlds," however, "is a comedown from the magical realism" of his earlier novels and "[t]he lack of baseball action also tends to be disappointing" (Schraufnagel 145). Despite such criticism, the novel does present a unique opportunity to re-examine the identities of Kinsella's two earlier protagonists, Ray Kinsella from *Shoeless Joe* and Gideon Clarke from *The Iowa Baseball Confederacy*, both of whom are occasional narrators in the story. Additionally, the novel's central character, Joe McCoy, also serves as its primary narrator, allowing the reader to examine Ray's and Gideon's identities, not only through their own words, but through McCoy's observations as well. Returning once more to the game as a significant part of the story line, Kinsella again uses the game to establish Joe McCoy's identity and to further emphasize how the game has continued to play an important role in the identities of the two earlier characters, Ray Kinsella and Gideon Clarke.

Joe "Kid" McCoy

Baseball's history is filled with players and managers who have commented on the ways in which the game allows for personal redemption in the most fundamental manner: through the hope of tomorrow. Former catcher and current announcer Tim McCarver has said, "There are bad days and good days, bad months and good months, bad years and good years. If you lose, pick yourself up and carry on. That's baseball. And that's life" (qtd. in Freeman 66). Walter Alston, who, similar to Moonlight Graham, played in one major league game, though he struck out in his only at-bat, later gained fame as a successful manager and said, "In baseball, there's always another game tomorrow, and if not tomorrow, then the next day. Some seasons you find yourself waiting for a lot of tomorrows" (qtd. in Freeman 66). Former major league infielder Manny Trillo echoes these sentiments, saying, "The best thing about baseball is that you can do something about yesterday tomorrow" (qtd. in Freeman 67). The game's ability to offer forgiveness and redemption to its players and fans is not unique to one aspect of level of the sport, and it often appears in baseball literature as a means of mirroring elements of these same acts outside of the game.

Kinsella's use of magic realism in his novels and short stories alike allows the plots of many of his works to occur in multiple places simultaneously. Perhaps the most well-known of these is when Ray Kinsella is able to go back in time to visit an aging Moonlight Graham to discuss what baseball means in the old doctor's life. Similarly, Gideon Clarke and Stan Rogalski find a portal at the end of an old railroad line, the Baseball Spur, which transports them back in time 70 years where they are able to stay for several weeks watching the Iowa Baseball Confederacy All-Stars in action. While borrowing characters from these earlier novels, W.P. Kinsella also returns to his earlier use of magic realism and time travel, something abandoned in the novel preceding this, *Box Socials*. Despite his choice to return to the motif that served him well in his first two books, *If Wishes Were Horses* has been criticized for Joe McCoy having lives in parallel dimensions, leaving the novel as "a comedown from the magical realism of Kinsella's best books" (Schraufnagel 145). Unlike *Shoeless Joe* and *The Iowa Baseball Confederacy*, both of which clearly separate the various worlds and time periods in which the stories are set, McCoy's lives are often so blended together and interspersed with his recounting of dreams he has at night that separating the lives into individual descriptions becomes difficult. Regardless of the worlds in which McCoy's life is set, however, each of his identities exists because of his life in the game of baseball.

With the novel's first four chapters alternating between narratives from Ray Kinsella and Gideon Clarke, it is not until Chapter Five that Joe McCoy speaks for himself; however, based on the two other characters' accounts of their initial phone conversations with him, McCoy is known for being two things: a former baseball player and a criminal on the run from the FBI. In his first narration, McCoy provides the vaguest of details surrounding his parallel lives, though additional details are interspersed throughout subsequent chapters. Upon meeting Ray and Gideon in person for the first time, McCoy considers introducing himself as a man who has a wife, a daughter, and an infant son, but he says "[a]t the moment all three are lost to [him]," due to his current existence in a parallel dimension in which he "[is] the someone else [he] would have been" without his high school sweetheart, his small town upbringing in Iowa, his children, and, most telling to his identity in both worlds, his "passion for baseball" (27). For Joe McCoy, the game is as much a part of who he is as the place where he grew up and the family he has there. Once more demonstrating baseball's complexities, specifically as they relate to one's individual identity, W. P. Kinsella constructs both of McCoy's identities, one positive and one negative, as rooted in the game.

Nearly all of Kinsella's characters have choices to establish an identity in the game or not. Ray has the option of *not* listening to the voice guiding him on his endeavor to build the field and resurrect both his father and Shoeless Joe; Jackson himself had the choice of not accepting the gamblers' money during the 1919 World Series; Stan Rogalski has the choice of forging an identity unrelated to baseball upon his return to 1978 Iowa after playing against the 1908 Cubs; and Moonlight followed through with the option of establishing an identity as a physician after his own brief major league career ended. Even when these characters make questionable decisions, Kinsella often uses the game to redeem whatever sins or errors are committed. For perhaps the only time in his fiction, however, through McCoy, he crafts a character who demonstrates that an identity formed in the game is not always one of forgiveness, redemption, and hope.

While growing up in Lone Tree, Iowa, Joe McCoy quickly establishes himself as a premier pitcher who has the ability to succeed at the game's highest level; however, he becomes so consumed by his own success that he refuses to pitch on fewer than four days' rest, regardless of how much it may benefit the team. In fact, in his senior year, McCoy helps his team reach the state finals but then refuses to take the mound again as it may lead to an arm injury that would derail his career. Disappointing the town, his teammates, and even his own mother, McCoy watches the game as his team loses in the championship game. Years later as he sits at the soda fountain with Ray and Gideon, and despite having played for a few years in the major leagues, McCoy wishes that he could begin his life over, choosing this time to pitch in the game, ruin his arm, leave baseball forever, get his degree in journalism at the University of Iowa, marry Maureen Renn, "and live happily ever after" (28). For the first time in his novels, Kinsella shows a character whose choice to remain in baseball has resulted in his unhappiness.

Like many other characters in Kinsella's literary canon, Joe McCoy is able to pinpoint with absolute precision the exact moment in his life when a specific decision led him to a point in his life when he realizes that baseball is inextricably linked to who he is and where he is in his life. For Ray, that moment is when he hears the voice telling him to build the field; for Gideon, it is when his father dies and he is immediately filled with that same information his father possessed only moments before; Truckbox Al McClintock's moment is when he hits five home runs in a game, giving him an opportunity to be recognized in the community and to play in the all-star game; and for Mike Houle, the moment he first considers the possibility of playing baseball for the Grand Mound Greenshirts is when he understands that baseball is as much a part of him as are his father and brother.

Joe McCoy, however, has two such moments—the first, in which he decides to put his own baseball career ahead of the team's success, and the other after he has arrived at the major league level and gives an interview to *Sports Illustrated* in which he is highly critical of team management, effectively ending his career by being blackballed from the sport. Had McCoy never made it to the major league level, this second moment would never have taken place; therefore, his wish is to replay the high school championship game on Ray's field, resulting in a championship for the team but ruining his own arm in the process. By accomplishing this, McCoy is able to eliminate his negative identity as a mediocre relief pitcher and anti-management mouthpiece in the majors, thereby leaving him only the identity as a former state champion pitcher who used his talent for the good of the team and not for his own personal gain. In this manner, much like Moonlight Graham, McCoy's identity in the game, though still an inseparable part of his personal identity, coexists with an identity in which he places others—the team, his town, and most importantly, his love, Maureen—ahead of himself. At the conclusion of his first meeting with Ray and Gideon, Joe admits that he gets occasional visions of another life he may have, a life in which he never left Iowa and never become a major league pitcher, but one in which he has a wife a children whom he loves. He asks Ray and Gideon if they think each person has a time in his or her life "when [he or she has] a choice [...] when [he or she] either follow[s] the life [he or she is] in or veer off in a completely different direction?" (44). Though his parallel lives drastically differ from one another, McCoy's identity in each is based on his decision at the state championship game during his senior year at Lone Tree High School.

Because McCoy's transformation back to the life he would have lived had he chosen to pitch in the championship game the first time does not take place until the novel's final pages, Kinsella's plot allows his protagonist several opportunities for people to identify him, always somehow related, either positively or negatively, to baseball. As he begins narrating the specifics of his baseball success in high school and, subsequently, his failures as a professional, Joe McCoy admits that he is reluctant to talk about the game because he gets "depressed just thinking about it" (53). His analysis of his own abilities, including telling coaches when he was unable to pitch effectively in a game, mirrors the same honesty that caused him to be critical of team management in the *Sports Illustrated* article; within the world of baseball, McCoy admits, "being honest is seen as a weakness" (54).

Reflecting back on his time as the star pitcher for Lone Tree High School, a time in which his individual identity was being formed, McCoy admits that he chose to play baseball over other sports simply "because it is essentially *not* a team sport," declaring that he "never had a fanatical dedication to team" (55). This selfish trait is unlike any of Kinsella's other characters who, like Moonlight Graham and Ray Kinsella, sacrifice themselves in a variety of ways to benefit others. His individualistic approach to the game follows him to the professional level where, combined with his mediocrity as a relief pitcher, he has a largely unsuccessful career in which he is soon labeled as "poison" (62) after granting his infamous interview. During his seven-year major league career, McCoy begins writing articles for various periodicals, giving readers an inside look at the game; much like New York Yankees and Seattle Pilots pitcher Jim Bouton in the 1970s, McCoy writes non-fiction books about his playing days. Unlike Bouton, who was labeled throughout baseball much like the fictional McCoy is, McCoy's writing never brings him success due in no small part because he is identified at best as a marginal player.

Even after leaving the game and beginning his career as an investigative newspaper writer in Los Angeles, Joe McCoy continues to be identified as a baseball player, once again reinforcing the importance of the game in his individual identification. Even in the midst of hijackers overtaking the airplane on which he and Francie Bly are traveling, a passenger asks, "Ain't you Joe McCoy?" noting that he had seen McCoy "play for the Rangers a couple of seasons back," and that McCoy "couldn't pitch a strike if [he] was throwin' at a boxcar" (76). Unlike in Lone Tree, where he was identified as the team's best player and its best hope for a championship, McCoy's identity is now based on his inability to play well at the highest level. Even more removed from this identity is when, in a nightclub with Franice, Joe is approached by a drunk who asks, "Didn't you used to be somebody?" (84). Whereas the man on the airplane is able to recall McCoy's playing days with some clarity, noting the team he played for as well as his ineffectiveness, the man in the bar knows only in the vaguest sense who Joe McCoy is. Only by connecting with Ray Kinsella and seizing the opportunity to replay the state championship, this time on the mound, is Joe McCoy able to erase his negative identity in the game and live only with the identity as the pitcher who placed the team's and the town's interests above his own.

Ray Kinsella

In *Shoeless Joe*, Ray Kinsella follows the voice that guides him through a series of events, much like a rite of passage, allowing him to offer redemption to his father, Joe Jackson, Moonlight Graham, and Eddie Scissons for mistakes and missed opportunities in their lives. In doing so, Ray is able to define himself as a healer of sorts, providing those who are drawn to his field, including his brother Richard, a peace they are otherwise unable to know. Re-emerging in *If Wishes Were Horses*, Ray takes on a secondary role to Joe McCoy, yet Ray serves as an important connection to help the former pitcher transcend from one life, and the identity from which he hopes to escape, to another life in which he is a former player who chose to stay in his beloved Iowa. Besides the geographical connection, the only similarity between Joe and Ray is their shared passion for baseball, a passion that is enough to allow McCoy literally to change who he is to who he wants to be. No longer in need of his own fulfillment, Ray is then able to bring the same forgiveness and redemption to Joe McCoy's life as is shown in the first novel.

It is not unusual for W.P. Kinsella to incorporate plots and characters from his short fiction into his novels; in fact, his award-winning first baseball novel, *Shoeless Joe*, does both, with the narrator and the entire first chapter coming from an earlier short story, "Shoeless Joe Jackson Comes to Iowa." *If Wishes Were Horses*, however, is unique in that it is the only one of his novels in which he revisits characters from earlier books, the most notable of whom is Ray Kinsella. *Shoeless Joe* clearly demonstrates how Ray's identity as a fan of the game and his passion for it and for his father's hero, Joe Jackson, are at the core of his personal identity, while *If Wishes Were Horses* simply reinforces the fact that, once the field and the farm are in no danger of being overtaken by the bank, Ray's identity to the outside world continues to be deeply rooted in the game.

Although Ray is not the primary protagonist in this novel, as with *Shoeless Joe*, his is the first voice the reader hears. In the earlier novel, Ray begins his narrative by remembering his father's story about seeing Shoeless Joe play baseball, but in this later novel, Ray's narrative begins by relating a personal account of when Joe McCoy first contacted him. Ray's story is told in real time, with the initial meeting between him, McCoy, and Gideon Clarke having taken place just that morning. Curious as to why McCoy, who is on the FBI's 10 Most Wanted List, would be interested in meeting him, Ray is reminded of the "rumors about unusual goings-on at [his] farm," that people from around the world visit the farm to experience the fantasies that unfold on the field, and "that weird things happen out there at night, that there are long-dead ballplayers" (3). Quickly understanding that McCoy is experiencing something as unexplainable as he did while hearing the voice that directed his own quest, Ray is amazed that in such a brief telephone conversation that McCoy "made me identity with him" (4). With no prior relationship between them, the only aspects of McCoy's life which Ray could have known are that he is wanted by the FBI and that he was once a major league baseball player. The shared connection, even a shared identity, in baseball is all that Ray needs to commit to meeting with McCoy and, as is clarified in the novel's second chapter, Gideon Clarke in Iowa City.

After Ray agrees to meet McCoy, Annie Kinsella expresses her reservations about her husband meeting someone who is known to have kidnapped a baby and spent several weeks running from the law. Ray, however, defends the man whom he has not yet met in person, recalling how people from his community previously identified him, "unable to grasp eccentricity, watching me plow under a portion of my corn in order to build a baseball field proposed by a disembodied voice" (7). During the building process, the local citizens, Ray's neighbors, viewed him as, at best, an eccentric; by the time McCoy calls him, Ray's field is known around the world and people come to visit it so that they, too, can experience the peace and nostalgia the game brings them. Though people's perceptions about him are diametrically opposed, both examples of the way in which Ray is identified are grounded on baseball.

Immediately following his invitation for Ray to meet at the Iowa City drugstore and soda fountain, Joe McCoy places a call to Gideon Clarke, another character from an earlier Kinsella novel. As with Ray, Gideon's entire identity in the game — his as a baseball researcher and historian — is already known to the reader. Further reinforcing Ray's identity and its basis in the game, Gideon asks McCoy if the Ray Kinsella of whom he speaks is "[t]he fellow who built the baseball diamond that attracts tourists" (14), later noting that "[i]t will be interesting to meet [him]" and that he has heard rumors of the field having "healing properties" (15). Gideon's comments, much like Ray's later comments about Gideon, support the identity that is established in the earlier novel and further demonstrates the importance baseball has in how others—tourists and Gideon, specifically—identify him. No longer is Ray Kinsella a farmer; now, he is completely identified by his connection with the field on the land where his crops used to be.

As the novel primarily focuses on Joe McCoy and his quest to return to the parallel life in Iowa of which he has been slowly made aware, Ray's life and identity are discussed in only the most limited of ways. In *Shoeless Joe* Ray and Annie Kinsella have only one child, Karin, but when McCoy calls him, Ray refers to the twins that are "smaller versions of Karin and Annie" (5), once more reinforcing the patriarchal structure within the game; only the male characters have a significant place in baseball, whereas the female characters—Annie, Karin, and the twin girls—are marginalized and discussed only as they appear on the periphery of the storyline. Ray's significance in the text, then, has nothing to do with his family or his life in general, but everything to do with the baseball field he built and how it can help another baseball sojourner, Joe McCoy, replay the high school championship, thereby allowing him to abandon the life he's been living and return to the life he knows exists in a parallel dimension.

Gideon Clarke

In the closing pages of *The Iowa Baseball Confederacy*, Gideon Clarke says that his "life is being stripped clean" (284); having proven the Confederacy's existence and both witnessed and participated in the 1908 All-Star game against the Cubs, Gideon returns home to Onamata to discover that his wife, Sunny, has left him again, presumably for good, and that his friend John Baron has killed himself. Unable to return to Big Inning 70 years before, Gideon is, unlike Ray Kinsella, left with the possibility of establishing a new identity completely unrelated to baseball. Joe McCoy's telephone call to Gideon, however, demonstrates that Gideon is still identified by his past connection to the game.

After identifying himself as a criminal, McCoy, who was raised in Lone

Tree, Iowa, and played against Gideon's local Onamata High School, tells Clarke he knows him as "a baseball historian" (13). Their lives in the game, McCoy's as a former major league pitcher and Gideon's as a researcher/historian, are all that connect them, yet this loose connection is enough to convince Gideon to meet McCoy and Ray Kinsella at the soda fountain in the Iowa City drugstore. Sensing his reluctance, McCoy alludes to how people thought of Gideon before validating the work on which he and his father collaborated: "you weren't always considered an authority on baseball history ... you were considered an oddball" (14). Mirroring Ray's identity in the game, Gideon's initial attempts at completing his quest are met with naysayers and negative comments from those in the community; however, once successful, his identity in the game is more positive and his work accepted by those in academia, where he has lectured at the University of Iowa, and by mainstream fans, evidenced by a cover story about him in *Sports Illustrated*. Though others' perceptions of him have changed from mockery to acceptance and respect, Gideon is still seen, not by his substantial fortune or the ability to play his trumpet, but by his work in the game of baseball.

Stan Rogalski

Many former players, including those who succeeded at the major league level and those who never advanced beyond the lowest levels of the minor league system, have found other identities in the game beyond that of a player. Many former players through the years, including Hall of Fame members Dizzy Dean and Joe Morgan, redefined themselves as successful and highly popular radio and television broadcasters. Former players like Chuck Tanner and Tony LaRussa who were only moderately successful on the field later won World Series titles as major league managers, while retired stars like Joe Torre, Lou Piniella, and Gil Hodges also achieved success as managers, thereby forging new identities though still connected with the game by which they first became known to the public. Similar to these players and others like them, W.P. Kinsella uses *If Wishes Were Horses* to afford one of his lesser-known characters an opportunity to remain identified by the game, albeit in a much different manner than when first used in a Kinsella novel.

Without question, the two most recognizable characters from Kinsella's earlier fiction who are found in *If Wishes Were Horses* are Ray Kinsella and Gideon Clarke. This novel continues to solidify the identities of each man as established in *Shoeless Joe* and *The Iowa Baseball Confederacy*, Ray as the heroic family man who, against all rational thinking, builds a field that allows people to find a sense of peace and fulfillment, and Gideon, the tortured soul who finds fulfillment in proving the validity of his father's research while left virtually alone as his family have all either died or abandoned him. While both Ray and Gideon are developed beyond their characters in the first two novels, neither one's identity as previously discussed is amended in any significant manner. The most drastic change in an individual's identity within the game is, surprisingly enough, a supporting character in *The Iowa Baseball Confederacy*, former minor league baseball player and Gideon's best friend, Stan Rogalski.

After spending 40 days playing baseball in 1908, where he is able to prove his hitting abilities are on a par with those of the Chicago Cubs, Stan reemerges in 1978 with Gideon Clarke, both men forever changed by the events of the past weeks. While Gideon comments that his own life is being "stripped clean" (284) with no real purpose guiding him now that the Confederacy has been proven to have existed and his family members are no longer in his life, Stan comments that he plans to go home to his wife where he can get "some reality for a change" (282). Knowing that a job with the railroad is waiting for Stan, Gideon encourages his friend to take the job. Throughout the entire novel, Gideon has repeated the same mantra to Stan whenever the topic of pursuing a career in the major leagues is broached, telling Stan that he is confident in the aging slugger's ability to play at the game's highest level. The return home signifies a complete redefinition of Stan's identity. Now, rather than clinging to the hopes of achieving his own dreams of playing in the major leagues, Stan proclaims a new goal of coaching in "[s]ome little town like Onamata" were he can "teach them to hit" and help some of them make the Big Leagues (282). If Stan's character were left at that particular moment, his primary identity would still be as a minor league outfielder who could hit well at the AAA level, but was not talented enough to perform at the next level; however, by reemerging in *If Wishes Were Horses*, Stan's new identity as a successful high school coach is evident and, therefore, demonstrates Kinsella's ability to redefine who his characters are without abandoning that game by which all of his characters are defined: baseball.

Compared with Ray and Gideon, Stan plays a minute role in this novel's plot. In fact, he only speaks once himself and there is only one other passage, with Gideon as the narrator, in which his identity is discussed. The relevance of these two scenes, however, underscores the manner in which one may be able to assume a new identity in the game without changing who he or she is as a person. Gideon reflects on the time late in the summer of 1978 when he and Stan were transported on the abandoned Baseball Spur railroad line. Before the previous weeks' events, Gideon imagined himself to be "a knight in shining armor" who, while searching for the validity of the Confederacy, continually reassures Stan "that he still had a chance, albeit a slight one, of making it to the major leagues" (11). To Gideon's great surprise, though, Stan is able to adjust much more easily than Gideon himself to life after the Iowa Baseball Confederacy. Stan, the reader is told, is cut from this minor league team, effectively ending his dreams as a player and forcing him into early retirement, and turns down the railroad job to begin coaching for Onamata High School. Unlike Eddie Scissons, who fails in his attempt to redefine his identity from a failed minor league player to an imagined career as a relief pitcher for the Cubs, Rogalski seamlessly transitions from his initial identity as a failed minor league prospect into an identity as a successful high school hitting coach.

Stan's role as a minor league player takes place in real time, including the time spent travelling to 1908 in which the majority of the earlier novel is set; his later identity as a coach, however, is alluded to by Gideon, but the only time the reader is actually able to witness Stan as a coach is in one of Joe McCoy's dreams in which he lives his life as it would have been had he decided to pitch the final game in the state championship 13 years earlier. In this specific dream, McCoy is a sports writer for the *Iowa City Press Citizen* and he covers a game in which Onamata High School is playing. McCoy's analysis of the team is that "[t]hey had pitiful pitching, mediocre fielding, and no particular skills as base runners. But they could hit" (87). Despite having no success in taking his own career to the major league level, McCoy's description of Onamata's team —"But they could hit"— is nearly verbatim from Ray Kinsella's retelling of his father seeing Shoeless Joe Jackson play in a commercial league years after being banned from the game: "but he could still hit" (*Shoeless* 3). In a purely Freudian sense, Stan has transferred the strongest aspect of his own abilities, his hitting, to the high school players with the goal of seeing his own failed dreams become successes for his protégés. After being asked why he is not a hitting coach in the major leagues, Stan recognizes that he has only been a coach for four seasons, a relatively brief period of time for a coach at any level, and realizes teams are beginning to recognize his talent in this new role. With one former player at the AAA level, expected to be called to the major leagues by the end of the season, Stan had already turned down an offer to coach in the Philadelphia Phillies' organization because of the time it would keep him from his family.

After McCoy wakes from this particular dream, Stan's character disappears from the rest of the plotline; however, despite the relatively insignificant role he plays in the story, Stan Rogalski's character in both novels demonstrates the only time in which one of W.P. Kinsella's characters assumes a different identity within the game. Though Joe Jackson has an opportunity to change the outcome of his decision to take money from the conspirators in 1919, he identity in the novel is still as that of a player. Similarly, Moonlight Graham is able to have a more significant role in the major leagues on Ray's field, compared to the one game in his actual career with the New York Giants, yet he, too, is still identified as a baseball player. Stan Rogalski is the only one of Kinsella's characters to fail in one identity as a player who finds success in another career as a coach. Once again, the themes of forgiveness and rebirth so often associated with baseball are personified as Stan is reborn as a coach, allowing him to continue to be identified by the game to which he has dedicated his entire life.

Individual Identity and Baseball in Magic Time

Following *If Wishes Were Horses*, Kinsella's only other novel set in Iowa, *Magic Time*, once again builds on a short story and transforms it into a novel. While the majority of players in the game are known for their abilities on the field, the Grand Mound Greenshirts are unique; they are a team made up solely of players and coaches who are notorious for underachieving in clutch game situations. Instead of being known for hitting game-winning home runs or pitching perfect games like the players in "The Fadeaway" and "Searching for January," the Greenshirts are known for failing in these pressure-filled situations. Ultimately, they are all defined by their inability to achieve significant success in baseball, though the game still serves as the means through which they are identified. Within the novel, Kinsella uses three of his short stories to lay the foundation for three of the specific characters whose identities are directly related to the game: Mike Houle, Roger Cash, and Barry McMartin.

Mike Houle

In the prologue and first chapter of *Magic Time*, Kinsella's narrator, Mike Houle, provides insight into his family history and how he came to be signed by the Grand Mound team; the next four chapters, however, are the retelling of a story from the narrator's youth, a story that was originally Kinsella's short story, "Distances." The most noticeable difference in the narrator in each version of the story is his name; *Magic Time* is narrated by Mike Houle, but "Distances" is told by Gideon Clarke, the name Kinsella chose for his protagonist in *The Iowa Baseball Confederacy*. Houle's brother, Byron, who is referenced in the novel, was originally named Stan Rogalski, a name also used by Kinsella in his earlier novel. The friendship in "Distances" between Gideon and Stan is developed in another fantasy plotline in *The Iowa Baseball Confederacy* while the short story itself is used nearly verbatim in *Magic Time*, with that friendship transformed into the Houle brothers. The fact that Kinsella recycles the names of his characters from his short story for his earlier novel and subsequently changes them for the later novel is evidence that the characters in his fiction are not identified in any great degree by family name; rather, Kinsella's characters are identified by something much more representative of who they are: baseball. Houle is the prime example of this fact as he is equally identified by his love for the game as for his inability to perform in key situations.

Like *Shoeless Joe* and *The Iowa Baseball Confederacy*, *Magic Time*'s plot is largely driven by a father-son relationship. What sets this bond in *Magic Time* apart from Kinsella's two prior novels, however, is that the son in the relationship, Mike Houle, is a player who has experienced some success at the collegiate level and who has garnered some interest from some major league organizations. Mike's identity in the game of baseball is both a blessing, as it was for Ray Kinsella, and a curse, as it was for Gideon Clarke, though all three characters share the common element of baseball as a means of identification. Though players used in Kinsella's fiction like Shoeless Joe Jackson, Moonlight Graham, Stan Rogalski, Roberto Clemente, and Christy Mathewson often have successful baseball careers at either the minor league or the major league levels, Houle represents a shift from this dynamic. Mike Houle is identified by the Grand Mound Greenshirts as a player worthy of being drafted, not because he has had a successful collegiate career by traditional standards; rather, Houle is drafted because he fits into the team's mold of finding players who are notorious for failing to meet expectations in high-pressure situations. Despite this rather unconventional method of identifying talent for a team, Mike's identity is nevertheless contingent upon his role in the game of baseball.

What Kinsella offers the reader about Houle's playing ability is told from the player's own perspective, including a surprisingly candid evaluation of his performance. Despite being a fourth-round draft choice for the Montreal Expos and offered a substantial signing bonus to leave college early, Houle returns to play at Louisiana State University, where he completes his degree in business management, though his hopes of being drafted quickly disappear in what he calls "one long, downward spiral" of his senior season (8). Even before his collegiate career, Mike says, he demonstrated a talent for playing the game, "roar[ing] through every league [he] played in" (22). As a young boy, Mike Houle understands that his performance in the game is what makes him unique from other boys his age:

> It came upon me like a revelation when I was about seven years old that I had more ability at hitting, fielding, and throwing than other kids my age. It wasn't long until I decided, that if I did each of those things perfectly, within the range of my abilities, I had a good chance to play professionally [59].

The tragic flaw in Mike's identification as a player, however, is that "[he] didn't play well under pressure" (23), and "didn't come through in the clutch" (60). When asked by his college girlfriend what his deepest secret is, Mike responds honestly, "During a game, when I get into a tight situation, a crucial situation, I choke" (66). Verbalizing his shortcoming signifies that Mike is very much aware of his real identity despite possessing the ability to conceal it from most of those around him on the team. For the major league scouts, this flaw signifies the end of Mike's baseball career; for the Grand Mound Greenshirts, however, it is precisely what draws them to him. While his business degree makes him an appealing prospect for his host, Emmett Powell, the local insurance agent with whom Mike will work, Mike's true identity is as a player notorious for underachieving in crucial moments.

Before Mike's first practice with the team in Grand Mound, the team's manager, Suicide Walston, immediately and subtly addresses Mike's identity in a private conference with the new infielder. Having watched a tape of four of Mike's college games and assured of the player's fundamental playing abilities, Walston assures Houle that he has "got the starting second-base spot locked up" and that he should "relax" because "the job's [his]" (91). By putting to rest Mike's fears of inadequacy under pressure, Walston is able to transition him efficiently into his role on the team. It is also important to note that Walston's evaluation of Mike is based only on Houle's playing ability. Walston identifies Houle by his performance on the field and not by anything unrelated to the game.

As the summer in Grand Mound progresses and Mike becomes aware that life in Grand Mound, while nearly perfect, is not what it first appeared to be upon his arrival, he realizes that the tragic flaw in his identity outside of the town is exactly what he shares with the other members of the squad: "I'm sure there is a tie-in between us ballplayers and the overwhelming enthusiasm for small-town life of Emmett and his friends from the Grand Mound Booster Club. But what is that connection? Is there some common denominator in our being chosen to play baseball here in Grand Mound?" (181). Throughout his entire life Mike has been identified as a baseball player; not wanting to collapse under the pressure of failing, his wish becomes to "play ... in Grand Mound, where baseball is fun [... w]here [he] feel[s] [he] belong[s]" (183). Even when he leaves the town in an effort to make one last attempt at reaching the major league level, Mike soon realizes that his identity as a choker is what separates him from the game outside of Grand Mound and connects him to those living in the town. His identity does not change; instead, Mike is left to decide how his identity is either accepted or rejected. Ultimately, the overwhelming feeling of being and the desire to be accepted brings him back to Grand Mound, where his identity is an endearment and not rejection. For Mike Houle, being a baseball player has been his only identity from childhood until his arrival in Grand Mound. Unlike Doc Graham, Houle does not initially realize that his identity as a person does not completely have to rely on his performance in the game. Only by accepting the premise for the non-league team in Grand Mound is he able to envision a life away from the diamond.

Roger Cash

The story Gideon Clarke narrates in "Distances," of a young boy helping a transient grifter passing through his hometown, is nearly identical to that of Mike Houle's version in *Magic Time*. The most important similarity is that the stranger who arrives in town to challenge a local team to a game of baseball is Roger Cash, his surname representing his reasons for traveling to various towns playing the game. Using the game as a commodity through which he can earn a living, albeit somewhat deceptively, Cash differs from such characters as Ray Kinsella, Gideon Clarke, and Moonlight Graham, each of whom views the game as being something more important than a means to financial gain. Although the short story ends immediately after Clarke confronts Cash about the questionable methods of fixing the game and taking the locals' money, in *Magic Time*, Kinsella introduces Cash to the town of Grand Mound, Iowa, where he once again comes into contact with the story's narrator, in this case Mike Houle. Though Cash is a former player who made his living running his scheme across the country, Kinsella uses him in the novel as the groundskeeper, a role that still provides for him and his family and keeps him connected with the game. In each profession, however, Cash's identity rests primarily on his role with baseball.

An overwhelming majority of Kinsella's characters for whom baseball serves as the primary element of their identity voice their love for the game itself and not what it may be able to provide for them financially. Shoeless Joe tells Ray that he would have forgone any financial compensation and played only for meals (*Shoeless* 15); Matthew Clarke tells Gideon, "Why not baseball? Name me a more perfect game!" (*Iowa* 41), but Roger Cash is Kinsella's first character in a novel who exploits the game for his own financial gain. Though Ray Kinsella's field on his farm does begin to draw a paying crowd at the end of *Shoeless Joe*, Cash purposely misrepresents himself through the game to establish an identity as a pitcher who rarely loses when playing any of the local teams in the towns he visits.

Cash arrives in Mike's neighborhood when the second baseman is in high school, quickly establishing himself with an uncanny ability to know the exact mileage distance between any two major American cities. Cash admits to Houle that he has gambled on his talent for memorizing mileages between cities and on the baseball games in which he pitches, clarifying that "never gamble[s] unless the odds are in my favor, substantially in [his] favor" (29). Using his memorization of mileage charts as a way of connecting with Mike and Byron Houle, Cash identifies himself as a pitcher who hopes to set up an exhibition game against an established team from the local commercial league, with only some local high school players playing on his own squad. Mike observes by the way Cash proceeds to unveil his plan that "[i]t was obvious he had done this thing many times before" (29), and "that his upper right arm and shoulder were huge, many inches larger than his left" (33). Only by catching Cash in the act does Mike realize that Cash's ability to win games is not due to the pitcher's talent, but because he adjusts the distance between the mound and home plate, moving it back six inches to play to his advantage and to diffuse the effectiveness of the opposing pitcher's off-speed pitches.

Despite being caught in his deception, Cash tells Mike "that cheating is making your opponent do something you don't have to. We both pitched from the same distance. It was just that I'm used to that distance, and it took him awhile to adjust" (52). By revealing that he has won the majority of the games in which he has employed the same deceit, it is clear that his identity as a successful pitcher is based more on his abilities to alter the circumstances under which he plays and less on his athletic talent. Unlike Joe Jackson or Stan Rogalski, there is no evidence that Cash would be able to achieve any level of success were it not for his altering the distance between the mound and home plate. In foreshadowing what is to come in Grand Mound, Cash leaves Chicago by telling the young infielder, "Maybe we'll run into each other again, Mike. Be cool. Life's all a matter of distances. Make them work for you" (53). In the coming years, however, Cash's identity in the game, dishonest as it may appear, will be forever changed through the game itself as he, too, assumes a role in the baseball hierarchy of Grand Mound, Iowa.

When Mike discovers the truth behind Grand Mound's deception, Roger Cash offers to talk with him about the circumstances surrounding Mike's identity as a player in the community. In explaining the situation, Cash reveals that he arrived in Grand Mound years earlier to take advantage of a small town in a baseball game, but his shoulder was injured during the game. Rather than trying to collect on the bets, Grand Mound declared that all wagers were void and provided Cash a place to recuperate, during which time he discovered that someone had already moved the pitcher's mound back to its original distance. Quickly becoming romantically involved with a local widow, Cash is welcomed into the community and is offered the groundskeeper's job when he becomes engaged. Through his new roles in the community, as a part of the Booster Club charged with maintaining the flow of players into the town and as the groundskeeper, Roger Cash is still identified through his relationship with baseball. By perpetuating the myth of Grand Mound's place in the Cornbelt League, Cash continues to fill a role that is arguably still based on deception, much like his original role as a pitcher who altered distances. In Grand Mound, however, Cash's deception is employed ultimately to benefit those players he helps draft into the community rather than for his own financial gain. Instead of being a commodity for himself, baseball becomes Roger Cash's means of producing a seemingly utopian society in the idyllic town. Like Ray Kinsella, whose field provided redemption for several former players, Cash uses his new identity in the game to enable players like Mike Houle, players who would have only limited success at best elsewhere, to find personal and professional happiness.

Barry McMartin

While all of Kinsella's baseball novels deal with various issues relating to race, class, and gender — issues that are integral parts of baseball and main staples in literary criticism, specifically that of cultural studies—*Magic Time* is unique in that he openly deals with an issue that Major League Baseball has long tried to ignore: homosexuality. Barry McMartin's character in the novel is, like Roger Cash, from an earlier Kinsella short story. In the original story, "Punchlines," McMartin's homosexuality is implied but never fully brought into the open. Instead, his sexual orientation is kept hidden for fear of ridicule by his teammates and penalty by team management. In the novel, however, he is embraced by the team and the town, eventually finding a partner in the small Iowa community. Kinsella's incorporating "Punchlines" into the narrative represents the way baseball ignores homosexuality rather than accepting gay players, as do the town and players in Grand Mound. McMartin's baseball abilities, even more than his sexual orientation, are what identify him within the Grand Mound community.

Despite baseball's attempt at presenting itself as an all-inclusive game, the first African-American player on a modern-day roster in the major leagues did not appear until 1947. It was 1959 before every team in the both the National League and the American League had a black player on its roster. In recent decades, beginning with Jim Bouton's tell-all book, *Ball Four*, and continuing through the current steroid scandal, it has become common knowledge that many players have had various levels of substance abuse problems. There have also been public scandals involving the heterosexual lives of various players, including Hall of Fame third baseman Wade Boggs, whose affair with Margo Adams made headlines in 1988 after she filed a $12 million dollar palimony suit against him and gave a tell-all interview to *Penthouse* magazine, assuring that she "still gets a mention almost every time Boggs' career is summarized" (Nipps), and New York Yankees teammates Mike Kekich and Fritz Peterson, who not only traded wives, but entire families, following the 1972 season. Their decision created such a firestorm of controversy that then-commissioner Bowie Kuhn "received more mail about the swap than about the American League's introduction of the [designated hitter rule]" which was implemented the following season (Heller).

While Major League Baseball has accepted minority players—an acceptance that was long overdue—and the players with various problems in their personal lives, it has been reluctant to accept an openly gay player. Players like Glenn Burke and Billy Bean publicly came out about their homosexuality only after their playing careers had ended. Burke, who felt his career with the Los Angeles Dodgers ended prematurely because of the rumors of his homosexuality, said in his 1995 autobiography, written as he was dying from AIDS, that "baseball, perhaps more than any other sport, promotes machoism and virility" (7). Similarly, Bean, who retired following the 1995 season, admits that, as a player, he "spent far too much time wondering whether [he] measured up to the guys around [him], whether [he] could match their toughness, ferocious competitiveness, and even their masculinity" (Bean 229). Brian Pronger, who has explored the role of homosexual men and boys in athletics, says, "[b]ecause gay men grow up in a predominantly heterosexual world, they have learned the standard language of masculinity" (145). Being a gay player in a decidedly heterosexual sport, players like Burke and Bean feel forced to either conform to the game's expectations or risk being ostracized by the structure of the game itself. "Afraid of losing their positions on teams, as a result of the compulsory heterosexuality of sport, many gay athletes find it necessary to hide their homosexuality by passing as straight" (Pronger 147). In dealing with a subject generally considered taboo in the clubhouse, Kinsella directly addresses the issue of presenting a false sexual identity through Barry McMartin's character in *Magic Time.*

In "Punchlines," there is no background given on Barry McMartin other than what he, as the story's narrator, offers the reader; however, Mike Houle, as the narrator in *Magic Time*, is able to provide a somewhat more objective viewpoint as to what makes McMartin unique from any of the other players on the team whose inabilities to perform anywhere else brought them to Grand Mound. In intersquad games where the umpire's decisions are rarely contested above that of minor protests, McMartin vehemently disagrees with one call to the point where he is physically restrained before breaking free and acting "completely berserk" (141). Following the game, Emmett Powell is address this aspect of McMartin's character, noting that "[McMartin] has a history of [violence]" and that the Boosters "thought we knew how to handle him," giving the talented player "a final chance here in Grand Mound" (142). Though the Booster Club is well aware of his volatile personality, Barry's true identity as the team's only gay player is not revealed until he arrives at the Powell home to talk with Mike Houle.

Providing Mike with his personal history, McMartin tells of several fights and physical confrontations during his baseball career. After one incident in which he ran through a glass wall, requiring 41 stitches, the General Manager of his previous minor league team tells the troubled star that the team will "tell the press [he was] being chased out of the building by an angry husband. It will fit [his] image" (150). The violent image, however, is another façade, much like Eddie Scissons had, hoping to hide his true identity. McMartin continues to perpetuate his false identity by demonstrating an overwhelming amount of masculine bravado and harassing homosexuals by calling out "queers" when he passes by a local gay bar, the King's Castle, and telling jokes at the expense of those within the homosexual community. McMartin later admits to Houle that the last time he passed the bar he once again harassed the men outside, but "[a] tawny-skinned young man in tight Levis, his open white shirt tied in a knot across his belly, leaned insolently against a wall" (160). McMartin then realizes that the openly gay man is keenly aware of the secret his teammates show no indication of knowing: "my eyes had flashed across those of the tawny-skinned boy, and I knew that he knew; that it is not a matter of will I or won't I, but only how long before I do" (160). Openly addressing his homosexual orientation for the first time to a teammate, McMartin confesses that he would have returned to the bar had he not had another fight and gotten kicked off the team.

The hyper-masculine traits McMartin demonstrates around his teammates may be explained though Brian Pronger's study of gay men in athletics, "Gay Jocks: A Phenomenology of Gay Men in Athletics: "[a]s a result of coming out in some contexts, gay men become more consciously aware of passing in others; gay men can start to see others' uses of masculinity as a technique for passing" (150). Since McMartin realizes that the man at the bar has identified him as being homosexual, his actions may be read as a subversive attempt at coming out to those on his team. Throughout his career, it is obvious that Barry McMartin's identity as a violent ballplayer has been an intentional façade behind whose stereotypical masculine bravado he can conceal his true identity as a gay baseball player. In either case, the common foundation for McMartin, violent or gay, is that he is first and foremost a baseball player. His identity as a gay player is actually magnified by the fact that the sport has traditionally been unwilling to accept openly gay athletes.

In a game that has traditionally been unreceptive towards the gay community, McMartin has played his career feeling the need to portray excessively masculine characteristics. In Grand Mound, however, Kinsella creates a community that welcomes McMartin and provides for his needs in the same way it welcomes and provides for the needs of his teammates and their families: the townspeople present Felix Ricon with a home and a steady job, helping his wife and children to move to town as well; Mike Houle is provided an opportunity to play the game he loves with no fear of failing or disappointing the team; Roger Cash is welcomed into the community he once tried to take advantage of and is given a chance to work with players on a daily basis; and Mike's father, Gil Houle, is afforded the opportunity of finding a new love in the widow who becomes his wife. Similar to Mr. Houle finding a romantic relationship within the insular community, Barry McMartin is welcomed into the town and into his host family, the Millers, who have an openly gay son to whom Barry confides his own sexual secrets and with whom he falls in love. The result is that McMartin, free from the burden of hiding his sexuality, "will soon be gone, headed for a couple of weeks of conditioning in Triple A and then to the Bigs" (220). Regardless of whether or not he is trying to hide part of his true identity to the outside world, McMartin remains, like all of the players on the team, identified by the fact that he is, first and foremost, a baseball player.

For Their Love of the Game

Considering the concept of an individual identity established in the game of baseball presents multiple lenses through which each character may be explored. While all of the characters share the common aspect of the general game, each character has multiple identities within the respective novels. A character may be analyzed concurrently as a teammate, son, and father, but at the root of each role is the relationship that character has with the game of baseball. W.P. Kinsella portrays successful players from history, some of whom demonstrate tragic flaws that lead to their separation from the game, fans of the game, marginally talented players, and footnotes from the game's history in his magic realism. Timothy Morris says that defining "a nation's essence in terms of a competitive sport makes it a nation of and for sport, one where the (unexamined) values of sport come to constitute national character" (13). I argue, however, that Kinsella's use of baseball allows the values and characteristics of the game to define the identities of his characters. If baseball is, as Morris argues, "the most perfectly meritocratic social organization in modern America," where "better players rise higher in the organization, become more famous, and make more money" (116), then characters like Ray Kinsella, Moonlight Graham, Stan Rogalski, and Mike Houle would, with regards to the game, be no better than middle class citizens at best, though many of them would fall well below that broad classification. Kinsella's characters, however, have value beyond the game. Baseball is at the root of their identities, but the game does not comprise the whole of who they are. Kinsella tells his love stories with baseball as a foundation to create characters with greater value to both community and family.

Former Boston Red Sox and Montreal Expos pitcher Bill "Spaceman" Lee last played in the major leagues in 1982, yet he continues to play the game in semi-professional and amateur leagues around the United States at more than 60 years old. In *Have Glove, Will Travel: Adventures of a Baseball Vagabond*, Lee concludes that he still plays the game, even away from the spotlights of the major league level, for a variety of reasons: "the game's mystery still entrances ... because whether you win or lose, the cold beer tastes better after a game ... because I have no choice. I am a ballplayer" (290–91). Like Lee, Kinsella's individual characters are not motivated by big paychecks or the notoriety that comes with being on a major league roster; all of his characters are driven by and identified through their love for the sport, be it as a player of any level or simply as a fan of the game. Though all of the men discussed in this chapter have their own unique connections to the game, all of them share the one common characteristic that unites them and their identities; as Shoeless Joe Jackson tells Ray when he is resurrected on the field, they "loved the game" (*Shoeless* 15). Greater than talent, desire, or appreciation for the game is the love of the national pastime through which all other character traits are viewed.

Chapter Five

Playing Short: Transforming Short Stories to Novels

Despite W. P. Kinsella's fame as a novelist — specifically following *Field of Dreams*' release in 1989 which exposed an entirely new audience to *Shoeless Joe* and his other novels— his early success, and the genre in which he has spent the majority of his writing career, was in writing short stories. In fact, despite his success with his first two novels, Kinsella mentioned in a June 1988 interview, during which time *Field of Dreams* was being filmed in Dyersville, Iowa, "I prefer writing stories, mainly because of the time commitment.... I have to be very sure I'm going to finish and almost positive that I'm going to succeed before I start on a novel" (Gray 11). With his primary medium being the short story, it is no surprise that of the five baseball novels he has written, four of them began in his preferred form. The most well-known of these is, of course, "Shoeless Joe Jackson Comes to Iowa," published in 1980 and the catalyst for his first baseball novel, *Shoeless Joe*, in 1982. Subsequently, "The Baseball Spur," published in his 1984 collection *The Thrill of the Grass*, is the foundation for his 1986 novel *The Iowa Baseball Confederacy*; his third novel, *Box Socials*, began as "a twenty-page short story about a kid getting a try-out with the Cardinals" (Gray 11), presumably "The First and Last Annual Six Towns Area Old-Timers' Game"; the 1991 short story, "The Dixon Cornbelt League," became his last novel, *Magic Time*, in 2001. Various chapters in these four novels also originate from Kinsella's short fiction, some with few notable changes whatsoever; as a result, many of the forms of identity previously analyzed are also seen in the short stories. *If Wishes Were Horses* is the one novel in which no specific short stories are integrated, though characters and references to plotlines from two other novels appear. Unlike most of the short stories he uses in his novels, Kinsella also has a body of shorter works in which he builds upon the identities of several players who had significant careers at the major league level, many of who are now enshrined at the Baseball Hall of Fame in Cooperstown, NY. Finally, in one of the smallest samplings of Kinsella's short fiction, just two stories, he inserts himself or references to his earlier writings, into the plot. While a complete analysis of his entire canon of baseball short fiction is best saved for another, more comprehensive study, an examination of these specific types of stories—those incorporated into his later novels, those in which he draws more from the identities of actual major league players, and those in which he inserts some specific aspect of himself or his work—serves as a means of exposing the commonalities between these two genres of Kinsella's fiction.

Until *Shoeless Joe* was published in 1982, all of Kinsella's baseball fiction was in short story form. Although this novel introduced him to the mainstream American reader, he had already released three collections of short stories related to Native Americans set in Canada. After reading "Shoeless Joe Jackson Comes to Iowa," originally rejected by the *New Yorker* for its sentimentality, Houghton Mifflin editor Larry Kessenich encouraged Kinsella to expand the story into a full-length novel. Kinsella's now famous response—"I'm a well-established short fiction writer, but I've never written anything successful longer than 25 pages" (Shannon, *Baseball* 158)—led to the development of the shorter piece into the novel, the first chapter of which "is 99.9 percent the same as the short story" (157), the lone change being that the short story's anonymous narrator is given a name, Ray Kinsella, by which he is identified in the book and the subsequent film: Ray Kinsella. While this is the most well-known example of Kinsella developing his short fiction into baseball novels, it is by no means the only example; in fact, no fewer than nine of his shorter pieces have been incorporated into four of the five novels discussed in earlier chapters. The short stories, as with "Shoeless Joe Jackson Comes to Iowa," are sometimes inserted verbatim while others undergo significant transformations, with only portions of some stories appearing in various novel chapters. Furthermore, some short fiction plots—"Distances," for instance—appear in one novel (*Magic Time*), while the characters within the story—Gideon Clarke and Stan Rogalski—appear in other novels (*The Iowa Baseball Confederacy* and *If Wishes Were Horses*). In nearly every example of his transforming his short stories into novels, however—the exception, *Box Socials*, incorporating elements of "The First and Last Annual Six Towns Area Old-Timers' Game" into its narrative—Kinsella's short fiction remains set in the rural farming landscape of Iowa. Despite the differences in genre and the obvious plot developments and character traits that are indicative of the novels, a close reading of the short stories and the novels demonstrates that the issues of identity already explored in earlier chapters are simply extensions of the identities seen in his short fiction.

Short Fiction in Shoeless Joe

Of all the short stories that find themselves integrated into later novels, no selection remains as unchanged from its initial form as "Shoeless Joe Jackson Comes to Iowa." In fact, as previously mentioned, the only alteration is that, in the novel, the story's narrator is finally given a name: Ray Kinsella. The story overall, however, is verbatim and acts in the novel as a starting point for the novel's primary objective — reuniting father and sons on Ray's field. What has become the novel's most defining trait, the sentimentality that led to its initial rejection from the *New Yorker*, is what drives the plot and serves as Ray's motivation for building the field. Ray's identity as established in the game remains unchanged and, in fact, the only additional information added in the novel about his role as the field's builder and owner is his name. Additional information such as the relationship with his brother, Richard, is also included, but none of his character developments in the novel provide any other means of identification than those already presented in the short story.

The short story ends exactly where the first chapter in the novel ends—with Ray sitting in the left-field bleacher watching Joe Jackson ready himself for the ball being hit in his direction. Their conversation up to this point focuses on Jackson's request for Ray to finish the field so that the other seven banned members of the 1919 White Sox can also return to the game they love; in return for the years of work that this entails, Jackson agrees that, upon the field's completion, Ray's father will be given a chance to try out for the team as well. Since the White Sox catcher, Ray Schalk, was never connected with the gambling scandal, the team has an open roster spot that John Kinsella could fill, provided Ray finishes the field. Although now identified by the strong description of the father-son relationship and how the entire plot moves towards their reunion on the field, something that also drives the film version, the short story started with no such thought. In fact, W.P. Kinsella admits that "the father-son business was an afterthought" (Shannon, *Baseball* 157) and that, despite the building of the field being "the absolute main point of the book ... [he] created the whole story without thinking about that" (157). As a result, Ray's identity remains unchanged while the plot's motivation for building the field is transformed from Jackson's arrival in Iowa to Ray and Richard reuniting with John Kinsella, their father, as the game allows the patriarch to transcend time, space, and even death itself to emerge on the diamond.

When writing *Shoeless Joe*, Kinsella wrote under the working title of *The Oldest Living Chicago Cub*, a title that became the basis for an entire section of the novel dealing with Eddie "Kid" Scissons. While Scissons is perhaps less analyzed and more marginalized in the shadows of Jackson, Moonlight Graham, and J. D. Salinger, he is the only other character in the novel besides Jackson himself who is named in one of Kinsella's short stories. Unlike the other examples of Kinsella using his short fiction in novels, however, Scissons appears in "The Eddie Scissons Syndrome," written after *Shoeless Joe* was published. The majority of Kinsella's characters who appear in both shorter pieces and novels, are first in the short fiction and then more fully developed in the novel; however, Eddie Scissons's character in the novel is mentioned as the plot's motivation in "The Eddie Scissons Syndrome." In the story, Lawrence "Dumpster" Kavanagh tells of how a devastating knee injury ends his promising baseball career after he hit .481 during his junior year of college and drew the attention of 12 American League teams who were interested in him as a designated hitter. Following the injury, however, Kavanagh continued working towards his degree requirements in sports psychology, working as a research assistant for Professor Eugene Willis.

In one of the rare instances in which Kinsella refers to himself or his actual writing, Kavanagh narrates how he worked with Willis on a phenomenon named "The Eddie Scissons Syndrome":

> The idea for the study and the name for it derived from a piece of fiction. A few years ago there was a novel about baseball called *Shoeless Joe*, in which a character ... claimed to be the oldest living Chicago Cub ... but it turned out he was a stone-cold liar who had never played major-league baseball" [Kinsella, "Eddie Scissons" 141].

Impressed by the novel, Professor Willis "actually tracked down the author at some university town in Iowa and discovered that Eddie Scissons was based on a real character, though his name had been changed in the book" (141). The rest of the short story is Kavanagh retelling how Willis sought out men who claimed to be former baseball players, only to humiliate them when he confronted them with the facts found during his archival research.

The fact that Scissons's character is referred to in the short story after the novel was published is only one of the unique elements of his character appearing elsewhere. In fact, Richard Crepeau and Rob Sheinkopf collaborated on an article, "The Eddie Scissions [sic] Syndrome: Life Imitating Art

Imitating Life," in which they consider the same construct Willis explores in the short fiction. Furthermore, Tim Wiles, the Director of Research for the A. Bartlett Giamatti Research Center at the National Baseball Hall of Fame and Museum admits that he often encounters people who come to search the archives in Cooperstown, New York, because a friend or family member has embellished some small role he had in the game or created elaborate lies in order to identify himself as a former player, much like Scissons does in *Shoeless Joe*. Using Scissons's lie as a type of template, these people have attempted to create an identity within the game that presents the lives they wished they had lived rather than the reality they know exists. Once more, by resurrecting an earlier character, Kinsella reinforces Scissons's identity and the identities of those like him in real life who use the game's redemptive characteristics to reinvent themselves to the world around them.

Short Fiction in The Iowa Baseball Confederacy

Generally, when incorporating short stories into his novels, Kinsella simply builds upon an existing plot and more fully develops it throughout the course of the novel, much like he does in *Shoeless Joe*; however, in the case of *The Iowa Baseball Confederacy*, he uses names and character traits from one short story, "Distances," and incorporates the actual plot into an entirely separate novel, *Magic Time*. First published in *Sport Magazine* and included in his 1988 collection *The Further Adventures of Slugger McBatt*, "Distances" is narrated by Gideon Clarke and describes an encounter he and his best friend have with a travelling grifter, Roger Cash, who wanders the country pitching against local teams, wagering large amounts of money, and then fixing the results of the games by moving the pitcher's mound back to 61 feet from home plate, longer than the regulation 60 feet 6 inches. As he is used to the increased distances, Cash rarely loses his money and then moves on to work the same scam in another town.

What makes his short story interesting is that Kinsella uses the two boys whom Cash enlists to help him — Gideon and Stan — as the two men who travel back in time to witness the Iowa Baseball Confederacy All-Stars play the 1908 Chicago Cubs in *The Iowa Baseball Confederacy*. As a result, notable character traits by which Gideon is identified in the stories are made clear. Whereas in the novel Gideon admits to having no real ability to play the game, in the short story he is a leadoff hitter who "hit[s] singles, and more importantly, [is able to draw a] walk" (Kinsella, "Distances" 13). Furthermore, Gideon mentions that his father, Matthew, "was engaged in a peculiar baseball research project, which took up most of his time," leaving "the operation of Clarke and Son Insurance to his secretary" (12). Readers familiar with Kinsella's second novel quickly realize that this "peculiar baseball research project" is his quest to prove the Iowa Baseball Confederacy's existence, something with which Gideon himself becomes obsessed in the novel. However, as the primary focus of "Distances" is Cash's game against a local industrial league team, only by reading the novel and the short story is the reader able to draw such conclusions. Stan Rogalski, also appearing in both stories as Gideon's friend, remains largely unchanged, being described by Gideon as a "really good hitter" who is "gonna make it to the Bigs" (5). While Gideon's identity as a player in the short story is changed into that of a fan and historian in the novel, a role by which he is also identified in *If Wishes Were Horses*, Stan's remains the same in all three stories, identified by his ability to hit a baseball. Known as a prodigious hitter in "Distances" and *The Iowa Baseball Confederacy* and as a high school hitting coach in *If Wishes Were Horses*, Stan's identity is more stable than that of his best friend, Gideon.

Removing Gideon's and Stan's names from this story when it is incorporated into *Magic Time*, Kinsella does not remove them or their identities from his canon of baseball fiction. In fact, even before *The Iowa Baseball Confederacy* was published in 1986, Gideon Clarke and Stan Roglaski appeared in "The Baseball Spur," originally published in *Descant* and included in the 1984 collection, *The Thrill of the Grass*. Unlike "Distances," in which Gideon and Stan appear as boys, "The Baseball Spur" describes them identically to how they are portrayed in the early pages of *The Iowa Baseball Confederacy*. Interestingly, however, while a majority of the short story's plot is integrated into the novel, only Stan's name appears in both. Gideon's character in the novel is known only as "Jack" or, to Stan, "Jackie" in the shorter piece. Both wives in the short story and novel — Gloria and Sunny — retain the same names in both, making Jack/Gideon the only character known by a different name once the story is expanded.

Though the plot in "The Baseball Spur" is largely driven by Jack's dealing with Sunny's transient nature — she leaves him again as the story unfolds — at the same time as Stan is accepting the fact that he, as a 36-year-old minor leaguer, has just been released from the team for which he has been playing, one significant character difference is evident upon a parallel reading. In the short story, Jack describes when he first met Sunny and he told her "about

[his] interest in baseball history ... of [his] plan to do a master's thesis on the history of the Iowa Baseball Confederacy, a semi-pro league that existed in Eastern Iowa shortly after the turn of the century" (32). Later reminiscing about the first time Sunny left him, Jack recalls staring into the study where he has "spent half [his] life pursuing the same elusive dream [his] father was never able to capture. The dream of the Iowa Baseball Confederacy" (36). In the novel, however, Gideon (formerly "Jack") is not the one who has written the thesis on the Confederacy; instead, his father spends most of his adult life defending the master's thesis that was denied approval from the university history department. When he is killed by the errant foul ball, all of Matthew Clarke's knowledge of baseball history, specifically that of the Confederacy, is immediately transferred into Gideon's mind. Since in the novel it is Matthew Clarke who writes the thesis, Gideon tells Sunny during their first night together of his "ongoing quest to prove the existence of the Iowa Baseball Confederacy" (71). While clearly following in his father's footsteps searching for verification of the Confederacy, Jack seemingly chooses to write his thesis on the subject; Gideon, however, has no such choice as the information fills his mind on its own. The burden of proving the Confederacy's existence in the short story is shared by Jack and his unnamed father, both of whom have apparently chosen this endeavor of their own volition; in the novel, however, only Matthew Clarke, the name given to the father figure, is able to choose as Gideon has no such option. For Gideon, the quest to verify his father's research is less about achieving his own objective — as with Ray building the field to bring his father back to life — and more about validating his father's work.

Elements of a third piece of short fiction, "Frank Pierce, Iowa," also appear in *The Iowa Baseball Confederacy* though not as much as the earlier two stories. The story originally appeared in a chapbook, *Five Stories*, published in 1986, the same year in which the novel was released. It was later included in 1988's *The Further Adventures of Slugger McBatt*, the same book in which "Distances" appears. Once more, Kinsella chooses to infuse selections from his primary genre, short fiction, into the second novel. This story, like both "The Baseball Spur" and "Distances," is set in Onamata, Iowa, the town in which *The Iowa Baseball Confederacy* is set and a town that reappears with multiple references in the 1996 novel, *If Wishes Were Horses*. Employing a frame-story technique, Kinsella once again has an unnamed narrator introduce a storyteller, Marylyle Baron, who tells a story of her girlhood growing up in Iowa. Also appearing in *The Iowa Baseball Confederacy*, Marylyle Baron is described as having a daughter, Missy, who has Down's Syndrome; conspicuously absent in the shorter work, though, is John Baron, Marylyle's husband and the man who, in the novel, helps Gideon and Stan slip through the cracks of time to emerge 70 years earlier on the evening before the all-star game against the Cubs. The actual plot of the short work is not included in the novel, but there are significant elements related both to Onamata and the aforementioned people that Kinsella places in *The Iowa Baseball Confederacy* and, in some cases, *If Wishes Were Horses.*

The narrator begins the story by introducing Marylyle Baron, a woman who spent several years leading up to her death telling him what he refers to as "the Oral History of Johnson County, Iowa" (Kinsella, "Frank Pierce, Iowa" 65). In the novel, following his father's death, Gideon lives with the Baron family for two years as he finishes school. It is during this time that Mrs. Baron shares with him "the oral history of Big Inning, Iowa" (Kinsella, *Iowa* 51). In both accounts, the Baron matriarch recognizes the absurdities of her stories, a trait that connects her to Gideon, whose own pursuit to prove the Confederacy existence appears to outsiders to be equally absurd. Although the magical events which she recounts were once accepted by the citizens of Johnson County, only a select few, Gideon may argue "chosen few," of the contemporary inhabitants consider them as anything other than legends from local folklore. When sharing more of her memories and the county history with Gideon in the novel, Marylyle states, "[t]here've always been a lot of odd goings-on here in Johnson County (Kinsella, *Iowa Baseball Confederacy* 64); similarly, in "Frank Pierce, Iowa," the narrator remembers Mrs. Baron's favorite expression when she recounted the tales, an expression that appears verbatim when Joe McCoy asks Ray Kinsella if he has ever heard it: "Things are out of kilter in Johnson County" ("Frank Pierce, Iowa" 73; *If Wishes Were Horses* 4). When Ray hears the phrase, he responds, "My wife uses it, her family have been here for generations" (Kinsella, *If Wishes* 4), connecting three novels' characters— Ray, Joe, Gideon and Marylyle — with this one line. More importantly, the notion of things being "out of kilter" reinforces the elements of fantasy that have appeared within the county for over 70 years— another reference to Kinsella's own brand of magical realism often finding itself woven into the backdrop of the Iowa landscape.

The narrator in "Frank Pierce, Iowa" introduces the reader to Missy, explaining that, following Marylyle's death at 90 years old, he took custody of the mentally handicapped woman who is herself middle-aged. Although the narrator is unnamed in this story, Gideon Clarke tells of her coming to live with him twice, once in each novel in which he appears. First, in the closing pages of *The Iowa Baseball Confederacy*, he returns from his trip back in time to 1908 to the period in which he lives, 1978 Onamata, Iowa, to find that John Baron has killed himself and Marylyle is staring out the window, mourning her husband's death. Realizing that Missy cannot be left alone, Gideon takes Missy home with him to care for her. In *If Wishes Were Horses*, some time has passed since Gideon's return and he recalls how "Missy came to live with [him] after her mother, Marylyle Baron, passed away" (9). Although she has only a minor role in this later novel, Missy, much like her mother's observation about the strange goings on in Johnson County, serves as a thread connecting the three novels, a thread that originates with this particular short story.

Many of Kinsella's shorter pieces are later revised or expanded to be included in his novels, though some selections from his short fiction canon are inserted into novels nearly verbatim. "Frank Pierce, Iowa," however, is unique in that only specific characters and locations found in a later novel are shared between the texts. The rural legend from Johnson County's folklore that Marylyle Baron tells in this story does not appear in the novel, though many of her other stories, all of which share the element of fantasy, do make their way into the novel. Of the four novels in which elements of his short stories appear, only *The Iowa Baseball Confederacy* uses characters from a shorter piece while not including the majority of the plot as well; however, *The Iowa Baseball Confederacy* also incorporates the two aforementioned stories, building on Kinsella's usual method of incorporating settings, characters, and full plots from the short stories into his novel's narratives.

Short Fiction in Box Socials

While this specific novel often deviates from Kinsella's other baseball novels—set in Canada rather than Iowa; baseball playing a far less prominent role in the plot; and having none of the magical realism found in the other four books—*Box Socials* also incorporates elements of one short story, providing background on various characters and aspects of the community history not found in the novel itself. In fact, perhaps more than any of the other books, Kinsella weaves into *Box Socials* a short story, "The First and Last Annual Six Towns Area Old Timers' Game," that reads more as a companion piece to be read with the novel than as a chapter of it. Originally appearing in a 1991 chapbook, this story was later included in the more widely circulated collection from 2000, *Japanese Baseball and Other Stories*. Although, like "Frank Pierce, Iowa" in the previous novel, this story provides details of the characters and the community not found in the novel, it also provides several details integrated into *Box Socials*, further reinforcing the identities of Truckbox Al McClintock and various characters from the Six Towns community.

Though *Box Socials* relies less on baseball as a plot device than the other four novels, the game is what drives the plot in "The First and Last Annual Six Towns Area Old-Timers' Game," showing a stronger relationship between the community and the game than seen in the novel and incorporating the game into the lives of more characters than McClintock and John O'Day, the narrator's father. The novel primarily deals with the various immigrant families within the Six Towns community, focusing on the Eastern European traditions each family brings to the Canadian culture. Wedding ceremonies, box socials, community dances, schooling, and the occasional baseball game are all components of Kinsella's third novel, though baseball is given no preference over the other cultural events within the community; arguably, baseball is marginalized, as the premier social events within the largely European dominated community are not games of sport but are instead the box socials used to bring families from all backgrounds together for fellowship, a meal, and dancing.

The most notable difference between "The First and Last Annual Six Towns Area Old-Timers' Game," the only one of Kinsella's short pieces to be incorporated into *Box Socials*, and the novel is that the short story emphasizes the game far more than does the novel; however, this difference is what connects it with the other four baseball novels in that the game serves as a means of establishing individual identities for the players, most notably Truckbox Al and Eddie Grassfires, along with the local men who play on the team and their friends and families who come to watch the game. The emphasis in the vignette then is how much the game plays a role within this specific Canadian community and how it serves in roles much like those found in the Iowa communities of Kinsella's other works.

As with the novel, Jamie O'Day narrates the short story, beginning with a reference to baseball. Whereas the novel begins with a reference to the only member of the community to be identified by the game—"This is the story of how Truckbox Al McClintock almost got a tryout with the genuine St. Louis Cardinals of the National Baseball League, but instead ended up batting against Bob Feller, of Cleveland Indian fame" (3)—the short story returns to a reference that was used in Kinsella's first two novels and one which appears in his last novel: the patriarchal figure and his role in the game. Jamie's first line in the story clearly shows the connection his family, specifically his father, has to baseball: "It was my daddy, Johnny O'Day, who came up with the idea of an old-timers' baseball game" (95). While he mentions in the novel that his father played baseball as a young man, there is no evidence that John O'Day has played the game in recent years, preferring instead to participate in other aspects of the community events. This short story, however, has him not only playing the game, but organizing it, inviting people to play, and eventually helping to win the game, albeit by questionable methods. Conversely, the novel's primary baseball player, Truckbox Al, is relegated within the shorter piece to a secondary role as a player on the New Oslo Blue Devils, the team against whom the old-timers' team plays its only game.

Despite not being the focus of the short story's plot — that role is given to the old-timers themselves, specifically Johnny O'Day — Truckbox Al's playing ability is the one constant related to the game that is found in both stories. In *Box Socials* his identity as a player is established after he hits five home runs in five at-bats against an all–Indian team for whom Eddie Grassfires pitches. This feat earns him a position on a local team, leading to a roster spot on the all-star team that played against a team of professionals, most notably Bob Feller. Eddie Grassfires is the pitcher for the old-timers' team in the short story, though no indication is given that he has any history of pitching against McClintock. It is only when Jamie O'Day mentions Grassfires's name that the men even think of him as an option to pitch for them. Truckbox Al, however, is known in both stories as a home run hitter and the one player from the Six Towns community with a chance of achieving notoriety in the game at the major league level.

Kinsella begins the novel by emphasizing Truckbok Al's chance to play against Bob Feller, hoping to earn a tryout with the St. Louis Cardinals. Al's father, a local mechanic, sells a variety of automobile parts to have money available to buy him a uniform, a new glove, and a pair of cleats for the game. Jamie also mentions that Curly McClintock "had already been gifted with the proceeds from the oldtimers' baseball game, which were to be used to buy the boy a new baseball uniform" (*Box Socials* 204). Further demonstrating the community's desire for its lone representative on the all-star team to do well, unnamed members of the Six Town's area provided money for Truckbox Al's bus fare and hotel room in Edmonton. The short story, however, shifts the focus from Truckbox Al playing in the all-star game to the old-timers' game raising the money to assist in the purchasing of a new uniform. The community's role, then, is much stronger in the story than in the novel. In fact, "the old-timers' game would have died a peaceful death" if not for Al being afforded an opportunity to play against the major league players who were coming to the area, thereby necessitating the new uniform and cleats ("Old Timers' Game" 109). In Al McClintock's lone at-bat described in the short story he, as in the five at-bats against Grassfires mentioned in the novel, hits a prodigious home run "a good twenty yards beyond the mowed area in centre field" (113). Even as a secondary character in the short piece his identity lies solely in his ability to hit a baseball, an ability that leads to him playing against Bob Feller.

When transitioning from "The First and Last Annual Six Towns Area Old-Timers' Game" to *Box Socials*, Kinsella places greater importance on Truckbox Al's role as a hitter and his one game in Edmonton, thereby marginalizing the other players from the area, most notably the old-timers and Eddie Grassfires. The novel ends with a description of McClintock's striking out on three pitches from Bob Feller, later having a tryout with the New Edmonton Hotel Eskimos where it was discovered that he was not able to hit a breaking ball. He is, therefore, resigned to playing a few times each summer at local picnics where he is able to show occasional flashes of brilliance against inferior pitching. The only reference in the short story to McClintock's career after the old-timers' game is when Jamie mentions Al "had his tryout in a brand-new white flannel uniform, [though] he never did become the next Babe Ruth" (118). Rather than distancing the community from the game as happens in the novel, Kinsella uses the game as a means by which the members of the Six Towns community can participate, providing money to help Truckbox Al achieve his goal. Very much like his other baseball fiction, this short story, though the plot is changed in the novel to emphasize Truckbox Al's game in Edmonton, once again demonstrates the game's unifying elements to a body of players and spectators alike.

Short Fiction in Magic Time

Beginning with *Shoeless Joe*, the result of an editor's request to expand upon the short story "Shoeless Joe Jackson Comes to Iowa," Kinsella's novels are all based on earlier works. The first three novels all have at least one—though usually more—of his shorter pieces integrated as either a chapter or as a means of expanding upon a character or idea found in the short fiction. After *Box Socials*, however, Kinsella abandons his use of short stories in *If Wishes Were Horses*, choosing instead to incorporate characters and elements of plots found in two earlier novels, *Shoeless Joe* and *The Iowa Baseball Confederacy*. This novel, then, is unique in that it weaves in parts of his earlier novels instead of the expected modus operandi of relying on his short stories as the basis for his novel. His next, and to date the most recent novel, *Magic Time*, not only returns to his use of short stories, but it also incorporates more shorter pieces, a total of four, than do any of his earlier books. Drawing on two stories from *The Further Adventures of Slugger McBatt* (1988) and *The Dixon Cornbelt League and Other Baseball Stories* (1993), Kinsella's last novel "is a return ... almost, to the quality of *Shoeless Joe*" (Schraufnagel 170).

Magic Time's plot is taken from "The Dixon Cornbelt League," the title story of Kinsella's 1993 collection of short fiction in which Mike Houle, an undrafted second baseman who had once been projected as a high pick in the major league draft, is signed to play in Grand Mound, Iowa, in the Dixon Cornbelt League. Houle quickly realizes, however, that Grand Mound's team plays only intrasquad games and is unaffiliated with any league at all. Confronting his host family's patriarch, Emmett Powell, about the legitimacy of the team and the league, Houle is told that the entire team is comprised of players who need "a place to play baseball where they'd never have a chance to choke" (Kinsella, "Dixon Cornbelt" 178). When expanded into the novel, the short story is divided into various sections, each of which is elaborated on in greater detail and some of which are blended with other short stories, helping to develop a more complex plot that reinforces Kinsella's magical realism while offering unsuccessful players a chance of happiness and fulfillment in the game.

The most notable difference between the short story and the novel is the transformation of the groundskeeper's character. While the story describes him as "a stoop-shouldered man named Jeremy" (167), little is known about his own life and what brought him to Grand Mound; however, *Magic Time*'s groundskeeper, Roger Cash, plays a much more important role in the plot and is originally found in "Distances," the first story in Kinsella's collection *The Further Adventures of Slugger McBatt*. While "Distances," more fully described earlier in this chapter, ends with Cash leaving town, there is no indication of where he goes next or how his life ends up. Cash's closing line to the narrator in both versions of the story remains nearly identical: "Maybe we'll run into each other again.... Be cool. [Life's] all a matter of distances. Make them work for you" ("Distances" 24; *Magic Time* 53). Mike Houle later uses this line to identify himself to Cash in Grand Mound and to know that he recognizes Cash from years earlier.

The plot used in "Distances" is nearly identical to its original form — the two boys' names, Gideon Clarke and Stan Rogalski, are changed to the brothers Mike and Byron Houle — but in the novel, Kinsella places Roger Cash into Jeremy's groundskeeper role. Though Cash's name is not mentioned when Mike first meets him in the novel, Mike notes that he does recognize the team's groundskeeper and that he "wondered if [Cash] recognized [him], then wondered if [he] wanted [Cash] to" (Kinsella, *Magic Time* 86). Discussing ways in which a few scattered pebbles on the infield can work to the home team's advantage when placed on the ground in between innings, Mike asks Cash, "does this happen to have anything to do with distances?" (94). Cash's response is simply to smile, Houle guessing that the groundskeeper "was holding back because he wasn't certain I'd wanted to acknowledge our past relationship" (94). Despite the various name changes and layering of various plots, both Roger Cash and Mike Houle continue to be identified by their roles in the game, Roger as pitcher-turned-groundskeeper and Mike as an infielder who fails to perform under pressure. Their previous relationship plays a significant role when Mike questions the validity of the Ground Mound Greenshirts and its place in the league. Whereas in "The Dixon Cornbelt League" Emmett Powell reveals the town's true purpose in recruiting him to play for its team, this responsibility in the novel is transferred to Cash. As one who was also drawn into the community unaware of its true motive, Cash can identify with Mike's adjustment to the reality that Grand Mound uses the game not for competitive purposes, but to maintain its current economic and social framework.

The first two short stories used in the novel intertwine the lives of two significant characters in the story; the other two stories Kinsella uses in *Magic Time,* however, introduce secondary characters used to reinforce Grand Mound's goal of using baseball as a means of keeping the town alive and not, like many other rural Iowa towns, fade away and die as younger people grow up and move away. Mentioned only one time in the novel, pitcher Crease Fowler recounts the story of Manny Embarquadero while on a night out in Grand Mound with the team's three other new players — Mike Houle, Stanley Wood, and Daniel Morgenstern. In a unique twist to Kinsella's standard integration of plots and characters from his short fiction into his novels, Fowler's role is simply as a conduit through which another player's story is told. The short story, "How Manny Embarquadero Overcame and Began His Climb to the Major Leagues," Crease narrates the story of how he discovered that his teammate on a minor league roster has been able to conceal his true age and nationality, passing himself off as a 17-year-old mute shortstop from Courteguay who had never before played professional baseball. Hearing Manny talk in his sleep, Fowler confronts his teammate the next day to discover that Manny is really Jimmy Williams, from Detroit, Michigan. Williams, mimicking Roger Cash's scam in "Distances," tells Fowler that he had been unable to generate interest from professional teams, concluding, "[i]f you ain't the most talented then you got to play the angles ... so I figured if I went over there and kept my mouth shut and pretended to be an inexperienced kid from the outback, I'd get a chance to play" ("Manny Embarquadero" 97; *Magic Time* 116). Continuing a theme found in a variety of Kinsella's works, Manny/Jimmy is identified, more than anything else, as a baseball player. Changing his name and creating a fictional biography does not mask the fact that he possesses the skills as a player which could provide him a direct path to the major league level.

After watching Manny kill the team owner's dog, Crease Fowler ends his narration in both versions of the story by saying he would be on the bus passing through town at four o'clock the next morning. While the short story ends here, like "Distances," leaving the reader ignorant as to what happens next in the character's life, *Magic Time* provides only a little more information. Having heard Fowler's story of Manny Embarquadero, Mike Houle asks him how he came to play in Grand Mound. Fowler replies he is uncertain of the exact reason, but that, "It was Dilly Eastwick who called Justin Birdsong and told him I would fit in perfectly" (125). Though this is the only time during the novel in which Crease Fowler plays a role, it is important to note that his agent, Justin Birdsong, is the same agent for the three players to whom he tells the story. Furthermore, the mystery of his involvement with Manny mirrors the shadowy nature of the town and its team, shadows that become clarified for Mike as he learns the town's true purpose for the Greenshirts. When read in the context of the entire novel, however, Manny Embarquadero's story offers little to the overall plot and storyline.

In an incorporation of another short story into *Magic Time*, nearly identical to how the previous short story is used, Kinsella chooses to develop a character far beyond merely inserting someone like Fowler. By using "Punchlines" as the majority of chapter 18 in the novel, four chapters after the Manny Embarquadero chapter, Kinsella not only uses another of his shorter pieces as a device to develop the novel's plot, but also introduces a type of player rarely seen in baseball fiction: a gay baseball player. Building on chapter four's discussion of gay players in Major League Baseball and Kinsella's representation of gay players in his fiction, analyzing his choice to include "Punchlines" as a chapter, thus incorporating Barry McMartin into *Magic Time*'s storyline, further reinforces baseball's alienation of gays. Although the short story by itself introduces the idea of a talented gay player struggling with his sexual identity while surrounded by the machismo of the professional baseball locker room, Kinsella's choice to include McMartin in the novel provides him an opportunity to show, as with Roger Cash and Mike Houle from other vignettes, what happens after the short story ends.

Like the majority of Kinsella's baseball fiction, "Punchlines" is told in first person voice, with Barry McMartin introducing himself by the third paragraph. Since much of McMartin's character has already been developed earlier in the novel, by the chapter in which the short story is placed, there is no need for him to provide details already known to the reader—McMartin's volatile temper has been on display as he physically attacked an umpire during an intrasquad practice game, threw bats onto the field, and was locked in the back of a Grand Mound police car. Though this incident is the first time Mike and the members of the community are exposed to McMartin's antics, Emmett Powell does mention that the Grand Mound Boosters had been aware of his history and that he had not fit in with the town in the manner in which they had hoped. "Punchlines" also spends more time providing information on McMartin's two teammates with whom he spends most of his free time: Pascoe and Martinez. In the novel, this information is condensed, thereby focusing even more on McMartin and his sexuality.

In both versions of the story, McMartin and Pascoe, an African-American player who will never rise above the AAA level, are roommates who have told the same jokes so often that they need only recite a joke's punchline for them to break into laughter. Martinez, a Dominican who speaks little English, completes the trio, presumably because these two teammates are the only ones who "pay any attention to him" ("Punchlines" 121). As McMartin soon discovers, told in the short story and retold again when he opens himself up to Mike Houle after the ugly incident in Grand Mound, Pascoe is paid by management to befriend McMartin in an effort to keep him out of trouble. With a history of violence and drunken rage, McMartin is most vocal about his hatred for homosexual men. The only punchline that is repeated in the story, "The trouble was the pilot was gay" ("Punchlines" 123, 135; *Magic Time* 145, 160), is told at the beginning and the end of McMartin's narration, reinforcing the façade he puts up for his teammates as he tries to repress his homosexual feelings.

Before becoming aware of Pascoe's connection with the team's management, McMartin appreciates his friend telling him which local bars to avoid, specifically the King's Castle, the largest gay bar in Vancouver, and the Royal Bar, an establishment frequented by "[b]ikers and Indians" ("Punchlines" 125). In the version told to Houle in *Magic Time*, McMartin recounts being told to avoid the King's Castle (for the aforementioned reasons) as well as the Crown Jewels Bar, primarily because its clientele includes "[l]esbians and bikers" (150). This slight change provides two examples of baseball disregarding the gay community, male and female. McMartin's response while passing the King's Castle is to loudly call out "[q]ueers," not caring who hears him ("Punchlines" 125; *Magic Time* 150). Following an incident in which he attacks a police officer and is put on the strictest possible probation by the team, McMartin tells of an angry encounter with another man while both are on a double date. McMartin refuses to watch *Kiss of the Spider Woman* because it is "about a couple of queers locked up in prison in Argentina or someplace" ("Punchlines" 131; *Magic Time* 156).

As the story closes in both versions (with only slight differences in the verbiage), McMartin and his teammates pass by the King's Castle when he makes eye contact with "[a] tawny-skinned young man in tight Levis, his open white shirt tied in a knot across his belly, leaning insolently against a wall" ("Punchlines" 135; *Magic Time* 160). With only the slightest variation of its verbiage in the novel, McMartin's concern remains the same in both: "it is not a matter of will I or won't I, but only how long before I do" ("Punchlines" 135; *Magic Time* 160). As with earlier short stories, Kinsella provides no further information to explain how the narrator addresses the issues raised in his story. Whereas Crease Fowler's story seems to have no other purpose than to serve as fodder for the novel's plot, McMartin's story demonstrates a problematic dynamic in baseball as the narrator, like former major leaguers Glenn Burke and Billy Bean, feels obligated to mask his homosexuality while living in the masculine culture of the baseball community. As every other player in Grand Mound has been specifically chosen to be on the roster for his inability to perform under the pressure of game situations, McMartin has known only success in the minor leagues and, in information given only in the novel, in Japan. His flaw, therefore, has nothing to do with his baseball performance and everything to do with the violent episodes occuring as the result of his using hyper–machismo outbursts to conceal his homosexual desires from his teammates and team management.

By inserting McMartin's story into the Grand Mound's search for a baseball utopia, Kinsella provides the player with an opportunity to reconcile who he is — a gay player struggling with his sexual identity — with who he has tried being — a gay player overcompensating for what he feels will be perceived by those in the game as a tragic flaw. In fact, McMartin is incredulous when Houle suggests that he come out of the closet in Grand Mound. When Houle reconciles himself at the novel's end with the fact that, despite his attempts to convince himself otherwise, he is a talented player only when there is no pressure on him to perform, he is informed that McMartin has left town to play at the AAA level before advancing to the major leagues, where he will soon earn a multimillion dollar contract. More importantly, however, McMartin will continue to call Grand Mound home as he found a partner in the town and openly revealed his homosexuality soon after. Much like he does by transplanting Roger Cash and Mike Houle from his short fiction into this novel, W. P. Kinsella's incorporating Barry McMartin into the Grand Mound community provides still another example of how individual identity is less about who these men appear to be — a traveling grifter earning a living betting on games in which he pitches; a talented second baseman unable to meet expectations in clutch game situations; and a talented, albeit violent, homophobic minor league player — and who they truly are: baseball players. The commonality in each of the four short stories used in *Magic Time* is that the narrators are all identified by their connection to the game. Even Crease Fowler, whose story is the most disconnected of all in the novel, is described as the only player in Grand Mound who never had aspirations of playing professionally and plays simply for the game's pleasure and "the one who fits in best" (219). More importantly, though, is that all of Kinsella's players fit into Grand Mound's goals, regardless of what emotional, psychological or sexual baggage they may be carrying, because they share the common bond of baseball, a game as unique and imperfect as each of them is.

From Fact to Fiction: Major League Identity in Kinsella's Short Fiction

An overwhelming number of Kinsella's short stories deal with fictitious players of his own creation, oftentimes playing at the minor league level. The most notable exception to this is his title character in "Shoeless Joe Jackson Comes to Iowa" and the novel which it inspired. For the most part, however, Kinsella's fiction is filled with fictitious players who are, at best, marginal in their ability to play the game. A small body of his short fiction, however, focuses on not only real-life major league talent but Hall of Fame-caliber players whom he weaves into his storylines. Such stories, unlike the ones involving fictional players whose identities are developed throughout the plot, emphasize players whose identities are already established within the game. In the majority of these stories, Kinsella uses as his characters players whose careers and, sometimes, lives were cut short due to some unforeseen circumstance, while other stories consider the possibility of how a fictional character may be able to impact the game's history through an interaction with the historical players Kinsella fuses into his work.

Obviously, as this study and others like it have explored, Shoeless Joe Jackson is the most popular and most often analyzed of all the players from the game's history that Kinsella uses in his work. The fact that Kinsella resurrects Jackson and provides him an opportunity to play the game he was prohibited from playing following the 1920 season reinforces the game's restorative qualities. Jackson, though, is not the only player to whom Kinsella offers this possibility; Christy Mathewson, Roberto Clemente, and Thurman Munson are all used in various short stories in ways that, once again relying on his trademark magical realism, offer them the possibility of reclaiming years in their lives and careers cut short by their untimely deaths.

Unlike Jackson, whose career was cut short but who lived to be 64 years old, Christy Mathewson pitched a full career and retired after 17 seasons during which time he won 373 games, including a stretch of 12 seasons (1903–1914) in which he won at least 22 games (*Christy Mathewson*). Following the 1916 season, Mathewson retired as a player, going on to manage the Cincinnati Reds for two more seasons. After enlisting in the Army in 1918, Mathewson was accidentally gassed while training, which contributed to his developing tuberculosis. One of the original five members elected into the Baseball Hall of Fame in 1936, his life was tragically cut short from the disease, dying in 1925 at 45 years old (*Christy Mathewson*). Similar to Jackson, however, Mathewson is incorporated into Kinsella's work as a man who offers an opportunity to a marginal player to perform at the game's highest level.

In "The Fadeaway," Mathewson appears only as a voice from the Cleveland Indians' bullpen in 2000, offering manager Tag Murtagh the chance for the worst pitcher on the team, Ed Jerusalem, to learn Mathewson's famously effective fadeaway pitch, comparable to a screwball in today's game. Promising to turn Jerusalem into a pitcher much like Dennis Eckersley, Mathewson convinces Murtagh to pitch Jerusalem, correctly predicting the outcome of the pitcher's effort. With no ties to the Cleveland organization during his own career, Mathewson explains that his motivation to help the often hapless Indians is because Murtagh is "basically honest and ... not greedy ... [and]

winning will be enough" (36). Know as "the Christian Gentleman" during his playing career, Mathewson is interested in helping out a manager and a player who are not motivated by any desire other than wanting to win baseball games.

Like Ray Kinsella, who builds a field after a voice tells him to do so, Murtagh elects to adhere to Mathewson's voice on the other end of the dugout telephone, learning how to teach Jerusalem the pitch that will help Cleveland win its first pennant in decades. Following Murtagh's promise to "do [his] best," Mathewson simply responds "No one can ask for more" before the line goes dead (36–7). Unfortunately for Murtagh, pitching coach Griff Wilson has spent nearly two hours watching Murtagh talk on the phone, presumably to himself, taping what appears to be the manager going insane. As a result, the team owner replaces Murtagh with Wilson as manager, effectively ending his major league managerial career and Jerusalem's pitching career.

Although Joe Jackson and Christy Mathewson are both considered among the best at their positions in the game's history, how Kinsella incorporates them into his fiction varies greatly. Jackson promises to help Ray's father try out for the team only if Ray first completes the field for the members of the White Sox; Mathewson, however, asks for nothing in return as he teaches his fadeaway pitch to the Indians' manager. Unable to complete his career on his own terms, Jackson's initial loyalty is to his own career and the careers of his banished teammates. Because he was able to retire at his own discretion, Mathewson does not feel as though the game owes him anything, choosing instead to pass on his knowledge of effective pitching to someone else for no other reason than Murtagh wants only to win with no consideration for money or fame.

While Jackson lived into his 60s but had his playing career cut short and Mathewson played a full career and had his life cut short, Kinsella also uses two players from baseball's history who had both their lives and careers cut short due to airplane crashes. On December 31, 1972, Pittsburgh Pirates right fielder and team leader Roberto Clemente was killed when his cargo plane crashed into the ocean shortly after taking off with a load of supplies for Nicaraguan earthquake victims, only three months after recording his 3000th hit in the final game of the season. Nearly seven years later, on August 2, 1979, a similar tragedy struck the New York Yankees when their team captain, catcher Thurman Munson, died when the Cessna airplane he was piloting crashed at the airport where he had been practicing landings. Both players, while arguably in the last years of their playing careers, lost their lives far sooner than anyone could have anticipated. Using these tragedies in two of his short stories, Kinsella ponders what the game would be like had both men lived.

"Searching for January" has yet another of Kinsella's unnamed narrators telling a story of an encounter with a legendary ballplayer. While walking along a beach during his vacation in March, 1987, the narrator sees a raft emerging from the mist, "like something from an Arthurian legend," carrying a dark-skinned, athletic man (111). Immediately, the stranger on the raft begins calling his name "Clemente!" from the raft, emerging on the shore and introducing himself as "the baseball player" (112). As with each of the other major league players Kinsella uses, Clemente is first identified by his role as a baseball player. The fact that he was on a relief mission to Nicaragua when the plane went down is mentioned only later in the story. Believing he has been missing for only a few days and that it must be January of 1973, Clemente is shocked to discover he's been dead for over 15 years.

Despite the 15 years that have elapsed since Clemente's death, the narrator "remembers watching [him] play. When [he] ran for a fly ball it was like [he] traveled three feet above the grass, [his] feet never touching" (118). In fact, Clemente's talent and impact on the game were so great that he is the only person to be elected to the Hall of Fame following the waiving of the mandatory five-year waiting period. Wanting to somehow return to 1973, where he hopes to resume not only his life with his wife and children but also his career with the Pirates, Clemente states, "I am destined to be found, maybe even on this beach, but fifteen years in your past. I intend to be found. I'll keep searching for January" (119). In the aforementioned short fiction, Kinsella brings players back from the dead so that they, like Jackson, may help others and themselves in the game or, like Mathewson, help someone for more altruistic reasons. With Clemente, though, Kinsella brings a player back from the dead for only a brief moment as that player searches for a way to return to the life and career that had been cut short years earlier.

When "Searching for January" ends, the reader is left with the possibility that Clemente may one day appear washed up on a beach in January of 1973, returning to his family, his relief efforts, and to the career that brought him such pleasure and notoriety. In a unique approach to the same idea, in "The Night Manny Mota Tied the Record," Kinsella explores the possibility of Thurman Munson's life and career being extended. In the opening paragraph, Kinsella's once again unnamed narrator notes that he is sitting in Dodger Stadium watching the Dodgers play the Houston Astros: "It is Mormon Family Night. The stadium is nearly full. It is five days since Thurman Munson died" (93). Though attending the game alone, the narrator is approached by an old man who sits next to him: "I can see the same sense of tragedy floating in his eyes as I have viewed on my own the past five mornings" (94). The stranger tells the narrator that Munson "*is* the finest catcher in the game" and that "[d]eath ... need not be as final as many of us are used to believing" (94) before suggesting "that it might just be possible to move time back ... and undo what has been done" (95). The stranger who finally introduces himself as Mr. Revere suggests that the narrator may be able to sacrifice his own life so that Munson's accident would never have happened and he could continue his career with the Yankees.

In one of the few places in his short baseball fiction where Kinsella inserts aspects of his own life into a character's description, the narrator suggests that if he gives up his own life for Munson, then someone would have to take the narrator's place: "I'm a writer. I've published four books.... Short stories, too ... I'm relatively famous ... I've made a contribution. I'm at least well known ... I *do* have a following" (97). Presented with evidence showing that President Gerald Ford had been saved after being assassinated in 1975 and the John Kennedy had been saved once before during World War II, the narrator begins to seriously consider saving a man whom he had never met and of whom he was, admittedly, not a great fan. Asking why he is the one being considered to trade his life for Munson's, the narrator is told, "Because you love the game for the sake of the game. There aren't many of us left. It is rather like finding a genuinely religious person" (104). Like Ray Kinsella and Gideon Clarke in the novels, this narrator is identified simply by his love for the game. Not a Yankees fan or a Munson hero-worshipper, he is identified solely because he loves the game in a pure, undefiled manner. While Mr. Revere tells him that he is "not the one" (105), the narrator's identity remains like that of Munson's: a purist. Known for his distaste for the press and his passion for the game, Munson's attitude is projected onto the narrator's description as one who loves the game for its own sake, no more and no less. Though Munson, unlike Clemente, remains dead at the end of the story, the reader is left with the possibility that Mr. Revere will, in fact, find "the one" who is able and willing to trade his life for the catcher's.

Though his stories often incorporate fictional players who have some type of tragic flaw or shortcoming, Kinsella occasionally uses some of the best players in major league history in his short stories. These players, while successful in their careers, have often had lives and careers cut short, leaving fans of the game with the "what if" questions—What if they hadn't died? What if something different could have happened? Incorporating the magical realism for which he is so widely known, Kinsella uses the game, a game marked by a new beginning every spring and a new start every day of the season, to resurrect the lives and careers of such players.

One of Us: Kinsella the Fan and Kinsella the Character

In his introduction to the collection of short fiction *The Thrill of the Grass*, W. P. Kinsella writes that one of the questions he is most often asked is "How much [of his writing] is autobiography?" (ix). He explains his own failure to understand why readers are fascinated with an author's autobiography when reading pieces that are, quite obviously, fiction. Despite several interviews and essays in which he expresses disdain for academicians and literary critics who overanalyze texts, finding symbolism where none was intended, many readers do see seemingly obvious connections between Kinsella's characters, often the narrator-protagonist, and his own life. Though some apparent connections between the fiction and Kinsella's personal life are mere coincidence — in *Shoeless Joe*, Ray and Richard Kinsella are named, not after W. P. Kinsella, but after two characters' names in J. D. Salinger's works— other connections are not so easily explained away. Such examples include Ray Kinsella's wife, Annie, being a derivation of W. P. Kinsella's first wife's name, Ann; Gideon Clarke's primary job as an insurance agent, a job for which he has little interest and no passion, is one that Kinsella himself had before making his living in the literary world; the overwhelming number of his stories being set in Iowa reflects Kinsella's own love for the state where he lived for many years and for which he continues to express a deep love; and, perhaps most importantly, most of Kinsella's narrators are, if not players, baseball fans, not unlike Kinsella himself.

Despite being puzzled by readers' fascination with autobiographical elements in his work, there are at least two stories in which there are specific references to himself or his work. In "The Eddie Scissons Syndrome," Lawrence "Dumpster" Kavanagh tells of his role as a research assistant for Professor Eugene Willis, who is researching a phenomenon "derived from a piece of fiction ... a novel about baseball called *Shoeless Joe*" (141). Intrigued by Eddie Scissons' character in the novel, Professor Willis "actually tracked down the author at some university town in Iowa" (141). The specific reference to Kinsella's novel coupled with the fact that he was, in fact, living in Iowa after the novel's 1982 release is one of the few times when he specifically refers to his own fiction in a separate fictional piece. In his first collection of baseball short stories following *Shoeless Joe*, Kinsella's *The Thrill of the Grass* (1984) includes a short story that may best demonstrate how Kinsella incorporates himself into his fiction as well as how he best identifies with his readership — as a fan of the game.

In "How I Got My Nickname," the narrator's name is William Patrick Kinsella, though he introduces himself to Leo Durocher as "W. P. Kinsella" (54). Though neither overweight nor diabetic as the narrator describes himself, Kinsella is, like his fictional counterpart, a teenage author who, despite having no actual playing experience, is a great fan of the game. While the real Kinsella grew up in Canada, the narrator Kinsella is a native Iowan from near Iowa City, specifically Onamata, the town referenced in *The Iowa Baseball Confederacy* and *If Wishes Were Horses*. In recognition for achieving an A average during his 11th grade year in high school, the 17-year-old narrator is rewarded by his father with an extended visit to New York where he stays with Kinsella family friends, the Robert Fitzgerald family, who also spend the summer hosting a young Georgia writer, Flannery O'Connor. During this trip, the narrator visits the Polo Grounds in August to watch the Giants, then 13 games behind the Brooklyn Dodgers in the standings.

While watching the team warm up, narrator Kinsella summons the nerve to ask manager Leo Durocher for an opportunity to take batting practice. Despite having never hit live pitching before, Kinsella "batted about .400 against [Giants pitchers], including a home run into the left centerfield stands" (52). Having amazed Durocher with his hitting ability as much as the fact that he had never before played baseball, Kinsella is offered a contract as a pinch-hitter for the Giants pennant stretch. During the course of his time with the team, Kinsella discovers that the Giants' roster is filled with well-read and remarkably educated players. Alvin Dark claims that "the average player on this squad is fluent in three languages" (53), and Kinsella notes that each player is engaged in reading a variety of canonical texts. Soon after Kinsella signs with the team, Durocher tells him that he is invited to dinner with J. D. Salinger who is "a big Giant fan" (56), once again referencing the reclusive writer the author Kinsella melded into *Shoeless Joe*'s plot. The narrator blends seamlessly into the team dynamic as he, like each of them, is educated and bookish. His only shortcoming is his name: W. P. Kinsella. Durocher, in fact, tells him, "You need a nickname, Kid. Bad" (54). The remainder of the story describes how the Giants come back to tie the Dodgers in the standings, forcing a playoff game, and how the team continually debates whether or not F. Scott Fitzgerald's *The Great Gatsby* is to be read as an allegory.

Having inserted himself into his own fiction, Kinsella's narrator finds himself in "the deciding game of the pennant playoff, trailing the Dodgers 4–1" (57). Similar to Ray Kinsella, Gideon Clarke, Joe McCoy, and Mike Houle, narrator Kinsella questions his purpose in the circumstances in which he finds himself: "Why am I here? ... I had some vague premonition that I was about to change history. I mean I wasn't a ballplayer. I was a writer" (57). Sent in to pinch-hit with the chance to tie the game, Kinsella hits a Don Newcombe pitch to Pee Wee Reese for an easy out. The narrator does change history, however, as he takes his place back on the bench. With Durocher preparing to send in another pinch-hitter to replace Bobby Thomson, Kinsella sticks out his foot to trip the unnamed replacement, sending him into the clubhouse with the trainer and sending Thomson into history as he hits the game-winning home run off Ralph Branca. Kinsella's narration concludes with his one-line statistical entry in *The Baseball Encyclopedia*, showing the nickname he had earned that day: "W. P. KINSELLA Kinsella, William Patrick 'Tripper,'" followed by his batting statistics (59).

In the majority of his fiction, both the novels and the shorter pieces, W. P. Kinsella creates fictional players (Mike Houle and Stan Rogalski) or he incorporates obscure players from baseball history (Moonlight Graham) or some of the game's legends (Shoeless Joe Jackson, Roberto Clemente, and Thurman Munson); however, in this rare insertion of himself into the storyline, Kinsella makes himself both fan, sharing a strong connection to Ray Kinsella and Gideon Clarke, and player, averaging over .300 for the 1951 Giants. By doing so, Kinsella bridges the gap between fan and player, melding the two in the same fashion in which he continually blends fantasy and realism. The result of this complexity is a story that identifies him in the game as well as in the literary world. His entry in baseball's statistical reference guide, though most clearly fictional, and the large body of baseball literature for which he is known connect him to players, historians, readers, and, most importantly, fans of the game.

Chapter Six

We the People: Nationalism Within the Narrative

In the past 30 years, the amount of scholarship related to sports in America has increased dramatically. In the introduction to his study, *Sport in Society: issues and controversies*, sociologist Jay J. Coakley says, "[f]or anyone living in American society, it does not take a sociologist to call attention to the extent to which sport has permeated our way of life" (1). In the nearly 30 years since Coakley's book was published, numerous networks, including ESPN and Fox Sports, and the internet have only increased the availability of various sports to Americans. More recently, Kathryn Jay says, "In modern American society, sports are far more than just a game.... [S]ports saturate our culture as well as our language" (1). With such an emphasis on sports in America today, it is obvious that our literature reflects the overwhelming proliferation of athletics in our country. Though some may continue to deny the significant impact of sports, including baseball, on our society, clearly the game is one of the greatest identifying traits we have as a nation.

As a graduate student living in Nashville, Tennessee, I was once asked what my specific area of interest in literature was. I replied that I was most interested in American literature, specifically baseball fiction. The man responded that he knew nothing at all about the game and, therefore, was not interested in that specific genre. He supported his position by saying, "I don't know the difference between Ted Williams and Joe DiMaggio," to which I replied that his even knowing those two players from the same era demonstrated, in some small way, a minute knowledge of the game. He did claim, though, to have enjoyed the film *Field of Dreams*, based on W. P. Kinsella's novel *Shoeless Joe*. His justification was that it was not a film about baseball, but about relationships. Despite the attempts of many academics and critics, including myself, who study the game and its role in both American culture and literature, there are those who are wary of placing too much emphasis on the game as a lens through which other larger issues may be viewed. In his introduction to Roger Angell's *Game Time: A Baseball Companion*, Richard Ford reflects on a former teacher of his during the 1960s who "used to say that baseball was just a stylized enactment of the basic Freudian paradigm" (xi). Since that experience, Ford claims to have

> stayed watchful of the deft balance sportswriting must achieve between its preoccupation with "the game" and the game's context, the outside world, where moms and dads and sons really do struggle, and where things matter a lot and are rarely soluble, and where baseball — its rules, history, conduct — isn't a very useful microcosm, and life's lessons can't be taught very well by overpaid twenty-two-year-old phenoms. Sport may occasionally be a little like life and occur within it. But it's a game. That's the fun part, its privileged irrelevancy and occasionally its beauty [xii].

The purpose of my own study has been to find a balance between the approach of writers like Jacques Barzun, who often focus on the beauty of the game as only a fan can, and the critical, more sociological approaches of those like Coakley, who examine the fallibility of the game and its role in American society.

A large portion of critical approaches to baseball film and fiction focuses on the pastoral elements of the game and how the game relates to various elements of American culture, including religion, family, politics, and commerce. The most overlooked aspect in these critical approaches, however, is how baseball acts as a vehicle establishing various forms of identity. Due in large part to the success of *Field of Dreams* in 1989, W. P. Kinsella has become the most popular contemporary writer within the genre of baseball fiction. Adult baseball fiction is generally considered to have started with the publication of Bernard Malamud's *The Natural* in 1952, but Kinsella has been the most productive writer in the genre for three decades, publishing five novels and dozens of short stories which employ baseball in some aspect in their plots, despite a 1997 accident that resulted in his no longer publishing fiction. Multiple writers within the genre use the game to deal with issues such as race (William Brashler's *Bingo Long's Traveling All-Stars and Motor Kings*), friendship (Mark Harris's Henry Wiggin novels), religion (David James Duncan's *The Brothers K*), and business (*The Natural*), but Kinsella uses the game to establish a complete identity for his characters on multiple levels—community, family, and individual — instead of narrowing his use of the sport. Despite the romantic, pastoral language often found in his fiction, Kinsella likewise resists the temptations to romanticize his baseball fiction, showing the game's shortcomings as well as its positive traits.

In 1989, Roger Angell, author of several successful baseball narratives himself, wrote:

> Organized baseball loves its image as a family-centered, non-violent, tradition-based entertainment, but I wonder at times if any of that matters much. Maybe it's a load. Other sports get along well, or well enough, without this old heavy-mohair mantle of goodness, and maybe the commissioner or somebody else could arrange to loan it out to one of them — to basketball or stock-car racing or croquet—for a season or two and see if our game didn't feel lighter and quicker on its feet without it. I like baseball, the game and the games, but I can't always understand why it's so hard to look at the pastime with a clear gaze. We seem to want to go on sweetening it up, frosting the flakes, because we want it to say things about ourselves that probably aren't true [56].

Although Angell speaks specifically to the vast number of baseball films released in the 1980s, including *The Natural* and *Field of Dreams*, much of what he says is also indicative of the types of criticism against baseball fiction. The game often becomes so romanticized within the genre that the characters, their identities, and the various themes within the texts somehow ring false. Kinsella, however, addresses such issues as racism, class divisions, and gender imbalances through the lens of the game so that the reader is able to have a more clear understanding of the inadequacies the game inherently shares with the country with which it is most often associated.

As has been discussed earlier in this study and in greater detail by other scholars, baseball represents both the good and the bad of American culture. Though the game was finally integrated in 1947, several generations of African-American players were afforded no opportunity to compete on or against white teams. While women are welcome as fans of the game, there has yet to be a woman play at the major league level, and few female umpires have reached as high as the AAA level. Though the game has opened itself to players of all ethnicities, it is still such a representation of masculinity that no gay players have felt enough support from the game to come out to their teammates while still playing on a major league roster.

More than 20 years ago, professional baseball was played in the shadow of a gambling scandal involving one of its most successful players on the field, Pete Rose. In recent years there have been Congressional hearings focusing on the alleged use of performance enhancing drugs in professional baseball, casting doubt on the legitimacy of home run hitters Rafael Palmeiro, Mark McGwire, Barry Bonds, Alex Rodriguez, and Manny Ramirez as well as pitchers like Roger Clemens; many of these players, once considered first ballot Hall of Famers, now find themselves being judged less by their abilities on the field and more by the public opinion of whether or not they took

PEDs. The statistics of players from this era, dubbed by many in the media as "the steroid era," will forever be called into question if for no other reason than the difficulty in knowing who did and who did not take these substances. In an interview for this study, former New York Yankee Bobby Murcer said,

> [The drug scandal] is an issue and it's going to be ... known as that era. There will always be an asterisk when you talk to your family about baseball and this particular era that we're living in now ... [n]ot that they're guilty, because they haven't been proven guilty, but they're guilty by association of the year and of the issue that's going on.

Despite the negative issues like the various drug rumors and the 1994 strike which cancelled the World Series for the first time ever, Tim Wiles, Director of Research for the National Baseball Hall of Fame and Museum, suggests that even the negativity contributes to the communal aspects of the game:

> Drugs and strikes and other disappointments about the game ... all of those things, I think, kind of have a unifying effect on fans in some ways. If everybody can complain about the strike together or about the steroids together, then it, in a perverse kind of ironic way, it turns into another way of having a discussion about this thing that we love or this thing that fascinates us.

Kinsella's fiction, despite these obvious problems in the game, uses baseball to address how these issues combine to form various identities. The game that, as Wiles says, "fascinates us" as members of the American community, becomes a representation of the balance of both the good and the bad in our society. Even the shortcomings within the game — racism, sexism, gambling, and drug use to name but a few—can, as Wiles notes, serve a valuable purpose by rallying a community of fans to address these problems and, more positively, the solutions.

D. Stanley Eitzen argues that sociologists are drawn to the way sport mirrors society because, in studying sport, "there [are] the basic elements and expressions of bureaucratization, commercialization, racism, sexism, homophobia, greed, exploitation of the powerless, alienation, and the ethnocentrism found in the larger society" (4). In addition to the varying degree of negative elements found within American sports, Eitzen further asserts that

> There is the human desire to identify with something larger than oneself. For athletes, it is to be part of a team, working and sacrificing together to achieve a common goal. For fans, by identifying with a team or a sports hero, they bond with others who share their allegiance; they belong and they have an identity [5].

Within the five novels and selected short stories analyzed in this study, Kinsella addresses the various forms of identity for players and fans alike.

While often using Hall of Fame-caliber players like Joe Jackson, Christy Mathewson or Roberto Clemente as primary characters, Kinsella is just as likely to use a marginally successful player like Moonlight Graham or to create a fictional player who is a failure as a player, like Kid Scissons or Stan Rogalski, in order to present multiple versions of a player's identity. Though Kinsella often uses players taken from the game's history, his more complex characters are fictional or, like Graham, have remained hidden from all but a few of the most enthusiastic baseball fans. Tim Wiles suggests that Graham's life, "which in many ways is rather ordinary, has become extraordinary because of [Kinsella finding his name in baseball history] and how that is theoretically possible for all those other guys who played one game, who are [in the Hall of Fame archives] and haven't had a movie [including their playing days]." Kinsella's characters have identities that are based on the game of baseball; these often ordinary men accomplish extraordinary tasks because they follow the direction set forth for them by the game.

While no sport is infallible, baseball continues to represent many of the ideologies of the United States as a whole. Using the broad term "baseball," however, is problematic in itself as the game continues to be played on various levels around the country and even the world. Tim Wiles observes that the term generally describes the game at the major league level:

> At a time like a baseball strike, people will say that baseball needs to do this, and they usually mean Major League Baseball, but the attendance at minor league baseball in this country is going up every year for the last, essentially the last ten or fifteen years, and really spiked in 1994 and '95 when Major League Baseball was on strike.

Despite the inherent negative issues found within the game at the highest level, baseball continues to thrive in America. Every summer, ESPN televises the majority of the games played at the Little League World Series in Williamsport, Pennsylvania. The Men's Senior Baseball League "started on Long Island and has gone national ... [has] a World Series and probably ten thousand teams from coast to coast" (Wiles), demonstrating a flourishing of the sport at the local level across the country away from the glaring spotlights of the major league level. It is at this level that Kinsella focuses his fiction and addresses the various elements of identity through the game.

John Fiske argues that "different life experiences often occur in different places, and the sports experience is often used to identify the meaning of place ... [s]port identifies place, gives it a significance that works only for those who live in it" (91). Because America recognizes baseball as its National

Pastime, the game serves as the primary sport through which the nation identifies its collective sense of place. Though many in our society, like the man with whom I had the conversation in Nashville, claim to know nothing about the game, it is virtually impossible to not understand that the game is a clear and fixed representation of America's most positive and negative traits. Jay Coakley writes that there are two predominant, opposing mindsets when considering the role that sport plays in American society. The first is "those who are generally uncritical of American society and see the popularity of sport resulting from its compatibility with the basic values of the system itself and from its contributions to the maintenance" (16). Those who adhere to this viewpoint "define sport as a social *inspiration*" (16). At the opposite end of the spectrum, however, are those "who are critical of the basic structure of American society ... [and who] see the popularity of sport as an outgrowth of the basic interests of those who make up a power elite in the system" (16). Rather than viewing sport as an inspiration, proponents of this mentality "see sport as an *opiate* sponsored by those in power to serve their own exploitive interests" (16). In the five Kinsella novels and various short stories analyzed in the previous chapters, it is clear that he understands that the game is an opiate to offer members of the society a sense of community identity and promote the ideologies of the powers in control of the sport. He does, however, counter this power structure — represented by the wealthy owner Charles Comiskey, who put his players in a position where they felt the need to fix the outcome of the World Series, and the academics who are against the Clarke family's quest to prove the existence of the Iowa Baseball Confederacy — with the inspiration of those who see the game for its redeeming qualities and then strive to promote those same values, people like Ray Kinsella and Gideon Clarke, each of whom rebels against the accepted norms to promote the positive qualities of the game, and the people in the town of Grand Mound, Iowa, who use the game as a means of promoting the traditionally conservative values of small-town, Midwestern America. While acknowledging the fact that the game reflects the racism, class division, and gender inequities in America, Kinsella's fiction offers hope that the game itself, not just as it is played at the major league level, will continue to offer the necessary inspiration to overcome these shortcomings.

Viewing baseball as a means of establishing a community, family, or individual identity is by no means the only form of identification in the novels. Characters may be identified by race, class, occupation, religion, or sexual orientation, but the one commonality shared between all of the characters, as groups and as individuals, is their relationship to the game of baseball. Matthew and Gideon Clarke may be identified as eccentric insurance salesmen, but both are more readily identified by their obsession with researching the Iowa Baseball Confederacy. Ray Kinsella is, on the surface, viewed only as a marginally successful farmer, but his true identity lies in his deep and abiding respect for and love of baseball which leads to his creating the ballpark on his farm. Even secondary characters in the novels, like Stan Rogalski and Barry McMartin, have multiple levels of identity. While Rogalski is presented as a failed player who never made it to the major league level, his identity relies more on the fundamental passion for the sport. McMartin, who has all of the necessary gifts to succeed at the game's highest level, is handicapped by his feeling that he cannot be open about his life as a homosexual baseball player in a traditionally heterosexual sport. The internal conflict of his identity with which he is faced, then, is magnified by the fact that the game has been slow to accept homosexuals, much the way it was slow to accept racial integration before 1947.

Although the focus of this current analysis is on specific male characters from *Shoeless Joe*, *The Iowa Baseball Confederacy*, *Box Socials*, *If Wishes Were Horses*, *Magic Time*, and numerous short stories, the various concepts of identity extend far beyond the pages of these works. Players, fans, historians, sociologists, and writers from numerous academic camps have explored these same types of identity and how baseball has served as a means of establishing them in their own lives. For former New York Yankee Bobby Murcer, who was a broadcaster for the team from his retirement in 1983 until his death in 2008, his identity to fans is as both a player and a broadcaster, identities that directly relate back to the sense of community:

> [Younger fans] never got a chance to see me play, like I never did really get a chance to see Joe DiMaggio play in person, but they've heard about it and they've seen all the different clips and heard about it from either a Yankee fan within their family, or in their block, or within their community.

Growing up as a Yankees fan in Oklahoma, Murcer identified with fellow Oklahoman Mickey Mantle, the Hall of Fame outfielder for the team. As a member of the Yankees family for over 40 years, Murcer recognized the importance of the team to the city of New York as well as to America as a whole: "The Yankees are important to the whole United States and Major League Baseball. I think they might set the standard for everybody else and have [done so] for many, many years because of their rich history and what they have done in the pinstripes and all of the World Championships that they've won." In her memoir *Wait Till Next Year*, Doris Kearns Goodwin shares a similar feeling of identifying with a New York team, though her childhood loyalties lay with the Brooklyn Dodgers. In describing the city's three teams during her youth — the Yankees, Dodgers, and Giants— Goodwin describes the Giants as a club whose own "identity [was] somewhat blurred, caught, as they were, between the Yankee 'haves' and the Dodger 'have-nots'" (63). For Goodwin, the three teams represented a clear division of social classes, and "each team was signified by a member of [her] small community" (63). Despite their opposing loyalties, both Murcer and Goodwin have recognized the family's role in passing its baseball identity from one generation to the next, using its unique characteristics to bond the family together. Murcer said,

> I think that's one of the great things the American pastime has given the American people and the family is a chance to be able to bond together on one common issue which, if you're a Yankee fan and you've heard about the Yankees in the household then you pretty much grow up to ... love that team because that's the one that your Dad loves, the one that he's talked to you about, and the one in the community.

Similarly, Goodwin appreciates the way the game united her community at its basic level but divided the same community when team affiliation was discussed:

> Baseball loyalties in our neighborhood were divided between the Yankees, Dodgers, and Giants. As earlier immigrants had brought their ethnic bonds with them to America, the settlers of suburbia had, for the most part, carried their baseball fidelity from their borough of origin — Yankee fans from the Bronx, Giant supporters from Manhattan, and, of course, the devotees of the Dodgers from Brooklyn. In each home, team affiliation was passed on from father to child, with the crucial moments in a team's history repeated like the liturgy of a church service. Over time, each team and its fans had taken on a distinct identity, a kind of stereotype into which the features of the team and the characteristics of its followers were molded to produce an exaggerated caricature [62–3].

Like Murcer and Goodwin, the families in Kinsella's fiction often share the common birthright of baseball, passed from generation to generation with the importance of a more traditional heirloom. John and Ray Kinsella share a love of the White Sox and of Shoeless Joe Jackson, a love that manifests itself in Ray's field, providing his father an opportunity to once again play the game. Matthew and Gideon Clarke share the blessing/curse of having knowledge of a league few others believe exists. This bond ultimately transports Gideon back to watch the league All-Stars play the Chicago Cubs, validating all that he and his father spent their entire lives defending. In each instance, from both memory and fiction, the game is unquestionably the common bond on which familial structure is built, a testament to the timeless elements of the family and of the game.

Political commentator and writer George F. Will argues that baseball "involves constant attention to the law of cumulation, which is: A lot of little things add up, through 162 games, 1,458 innings, to big differences. A 162-game season is, like life, an exercise in cumulation" (3). Tim Wiles continues Will's description of the game, saying, "there is simply more history for a person to connect with ... it is a game that is played every day as opposed to the other sports. Football is once a week, basketball and hockey are two or three times a week." As part of a community, family, or individual whose identity is rooted in the game, it is no more possible for a character to separate himself from the game than it is for a group or an individual to separate themselves from who they are socially, racially, or sexually. Though these elements of identity are often kept hidden or ignored, the game serves as a means of confronting these issues in their various forms. Despite its exclusion of female players at the major league level, the marginalization of minorities prior to 1947, the current marginalization of minorities in management positions, and the class divisions seen dating back to before the 1919 Black Sox scandal, the game "is to be spared, to live on in future generations" (Hye 122). Kinsella's baseball fiction, like America itself, is defined by these various shortcomings that alienate part of the population and promote the specific agendas of others; however, the game also becomes a means by which people on opposing ends of any sociological spectrum are defined and may reach a common understanding.

Like Barry McMartin in *Magic Time*, Billy Bean kept his homosexuality hidden from his teammates. Unlike McMartin, however, Bean publicly revealed his sexual orientation after his playing days had ended. Not knowing how to reconcile his life as a ballplayer with his life as a gay man, Bean has examined the role the game played in his life: "Baseball had been my everything: my physical outlet, my mental challenge, my source of income, and my social life. It wasn't just my reason for being. It *was* my being" (203–4). For McMartin, Kinsella has created a team of which he is a part, made up of players who have some obvious flaw, either psychologically or physically, in their personas. That he is placed in this community further emphasizes baseball's own reluctance to welcome an openly gay player into its clubhouses, something of which Bean is keenly aware. Baseball was not just a fragment of Bean's life; to those involved in the game and to fans themselves, baseball completely represents who he was as a person before he publicly addressed his homosexuality. The fact that he had been a gay player became the subject of controversy, not for him, but for those who continue to view the game as limited only to heterosexual players. Former Boston Red Sox pitcher Bill "Spaceman" Lee, retired from the major league level since 1982, shares Bean's view that the game is who he is, not in part, but completely. While he continues to play in recreational leagues around the country, Lee does so not for financial gain or notoriety, but because it is impossible to separate the game from who he is as a man:

> I love running out ground balls. My spikes bite and dig deep into the ground to produce perfect traction. My ankles and calves shove against the earth, and I explode out of the batter's box. Running down the baseline, the wind blows off my cap and scurries on its tiptoes to catch me, but I am fast and I am elusive and I am free and I am beyond the reach of the wind and pain and time and I am eighteen again forever.
>
> I still play because I have no choice.
>
> I am a ballplayer [291].

The characters in Kinsella's novels—rich or poor, black or white, gay or straight—are identified through the game because, like their social status, race, and sexual preference, it is a part of who they are. It is the one element through which all of the other areas in their identities may be analyzed and defined.

In *The Tour to End All Tours: The Story of Major League Baseball's 1913–1914 World Tour*, James Elfers writes that, during the early years of the twentieth century, "in all of America only one sport was followed with equal passion by poor and rich and black and white alike, the game Americans had invented and the one game that virtually every American believed was superior to all other games on the face of the globe—baseball" (2). The passion of American fans for "their" game led to writers such as Ring Lardner and Zane Grey contributing some of the earliest, most fundamental pieces of baseball fiction. The genre continued to grow, as did the game, taking on issues of more significant cultural importance, such as those addressed in numerous scholarly works. Todd Avery suggests that England and the United States have "long shared a common fascination with sports," and that "cricket and baseball have each generated a rich literary tradition. For every Eric Greenberg, W.P. Kinsella, or Bernard Malamud, England has produced a novelist whose passion for cricket invests his or her work with equal symbolic significance" (31). As a North American writer, Kinsella is obviously drawn to the game most associated with the United States, specifically the Midwest where he spent time during the 1970s in the Iowa Writers Workshop. In fact, Kinsella says, "it was probably [his] being in Iowa that precipitated [his] whole baseball-writing career" (Shannon, *Spitball* 55). Forms of identity within his short fiction and novels based on the game, then, are the types of identity that resonate with the readers, all of whom are simultaneously unique individuals and members of communities and families. The game, representing American cultural ideologies, then becomes the foundation for the fiction that encompasses each of the identities detailed in the three previous chapters.

In explaining his fiction and the role the game has in it, Kinsella says, "[b]aseball fans have to be more intelligent than other sports fans because they have to have imagination. There are no baseball fans without imaginations, except for the ones who are drunk and falling asleep in their seats" (Shannon, *Baseball* 160); however, he continues by saying, "[f]iction writers are essentially writing for people who don't have a whole lot of imagination.... Reading fiction is sort of like vicarious living, and I would think that most people have some sort of dream like Ray and Gideon, but, unlike Ray and Gid, they never do anything toward realizing it" (161). While a non-baseball fan may be, despite not fully comprehending baseball's idiosyncrasies, able to live vicariously through Kinsella's characters, baseball fans understand the game's subtleties and complexities and are able to understand that the central issues in the novels transcend the fulfilling of wishful fantasies; the game's fans are more able to grasp that Kinsella's fiction is no more about baseball than Melville's *Moby Dick* is a novel about fishing. For fans of the game, the novels speak to the issues of love, greed, family, disappointment, community, and every other aspect of our lives, using the game as the vehicle through which we arrive at a deeper understanding of and appreciation for these issues.

Kinsella's fiction has generated several critical examinations from disciplines varying from religion, sociology, and gender studies, a sampling of which has been discussed in Chapter One of this book. Despite these approaches, Kinsella himself makes it a point to clarify that his primary objective as a writer is to provide enjoyment to his readers: "I don't want to be a sociologist or a moralist or a naval-gazer. The fiction writer's role is simply to entertain" (Murray 50). Clearly, however, Kinsella's fiction, entertainment value aside, continues to elicit unique and often complex interpretations from critics, something not lost on Kinsella: "I actually enjoy reading good critical work, especially academic criticism ... I often laugh myself silly over interpretations of my work and wind up saying, 'What absolute idiocy!' It's very funny to watch a critic probe for hidden meanings which you had no intention to hide" (51). The purpose of this study has been not to misinterpret Kinsella's goal of entertaining the reader; instead, my goal has been to offer a closer examination of his five novels and selected short stories, in all of which baseball plays a part, and how the game offers another approach to community, family, and individual identities in its society.

In "Postmodernist Baseball," Richard Alan Schwartz says, "[i]n the twentieth century ... because of industrialization, urbanization, world-wide wars that radically altered social institutions and living patterns, and other such developments, our experiences often seem disjointed, fragmented, and isolated from the past and often from other people's experiences" (138). For writers like Giamatti, Will, and Goodwin, former players like Bouton, Lee, and Murcer, and fans of the game like Wiles and myself, the game is able, in some small way, to unify these experiences. George Grella observes that the game "denies players perfection, and luck plays so large a part in the game, no one can escape being wrong many times throughout the season" (564). The game, like America itself, is imperfect but continues to offer the possibility for renewal, redemption, and reemergence so that each of us connected to it may, in some way, improve on past failures with the hopes of the elusive "perfect game."

The opening lines of the companion book to Ken Burns's documentary, *Baseball*, offer this description of its role in America:

> Americans have played baseball for more than 200 years, while they conquered a continent, warred with one another and with enemies abroad, struggled over labor and civil rights and the meaning of freedom. At the game's heart lies mythic contradiction: a pastoral game, born in crowded cities; an exhilarating democratic sport that tolerates cheating and has excluded as many as it has included; a profoundly conservative game that sometimes manages to be years ahead of its time.
>
> It is an American odyssey that links sons and daughters to fathers and grandfathers. And it reflects a host of age-old American tensions: between workers and owners, scandal and reform, the individual and the collective. It is a haunted game in which every player is measured against the ghosts of all who have gone before. Most of all, it is about time and timelessness, speed and grace, failure and loss, imperishable hope—and coming home [Ward and Burns xiv].

Through its history, baseball in America has endured, among other things, a fixing scandal that led to the permanent banishment of some of its most popular players, racism which remained even after its highest level was integrated in 1947, misogynistic mindsets that continue to plague its foundation, labor disputes that have led to numerous strikes and the cancellation of one World Series, gambling scandals that resulted in eight members of the 1919 Chicago White Sox from ever being able play the game, and in the game's all-time hits leader, Pete Rose, being banned from ever being considered for enshrinement in the Hall of Fame, and accusations that have led to Congressional hearings and cast doubt on the legitimacy of many of the game's statistics.

Yet for all of these imperfections, the game continues to be an integral part of our society. Tim Wiles argues that, even with these shadows over the game and its history, "the game will survive." The survival of the game in Kinsella's fiction mirrors the survival of American society itself. Despite the game's inadequacies and fallibilities, it continues to reflect the nation that adapts to the present while maintaining its strong connections to the past.

Bibliography

Aitken, Brian. "Baseball as Sacred Doorway in the Writing of W.P. Kinsella." *Aethlon* 8, no. 1 (Fall 1990).

Althusser, Louis. From "Ideology and Ideological State Apparatuses." *The Norton Anthology of Theory and Criticism*. edited by Vincent B. Leitch, et al. New York: W.W. Norton, 2001.

Angell, Roger. "No, But I Saw the Game." *The New Yorker*. 31 July 1989.

Avery, Todd. "'The Girls in Europe Is Nuts over Ball Players': Ring Lardner and Virginia Woolf." *Nine* 13(2005).

Barzun, Jacques. *God's Country and Mine: A Declaration of Love Spiced with a Few Harsh Words*. Boston: Little, Brown, 1954.

Beach, Charles Franklyn. "Joyful vs. Joyless Religion in W.P. Kinsella's *Shoeless Joe*. *Aethlon* 16, no. 1 (Fall 1998).

Bean, Billy. *Going the Other Way: Lessons from a Life In and Out of Major-League Baseball*. New York: Marlowe & Company, 2003.

Bellah, Robert N., et al. *Habits of the Heart: Individualism and Commitment in American Life*. New York: Harper & Row, 1985.

Bloom, Barry M. "Mitchell Report proposes solutions." *The Official Site of Major League Baseball*. Major League Baseball. 13 Dec. 2007. Web: 22 Jan. 2011.

Bouton, Jim. *Ball Four: The Final Pitch*. North Egremont, MA: Bulldog, 2000.

Bowering, George. "Baseball and the Canadian Imagination." *Canadian Literature* 108 (1986).

Buckley, Steve. "She Rox." *Boston Sunday Herald*. 7 June 2009.

Burk, Robert F. *Never Just a Game: Players, Owners, and American Baseball to 1920*. Chapel Hill: The University of North Carolina Press, 1994.

Burke, Glenn. *Out at Home: The Glenn Burke Story*. New York: Excel, 1995.

Cameron, Elspeth. "Diamonds are Forever." *Saturday Night*, Aug. 1986.

Candelaria, Cordelia. "Literary Fungoes: Allusions to Baseball in American Fiction." *Midwest Quarterly* 23, no. 4 (1982).

_____. *Seeking the Perfect Game: Baseball in American Literature*. New York: Greenwood Press, 1989.

Christy Mathewson. N. p., n. d. Web: 22 Jan. 2011.

Coakley, Jay J. *Sport in Society: Issues and Controversies*. St. Louis: Mosby, 1978.

Colorado Silver Bullets. N. p. 28 Apr. 2002. Web: 21 Oct. 2010.

Crawford, Russ. "The Nationalist Pastime: The Use of Baseball to Promote Nationalism Globally." *The Politics of Baseball: Essays on the Pastime and Power at Home and Abroad*, edited by Ron Briley. Jefferson, NC: McFarland, 2010.

Crepeau, Richard, and Rob Sheinkopf. "'The Eddie Scissons Syndrome: Life Imitating Art Imitating Life.'" *Aethlon* 8 (1990).

Dahlin, Robert. "PW Interviews: W.P. Kinsella." *Publisher's Weekly,* 16 Apr. 1982.

Easton, Rebecca. "*Shoeless Joe* As Allegory: A Framework for the Writing of Fiction." *Aethlon* 17, no. 1 (Fall 1999).

Eitzen, D. Stanley. "American Sport at Century's End." *sport in contemporary society,* edited by. D. Stanley Eitzen. 6th ed. New York: Worth, 2001.

Elfers, James. *The Tour to End All Tours: The Story of Major League Baseball's 1913–1914 World Tour.* Lincoln: University of Nebraska Press, 2003.

Evans, Christopher, and William Herzog II, eds. *The Faith of 50 Million: Baseball, Religion, and American Culture.* Louisville: Westminster John Knox Press, 2002.

Evans, Walter. "The All-American Boys: A Study of Boys' Sports Fiction." *Journal of Popular Culture* 6 (Summer 1972).

Farrell, James T. "Baseball As It's Played in Book—Some Cheers, Jeers and Hopes." *New York Times Book Review,* 10 Aug. 1958.

Fiske, John. *Power Plays, Power Works.* London: Verso, 1993.

Fitzgerald, F. Scott. *The Great Gatsby.* New York: Scribner's. 1925.

Folsom, Ed. "The Manly and Healthy Game: Walt Whitman and the Development of American Baseball." *Arete* (Fall 1984).

Ford, Richard. Introduction. *Game Time: A Baseball Companion,* by Roger Angell. Orlando: Harcourt, 2003.

Freeman, Criswell, ed. *The Wisdom of Old-Time Baseball: Common Sense and Uncommon Genius from 101 Baseball Greats.* Nashville: Walnut Grove Press, 1996.

French, Warren. *J. D. Salinger.* Revised edition. Boston: Twayne, 1976.

Friedlander, Brett, and Robert Reising. *Chasing Moonlight: The True Story of* Field of Dreams' *Doc Graham.* Winston-Salem: John F. Blair, 2009.

Frost, Robert. *The Poetry of Robert Frost,* edited by Edward Connery Lathem. New York: Holt, Rinehart and Winston, 1969.

Gandil, Arnold. "This Is My Story of the Black Sox Series (as told to Melvin Durslag)." *Sports Illustrated,* 7 Sept. 1956.

Garman, Bryan K. "Myth Building and Cultural Politics in W.P. Kinsella's *Shoeless Joe.*" *Canadian Review of American Studies* 24 (1994).

Giamatti, A. Bartlett. *Take Time for Paradise: Americans and Their Games.* New York: Summit, 1989.

Gilbert, Sandra M., and Susan Gubar. "The Madwoman in the Attic." *The Norton Anthology of Theory and Criticism,* edited by Vincent B. Leitch, et al. New York: W. W. Norton, 2001.

Goodwin, Doris Kearns. *Wait Till Next Year: A Memoir.* New York: Simon & Schuster, 1997.

Gould, Stephen Jay. *Triumph and Tragedy in Mudville: A Lifelong Passion for Baseball.* New York: Norton, 2003.

Graham, Archibald. [Player File]. Cooperstown, NY: Library at National Baseball Hall of Fame and Museum. 20 Sept. 2004.

Gray, Lynn. "Interview: W.P. Kinsella." *The Short Story Review.* 5, no. 3 (June 1988).

Grella, George. "Baseball and the American Dream." *The Massachusetts Review* 16, no. 4 (Summer 1975).

Gretton, Viveca. "You Could Look It Up: Notes Towards a Reading of Baseball, History, and Ideology in the Dominant Cinema." *CineAction!* Summer/Fall 1990.

Grunwald, Henry Anatole, ed. *Salinger: A Critical and Personal Portrait.* New York: Pocket, 1963.
Hall, Donald. *Fathers Playing Catch with Sons.* San Francisco: North Point, 1985.
Hamblin, Robert. "'Magic Realism,' or, The Split-Fingered Fastball of W.P. Kinsella." *Aethlon* 9 (1992).
Hampl, Patricia. "Memory and Imagination." *Transitions: Lives in America,* edited by Irina L. Raicu and Gregory Grewell. Mountain View, CA: Mayfield, 1997.
Harris, Mark. "Horatio at the Bat; or, Why Such a Lengthy Embryonic Period for the Serious Baseball Novel." *Aethlon* 5 (1988).
Heller, Dick. "Kekich and Peterson made strangest trade in '73." *The Washington Times* 7 Mar. 2005. Web: 9 Sept. 2006.
Hemingway, Ernest. *The Old Man and the Sea.* New York: Scribner's, 1952.
Herzog, William R, II. "From Scapegoat to Icon: The Strange Journey of Shoeless Joe Jackson." Evans and Herzog II, 97–141.
Hohenstein, Kurt. *The Rules of the Game: Simple Truths Learned from Little League.* Nashville: Thomas Nelson, 1996.
Honig, Donald. *Baseball America: The Heroes of the Game and the Times of Their Glory.* New York: Galahad, 1985.
Horvath, Brooke K., and William J. Palmer. "Three On: An Interview with David Carkeet, Mark Harris, and W.P. Kinsella." *Modern Fiction Studies* 33 (1987).
Hye, Allen E. *The Great God Baseball: Religion in Modern Baseball Fiction.* Macon: Mercer University Press, 2004.
Jay, Kathryn. *More Than Just a Game: Sports in American Life Since 1945.* New York: Columbia University Press, 2004. 1–8. Print.
"Joe Jackson Stats." *Baseball Almanac.* N. p., n. d. Web: 29 Jan. 2011.
Kellman, Steven G. "Posessive ghosts of nostalgia." *Commonweal* 11 June 1986.
Kimmel, Michael S. "Baseball and the Reconstruction of American Masculinity, 1880–1920." *Sport, Men, and the Gender Order: Critical Feminist Perspectives,* edited by Michael A. Messner and Donald F. Sabo. Champaign, IL: Human Kinetics, 1990.
Kinsella, W.P. "The Baseball Spur." Kinsella, *The Thrill of the Grass,* 23–45.
_____. *Box Socials.* New York: Ballantine, 1991.
_____. "Distances." Kinsella, *The Further Adventures,* 1–24.
_____. "The Dixon Cornbelt League." Kinsella, *The Dixon Cornbelt League,* 157–180.
_____. *The Dixon Cornbelt League and Other Baseball Stories.* New York: HarperCollins, 1993.
_____. "The Eddie Scissons Syndrome." Kinsella, *The Further,* 137–152.
_____. "The Fadeaway." Kinsella, *The Dixon Cornbelt League,* 23–39.
_____. "The First and Last Annual Six Towns Area Old-Timers' Game." Kinsella, *Japanese Baseball,* 95–118.
_____. "Frank Pierce, Iowa." Kinsella, *The Further Adventures,* 63–74.
_____. *The Further Adventures of Slugger McBatt.* Boston: Houghton Mifflin, 1988.
_____. "How I Got My Nickname." Kinsella, *The Thrill of the Grass,* 47–49.
_____. "How Manny Embarquadero Overcame and Began His Climb to the Major Leagues." Kinsella, *The Dixon Cornbelt League,* 87–107.
_____. *If Wishes Were Horses.* Toronto: HarperPerennial, 1996.
_____. *The Iowa Baseball Confederacy.* New York: Ballantine, 1986.
_____. *Japanese Baseball and other stories.* Saskatoon, Saskatchewan: Thistledown, 2000.
_____. *Magic Time.* Stillwater, MN: Voyageur, 2001.

_____. "The Night Manny Mota Tied the Record." Kinsella, *The Thrill of the Grass*, 91–106.

_____. "Punchlines." Kinsella, *The Further Adventures of Slugger McBatt*, 119–135.

_____. "Searching for January." *The Dixon Cornbelt League*, 109–120.

_____. *Shoeless Joe*. New York: Ballantine, 1982.

_____. *Shoeless Joe Jackson Comes to Iowa*. Dallas: Southern Methodist University Press, 1993.

_____. "Shoeless Joe Jackson Comes to Iowa." Kinsella, *Shoeless Joe Jackson Comes to Iowa*, 32–47.

_____. *The Thrill of the Grass*. Toronto: Penguin, 1984.

Kirsch, George B. *Baseball in Blue and Gray: The National Pastime during the Civil War*. Princeton: Princeton University Press, 2003.

Lauricella, John A. *Home Games: Essays on Baseball Fiction*. Jefferson, NC: McFarland, 1999.

Lee, Bill, and Richard Lally. *Have Glove, Will Travel: Adventures of a Baseball Vagabond*. New York: Crown, 2005.

Leitner, Irving A. *Baseball: A Diamond in the Rough*. New York: Criterion Books, 1972.

Lord, Timothy C. "Hegel. Marx, and Shoeless Joe: Religious Ideology in Kinsella's Baseball Fantasy." *Aethlon* 10 (1992).

Mandel, Brett H. *Is This Heaven? The Magic of the Field of Dreams*. Lanham, MD: Diamond Communications, 2002.

McCue, Andy. *Baseball by the Books*. Dubuque, IA: William C. Brown, 1991.

McGimpsey, David. *Imagining Baseball: America's Pastime and Popular Culture*. Bloomington: Indiana University Press, 2000.

Miracle, Andrew W., Jr., and C. Roger Rees. *Lessons of the Locker Room: The Myth of School Sports*. Amherst, MA: Prometheus, 1994.

Morris, Timothy. *Making the Team: The Cultural Work of Baseball Fiction*. Urbana: University of Illinois Press, 1997.

Mount, Nicholas J. "'Are the Green Fields Gone?': Pastoralism in the Baseball Novel." *Aethlon* 11, no. 1 (1993).

Murcer, Bobby. Personal interview by the author. 5 Aug. 2006.

Murray, Don. *The Fiction of W.P. Kinsella: Tall Tales in Various Voices*. Fredericton, New Brunswick: York Press, 1987.

"Negro Leagues History." *Negro Leagues Baseball Museum*. NLBM, n. d. Web: 22. Jan. 2011.

Nipps, Emily. "She's been his closest fan for 30 years." *St. Petersburg Times Online* 28 July 2005. Web: 13 Sept. 2006.

Pellow, C. Kenneth. "Shoeless Joe in Film and Fiction." *Aethlon* 9(1991).

Peterson, Richard. *Extra Innings: Writing on Baseball*. Urbana: University of Illinois Press, 2001.

Plaut, David, ed. *Baseball Wit and Wisdom*. Philadelphia: Running, 1992.

Podhoretz, Norman. "Achilles in Left Field." *Commentary* 15 (Mar. 1953).

Pronger, Brian. "Gay Jocks: A Phenomenology of Gay Men in Athletics." *Sport, Men, and the Gender Order*, edited by Michael A. Messner and Donald F. Sabo. Champaign, IL: Human Kinetics, 1990.

Reston, James, Jr. *Collision at Home: The Lives of Pete Rose and Bart Giamatti*. New York: HarperCollins, 1991.

Rossi, John P. *The National Game: Baseball and American Culture*. Chicago: Dee, 2000.

Schraufnagel, Noel. *The Baseball Novel: A History and Annotated Bibliography of Adult Fiction*. Jefferson, NC: McFarland, 2008.

Schwartz, Richard Alan. "Postmodernist Baseball." *Modern Fiction Studies* 33 (1987).
Shannon, Mike. *Baseball: The Writer's Game*. Washington, D.C.: Brassey's, 2002.
_____, ed. *The Best of* Spitball: *The Literary Baseball Magazine*. New York: Pocket Books, 1988.
Sheed, Wilfrid. *My Life as a Fan: A Memoir*. New York: Simon & Schuster, 1993.
Spalding, Albert G. *America's National Game*. New York: American Sports, 1911. Lincoln: University of Nebraska Press, 1992.
Springwood, Charles Fruehling. *Cooperstown to Dyersville: A Geography of Baseball Nostalgia*. Boulder: Westview Press, 1996.
Sullivan, Kathleen. *Women Characters in Baseball Literature: A Critical Study*. McFarland: Jefferson, NC, 2005.
Sullivan, Steve. *Talking Baseball Amongst Friends*. Santa Ana, CA: Shamrock, 2006.
"Timeline of Events in Professional Black Baseball." *Negro League Baseball*. P. Mills., n. d. Web: 25 Jan. 2011.
Trujillo, Nick, and Bob Krizek. "Emotionality in the Stands and in the Field: Expressing Self Through Baseball." *Journal of Sport & Social Issues* 18, no. 4 (1994).
Wallach, Jeffrey. "Game Without Limits." *American Book Review* Mar. 1987.
Ward, Geoffrey C., and Ken Burns. *Baseball: An Illustrated History*. New York: Knopf, 1994.
Westbrook, Deeanne. *Ground Rules: Baseball & Myth*. Urbana: University of Illinois Press, 1996.
White, Philip G., and Anne B. Vagi. "Rugby in the 19th-Century British Boarding-School System: A Feminist Psychoanalytic Perspective." *Sport, Men, and the Gender Order: Critical Feminist Perspectives*, edited by Michael A. Messner and Donald Sabo. Champaign, IL: Human Kinetics, 1990.
Wiles, Tim. Personal interview by author. 15 Sept. 2006.
Will, George F. *Men at Work: The Craft of Baseball*. New York: HarperCollins, 1990.
Zoss, Joel, and John Bowman. *Diamonds in the Rough: The Untold History of Baseball*. Lincoln: University of Nebraska Press, 1989.

Index